I'm not afraid, she told herself. *I'm Vermillion. I'm not afraid of any man, and especially not Caleb Tanner.*

She tossed her head, wishing her hair was fashionably done up and she was wearing rice powder and rouge. "Don't be silly. I wasn't afraid. I was enjoying a bit of sport, is all. I wanted to see what it might be like to kiss you."

He stiffened and a muscle tightened in his cheek. "That's what you were doing? Having a bit of sport?" Caleb stalked her, looking hard, even dangerous. "Then tell me, Miss Durant, did my kisses meet with your approval?"

She shrugged her shoulders. "I suppose so. Andrew's kisses are a bit more forceful. Yours were—"

Caleb jerked her hard against him, cutting off her words. "So you like things rough—is that it? Then rough is what you'll get."

She tried to turn away, but he caught her jaw, holding her immobile, and his mouth crushed down with brutal force.

It was a hard, taking kiss. A fierce, plundering kiss with none of the gentleness he had shown her before and yet her whole body went liquid with heat. Her fingers dug into the front of his shirt and she wasn't sure if she were trying to pull him closer or push him away....

Books by Kat Martin

The Fire Inside
Fanning the Flame
Secret Ways

Available from Pocket Books

KAT MARTIN

SECRET Ways

POCKET STAR BOOKS

New York London Toronto Sydney Singapore

An *Original* Publication of POCKET BOOKS

A Pocket Star Book published by
POCKET BOOKS, a division of Simon & Schuster, Inc.
1230 Avenue of the Americas, New York, NY 10020

Copyright © 2003 by Kat Martin

ISBN: 0-7434-1917-0

First Pocket Books printing April 2003

10 9 8 7 6 5 4 3 2 1

POCKET STAR BOOKS and colophon are registered
trademarks of Simon & Schuster, Inc.

For information regarding special discounts for bulk purchases,
please contact Simon & Schuster Special Sales at 1-800-456-6798
or business@simonandschuster.com

Front cover illustration by Tom Hallman;
tip-in illustration by John Ennis

Printed in the U.S.A.

To my mother.
For her years of love and constant encouragement,
and for always being there when I needed her.
I love you, Mom.

1

Outskirts of London
May 1809

Her name was Vermillion. It came from the Old French, a color, a bright Chinese red; cinnabar, some called it.

Vermillion. The word conjured sultry, mysterious images. Hot, lurid, untamed images.

She had always hated the name.

In private, she called herself Lee. Simple. Straightforward. The middle name she carried that was more like the person she was inside. Vermillion Lee Durant, a pretty name, she supposed.

If only it belonged to someone else.

"Hurry, Vermillion, darling. We mustn't keep the colonel waiting."

Lee sighed. No, one must never keep a gentleman waiting. At least not here, in the world of the demi-monde, where every man was king, or at least made to believe he was.

Lee paused in front of the tall cheval glass to check the fit of her scarlet velvet gown, a complement to the thick dark red curls swept up on her head, the style not really à la mode, as was the gown, but softer, more alluring, more pleasing to the gentlemen.

The elaborate coiffure was laced with gold ribbon to match the trim beneath the high waist of her gown, which was cut shockingly low, displaying an abundance of cleavage. The slim skirt, slashed nearly to the knee, was the height of London fashion, though hardly suitable for a young unmarried woman of Lee's mere eighteen years.

Still, she was used to the clothes and her sophisticated appearance. She stood patiently as her little French maid, Jeannie, swung the gold-lined, red velvet cape around her shoulders and fastened the diamond and garnet pin at her throat.

" 'Ave a good time, *chérie*," the woman said, though surely by now she knew it wouldn't be the least bit of fun for Lee.

"Good night, Jeannie." Pasting on the practiced, enigmatic smile her aunt and her admirers expected to see, she paused at the bedchamber door. "I'll be late coming home. I'll ring if I need help getting out of the gown."

Her artificial smile firmly in place, Vermillion swept out into the hallway and descended the curving staircase into the entry of her aunt's elegant mansion in Parkwood, a small village on the outskirts of London. Gowned in sapphire silk scattered with brilliants, Aunt Gabriella waited at the bottom of the stairs, her own, far more sincere smile in place.

Gabriella Durant was forty-six years old, taller than Vermillion and more slender, her breasts still high, her blond hair thick and luxurious, woven with only a few strands of silver gray. But fine lines had begun to appear around her mouth and eyes, and the flesh had loosened beneath her jaw. Though Gabriella loathed each small flaw, she was still a beautiful woman.

"You look lovely, darling." Aunt Gabby surveyed the ruby velvet gown and the upsweep of Vermillion's flame-red hair. "More beautiful every year."

Vermillion made no reply. The Durant women were known for their beauty. It was a simple statement of fact that Lee saw as more of a curse than a blessing. The butler, Wendell Perkin Jones, a thin, elegant little man who wore his dark hair parted down the middle and curled at the sides like an emperor, pulled open the door, and Vermillion caught a glimpse of the carriage, a sleek black barouche pulled by a pair of matched gray horses, a gift from the Earl of Claymont, her aunt's current *cher ami.*

"The coach is waiting," Aunt Gabby said. "Claymont is meeting us at the theater." Gabriella smiled, looking forward to the evening with a relish Vermillion rarely felt. She would rather stay at home, ride one of her precious horses if the sun were still up, or read a book, perhaps, or enjoy an hour on the harp, though none of those thoughts appeared on her face.

Instead, her smile widened as she settled into her role, almost second nature after so many years of learning the part. "I'm ready to go anytime you are. As you say, we mustn't keep the gentlemen waiting." Sweeping her cloak out behind her, Vermillion joined her aunt in the entry and the two Durant women walked gracefully out the door, into the glittering London night that awaited.

Captain Caleb Tanner held the harness of the lead horse of the pair in front of the carriage, keeping the flashy grays calm in their traces. The expensive black barouche sat in front of the Durant mansion, which was fashioned of brick, stood three stories high, and sat on several hundred acres of rolling green hills just outside London. Tall white Corinthian columns held up a decorative portico designed to shelter arriving visitors from inclement weather and a long curving driveway led up from the road.

The owner, Gabriella Durant, had inherited the mansion along with a very tidy fortune from her mother, a well-known courtesan of her day. Gabriella had followed in her mother's footsteps, amassing even greater wealth and continuing what appeared to have become a family tradition, currently being carried on by Gabriella's red-haired niece, Vermillion.

Caleb knew a great deal about the Durants, who traced their ancestry back to the time displaced French nobles arrived penniless in London to escape the guillotine. Using her great beauty and charm, Simone Durant had saved the near-destitute family and prospered, her skill as a lover legendary in the world of the demimonde. After Simone's death, her daughter, Gabriella, had become the reigning queen, La Belle, the toast of London.

Caleb cast a glance toward the door of the mansion, waiting for the women to appear. Rumor was, the niece Gabriella had raised as a daughter intended to claim the throne for the third generation.

Caleb had never seen Vermillion, but he had heard stories about her, gossip about her loveliness and skill in the boudoir.

He knew she must be beautiful.

But he wasn't prepared for the impact that hit him like a fall from his horse the moment she stepped out onto the porch. As he watched her in the glow of the whale oil lanterns beside the door, Caleb couldn't seem to tear his eyes away. He had never seen such fiery hair or skin so flawless. He had never seen eyes the color of aquamarines.

She was smaller than he had imagined, her figure fuller, more womanly. Beneath the clasp of her scarlet velvet opera cape, her breasts were high and lush and nearly spilled out of the bodice of her gown. His hands itched to cup them. He wanted to pluck the pins from her fiery hair and run his fingers through it. The true color of her lips was masked by the rouge that turned them a dark ruby red, but they curved in a sultry smile that made a man want to own them.

Caleb shook himself, a feeling of distaste rising inside him. Vermillion Durant was nothing but an expensive plaything, an object to satisfy men's lust, a woman who used her body to gain power over foolish, unwary men. Perhaps she was even a spy.

Which was the reason Caleb Tanner stood next to the horses, the newly hired head groom of Parklands, the name used by those who attended the lavish and notorious balls, ridottos, and house parties hosted by Gabriella Durant.

This assignment was different than any he had had before. Caleb had been ordered back to England during his tenure in Spain, having served in the cavalry under General Sir Arthur Wellesley through the Oporto campaign. The youngest son of the Earl of Selhurst, he had enlisted in the army just out of Oxford. Caleb had served in India and the Netherlands. On orders from the general, he was in England now.

At Parklands—trying to catch a traitor.

Caleb watched the women walking toward the carriage, felt the pull of Vermillion's aqua eyes the moment they touched his face, and a second jolt of lust hit him, making his dislike of her harden even more than the erection pressing against the front of his breeches.

Inwardly he cursed.

But he didn't look away.

Vermillion paused as she reached the carriage, her glance straying to the beautiful matched grays standing calmly in their traces. She loved horses. The animals at Parklands were her pride and her passion, but she didn't recognize the groom who stood next to the grays and she knew every man and boy who worked in the stable. She had personally hired each one.

Except for this man. This tall, broad-shouldered stranger with the hard, dark eyes and faintly insolent smile.

Instead of following her aunt into the carriage, Vermillion kept walking, pausing when she reached the man beside the horses.

"Where is Jacob?" Jacob had been the head groom and trainer at Parklands for the past fifteen years. "Why are you here? Has Jacob fallen ill?"

"He was fine the last time I saw him."

She didn't like his tone any better than she liked the smug look on his face. "Then where is he? And just exactly who are you?"

His gaze ran over her, starting at her toes, moving to the top of her sophisticated coiffure, then returning to her breasts. She received that same too-bold perusal from a gallery of males every night, yet when this man did it, it made her cheeks begin to burn. He wasn't one of her admirers—he made that clear by the casualness of his regard and the faintly cynical twist of his lips.

"I'm Caleb Tanner. Parklands's new head groom. Jacob had some family problems in Surrey he needed to attend. He hired me to take his place until he is able to return."

She lifted her chin, wishing for once she were taller. "I'm in charge of the stable. If Jacob had some sort of problem, he should have come to me. Do you have papers to recommend you? How do I know you can handle the job?"

He was a big man, not brawny, just tall and broad-shouldered, perhaps in his late twenties, with brown hair a little too long that curled against the nape of his neck.

"I was raised around horses," he said. "I worked mainly in the north . . . York, mostly. My specialty is racing stock."

"So you're a trainer as well?"

"That's right. Jacob spoke of a stallion named Noir you'll be racing at Epsom this week. At least give me till after the race to prove I can handle the position."

That seemed fair enough. Jacob had a knack with horses and he loved them as much as she did. He wouldn't turn them over to just anyone and certainly not to a man he didn't trust completely. Still, there was something about this man. . . .

"All right. You have till the end of the week. If Noir wins the race, you stay on until Jacob returns."

A dark brown eyebrow arched up. "You believe if the stallion loses, the fault will be mine?"

Of course not. He would have been there less than a week, but it would be a way to get rid of him and for reasons she couldn't seem to explain, she wanted exactly that.

"Noir is a champion. It's up to his trainer to see that he wins. If he does, you can stay."

His mouth barely curved. "Then I had better make certain he wins."

It was said as if there were no doubt he could do it, as if the outcome had already been decided. Vermillion made no reply, just turned and started back to the carriage, her scarlet cape whirling out behind her. They were heading into London, to the box they kept at the Royal Opera House. Though they would be snubbed by the nobles and other members of the *ton*, on the third floor of the building, where certain wealthy but less socially acceptable members of society watched the performance, they would be treated like royalty.

"Hurry up, darling, we're going to be late." Aunt Gabby's voice floated out through the carriage window.

Vermillion cast a last glance over her shoulder at the groom, who was stroking the neck of the gray, speaking softly into the animal's ear. Both horses had impressive bloodlines. They were beautiful, spirited, and often difficult to handle. Not tonight. Tonight, they stood with their elegant heads hanging down while the groom's long fingers scratched between their ears.

Perhaps the man was as capable as he appeared, his oversized ego well deserved. As she settled back against the tufted red leather seat, Vermillion found the notion irritating in the extreme.

The purple flush of dawn brightened the sky by the time Vermillion returned to Parklands the following morning. After the opera, Spontini's *La Vestale*, Aunt Gabby had insisted they attend a party given by Elizabeth Sorenson, Countess of Rotham, a woman with a scandalous reputation whom Lee and Gabriella both adored.

The party was an outrageous affair held at the countess's town house, with boundless amounts of Russian caviar, crystal goblets overflowing with champagne, and no shortage of attractive men.

A number of Vermillion's admirers were there: Jonathan Parker, Viscount Nash; Oliver Wingate, a colonel of the Life Guards; and the outrageously handsome and utterly notorious rake Lord Andrew Mondale.

There were other men, of course, dozens of them, but these were the three who vied most strongly for a place in Vermillion's bed.

Lee shoved the distasteful thought away as she wearily climbed the stairs to her bedchamber. From the corner of her eye, she caught sight of the fresh bouquet of flowers Jeannie had placed on the rosewood dresser. The deep mauve counterpane was welcomingly turned back beneath the matching satin bed curtains.

Jeannie would be sleeping and Lee hated to wake her at such a late hour. She struggled with the gown and finally managed to undo the buttons, put on a long white night rail and climbed beneath the sheets. Exhausted from the events of the evening, the champagne and the dancing, she slept the sleep of the dead, lacking even the energy for her usual morning ride, and didn't wake up until nearly noon.

She had indulged herself on purpose, knowing tonight would be another late night. Colonel Wingate would be escorting them to an evening of gaming in Jermyn Street. Then tomorrow night she and her aunt would be attending the theater. Lee had lost track of her schedule after that, but she knew that at each event, her tireless pursuers would be present.

While other girls her age entered the Season in search of a husband, Vermillion searched for a protector—the man who would become her first lover.

An image of the arrogant groom popped into her head. Why, she couldn't imagine. It was a fleeting vision, instantly forgotten.

She didn't think of Tanner again until three days later, when she saw him in the stable. The late afternoon sun had begun to fade and the soft glow of evening settled over the landscape. Aunt Gabby was giving a house party, so the servants were busy inside. Though none of the guests had yet arrived, they were sure to appear very soon. Dressed in a low-cut turquoise silk gown trimmed in black lace in preparation for the festivities, Lee slipped away from the house and made her way out to the stable.

She was worried about her beautiful horses, still not confident of Jacob's replacement.

She didn't expect to see the man himself, Caleb Tanner, standing in the middle of the exercise ring. He faced away from her, his collarless, full-sleeved shirt damp with perspiration and clinging to the extraordinary width of his back. The shirt was tucked into simple brown breeches that showed a narrow waist, curved over a round behind, and outlined a pair of long, muscular legs.

When he turned, she could see a vee of darkly tanned skin at his throat where the neck of the shirt stood open. The man was impressive. There was no denying that. Lee knew men—dozens of them—but she couldn't name one more beautifully built than Caleb Tanner.

He was busily working, Noir circling at the end of Tanner's lead line, the Thoroughbred's shiny black coat glistening in the fading rays of sunlight. Tanner didn't see her approaching. Or if he did, he simply ignored her.

Vermillion wasn't used to being ignored.

"You're jerking the line too much," she said as she came up to the fence. "He works better with a gentler touch."

The corner of his mouth curved up in a mocking half smile. "I'll keep that in mind." His dark gaze said he knew she had just made that up, which of course, she had. The stallion was working beautifully, doing his new trainer's bidding without the slightest hesitation. The man hadn't lied. He definitely knew horses. Noir could be fussy, and the stallion had never really liked being exercised on a lead.

Now the horse seemed to be enjoying every lap he made round the practice ring. Lee watched them for a while, unable to take her eyes off man and horse working so perfectly together. Then Tanner tugged on the rope and the stallion began to slow. Noir nickered and trotted over to where the groom stood in the center of the ring. Tanner reached into his pocket, pulled out a treat, and fed it to Noir on the flat of his hand. Speaking to the horse in that soft way of his, he ran his fingers through the stallion's course black mane.

Tanner led the animal over to the fence and stopped in front of her, and Lee tried not to think what a magnificent pair they made.

"He's in excellent condition," Caleb Tanner said,

patting the horse's neck. "Jacob's done a fine job with him."

"Then you think he's going to win."

"I think he has a very good chance. Who's riding him?"

"Mickey Warner."

"Warner's good, one of the best riders in the country." His eyes moved from her face down to the cleavage swelling up at the front of her turquoise gown. She rarely dressed this way when she came to the stable. Lee had forgotten that tonight she was Vermillion.

His smile held a trace of insolence it was impossible to miss. "But then, I imagine you know a great deal about riding . . . wouldn't you say so, Miss Durant?"

Her cheeks went warm. She knew what he was implying. At least she understood he was referring to the act of making love. She'd been raised in the world of the demimonde. Her aunt, though wealthy and many years now with the same man, was once a notorious courtesan with a long string of lovers. All of London believed that Vermillion was a courtesan as well, as very soon she would be. Having accepted that future long ago, a subtle innuendo here and there, spoken by one of her admirers, had never upset her before.

But when Caleb Tanner looked at her the way he was now, as if she were less than the manure on his boots, her face flamed the same fiery color as her hair.

"Win the race," she said simply. "Or get a job somewhere else." Turning, she forgot to walk with her usual provocative, hip-swaying gait, and stomped all the way back to the house.

*   *   *

Caleb cursed himself. Dammit, Colonel Cox had gone to a great deal of trouble to arrange for the trainer, Jacob Boswell, to relinquish his position at Parklands for the next few weeks so that Caleb could work in his stead. All he needed was for the little chit to fire him.

He had to start controlling his tongue, he knew, but somehow, whenever he looked at Vermillion's exotically beautiful face, her luscious breasts displayed like pale, ripe fruit, he couldn't seem to do it.

It bothered him that she was so young. Even with the rouge on her lips and cheeks, he guessed her not yet twenty. It bothered him that she had so willingly abandoned the chance for a respectable life in pursuit of power and greed.

It bothered him that his body wanted her just as much as every other man in London while his mind absolutely did not.

A shuffling sound alerted him to someone's arrival in the big stone barn.

"Ye want ta be keepin' yer job, ye young buck, ye'd best be keepin' a civil tongue in yer head when ye speak ta Miss Lee." Arlie Spooner, retired Parklands groom, tottered toward him, his few sparse strands of dull gray hair whipping in the breeze coming in through the open stable door. He had a wrinkled, liver-spotted face and a spine that looked painfully curved. The old man was no longer able to work in the stable, but still retained a position. At least the Durant women had conscience enough to take care of a man who had been loyal to them for so long.

"Who's Miss Lee?"

"Miss Vermillion." Arlie continued to shuffle past the stall where Caleb stood brushing Noir and continued on his way toward the small room he occupied at the far end of the barn. "Miss Lee won't tolerate yer disrespect. Ye weren't so blasted good with them horses a' hers, ye'd already be lookin' fer someplace else ta work."

The old man was loyal, all right. Caleb hadn't missed the affection in the old man's voice when he spoke his employer's name. Caleb wondered how much Arlie Spooner knew about Vermillion and her aunt and determined that as soon as he got the chance he would see what he could find out.

In the meantime, he would keep his eyes and ears open, as he was there to do. Caleb's superiors, including General Sir Arthur Wellesley, believed information was being leaked to the French. The casualties in Spain had been staggering—more than five thousand British troops. Wellesley was convinced the numbers at Oporto would have been far less if a person—or persons—hadn't provided information directly to Napoleon.

Colonel Richard Cox and Major Mark Sutton had been assigned to find the traitors responsible, and both Cox and Sutton were convinced the source could be found at Parklands. It was Caleb's knowledge of horses and racing that had brought him into the equation and home to England.

Caleb watched old Arlie disappear into his room and finished brushing the stallion, thinking of Vermillion and the dozens of men who frequented the house, many of them military officers and gentlemen highly placed in the government. Had one of them traded his soul for the chance to satisfy himself in Vermillion's tantalizing young body?

As Caleb stood in the shadows outside the house

later that night, watching carriage after carriage roll up the circular drive and its elegantly garbed occupants make their way up the steps to the entry, as he felt the pull of Vermillion's cool, smoky laughter coming from inside the house, he thought that it just might be true.

2

Vermillion, darling, I don't believe you've met Lord Derry." In the midst of her circle of admirers, Aunt Gabby stood smiling, enjoying the gaiety around her. The high-ceilinged drawing room rang with noise and laughter, a crush of men and women dressed in expensive satins and silks. If the ladies' gowns were cut a little lower, the fabrics a bit more colorful than those one might find in a fashionable London drawing room, it went unremarked.

Vermillion studied Lord Derry from beneath her lowered lashes and her lips curved into a provocative smile. "No, I don't believe we've yet been introduced. Lord Derry." She sank into a curtsey and offered him a black-gloved hand. The Earl of Derry bowed over it, all the while keeping his eyes fixed on the breasts nearly spilling out of the top of her gown.

"A pleasure, Miss Durant."

"Not at all, my lord. The pleasure is most certainly mine." It wasn't, of course. The earl was a decrepit old bag of bones, his shoulders, breeches, and calves padded so heavily he looked like an overstuffed mattress with feet.

"The earl has just returned to England," Aunt Gabby said. "He owns a very successful cocoa plantation in the West Indies."

"How terribly exciting," Vermillion lied, wondering, as she had a thousand times, how her aunt could possibly be enjoying herself. Yet Vermillion knew that she was. Lee had lived with her aunt since she was four years old, when her mother had died and Aunt Gabriella had appeared like a golden-haired angel at the orphanage and taken Vermillion into her home. The two sisters were nothing alike. Angelique Durant was shy and reserved while Gabriella was La Belle, celebrated and adored in the world in which she lived.

She surrounded herself with the wealthy elite and made friends of artisans, actors, and aristocrats, most of them men, of course. She loved her life and the power she wielded, and she couldn't imagine that Vermillion would want to live any other sort of existence.

"Would you care to dance, my dear?" Lord Derry asked, hovering far too close to suit her. "Afterward I shall be happy to tell you all about life in the Indies."

Vermillion inwardly groaned, imagining an hour-long discourse on heat and bugs and the necessity of owning other human beings. But her smile remained in place. "I should adore dancing with you, my lord." The words came out with a throaty purr that seemed to change men from lions into lambs.

She let the earl guide her away from her aunt and her friends, onto the parquet floor at the end of the salon where a four-piece orchestra, garbed in pale blue livery, played the upbeat strains of a contradanse.

Vermillion smiled her practiced smile and fell into the steps of the dance, but her mind was as far from Lord Derry's plantation as it could possibly get. It was a trick her aunt's friend, Lisette Moreau, had taught her. *Separate yourself, assume an outward appearance designed to please the gentlemen while inside you go wherever you most wish to be.*

As she executed the steps her dancing master had hammered into her, Lee rode like the wind over the green fields of Parklands. Tomorrow morning, she vowed, no matter how tired she was, she would indulge herself in her heart's greatest pleasure.

At the edge of her mind, she heard the music, felt his lordship's bony fingers leading her into a turn. Letting her lashes sweep down to veil her eyes, she moistened her lips, and mentally went back to the feel of the wind in her hair and the sound of thundering hoofbeats. Mounted on Noir, she approached a high rock wall. She could feel the horse straining beneath her, his powerful muscles collecting as they soared over the wall, came down on the opposite side, and made a perfectly executed landing.

"That was marvelous, my dear," Lord Derry was saying, placing a kiss on the back of her hand.

"Yes, it was," she said, remembering the thrill of a perfectly executed jump. "Thank you, my lord."

His lordship's watery blue eyes remained glued to her breasts. "Now . . . about my cocoa plantation . . . Perhaps a turn round the terrace would—"

"Sorry to interrupt, but Miss Durant has promised her next dance to me." Jonathan Parker, Viscount Nash, stood just a few feet away, a warm smile on his face. Of all the men of her acquaintance, Nash was among those Vermillion liked best.

"They are playing a waltz, I believe." He took hold of her hand. "Shall we?" The viscount was a tall, attractive man in his late thirties with dark hair silvered at the temples. He was a true gentleman, she thought, a widower these past three years. Jon was intelligent and kind and he had made it clear he was among those men who wished to become her protector.

Perhaps he is the one I should choose, she thought. Jon would be good to her and his demands in the boudoir would likely be less than those of a young stallion like Lord Andrew Mondale.

It was in that moment she spotted that particular gentleman striding toward her, Andrew Mondale, blond and handsome, if a bit foppishly dressed in a grass-green tailcoat with glittering gold and emerald buttons.

Vermillion inwardly sighed, steeled herself, and gave him a sultry smile. The night, it seemed, was going to be a long one.

In the end, to her good fortune, the evening had ended earlier than she had imagined. Midway through the dancing, while her aunt was holding court with her never-ending circle of friends, Lee had given in to her secret wish to retire, pled the headache, and slipped upstairs to her bedchamber.

This morning, amazingly alert and energetic, she climbed out of bed before dawn looking forward to the outing she had promised herself. Eager to reach the stable, she finished her brief toilette, ignored the expensive forest green velvet riding habit that had just arrived from London, and chose instead the form-fitting breeches and full-sleeved shirt she'd had custom-made for her several years ago at L.T. Piver's in London.

Lee had to admit there were advantages to the world in which she lived. One of them was that social dictates did not apply. By the nature of their business, the Durant women were exempt. Walking past the rosewood armoire that contained the cumbersome habit, her long red hair plaited into a single thick braid, Lee reached into a drawer of her rosewood dresser and grabbed a woolen cap in concession to the morning chill, pulled on her kidskin riding boots, and set off for the servants' stairs at the rear of the house.

The mid-May weather was crisp and clear, the sky a purple-tinged haze just beginning to brighten. She preferred to leave before the servants were up and beginning their chores, while the stable was still quiet, giving her a sense of freedom she found only out here with her beautiful horses.

She loved them all but especially Noir Diamant, Black Diamond, her prize Thoroughbred stallion, and Grand Coeur, Great Heart, the tall gray jumper she usually rode. She paused in front of Noir's stall to rub his velvety nose, but the stallion would be racing later in the week, so she chose Grand Coeur instead.

Coeur was an amazing horse that could run like the wind and jump the way she had imagined last night. Her gaze skipped to her comfortable sidesaddle with its padded tapestry seat, but Lee ignored it, just bridled Coeur and led him from his stall. She had worn the shirt and breeches so that she could ride bareback, completely unfettered and free.

Lee smoothed the stallion's dapple-gray coat, spoke to him gently, and led him out of the barn into the pale golden glow of early morning. Coeur nudged her with his beautiful head, danced and sidestepped, as eager for the morning's exercise as she.

Looping the reins over the horse's neck, she climbed up on the mounting block and settled herself on the stallion's back. The gray looked back at her and flicked his ears. Beneath her, his long, sleek muscles bunched in anticipation.

"You want this as much as I do, don't you, boy?"

As if in answer, the stallion nickered softly. Lee nudged her bootheels into the horse's ribs, urging him into a trot that carried them away from the barn and out into the open fields. Pulling on her woolen cap to keep her ears warm, she bent over the stallion's neck, urging him to pick up his pace. The horse responded to her subtle commands as if he could read her thoughts and her troubles began to fade.

She felt the rush of wind past her cheeks, felt a stray curl flutter at the base of her neck, and began to smile.

Pouring water into the porcelain basin in his room at the far end of the stable, Caleb splashed water on his face to chase away the cobwebs of sleep and dressed to begin the day. The night had been a long one, spent in the damp shadows outside the mansion, watching for anything that might be amiss inside, watching Vermillion charm her endless admirers with the cool smiles and throaty laughter that seemed to ripple through his insides.

She had gone to bed earlier than he expected. Caleb had scraped his knuckles and ripped his breeches, climbing the trellis behind the house to reach the balcony outside her bedchamber only to discover that she slept alone. It bothered him how much he wanted to slip into the room and join her in her satin-draped bed.

He was thinking about her as he walked from stall to stall to check on the horses, stopping stock-still when he noticed the door to Grand Coeur's stall stood open and the stallion was nowhere in sight. Caleb quickly scanned the interior of the barn. Noir stood lazily in his stall, one of half-dozen other horses who stuck their heads over the open stall doors to see who had entered.

One of the stalls was empty except for a fat yellow cat contentedly sleeping in the straw, her stomach stretched to near bursting with the kittens that appeared long overdue. Everything was the same as it had been last night—except that the expensive gray was missing.

Bloody hell! Caleb clenched his jaw as he turned toward the door. He could just imagine what his petite employer would say if she discovered he had lost one of her most valuable horses. He didn't much like the idea himself.

Striding out of the barn, Caleb made his way outside to survey the rolling fields in the ridiculous hope he would spot the animal placidly grazing in the pasture. He was amazed to see the gray disappearing over a rise, a rider clinging to his back, the horse in a flat-out run.

Caleb cursed again, more foully this time, and raced back into the barn. Grabbing a bridle off the rack, he hurriedly dragged it over the head of a big bay gelding that was one of the stable's fastest runners and swung up on the animal's back. In seconds, he rode in pursuit of the thief who was making off with Coeur. Somewhere behind him, he heard old Arlie shuffle out of the barn. He was shouting something, but the sound disappeared in the rush of wind and the thunder of the big bay's hooves.

Caleb urged the horse faster, settling into the chase, beginning to enjoy himself, now that he was sure of the outcome. With the horse's long, ground-eating strides, it didn't take long before he spotted the thief in the distance, the figure atop the horse smaller than he had imagined, a village lad, perhaps. One who was about to wish he had never tangled with Caleb Tanner.

Unaware he was being pursued, the youth reined the horse off to the right, riding straight for a low rock wall. Up and over he went, clearing the barrier with ease. Caleb's temper heated as the lad turned the animal to the left and sailed over a wide, meandering stream, then leaped up the bank on the opposite side, startling a hedgehog out of its burrow.

The horse could jump. Caleb had never seen such power in motion, such fluid grace. And he wasn't about to lose such a magnificent beast to the likes of some village miscreant. His jaw tightened, his anger building by the moment. Caleb gained a little more ground but the lad still didn't spot him. Or if he did, he was cocky enough to believe he could get away.

Horse and rider pounded on, Caleb in determined pursuit. The pair would soon reach the end of the field where a high rock wall separated the lower pasture from the one above. Caleb swore and urged the bay faster as he realized the lad's intent. The obstacle would pose a difficult hazard for even the most skillful rider. The horse could be injured—both of them could be killed. The boy seemed not to care.

Caleb's hands tightened on the reins as horse and rider approached the wall, and for an instant the breath froze in his lungs. If the boy brought harm to the horse, Caleb vowed, he would personally thrash the little thief within an inch of his reckless life!

To his relief and amazement, the pair sailed over the wall with absolute precision and made an impeccable landing on the opposite side.

That's it, boyo, your luck has just run out. Caleb's fury was so great he could feel it burning into the back of his neck. Reining away from the wall, he urged the bay along a path that led him through a copse of trees, a line that would cut off the youth's anticipated route of escape.

Watching through the trees as the lad took several more hazards, Caleb began to think perhaps the young man hadn't meant to steal the horse, but had merely taken him out for the pleasure of a wild morning ride. Either way, there was going to be hell to pay and the boy was about to pay it.

Lee glanced behind her, her body shaking with laughter. Tanner was gone. She had lost him. She couldn't remember having this much fun in years. It had taken less than an instant to recognize the tall figure with the wide shoulders mounted on the bay, riding like fury behind her. From the start, she had led him a merry chase. Another rider would have been hard-pressed to follow, but Tanner had stayed right on her tail. She had to give him credit. The man was a magnificent horseman.

Still, in the end, she had lost him, as she had intended from the moment she had spotted him behind her.

Lee reined in the gray, slowing the animal to a canter, letting him blow a little before she found a nice shady place for them to rest. Coeur had worked beautifully this morning, an exhilarating outing for both of them.

She grinned. More so with Caleb Tanner in relentless pursuit.

Whatever his reason for following her, it could wait until she returned to the stable. From morning to night, she was at someone else's beck and call. She had claimed this morning for herself and she would tolerate no interference.

At least those were her thoughts before a rider burst out of the woods and raced his horse up next to Coeur. She recognized Caleb Tanner's furious face the instant before his arm snaked out and he jerked her off her horse. With a shriek of outrage, her cap flying into the air, Lee landed facedown across Caleb Tanner's hard thighs, the air whooshing out of her lungs.

The last thing she expected was the impact of his big hand slamming down on her bottom, burning like fire through her breeches.

She shrieked as he delivered a second stinging blow and his palm went up again.

"Don't you dare!" she shouted, freezing his hand in midair. "You . . . you . . . madman! You jackanapes!"

Over her shoulder she saw a look of pure astonishment appear on his handsome face. "What the bloody—?"

"Put me down this instant!"

The horse danced beneath them, but Tanner made no move to release her, just kept staring at her as if he had never seen her before.

"Did you hear what I said? Put me down!"

He jerked her up so quickly her braid, already loose, came completely undone. The next thing she knew, she was standing on her feet beside his horse, her long hair curling around her shoulders, Caleb Tanner sliding off the bay and turning to face her, his expression as dark as a thundercloud.

Lee's own temper heated. "Why were you following me? What did you think you were doing?"

Hard brown eyes locked on her face. "I thought you were a thief."

"A thief!"

"That's right. When I went into the barn, the gray was missing. I saw you riding away, roaring over the fields like a Bedlamite, and I thought you were trying to steal him."

She could feel his eyes on her, taking in her clean, unmade-up face, the freckles across her nose that rice powder usually covered, the pinkness of her unrouged lips and the heightened color in her cheeks.

Something shifted in his features and some of the harshness eased from his expression. "I thought you were a boy."

She hoisted her chin, wishing she could grow about a foot, just for a moment or two. "Well, I'm not a thief and I'm not a boy."

His gaze moved down her body, taking in the breeches that fit so snugly over her legs and rump. His mouth curved into an insolent smile and she knew he was thinking of the way she had looked draped over his thighs and the stinging blows he had delivered to her bottom. "So I noticed."

More color washed into her face. She couldn't imagine how he managed to do that when no other male seemed able. "The horse is mine to do with as I please, just like all of the animals in the stable. I ride every morning and I shall continue to do so whether that meets with your approval or not."

He made a slight bow of his head, but the mocking glint in his eyes remained. "Whatever you say, Miss Durant."

"I won't stand for insolence from the men I employ. I ought to dismiss you for what you did." His expression remained inscrutable, but she thought she caught a hint of uneasiness in his eyes.

"I didn't want to lose the horse," he said.

"I gathered that." She sighed. "I'll admit it seems unfair to dismiss a man for doing his job, perhaps even putting himself at risk to do it. If I *had* been a thief, you could have been injured or even killed."

He looked into her face. "And I suppose you would have cared."

Lee forced herself not to glance away from those dark, probing eyes. "Of course I would have cared. As long as you're working at Parklands, you're my responsibility. I do, however, expect an apology. There was hardly a need to manhandle me the way you did."

The tension eased from his shoulders and a corner of his mouth edged up. His eyes looked warmer, a rich chocolate brown circled by a fringe of thick black lashes. "I assure you, Miss Durant, had I known you were a woman, I would have restrained myself. Dressed as you are, I don't think you can fault my assumptions. You're lucky your hat flew off. If it hadn't, I might have given you the thrashing I intended to give the thief."

Her bottom still burned from the blows he had delivered and his impudent smile said he knew. "If that is your idea of an apology, Mr. Tanner, perhaps you had better find employment—"

"I'm sorry. You're right, I should have been more careful. I should have checked to be sure the boy I thought was stealing a valuable horse wasn't the mistress of the house dressed up like a man."

Irritation bubbled through her. It occurred to her the man was amazingly well-spoken for a groom and she wondered vaguely where he might have come from. Wherever it was, he could return, for all she cared. Let him find another job somewhere far distant from Parklands.

"This discussion is over, Mr. Tanner. You may pick up your things when you get back to the barn." Lee turned to reach for Coeur's reins, intending to swing up on his back and ride away. She didn't need a surly head groom. Even if he was one of the best horse handlers she had ever seen, she would manage somehow without him.

Tanner caught her wrist. His hand felt big and warm and a tingle of awareness went through her. "I need this job, Miss Durant. I promise I won't interfere with your riding again."

Lee sighed. She didn't like the man, but he *was* good at his job. And with Jacob gone, she really did need him. "All right, I suppose that will have to do."

Caleb Tanner smiled and something warm slid into her stomach.

"Thank you for letting me stay," he said. Reaching toward the gray, he caught Coeur's reins and handed them over. "You're a very good rider, by the way. You and the horse performed extremely well together."

"Thank you." She found herself smiling at the compliment and realized it wasn't the usual pasted-on sort but actually sincere. "I enjoyed the chase . . . all but the end."

His mouth twitched. His lips had a sensuous curve she had noticed the first time she saw him.

"If that is the case," he said, "perhaps I could join you some morning. Maybe you could give me some pointers, help me improve my seat."

As if he needed any help. They both knew he was every bit as competent a rider as she, maybe better.

"Perhaps I could," she said loftily, just to annoy him. Reaching out to catch the reins, she waited while Tanner cupped his hands, then placed her knee in his locked palms and allowed him to lift her up onto the horse. "Good day, Mr. Tanner."

"Good day, Miss Durant."

And then she reined away, she and Coeur running like fire back toward the stable, wishing she didn't have to go, that she could stay outside in the sun and the fresh spring air.

That she didn't have to return to the house and once more become Vermillion.

Caleb watched the girl ride away. He still couldn't believe the fresh-faced young woman he had pulled off the gray was the infamous courtesan Vermillion. Without her face paint, she didn't look nearly as sophisticated as she had through the windows of the house last night, nor nearly as stunningly beautiful. Without the kohl beneath her eyes, they weren't the same too-bold blue-green, nor half as seductive as they had seemed.

She looked young and fresh and innocent. She looked sweet and lovely—and infinitely appealing. If he didn't know who she was, if he didn't suspect she might be involved in selling information to the French, he would have found himself completely enthralled.

As it was, as he rode at a distance behind her back to the stable, he found himself wondering about her, wondering at the life she had chosen, at the men she invited into her bed.

By the time he arrived at the stable, he expected to find her gone. Instead, she was there in the stall with the gray, brushing the horse's dappled coat to a brilliant sheen and currying its mane.

Caleb stepped up behind her, took the currycomb from her hand. She smelled of soap and horses, but he caught the faint whiff of rosewater. She had replaited her hair, he noticed, but the image remained of the way it looked tumbled free, in a riot of fiery curls around her shoulders.

"I'll take care of the horse," he said. "That's what I get paid for."

"Thank you, but I enjoy it." She retrieved the comb from his hand and started pulling it through the animal's mane. Standing behind her, he could feel the warmth of her body and his loins began to fill. He was hard by the time he stepped away, grateful when Arlie Spooner's head appeared over the top of the stall.

"Beg pardon, Miss Lee. Your aunt's askin' after ye, wantin' ta know when ye'll be comin' back ta the house."

Vermillion made a sound that might have been a sigh of regret. "Tell her I'll only be a few more minutes."

"Aye, Miss." Arlie tottered away in his slow, shuffling gait, his back hunched over, making him a full foot shorter than Caleb.

"Why does he call you that?" Caleb asked. "Why does he call you Lee?"

The currycomb paused. "Lee is my middle name. It's the name I prefer. It's what my friends call me."

"And Arlie Spooner is your friend?"

She looked up at him from the shadows of the barn and even without the kohl her eyes were the color of aquamarines. "Of course. Arlie has worked at Parklands since I was a little girl. He loves horses as much as I do. I consider him a very dear friend."

Caleb frowned. She was Vermillion, a seductress, a power-hungry female who took countless lovers and tossed them away like tattered clothes. She wasn't supposed to love horses and claim servants as her friends.

"Did I say something to displease you?"

Caleb shook his head. "No, not at all." His fingers brushed hers as he took the currycomb from her hand, and he tried not to notice how soft her skin felt. "You'd better go. Your aunt will be looking for you."

She tossed him a look. "Thank you for reminding me. I suppose for the short duration that you will be employed here, I shall have to get used to taking orders."

Caleb glanced away. "Sorry." He said nothing more but inwardly he cursed. He was too damned used to taking charge, too used to being in command. If he wasn't careful, Vermillion was going to suspect he was more than just a servant.

Vermillion. But the young woman he had seen this morning bore little resemblance to the image conjured by the name. As he finished grooming the gray and started on the tall bay gelding, Caleb found himself wondering about the pretty young woman who called herself Lee.

3

The horse races at Epsom Downs were attended by patrons from every level of society. From the lowliest ragpicker who stood watching from behind the rail to the royal party in their private boxes above the starting line.

The Durant women, longtime racing aficionados and owners of some of the finest racing stock in the country, sat with their own entourage, guests for the occasion who had traveled behind them in a string of expensive black carriages along the route to the track.

Activity swirled around them: apple sellers cooking on their tiny coal stoves, ale men selling beer at a penny a pot; an organ-grinder making music while one of those silly little monkeys jumped up and down on his shoulder. There were pickpockets and blacklegs, too, lying in wait for the unwary. Lee marveled at all of it, enjoying the cacophony of sights and sounds.

Anxiously awaiting the most important event of the day—the sweepstakes race in which Noir would be running—she sat next to Colonel Wingate, one of the three men most seriously vying for her affections.

A position soon to be filled.

At her aunt's insistence, Vermillion had agreed to announce her choice of lover on her upcoming nineteenth birthday. It was time she made a place for herself in the world, her aunt believed, past time, in fact.

On that particular point, Vermillion agreed. Aunt Gabby had her own life to live. She couldn't be expected to shelter her niece beneath her protective wing forever. For more than a year, Gabriella had scrupulously worked toward the goal of setting her young charge free. Vermillion would choose her first lover and assume her place as the toast of the demimonde.

And Colonel Wingate, Viscount Nash, and Lord Andrew Mondale each believed he was the man she would choose.

Vermillion sighed as she listened to the merry tune of the organ-grinder. She appreciated her suitors' confidence, but even she was not yet certain. Wingate was an attractive, imposing man somewhere near Lord Nash's age, perhaps close to forty, a military officer who had traveled extensively and was worth a goodly sum. He was intelligent and solicitous. He was also gone a great deal, which infinitely suited Vermillion.

Nash she considered a friend. He was in his late thirties, attractive in a genteel sort of way, and always interesting to talk to. The viscount was involved in politics and currently served as an advisor to the Lord Chancellor of England.

She liked Lord Nash. She just wasn't sure she wished to risk destroying the friendship she felt for him by turning it into a more intimate sort of relationship.

And then there was Mondale. Andrew was the youngest of the trio, perhaps seven and twenty, the best-looking of the three, the man she found the most attractive. Lord Andrew constantly professed his grand *amour* and he had kissed her more than once. They weren't the sort of kisses she had dreamed of, mashing her lips against her teeth and holding her a little too tightly, certainly not the sort her aunt described that made her knees feel weak, but her heart had certainly beat faster and her palms had grown a little damp.

Aunt Gabby's timely arrival in the garden had made certain the kisses were brief. There was no doubt what Mondale would do if he were given the least encouragement, but Vermillion wasn't yet ready to make that sort of commitment. Still, he was probably the man she should choose, being tall, blond, and handsome, and possessed of a passionate nature she imagined would make a good first lover.

He was also a complete and utter rogue where women were concerned, and though he read poetry to her and vowed to be faithful for the duration of their arrangement, she didn't believe for a moment that he would be.

But then, in the world of the demimonde, fidelity wasn't considered important.

"Are you comfortable?" Seated beside her in the grandstand, Lord Andrew cast a look at his competition. "The view might be better a bit farther to the right. I'm sure Colonel Wingate would be happy to give up his seat so that you might better view the race."

"Of course," the colonel said, drilling Mondale with a glare. "I should be happy to move, dearest, if that is your pleasure." Wingate's hair was black and he wore it slicked back and neatly trimmed. His eyes were light green and he had very handsome side-whiskers and a small mustache. "Or perhaps Lord Andrew's seat would better suit."

Used to the men's squabbling attentions, Vermillion simply smiled. "Thank you both for your concern, but I can see perfectly well where I am." She gazed off toward the track, then over to the stables where Noir and other competing horses were being readied for the race. She tried not to wish she were there with them instead of here with her aunt and her friends. "Besides, from here I can watch them leading the horses onto the racecourse."

Aunt Gabriella shifted on her seat in front of Lee. "Does anyone have the time?" she asked. Gowned in lavender silk with a matching silk bonnet, she sat next to Lord Claymont on her right and the colonel's aide, a young Lieutenant named Oxley on her left, next to the Countess, Lady Rotham.

" 'Tis nearly post time," the young lieutenant said, not bothering to hide his excitement.

Aunt Gabby smiled at Vermillion. "You're looking far too serious, darling. You mustn't worry. Noir is going to win."

"Of course he is," Lord Andrew said firmly. "As a matter of fact, I have placed a goodly wager to that end."

"As have I," the colonel chimed in.

"Oh, dear, that reminds me. I meant to send one of the footmen to the betting shop yesterday to place my wager—I can't imagine how I could have forgot."

Seizing on the chance for a moment's escape, Vermillion surged to her feet. "If you gentlemen will excuse me, I promise I shan't be gone more than a moment."

"Allow me to escort you," Lord Andrew said, snapping to attention beside her. "It would be highly unseemly for a lady to place such a bet on her own."

"Mondale is right," the colonel grudgingly agreed. "You must allow one of us to escort you." His look said he clearly preferred that she chose him while next to her, Lord Nash merely smiled, his manner, as always, gracious in the extreme.

Perhaps she should reconsider. Mondale might be handsome, but Nash would be gentle and constant.

"Hurry back, luvie. You don't want to miss the start." This from Lisette Moreau, a well-known courtesan and close friend of her aunt's, who sat next to Sir Peter Peasley, another of Gabriella's inner circle of acquaintances.

"The charming Mrs. Moreau is quite correct." Lord Andrew offered Lee his arm. "We had best be off." Accepting defeat, she placed a gloved hand on the sleeve of his saffron kerseymere tailcoat and they started making their way out of the stands.

"Please, pet, allow me to place the wager in your name."

Some of Vermillion's excitement seeped away. *Those are the things a man is supposed to do for a woman,* her aunt would have said. Charm her, lavish her with money and jewels. Vermillion figured she had enough money and jewelry already and she enjoyed the betting far more when the money at risk was her own.

Knowing it would do no good to argue, she simply smiled. "The betting post is just over there." She pointed in that direction and let him lead her toward their destination.

The day was warm and sunny, the sky an azure blue with just a few wispy clouds floating above the race-course. As Mondale guided her across the grass to place her wager, Vermillion's gaze strayed toward the horse barns. The first of the Thoroughbreds entered in the sweepstakes were being led out of their stalls and into the sunlight. Her gaze went in search of Noir and she spotted his gleaming black coat emerging through the wide double doors, prancing along beside his trainer.

The horse shied once, but Tanner spoke to him softly and Noir settled back down. Lee watched Tanner control the powerful horse with a skill she had rarely seen, saw the way his big hands slid so gently along the stallion's neck, and her stomach fluttered oddly. Vermillion fixed her eyes on Noir and stood rigidly next to Mondale as trainer and stallion approached.

For an instant, Tanner's dark gaze sliced to Lord Andrew before returning to her, and an expression of disdain appeared on the hard, handsome planes of his face.

"He is really quite something," Mondale said. "Prime horseflesh and no doubt." He reached out to pet the horse's nose. Noir snorted, tossed his beautiful head, and tried to back away.

"Easy, boy," Tanner said in a voice as soft and smooth as honey left out in the sun. He flicked a glance at Lord Andrew. "The color of your coat hurts his eyes. Maybe you'd better not get too close."

Though Mondale's features tightened, Vermillion fought down a laugh. She tried to be offended in Andrew's behalf, but the saffron yellow coat *was* atrocious. The amazing thing was that Tanner had the audacity to point it out.

"As Lord Andrew was, until now, unaware of Noir's taste in men's fashion," she said, "I'm sure the color of his tailcoat can be overlooked just this once."

The corner of Tanner's mouth edged up.

Andrew fixed the trainer with a warning glare, then returned his attention to her. "Your stallion looks in fine form, pet. I daresay, he's a rare galloper. I think he has a very good chance of winning."

"Chance has little to do with it," Tanner put in from a few feet away. "Noir has by far the best breeding. He's the fastest of the lot and the best prepared."

Andrew's face began to turn red. He wasn't used to receiving setdowns from the servants. Vermillion cast Tanner a look that told him he had better remember his place and stepped into the breach.

"He is definitely facing a difficult field of competitors," she said to Lord Andrew, "but Noir loves to race and he's going to win. Which is why we must hurry, my lord, and get our bets in place before the race begins."

Mondale cast a last disdainful glance at Tanner. "Exactly so." He extended his arm. "Come, my beauty."

Lee felt Tanner's eyes on her the moment she took Andrew's arm. She didn't miss the disapproval on his face as they walked away. She tried to smile, but it wasn't that easy to do.

Noir won the race, beating the next two horses, both top competitors in the field, by more than three lengths. Caleb kept his job and even received a faintly grudging compliment from the stallion's pretty owner, who hadn't spoken to him since.

By day he continued his work with the horses. As the youngest son of the Earl of Selhurst, he had been raised at the family estate in York. At Selhurst Manor, his father owned and bred some of the finest racing stock in England. Love of horses and racing were the two things he and his father had in common.

Horses had led him to a commission in the cavalry and a decision to make the service his career. Now, in a strange, unexpected way, he was enjoying his simple day's work in the stable, enjoying the thrill of seeing an animal he had worked with pit itself against a field of the very best livestock— and win.

It was the nights that left him tense and edgy, frustrated with the lack of progress he was making in his assignment.

On top of that, watching Vermillion with her endless string of wilting admirers left a bad taste in his mouth. At Epsom, she had spent most of her time with Mondale. Having lived only briefly in London and rarely moving about in Society, Caleb had never met the man, but gossip about him was rampant. Mondale was one of the most notorious rakes in London.

Caleb couldn't imagine what Vermillion saw in the simpering fop. He was a swaggering boor, as far as Caleb was concerned, and just thinking about the two of them together made a knot form in his stomach. He tried not to think of the man's pale hands on Vermillion's luscious breasts, tried not to imagine him lying next to her in bed. Determinedly he shoved the unwelcome image away and forced himself to concentrate on the job he had come there to do.

It was almost midnight. Darkness had settled over the fields and meadows around the house and quiet enveloped the landscape. Caleb moved away from the window at the rear of the mansion. With a dense growth of leafy foliage surrounding the mullioned panes, it was a safe place to view the drawing room and the stairwell leading to the second floor. The house was quiet tonight—an unusual occurrence—the Durant women retired upstairs to their respective bedchambers.

Earlier, he had seen Lord Claymont arrive, an imposing man in his late forties, and watched him make his way to the rear of the mansion to a private entrance heavily overgrown with ivy. There was a staircase just inside the door, Caleb saw, presumably to the room occupied by his mistress, Gabriella Durant.

Word was, for the past four years, Gabriella had forsaken her other lovers in favor of a long-term liaison with Claymont. From Caleb's observations thus far, the gossip appeared to be true. The woman was getting older, her looks very subtly beginning to fade. Perhaps she felt it was time to fix her interest on an individual. Whatever the reason, Gabriella was in bed with her lover and Vermillion had gone upstairs as well, and as she had done each night since his arrival, she had retired alone.

Caleb still wasn't certain what that meant. During the briefing he had received on his arrival in London, Colonel Cox had relayed a rumor that Vermillion meant to end her string of affairs. On the occasion of her birthday, she had vowed to choose a protector from one of her current lovers. Perhaps she had decided to remain celibate until then.

Whatever the reason, there was little he could discover tonight. Caleb turned away from the house and made his way across the courtyard to the stable, de-

termined to get some long-overdue sleep. Expecting
the barn to be dark, he slowed when he noticed the
glow of a lantern burning in one of the stalls and
heard the soft sound of straw being shuffled about.

Entering quietly, Caleb approached the stall. It was
the empty one, he saw, the one the fat yellow cat had
commandeered for herself. The animal was stretched
out on a bed of fresh hay, her insides heaving in and
out as if she had just finished a race. Five tiny yellow
kittens lay beside her, and stroking the cat's striped
fur, Vermillion bent over, giving Caleb a glimpse of
her thick red braid. Dressed in a simple brown skirt
and white blouse, she looked more like a servant than
an occupant of the house.

He must have made some sound. Her head jerked
up and her gaze turned toward him. He saw that her
face was free of paint. Her expression was bleak, her
aqua eyes luminous with tears. This woman was Lee,
not Vermillion, and her obvious distress bothered him
in a way he hadn't expected.

"What's wrong?" His stride lengthened as he
walked toward her. "What's happened?"

She swallowed, shook her head. "It's Muffin. I
came out to check on her and found her in labor. It
must have been going on for hours. She's had five kittens so far, but there's still one more. It think it may
be breached or something. She can't push it out. I
think she's dying."

Caleb moved farther into the stall and quietly knelt
next to the cat and her tiny newborn kittens, still trying to wrap his mind around the fact that Vermillion
was out here in the middle of the night, helping to
birth a litter of kittens. "What have you done so far?"

"I fixed her some warm milk laced with chokecherry and honey. I thought it might help with the pain, but I couldn't get her to take it." She gnawed her bottom lip. "I've seen Jacob reach into a mare to turn a foal. I know that can sometimes be done with a woman who's with child, but Muffin is too small."

Caleb ran his hand over the cat's protruding stomach. He could feel her fluttering heartbeat, her too-rapid panting breaths. The cat looked up at him and he could have sworn he saw resignation in her deep blue eyes.

"My hands are too large, but yours might not be." He reached over and caught her wrist, lifted her small, pale hand and examined it. Her fingers were slim, the nails carefully trimmed and buffed to a glossy sheen. The backs had a few stray freckles Caleb somehow found appealing. Her skin felt soft. He had the oddest urge to press his lips against her palm, to suck on the tips of her fingers.

He let go of her hand as if it had just caught flame. "I think you should try it. Perhaps if you could manage to get your fingers inside the womb, you could stretch the opening. Perhaps you could adjust the kitten and it would be able to slide out as the others have done."

She sniffed, dried her eyes on the sleeve of her blouse and looked up at him. He could read the spark of hope he had just ignited, and something tightened in his chest.

"All right. Yes . . . let's give it a try." She blotted her eyes again, bent over and petted the cat, stroking its soft fur, whispering encouragement into its ear. Licking her fingers, she eased them inside the mother cat. She stretched the opening and began to probe the womb.

Muffin meowed, but barely moved. Caleb gentled the cat, praying her efforts would work.

"I think the kitten is turned a little bit sideways," Vermillion said. "Maybe it's caught or something."

"Can you move it?"

"I'm not sure." Moving very slowly, Vermillion continued to work. Beads of sweat appeared on her forehead and he thought she might give up. She stopped once during a contraction and spoke a few encouraging words to the cat. Then she took a deep breath and started all over again.

"I think I moved it," she said, looking up. "I think I turned it so it's lined up in the proper direction." She removed her fingers and leaned down to stroke the cat. "Now if Muffin just has enough strength left to push the kitten out."

But it was only a few seconds later that the pouch slid onto the straw, the tiny kitten enclosed in its protective sack.

Vermillion grinned and laughed with relief. "We did it, Caleb, we did it!"

It was the first time she had used his first name and the intimacy washed over him like a gentle spring breeze. "Yes . . ." he said softly. "We did."

Very carefully, she helped the exhausted mother cat turn around in the straw enough to lick the sack from the kitten, then sat back on her heels in the stall, her entire face wreathed in a smile.

"She's going to be all right," she said. "I can hardly believe it." She turned to look at him and he thought she appeared almost shy. "Thank you, Caleb. She would have died if you hadn't come to help."

"You did all the work."

Vermillion made no reply, just turned and gazed

softly down at the kittens. "They're beautiful, aren't they?" But he was thinking it was she who was lovely, this girl who cried over a barnyard cat, who sat in the straw like a servant, who called him Caleb and smiled so sweetly an ache formed in his chest.

Vermillion turned to the yellow-striped cat. "*Mon Petit Pain,*" she whispered, saying the cat's name in French. More French words poured out, the endearments reminding him of who she really was and why he was there at Parklands, jolting him out of the fantasy he had allowed to creep into his head.

"It looks like your cat is going to be fine," he said brusquely. "If you don't require my services any longer, I think it's time I went to bed."

She glanced up, saw the harshness that had seeped into his features, and her gaze turned uncertain. "No . . . I won't be needing you any more tonight. You're free to go anytime you wish."

He made a curt nod of his head. "Good night, Miss Durant."

She stiffened a little where she sat in the straw. "Good night, Mr. Tanner."

He started walking, trying not to wish she had called him Caleb instead.

Caleb saw Vermillion again the next day. She came to check on the kittens and their mother, all of whom appeared to be doing very well, then ordered Jimmy Murphy, the youngest of the grooms, to saddle Grand Coeur for a late-morning ride. She was wearing her tailored men's breeches and a pair of Spanish riding boots, her hair in a single thick braid. She had never brought one of her lovers into the stable and he thought that perhaps this was her refuge, the place she could simply be Lee.

Unless, of course, she rode out each day for some more nefarious purpose.

Caleb's jaw hardened. There was every chance the woman was a spy, that she or her aunt were responsible for the deaths of thousands of British troops, a thought that sent him striding through the barn in search of a suitable mount. Saddling the big bay gelding he had ridden before, he set off behind his quarry, riding at a leisurely pace some distance away.

Careful to keep her in his sight but remaining far enough back that she wouldn't know she was being followed, he watched her gallop over the rise and for a moment disappear out of sight. When Caleb saw her again, she was riding less recklessly than she had been before but no less skillfully, putting the horse through its paces with perfect timing and precision, apparently enjoying the sun and the wind in her face.

She met no one during the ride, encountered none of her lovers or anyone else, and as she turned and started back to the stable, Caleb sat a little easier in his saddle. As yet some distance from home, he watched her ride into a copse of trees and gave in to a sudden urge to follow, knowing she would spot him the minute he rode out on the opposite side.

She was waiting, as he had expected, sitting astride the gray, her back ramrod straight and her pretty mouth thinned into an angry line.

"You're following me again. I believe you gave me your word that you wouldn't interfere."

"I'm not trying to interfere. If you recall, you agreed to give me some pointers. Or are you the one who intends to break her word?"

Her spine went even stiffer. "I believe I said I *might*

be willing to give you some pointers. We both know you ride as well as or better than I do."

He shrugged his shoulders. "I can hardly argue with a compliment." He looked out over the rolling fields, at the sheep that grazed in one of the upper pastures and the black-and-white dog there to watch over them.

"I guess, since you don't think I'm in need of a lesson, we could simply enjoy ourselves, take a couple of fences before we head back to the stable."

She eyed him with a look of suspicion that turned to one of interest. She glanced toward the stable, judging the distance. "The bay is faster than Coeur but I'm a good bit lighter, so we should be fairly evenly matched. What do you say we race back to the barn?"

Caleb looked at her small frame perched on the gray and found himself smiling. "All right—if you promise not to fire me if you lose."

Vermillion rolled her eyes. "I vow your employment is in no jeopardy. Now . . . what shall we wager? It is always more fun if one has something at risk."

He knew exactly what he'd like to win—a good, long taste of her, but the woman in his bed would have to be Lee, not Vermillion.

"I have it!" she said with a grin. "If I win, you muck out the stalls for Jimmy Murphy the rest of the week."

Caleb cocked an eyebrow. He didn't mind the work. He had done his share in his father's barn as punishment for one indiscretion or another. Besides, he didn't plan to lose. "And if I win?"

"If you are the winner, you may take the balance of the week for yourself—with pay, of course."

He shook his head. "Not good enough. If I win . . . let me see . . . How about, if I win, *you* muck out the stalls for Jimmy Murphy for the rest of the week?"

The gray pawed the ground, eager to be away. "You can't be serious."

"What's the matter? Afraid you'll lose?" He could almost see her mind working, spinning around the possibilities, intrigued by the challenge. Unable to resist.

"All right, fine. If I lose, I'll muck out the stalls for the rest of the week." She whirled her horse toward the stable. "Are you ready?"

Caleb turned the bay. "Whenever you say the word."

Vermillion grinned. "Go!" she shouted and dug her small heels into the side of the gray. The animal leaped into action and she settled low over its neck, urging the horse into a flat-out run. Caleb watched the mesmerizing sight for an instant longer than he should have, then set his heels to the bay.

It took longer than he thought it would to catch her. With her lighter frame and skillful handling of the horse, the pair flew over low rock walls and thundered across the open green fields. They were riding neck and neck, saddles groaning, legs brushing, hooves thundering as they approached the final stretch of the race and headed toward the big stone barn behind the house.

The bay began pulling ahead. He was going to beat her, but not by much. An image appeared of her small figure shoveling the heavy muck out of a stall and at the very last minute he found himself easing back on the reins. Vermillion shot past him with a whoop of glee, streaking into the courtyard in front of the stable, her braid bouncing up and down on her back.

Tendrils of fiery hair whipped around her smiling face and he found himself smiling, too.

"I did it! I won!"

Caleb pulled his horse to a stop and swung down from the saddle, the laughter still in his eyes. "Yes, I guess you did."

Vermillion kept a tight rein on Grand Coeur, who snorted and blew and danced beneath her, then finally began to settle down. Caleb reached up and clamped his hands around her waist to lift her down and tried not to notice the feminine flare of her hips, how light she felt in his hands. For a moment, her breasts crushed into his chest as he swung her to the ground and he could feel the weight of them, the softness. They were round and full and he went instantly hard.

Swearing softly, Caleb took a step away.

"That was marvelous," Vermillion said, oblivious to the havoc she wreaked in his body. "Grand Coeur ran like the wind." Leading her horse next to his toward the door of the stable, she gave him a saucy grin. "Tomorrow morning, I expect you shall make Jimmy Murphy very happy."

Caleb chuckled. They continued leading the horses and had nearly reached the entrance when a man stepped out of the shadowy interior of the barn. It was Oliver Wingate, a colonel of the Life Guards. Spying Vermillion without her sophisticated rice powder and rouge and dressed in men's clothes, his face went utterly pale.

"My God, Vermillion! I can't believe it. Is that really you?"

She blinked as if waking from a dream. Caleb saw the transformation in the squaring of her shoulders, the haughty look she gave the colonel down her small, lightly freckled nose.

When it came to men, Vermillion gave no quarter.

"I wasn't expecting you, Oliver. Had you sent word ahead of your arrival, I should have been able to greet you in a more proper manner. The fault lies with you and not me."

The colonel's gaze ran over the tight brown breeches that curved over her small round bottom and Caleb could see the lust seep into his eyes. Caleb had never met Oliver Wingate, though he had a full dossier on the man and had seen him many times there at the house. Wingate, a high-ranking officer of the Guards, had access to a good deal of sensitive information.

"My apologies," the colonel said, making a very slight bow. "I can't say I approve your choice of garments, my dear, but I daresay I shouldn't quibble if you wished to wear them for me in private sometime." His look said he wouldn't mind peeling them off her right now, and Caleb's jaw knotted.

Vermillion paid not the slightest attention. Turning away from the colonel, she handed Caleb her reins. "Give Coeur an extra ration of oats, won't you? And see he gets a good long rubdown."

Caleb made a slightly mocking bow, wishing he hadn't let her win the race, wishing instead the colonel had come upon her shoveling manure out of one of the stalls.

"Your wish is my command . . . Miss Durant." Of course she probably would have reneged on the bet, at any rate. Undoubtedly would have, he told himself.

Vermillion didn't miss the sarcasm in his voice. As if they hadn't been laughing together just moments ago, she cast him a speaking glance and started walking back toward the house, allowing Colonel Wingate to trail along in her wake. All the way back to the mansion, Wingate's eyes remained glued to her rump and Caleb knew the man was thinking of the hours he hoped to spend in her bed.

Caleb made a mental note to find out what secrets the colonel might know that could be valuable to the French. What might Wingate be willing to divulge for a chance to spill his seed in Vermillion's delectable little body?

As Caleb turned to lead the horses back into the barn, unconsciously his hand tightened into a fist.

4

~•~

Caleb received a summons from the footman the following morning. Miss Durant would be traveling to Tattersall's Auction House in the matter of the purchase of several more head of blooded stock and she required his expertise in helping her make her selections.

As soon as his duties in the stable had been performed—including, to Jimmy Murphy's great delight, mucking out the stalls—Caleb freshened and changed into clean clothing and made his way up to the rear of the house.

"Miss Durant has summoned the carriage," the butler told him when he reached the back door. "She instructs you to await her out front."

He made his way round to the front of the house and Vermillion arrived a few minutes later, in company with a slight, brown-haired woman who appeared to be her maid. He was mildly surprised to see the maid, having expected Vermillion, never one to succumb to convention, to be traveling unchaperoned.

Then he saw that today she wasn't dressed in the bold, bright colors she usually wore, but gowned very simply in a high-waisted garment of pale green muslin, her red hair covered by a matching flowered bonnet. Her unadorned features were shaded by the parasol resting on one of her small shoulders, an unremarkable young lady at first glance.

Unfortunately, Caleb thought she looked more appealing than he had ever seen her.

"Good morning, Mr. Tanner."

"Good morning, Miss Durant."

"This is Jeannie Fontenelle. She'll be accompanying us today. Jeannie, this is Mr. Tanner. He's taking Jacob's place for a while."

"Bonjour, M'sieur," the little maid said in French, reminding him again of the undercurrents swirling through the house and the Durant women's possible sympathies toward the French. The maid was slender and pretty, a few years older than Vermillion, with brown hair and warm brown eyes. He managed a smile, only a little surprised to have been introduced to a person who was, perhaps, another servant Vermillion considered a friend.

She carefully folded her parasol and he helped her climb into the open carriage, followed by her little French maid. The conveyance wasn't the fancy barouche she traveled in most evenings with her aunt, but a shiny black calèche. Caleb took a place next to the coachman, who smartly slapped the reins against the rumps of a nicely matched set of bays and they set off for Tattersall's.

Caleb had been to the auction house on several occasions: as a boy once with his father, in later years with one or another of his three brothers. Lucas, the eldest, enjoyed horse racing nearly as much as Caleb. Christian and Ethan also owned some very fine bloodstock.

Caleb thought of his father and brothers as the horses clopped along the road between the low stone walls surrounding the rolling green fields, wishing he'd had time to pay his family a visit before he had begun his assignment. Hopefully, there would be time to see them before his return to Spain.

The sun had warmed the air by the time the carriage arrived at Tattersall's and Caleb helped Vermillion and her maid descend the iron stairs onto the grass. Two ladies among the throng of mostly well-dressed men caused a momentary buzz, but there were several other women in attendance and soon their presence at the edge of the crowd was forgotten.

"This is the big spring sale," Vermillion said. "They'll be auctioning broodmares, foals, and yearlings. I was hoping you could make a cursory examination of the horses coming up for bid and then I could take a look at the ones you've initially selected."

"All right, that sounds like a workable plan. I won't be gone long." He cast her a glance. "In a crowd like this, there are bound to be pickpockets and sharpers. You and Jeannie had better stay here." Where hopefully they would stay out of trouble and he would be able to find them.

But the crowd was different at the auction house, a little more sophisticated than it was at the races, so he wasn't all that worried—aristocrats and men of the upper classes, a few in company with ladies, men with purses hefty enough to pay the price demanded by the very high caliber of breeding stock Tattersall's made available through its sales. Still, he didn't like leaving the women alone for too long.

With that thought in mind, Caleb made his way along the line of horses coming up for bid, making a brief examination of each and a mental note of those he thought might be of benefit to a stable the quality of the one at Parklands.

As he had vowed, he wasn't gone long. Still, when he returned to the spot where he had left her, Vermillion was nowhere to be seen.

Caleb softly cursed. As fashionable as the crowd appeared, there were always blacklegs ready to fleece the unwary. And a woman unaccompanied by a man was always fair game.

He released a sigh of relief when he spotted Vermillion standing near the fence examining a newborn foal and its mother about to come up for bid. Caleb could tell by the look on her face as she stared at the white-stockinged sorrel and its spindly-legged colt that she had already fallen in love.

"What do you think of Hannibal's Lady?" she asked, clearly having already made the decision to bid on both horses.

Caleb stepped closer, examined the mare's teeth, walked around her, ran his hands up and down each of her legs, checked her hooves. He took a few minutes to assess the tiny stud colt the horse had foaled.

"The mare has excellent confirmation. She looks sound and so does the foal. What about the breeding?"

"She's out of Hannibal's Bride, sired by Lochinvar. The breeding book shows a direct line to the Godolphin Arabian."

"I know Lochinvar. He won the Derby at Epsom

four years ago. With that sort of breeding, they're going to be expensive. I've found a couple of others you might be able to buy at a better price."

Her chin went up. "I want Hannibal's Lady and her foal, Lochinvar's Fist. I think whatever they cost will be worth paying."

It galled him to admit she likely might be right. He couldn't help feeling a grudging admiration at her selection. "If that is the case, why don't we go somewhere where we can enter the bidding?" He started to turn, but she caught his arm.

"I'd like you to handle that for me."

He hadn't thought of that, though he should have. A woman didn't enter the bidding, it wouldn't be seemly, perhaps wasn't even allowed. And she didn't want to be recognized as Vermillion—not that there was much chance of that. Still, she was always more circumspect when she was Lee.

Considering he also had no desire to be discovered, Caleb had hoped to stay in the background himself. Unfortunately, Vermillion hadn't left him any choice.

"As you wish," he said, not really all that concerned. His acquaintances were mostly in the military and he hardly looked like an officer of the British Army with his overlong hair and dressed in the clothes of a groom. "Come. Let's find a place to stand before Hannibal's Lady and her foal come up for bid."

The horses entered the ring not long after. By waiting for the bidding to near an end, he was able to step in without driving up the price, which seemed to please Vermillion. The financial deals were concluded and a promise made to pick up both horses on the morrow.

"It's been a good day," Vermillion said as Caleb returned the women to the carriage.

"You're sure you don't want to look at any of the others?"

"I'm satisfied for now. Perhaps another day."

"You chose exceptionally well. The mare and her foal are well worth the price you paid."

"Actually, I would have gone higher. You're a shrewd negotiator, Mr. Tanner."

He didn't mention that he had learned the trick from his father. The earl was a master of manipulation. Caleb knew that firsthand. He had joined the army to please his father and though it suited him very well, he often wondered if he would have made the same choice if it hadn't been for his father's subtle hand.

Continuing through the crowd, they had almost reached the coach when he heard someone shouting his name. Recognizing his brother Lucas's voice, Caleb silently cursed.

"That man," Vermillion said, her footsteps beginning to slow. "He seems to know you."

There was no avoiding the confrontation. Damn, Lucas. His eldest brother had a knack for stirring up trouble. Praying Lucas would follow his lead, Caleb turned and smiled.

"Lord Halford," he said, using his brother's courtesy title. "It's good to see you, sir."

His brother's dark eyebrows narrowed for an instant as he took in Caleb's homespun shirt and course brown breeches, and his hair, usually kept short, curling now at the nape of his neck. Lucas wasn't a fool. His look said whatever might be transpiring, he would play along for now—though Caleb couldn't begin to imagine the scenarios that must be swirling through his head.

"It's good to see you as well," Lucas replied easily, giving him a chance to invent whatever story he liked. His brother made a quick perusal of Vermillion, and the faint darkening of his pupils said he recognized the beauty she seemed unaware of, dressed as simply as she was.

"I used to work as a trainer for his lordship in York," Caleb supplied, making no attempt at introductions that would scarcely be appropriate for a groom.

"That's right," Lucas agreed. "I was sorry to lose you. I was hoping perhaps you might be ready to return to the north again."

"No, sir, not at present, but I'm flattered by your interest."

Lucas, ever a man with an eye for beauty, turned the full force of his charm on Vermillion. Luc was as tall as Caleb, his hair as dark. His shoulders were wide, though Lucas was slimmer, more leanly built. He also had a wicked reputation with the ladies nearly as sordid as Andrew Mondale's.

"I don't believe I've had the pleasure of your acquaintance," Lucas said, making her a very dashing bow. "Viscount Halford at your service, madam." His brother was beginning to enjoy himself. Considering his scandalous reputation and the fact he often sampled the delights of a beautiful Cyprian, he might already have met her, even spent the night in her bed. If not, he clearly wished to. Caleb felt a sudden urge to hit him.

"I'm afraid you'll have to excuse us, my lord," Vermillion said, determined not to give him her name;

certainly it wouldn't have been proper if she had done so. "My aunt will be worried should I be gone overly long." Turning away, she started walking, almost bolting for the carriage, Jeannie close at her skirts.

"Beautiful woman," Luc said, his gaze still following Vermillion. Caleb could see by the interest in his eyes he had never made her acquaintance. He was surprised by the enormity of his relief.

Lucas shifted his gaze back to Caleb. "So what are you doing with a chit just out of the schoolroom? Or are you so besotted you are posing as her groom simply to be near her?"

"Sorry to disillusion you, brother, but she isn't the innocent she seems. I'll explain everything later. In the meantime, it would be best if you forgot you ever saw me."

Luc smiled. "That shouldn't be too hard to do. Now the lady . . . that might be a more difficult matter. What did you say was her name . . . ?"

The corner of Caleb's mouth barely curved. "I'll see you when this is over. Not a word of the matter until then." His brother's smile faded as he recognized the seriousness in Caleb's tone.

"I gather there is more at stake than at first it might appear. Take care of yourself, brother." Lucas gently grasped his shoulder.

"You as well, Luc." Turning away, Caleb headed for his seat on the carriage next to the driver, grateful it had been Lucas he had encountered and not another of his brothers or one of his more rapscallion friends.

Yesterday had been more enjoyable than she had expected and Lee was delighted by the purchase of the mare and her foal. But the pleasant interlude was over and tonight her life had returned to normal. Aunt Gabriella was holding a small soiree in honor of the occasion of Lady Rotham's birthday. The countess would be turning thirty years old, not an auspicious event for some, but Elizabeth Sorenson seemed to see it as a portal into another, more hopeful phase of her existence.

"Charles has always thought of me as a child," she explained as they stood beneath one of the chandeliers in the drawing room, a crush of guests swirling around them.

Most of them were men, of course, but there were women as well, a novelist and poet named Sally Grisham, who thought herself something of a bohemian; Lisette Moreau, Sir Peter Peasley's current *chère amie;* and a couple of actresses up from Drury Lane. Colonel Wingate was there along with his aide, Lieutenant Oxley; and Jonathan Parker, Viscount Nash.

"Now that I have entered into my middle years," Elizabeth continued, "Charles shall be forced to see me as the woman I have become, rather than the innocent I was when we married."

Elizabeth rarely spoke of the man she had wed at her parents' insistence. It was interesting, Vermillion thought. Lady Rotham flouted convention at every turn. As soon as she had delivered her husband of an heir and a spare, she had begun to take lovers. She had a reputation for being shamelessly wicked and embroiling herself in one scandal after another, yet Vermillion thought that perhaps she had once been desperately in love with her husband.

Lee cast a glance at the Earl of Rotham. Charles Sorenson was refined and handsome, with light brown hair and pale blue eyes. Though he had always been more discreet than his wife in his affairs, it was rumored that just days after his marriage, Charles had returned to his mistress, a widow named Molly Cinders. Vermillion wondered if perhaps Elizabeth had been crushed by the faithless act.

"Vermillion, my beauty! At last I've found you. I've been looking all over." Mondale strode toward her. Tonight he was dressed in a peacock blue tailcoat, even brighter than his brilliant blue eyes. "The music has begun. The orchestra is playing a waltz and I believe you have promised this particular dance to me."

He cut quite a dashing figure with his handsome face and gleaming blond hair. Distantly she wondered why it was that Caleb Tanner seemed more appealing in a pair of coarse brown breeches and a simple homespun shirt.

"Good evening, my lord."

He made an extravagant bow over her hand. "You look ravishing, as always."

Lee thought that she did look pretty tonight, in a simpler gown than she usually wore, a tunic dress she had ordered in a moment of weakness that looked rather placid in contrast to Vermillion's usual extravagant attire. Though the bodice was so low it barely concealed her nipples, the silk was a soft shade of aquamarine. The tunic fit over a slightly darker lingerie skirt, both of them trimmed with cream lace. There were tiny bowknots down the front of the tunic and pearls sewn into the lace.

"Thank you, my lord. You look extremely dashing yourself." The coat might be a little bright, but it was a lovely shade of blue, slightly darker than his eyes, and the fit was perfect. Behind him, she could hear the strains of the waltz as Mondale reached for her hand.

In a way she didn't mind. She loved to waltz, scandalous as many thought it was, and Lord Andrew was an excellent dancer.

Leading her onto the polished wood floor, he pulled her into his arms, swept her into the rhythm of the music, and she felt as if she were floating. She tried to imagine what it might be like if Andrew were her lover, but her aunt had always been protective of her in that regard. She had seen a stallion mounting a mare, and during a party or ball, some of the guests might sneak away to the rooms upstairs. She had heard the odd sounds they made and of course Gabriella's friends often talked about it, so at least she knew what occurred. Still, there was no real way to envision what it might be like should they make love.

She felt Andrew's hand at her waist, drawing her shamelessly close.

"You don't have to wait, you know . . . till your birthday, I mean. We could simply go off together. We could leave tonight, if you wanted." He led her into a sweeping turn and she felt his hardened male anatomy pressing against her hip. She tried not to flush but a hint of color crept into her cheeks.

"It's too soon, Andrew. I'm not ready to make my choice." He was pressing her more and more. The men in the drawing room all believed she was a seasoned courtesan, an illusion her aunt had skillfully woven. They believed she held herself back from her string of eager admirers only to heighten the excitement when she chose her next lover.

But as Vermillion felt Lord Andrew's growing arousal and recalled what the stallion had done to the mare, she felt more and more uncertain.

When the dance came to a close, she stepped away. "I'm afraid you'll have to excuse me, my lord. There's a somewhat pressing matter I need to attend."

"Remember what I said." Andrew smiled, certain she was headed for the ladies' retiring room. "I shall remain just here, eagerly awaiting your return. Perhaps when you arrive, you will join me for a walk in the garden."

She should, she knew. The time to make her decision grew nearer each day. Perhaps if she were better acquainted with Andrew, if she allowed him to take certain liberties with her person, she would be more reassured in her choice.

She glanced up at him, remembered the dampness of his hands as his stiff length rubbed against her, and fled the drawing room instead. With a glance around to be certain no one witnessed her escape, she disappeared down the hall to the study and quietly made her way out to the garden.

Lee didn't stop until she was well away from the house, away from the light of the crystal chandeliers glowing like jewels through the drawing room windows. It was quiet in this distant part of the garden, except for the sound of her slippers crunching on the gravel path. She could see the roof of the gazebo through the branches of a sycamore tree, hear the hum of crickets and the distant hoot of an owl.

Seating herself on a wrought-iron bench near the fountain, she inhaled the musk of damp leaves, the soft scent of lilacs just beginning to blossom.

She felt better out here among the flowers, able to escape her turbulent thoughts for a while. She was listening to the trickle of water into the bowl of the fountain, beginning to relax, when she heard the rustle of leaves and recognized the sound as someone moving along the path toward the rear of the garden.

She knew she shouldn't be out there by herself. She was too far away from the house. If it were Mondale or Wingate, she might find herself with a problem. She started to rise from the bench when she heard Caleb Tanner's familiar, insolent drawl.

"You don't have to go. Not on my account."

She stood up anyway, not wishing to be at such a disadvantage. As he strolled toward her along the path, a distant torch illuminated his profile, but she couldn't read his face.

"What are you doing out here in the garden?" She tried to look affronted and ignore the little leap her heart made at his approach.

"I was listening to the music . . . watching the dancing."

"You're not supposed to be out here. You're hardly one of the guests."

"True enough." He sauntered toward her, stopped a few feet away. Propping a wide shoulder against the trunk of a tree, he gave her a sweeping perusal, then his dark gaze returned to her breasts. For an instant, she couldn't seem to breathe. When she did, each breath came much too fast and forced her bosom even nearer the top of her dress.

Tanner's eyes went dark. "And, of course, there is always the chance that someone might see me. Lord Andrew would scarcely approve your being out here alone, conversing with one of the servants."

But Caleb Tanner was as far from a servant as she had ever encountered. He was arrogant and impertinent. He was overbearing and at times even rude. In short, he was nothing at all like any man she had ever met and every time she saw him, her attraction to him grew.

It was ridiculous. She was a wealthy woman with a circle of admirers that stretched across the whole of London. She couldn't imagine how it was that he could make her feel so off balance every time they chanced to meet.

He pushed away from the tree and strolled toward her, looking dark and male and unbelievably handsome. Since the day they had spent together at Tattersall's, she hadn't been able to stop thinking about him.

"And then there is Wingate," he drawled, moving closer still. "Perhaps he'll be the one to follow you outside. I'm sure the colonel would like nothing better than to catch you alone out here, perhaps convince you to give him a tumble on the cushions in the gazebo. Or perhaps he has already done that. Perhaps he would prefer to take you right here by the fountain."

Anger shot through her, dissolving any of the ridiculous attraction she might have felt for him. "How dare you speak to me that way!" Caleb stood right in front of her, close enough that when her hand swept out, it made a resounding crack across his cheek.

He didn't move, not a muscle. He didn't even flinch. But she could see into his eyes and they had turned as black as pitch.

"My apologies," he said coolly. "More likely it will be Nash who follows, come to check on your welfare. Perhaps he hopes you will reward him for his concern."

The anger mixed with hurt. Was that the way he thought of her? No better than a whore? Her bottom lip threatened to tremble. She reminded herself that she was Vermillion. She didn't tolerate condemnation from a servant, and especially not this one.

"You have two choices, Mr. Tanner. You may remove yourself from my sight this instant, or you may pack your things and leave Parklands for good."

Something flickered in his eyes. Tanner stared down at her for several long moments and there was turmoil in his gaze.

"Why do you do it?" he asked very softly. "You don't need the money. Is it really so exciting? Is it worth the price you pay?"

Why did she pretend to be the most sought after courtesan in London? Why, on the night of her nineteenth birthday, would she meekly accept the life her aunt had so neatly laid out for her?

Because it was what Aunt Gabby wanted. What Gabriella Durant needed as other people needed to breathe.

The years were stealing away her aunt's beauty. Little by little, Gabriella was losing her vaunted position as La Belle, but through Vermillion she could continue the life she loved.

Because Lee owed her everything.

Because Gabriella had saved her from the terrors and loneliness of the orphanage she had been taken to after her mother had died, had brought her instead to London and given her a home. Because she had provided Lee with a brilliant education and set up a trust fund that would protect her as her own mother could not.

Because, should Lee choose another, different sort of future, she would be showing contempt for the life her aunt had chosen, spitting on the woman who had been the only real family she had ever known.

There were a thousand different reasons that Lee had become Vermillion, but none that Caleb Tanner would understand.

"I'm a Durant," she answered softly. "It's what Durant women do."

Caleb said nothing, just stood there in the shadows silently searching her face.

There was something in his expression as he turned and walked out of the garden. Vermillion couldn't tell if it was contempt or if it was pity.

5

❧❦❧

"Good afternoon, Captain Tanner."

"Good afternoon, Colonel. I apologize for my appearance. I didn't have time to change." Still wearing his homespun shirt and breeches, Caleb stood in front of Colonel Cox's desk in an office in Whitehall that Cox had commandeered for his use. Two chairs sat on the opposite side, one of them empty, the other occupied by Major Mark Sutton, the third member of this small band of men under special orders from General Sir Arthur Wellesley.

"Yes, well, that is understandable, given the nature of your assignment. We had hoped to hear from you sooner, but perhaps that was a bit optimistic. What have you got to report?"

"I'm sorry to say, Colonel, I haven't learned all that much." Dressed in the clothes of a groom, Caleb felt vaguely uncomfortable in the presence of his direct superiors, but his time away from Parklands without arousing suspicion was limited, as both of them understood. "The potential for collecting information is certainly there. Both of the women keep company with men who are highly connected, either in the military or in the government."

"You're speaking mainly of Nash and Wingate." The colonel was a man in his late fifties, silver-haired and strong-featured, with an air of vitality that seemed almost palpable.

"In Vermillion's case. The Earl of Claymont is also well connected. For the last several years, he has been keeping a close association with Gabriella Durant."

"You mean she is his mistress," the major put in. Sutton was only a few years older than Caleb, perhaps thirty-one or -two, a tall man with curly black hair. He had been studying to become a barrister before his enlistment. No one seemed to know why he'd changed his mind, but he seemed to have a number of interesting—if seemingly illicit—connections that had, on numerous occasions, proved useful in assignments like these.

"From what I've been able to discern," Caleb said, "Claymont and Gabriella Durant share a mutually exclusive relationship."

Colonel Cox plucked a quill pen from the shiny brass holder on his desk. "That would make a certain amount of sense. According to gossip, Claymont's been in love with the woman for years."

"Hardly surprising," Caleb said. "Both the Durant women are highly skilled in the art of pleasing a man."

Cox's paused in the act of dipping the pen into a crystal inkwell and one of his bushy gray eyebrows went up. "Are you speaking from personal experience, Captain?"

Caleb thought of the well-deserved slap he had received in the garden and shook his head. "No, sir. Merely from observation."

"For the present, you should probably keep it that way. You need to remain objective. That might become more difficult if you are bedding one of the wenches."

Major Sutton uncrossed his legs. "On the other hand, it might prove an interesting means of obtaining information. It is, after all, the means we suspect the Durant women may be employing to aid the French."

Cox scratched something on the sheet of foolscap in front of him. "I don't believe seducing a woman falls under the category of Captain Tanner's current duties, though as the major says, it does pose certain possibilities."

Caleb thought of Vermillion as she had looked in her snug boy's breeches and ignored a subtle throbbing in his groin. He fixed his attention firmly on the colonel.

"I was wondering, sir, if perhaps you might know what sort of information Colonel Wingate might have access to that might be valuable to the French."

The pen stopped moving. Cox looked up. "Colonel Wingate was injured six months ago during a training exercise when he suffered a fall from his horse. At that time, he was reassigned to the command of General Ulysses Stevens of the Royal Life Guards. The general is among those men whose advice is highly valued. He is kept abreast of troop movements on the Continent and would have had full knowledge of Wellesley's intention to confront the enemy at Oporto."

"Are you saying Wingate would also have that sort of knowledge?"

"I'm sure he does." Cox stuck the quill pen back into its holder. "Unfortunately, Captain Tanner, unless one of us can prove Colonel Wingate relayed that information to a person or persons other than those in proper circles, we cannot impinge upon his honor by making any sort of accusation."

"I understand, sir."

"What do you think of Lord Nash?" Cox asked. "Jonathan Parker is far more subtle than most of the Durant girl's admirers, but the plain truth is, he is just as eager to have her as the next man."

"Nash has made it clear he wishes to become her protector," Caleb said. "I'm uncertain whether or not he has ever been one of her lovers."

The colonel plucked a bit of lint off the front of his scarlet uniform jacket. "I realize Nash is a close friend of your father's, Captain, but as an advisor to the chancellor, he has access to a good deal of useful information. Is there any possibility he might be passing some of that along to the French, either through Vermillion or Gabriella Durant?"

"Lord Nash has always been a loyal Englishman, sir. I don't believe he would ever betray his country." And Caleb admired him greatly, had since he was a boy.

While his father was busy with his horses or running his earldom, Nash, the son of a peer who was his father's friend, always managed to find a spare moment for him.

That was years ago, of course. Caleb had rarely seen the man since. He doubted Nash would even recognize him now, though he made a point of avoiding him at Parklands.

"Just remember," the colonel warned, "Nash wants the girl—perhaps more than any other of her admirers—and when it comes to a woman he wants, no man is completely immune."

No, Caleb thought. *It would be difficult for any man to be completely immune to Vermillion.* "I'll keep that in mind, sir."

"Make certain that you do. Now, I suppose you had better hie yourself back to Parklands before you are missed."

"Yes, sir."

"Keep your eyes and ears open, Captain."

"I will, sir."

"That is all. You are dismissed."

Cox watched the youngest of the three men assigned to help him uncover a traitor, or more likely a ring of them, and thought that Wellesley had chosen extremely well. Captain Tanner was a fine officer, a skilled cavalryman and decorated hero of the war. He knew horses and racing—the reason he had been chosen—was intelligent and loyal, with a father who was a powerful friend to the Tories and extremely proud of his son. The captain would do the job that had been assigned him.

Across the desk, the major shifted in his chair. "Perhaps he'll wind up seducing one of them. I still think a more intimate relationship might be the answer to our prayers."

Cox raised an eyebrow. "You may be right, Major. If you are, Tanner is likely the man for the job. I don't believe even the practiced skills of a courtesan could seduce our handsome young captain away from his duties."

"Tanner's a good man," Sutton agreed. "And you're right. His career means everything to him. He won't let a woman come between him and his job."

*   *   *

It was past time she made a trip into London. Lee tried to go at least once a week, but somehow the days had rushed past and she had been unable to slip away. Forgoing her usual morning ride, she dressed in a simple gown of yellow muslin, summoned her smart little park phaeton, and along with Jeannie set out for the house she had rented in a quiet neighborhood at the edge of Bloomsbury a little over two years ago.

Though the three-story brick structure didn't perch on a street in Mayfair or any of the fashionable districts of London, the buildings in the area were clean and well cared for, the occupants mostly of the working classes, and there was a small park just a few blocks to the east.

"We should 'ave come in zee carriage," Jeannie grumbled in her heavy French accent, looking up at a sky that had begun to grow cloudy. "It will probably rain before we get back to the 'ouse."

"If it does," Lee said cheerfully, "we will simply put up the top. It might get a little damp going home but I'm sure we'll survive it."

Jeannie muttered something Vermillion ignored. Like a number of the servants in her aunt's employ, Jeannie was the child of a French immigrant who had fled to England during the Revolution. The ongoing troubles with Napoleon often made it difficult for French-speaking persons to find employment. Being part French herself, Gabriella felt it her duty to help whenever she could.

It was a similar sort of empathy that had led Vermillion to rent the house in Buford Street. Stepping up on the porch, she used the lion's head knocker to announce her arrival, and a few minutes later, the wooden door swung wide.

"Lee! We've missed you! Please come in." This from Helen Wilson, a plump, smiling young woman three years Lee's senior who had worked as a chambermaid for Lisette Moreau. Helen wasn't French but she had been in need, and Lee had decided to help her.

Since that time, four other young women, each *enceinte* and unmarried, had come to her for help. All of them now lived in the house in Buford Street.

"How are you, Helen? How is the baby?"

"Robbie is fine. So am I. Come and see. He always gets so excited when you come for a visit."

Lee smiled, pleased at the words. She loved little Robert Wilson, loved all of the children in the house. Helen set the boy on his feet and the baby of twenty-two months waddled toward her, a slobbery grin on his face. He held up his chubby little arms and she scooped him high against her breast.

"Hello, sweetheart. I've missed you so much. What a big boy you're getting to be."

Robbie giggled and banged his little fists up and down on her shoulders. Lee hugged him fiercely, then set him back down on his feet. Turning away, the little boy toddled over to where little Jilly, two months old, lay on a blanket near her mother's feet.

Lee stopped to talk to Jilly's mother, Annie Hickam, where she sat bent over her sewing. Born in a Southwark slum, Annie was a former prostitute who had earned her living on the street. Never a beauty, she was rawboned and rough-skinned, but she fiercely loved her child and she had vowed to make a better life for both of them.

" 'Tis good to see ya, Miss," Annie said. They talked about the baby and the colic she had suffered last week.

"She's fine now, don't ya see? Such a good lass, she is." She reached down, picked up the blanket-wrapped infant, and cuddled the child against her breast. "Aren't ya, sweet luv?"

Lee held the baby for a while, then handed her back to her mother and went over to check on the other two newborns in the house, Joshua Sweet and Benjamin Carey, and their mothers, Sarah and Rose. When she finished, she walked over to chat with a young pregnant woman named Mary Goodhouse, the newest addition to the group.

Mary was a chambermaid from Parklands who had gotten involved with a young man named Fredrick Hully, a lad from the village. A few months with Freddie, and Mary found herself with child, her belly swollen, and Freddie gone off to seek his fortune in the Colonies.

"He promised he would send for me," Mary had said, her soft brown eyes glossy with tears. "If he had known about the babe, he would have taken me with him."

Perhaps he would have, but Lee didn't think so. In the meantime, the house in Buford Street was the answer to Mary's prayers.

"How are you feeling, Mary?" She was small and brown-haired, her round belly ill-concealed by the apron she wore over her skirt. "You aren't still having those bouts of sickness in the mornings?"

"Oh, no, Miss. Not anymore. Annie made me 'er special tea, and I 'aven't 'ad nary a problem since."

"I'm glad to hear it. Have you chosen a name yet?"

"I was thinkin' maybe Jack, if it's a boy. I thought I might call 'er Lee if it's a girl." She glanced up, a little embarrassed. "That is, if ye wouldn't mind."

"I wouldn't mind at all," Lee said softly, touched by the gesture. "I'd be extremely pleased."

Mary flushed and turned away and all of the women busied themselves with their work. Lee paid the rent, but the women took care of the rest of the expenses. They took in sewing and word of their skill had spread. Lee thought that perhaps in time, they wouldn't need her help at all, which meant she would probably not see them as often. Considering how fond she had grown of the children, it was a notion she found oddly depressing.

A courtesan used every trick she knew *not* to become *enceinte,* but Lee had always thought it would be wonderful to have a child of her own. At least if it happened, she thought, she wouldn't need a man's financial support. But what about the child?

Secretly, she had always yearned for a father. Wouldn't a child, even one born out of wedlock as she had been, benefit from some sort of relationship with its sire?

Lee pondered the question a little while later as she and Jeannie left the house and made their way out to the carriage. What if by accident—and the women she had just left proved how easily it could occur— she were to find herself with child?

Mondale might be handsome, but he wasn't the sort to be bothered with children. Wingate would rarely be around. Lord Nash, widowed and childless, would undoubtedly be a solid, responsible father to any offspring he might sire.

As she settled herself on the seat of the phaeton

and picked up the reins, a memory flashed of Caleb Tanner, kneeling in the straw next to the kittens. She thought of his gentleness with the foal.

Very firmly, she slapped the reins, setting the carriage into motion and pushing the unwelcome images away.

Caleb watched the smart little phaeton disappear down the street and simply shook his head. Of all the scenarios he had envisioned as he had followed Vermillion to London, traveling to the city to visit a home for unwed mothers was scarcely among them.

In truth, even though today she wasn't dressed in the garb of an expensive courtesan, he had imagined she might be meeting a secret lover, perhaps the man who transported information she or her aunt garnered from one of their numerous beaux. On her arrival at the house in Buford Street, determined to find out who that man might be, Caleb had made his way down the alley to the rear of the house. Checking the windows, he found one of them unlocked and quietly slipped inside.

From a downstairs bedchamber, he could see along the hall into a parlor that was—to his utter dismay— filled with women and babies. It didn't take a master of deduction to realize Vermillion wasn't there to meet a lover. Caleb had listened to a portion of the women's conversation, just to be sure, then returned outside and waited until she left.

As soon as her carriage rolled out of sight, he knocked on the kitchen door and the woman called Annie pulled it open.

"I hope you can help me. I must have made a wrong turn somewhere. I'm looking for Langston

Street in Covent Garden. Can you point me in that direction?"

Annie smiled. She was a big, rough-edged woman, and there was a look of weariness in her eyes that spoke of the hard life she had lived. Annie was cordial and accommodating, giving him directions, even a crust of bread and a hunk of cheese to take with him. She seemed a little lonely and he took advantage of her need for conversation, letting her tell him about her friends.

When he mentioned the young woman he had seen leaving the house, Annie told him her name was Lee Durant and she was their guardian angel, the one who paid their quarterly rent.

"I'd think such a pretty little thing would have a gentleman escort," he said.

"Oh, no, not Miss Lee. She comes just with her maid. That way she can spend more time with the babies."

Caleb bade Annie farewell and returned to where he had left his horse. As he mounted the gelding and started the journey back to Parklands, he couldn't help thinking about the women, wondering at Vermillion's motives. None of the mothers appeared to be French. And only the girl named Mary had come from Parklands.

Perhaps, as she had with the cat and its kittens, Lee was simply the sort who took in strays.

Caleb wished it weren't so easy to believe.

6

From the window of her bedchamber, Lee looked out across the rolling green fields. She could see the racecourse her aunt had constructed three years ago when Lee had convinced her— with the help of Lord Claymont—they should not only breed Thoroughbreds, but race them as well.

The track wasn't large, but it was sufficient for flat-race training and Caleb Tanner was there, working with Noir. She couldn't be certain, but she caught a glimpse of bright red hair and thought Jimmy Murphy must be riding him. Jimmy had started as a stable boy, doing the most menial tasks, but Tanner had recognized a talent that had thus far been overlooked.

At sixteen, Jimmy was small for his age, and with older brothers who were also small, there was every chance he wasn't going to get a whole lot larger. From the upstairs window, Lee watched horse and rider pounding around the course east of the stable. Most of the morning was already gone, but there was still time to get in a ride if she hurried.

In concession to the lateness of the hour and the fact that the household was awake, she dressed in her forest green riding habit and made her way out to the stable. Coeur poked his head over the stall and nickered softly. She led him out and brushed his coat, hoping one of the grooms would appear to help her with the cumbersome sidesaddle. Instead, old Arlie creaked toward her.

" 'Ere, Miss, let me saddle 'im fer ye."

The sidesaddle was heavy. There was no way Arlie could lift it. Together they might manage, but she didn't want to hurt the old man's feelings.

"It's all right, Arlie. I think Billy is around here somewhere. Why don't we let him take care of it?"

"Don't be daft, gel. How many 'orses 'ave I saddled fer ye over the years?" Before she could stop him, Arlie hefted the heavy saddle off the wall. For a moment, he teetered backward, then he swayed forward, his thin legs wobbling with the effort of holding the heavy saddle against his bony chest.

"Arlie!" Lee cried as he teetered backward again. Racing forward, she reached up to help him hold the saddle. An instant later, Lee, Arlie, and the heavy sidesaddle with its padded tapestry seat all went crashing to the ground.

For several seconds, Lee just lay there beneath the saddle, on top of Arlie, the breath knocked out of her lungs, terrified she had killed her ancient groom.

Then the sidesaddle lifted away. A grinning Caleb Tanner stood above her, the saddle hoisted up on one of his wide shoulders. "Need some help?"

Reaching down, he took her hand and hauled her to her feet. Embarrassed, wishing she could wipe the grin off his handsome face, she turned her attention to

Arlie, still sprawled on the floor of the barn, blinking owlishly up at her as if he had no idea where he was.

"Arlie! Are you all right?"

He reached for the hand Caleb offered him and struggled back to his feet. "Just fine, Miss. Right as rain. Fit as a fiddle. Got a mite off balance, is all."

"Yes, I could see that." She turned, saw that Caleb was fighting another grin. "What are you staring at, Mr. Tanner? Since you don't seem to have any trouble hoisting that saddle, why don't you rig out Grand Coeur?"

"Yes, ma'am," he said, though the corner of his mouth twitched. Caleb turned to his task while Lee brushed straw and dirt off her habit, and a few minutes later, the tall dappled stallion was saddled and ready to go.

Walking beside her, Caleb led him over to the mounting block. "Nice day for a ride," he said.

"Yes . . . yes, it is."

"That big red gelding could use some exercise. I don't suppose you'd want company."

Her stomach contracted. Women often rode out with their grooms. It was a matter of protection. But most grooms didn't look like Caleb Tanner. They weren't the sort to make a woman's insides tremble or her heart start to sputter. And after his cruel words in the garden . . .

But Caleb always seemed different out here.

Then again, so was she.

"As you say, the red could probably use some exercise." She cast him a look and couldn't resist adding, "And there is a chance I might be willing to give you a pointer or two on how to improve your seat."

A corner of his mouth edged up. "One thing I

know for sure . . . yours doesn't need the least bit of improvement."

She could tell by the wicked glint in his eyes he wasn't talking about riding. She opened her mouth but couldn't seem to think of a single thing to say. She felt his big hands at her waist, lifting her up onto the sidesaddle, then he turned and walked away.

"I'll catch up with you at the top of the rise," he said to her over his shoulder.

Setting a leisurely pace up the hill, Lee reined up to wait for him there, letting Grand Coeur graze contentedly among the deep green grasses. As Caleb rode up the hill to meet her, she couldn't help admiring the ease with which he sat his horse, the way his shoulders remained erect while his body moved gracefully with the rhythm of the animal beneath him.

He rode with the confidence of an aristocrat, and she wondered, as she had more than once, who he was and where he had come from. There was something about him . . . something that simply did not fit. His speech was that of a gentleman and when he wasn't being surly, his manners were the equal of any of Aunt Gabriella's wealthy guests. Perhaps he was the son of a nobleman fallen on hard times, she thought romantically, trying to imagine what travails he might have suffered that had forced him into the ranks of the lower classes.

He reined up beside her and patted the big gelding's neck. "Duke is full of himself this morning. Perhaps a jump or two will help even out his disposition."

The horse's real name was Le Duc de Gar, but that was too long to say, so they just called him Duke. She smiled, liking the idea. "Let's head north, toward the boundary line." An uphill journey, crisscrossed with streams and low rock walls. "That little run should take some of the starch out of him."

Caleb nodded and they rode off in that direction. The sun was warm on her back and the breeze felt cool against her cheeks. Coeur performed solidly and as Caleb put the bay through its paces, the horse settled into an easy gallop.

Lee was breathing a little faster, exhilarated by the thrill of the chase. They reached a small copse of trees at the north end of the property and Caleb pulled rein on his horse in the shade of the trees.

"I thought we'd rest here for a while," he said. "Let the horses graze a little."

"Sounds like a good idea."

Caleb swung down from his saddle, walked over and caught her round the waist. As she rested her hands on his shoulders to balance herself, his gaze locked on her face. She could see a faint ring of gold in the centers of his eyes, see the way they began to darken. Something thickened in the air between them, grew warm and soft, seemed to swirl around them like an invisible red-hot mist.

Slowly, inch by inch, Caleb lowered her to the ground, his body so close she brushed against him the length of her slow descent. She could feel the heat of him, the solid wall of his chest. She couldn't breathe. The air seemed to burn in her lungs. Caleb set her on her feet but didn't let her go. Instead his hand came up and very gently caught her chin.

He was close. So close that if he lowered his head the least little bit ...

"Caleb . . ." she whispered the instant before his mouth settled softly over hers.

Lee closed her eyes. She could feel the fullness of

his bottom lip, the softness, the heat of his mouth moving over hers. His thumb felt warm where it lightly brushed her jaw, controlling the kiss, allowing him to take what he wanted, and yet it was nothing like any other kiss she'd had before.

He tilted her head back and kissed her again, sampling her lips, the corners of her mouth, coaxing her to open for him. She felt the slick heat of his tongue sliding over hers, taking what she had never given a man before. She hadn't expected the quick surge of pleasure, the soft heat coiling in her belly, the urgent pull low in her womb.

He smelled faintly of leather and horses, a pleasant, masculine scent, and where her palms rested on his chest, bands of muscle flexed beneath her fingers.

She knew she should stop him. Mondale would be furious and Wingate would go into a snit. Aunt Gabriella would be wildly disappointed. But she made no protest when Caleb pulled her closer and deepened the kiss, and a sweep of desire washed over her.

Lee clung to his powerful shoulders, drowning in the slow, deep, lingering feel of his mouth and tongue, wishing the moment never had to end. He kissed her one way and then another, kissed her fiercely then gently, kissed her the way she had dreamed a man should kiss. It made her head spin and her knees go weak. It made her heart pound so hard she was sure it would tear through her chest.

"Caleb . . ."

He didn't answer, but she felt his mouth against the side of her neck, felt the warmth of soft, moist kisses on the skin beneath her ear. She moaned when he took her mouth again, more possessively this time, and her legs began to tremble. One of his big hands moved up to cup her breast while the other began to work the buttons on the front of the short velvet jacket of her riding habit.

Dear God, it was time to bring this to an end. Plans had been made for her future, plans that didn't include Caleb Tanner.

Trembling all over, she turned her face away, ending the kiss, then breaking free of his arms, dizzy for a moment, swaying a little on her feet.

"Easy," he said, reaching out to steady her. "Why don't we go someplace where we can be private? There's a little shepherds' cabin not far away. I saw it the last time I was out here."

She only shook her head. "I have to go," she said, backing away, wetting her kiss-swollen lips, tasting him there. "They'll be . . . they'll be wondering where I've got off to."

Caleb frowned. "You're frightened," he said, his eyebrows drawing together as she stepped even farther away. "I didn't mean to scare you."

I'm not afraid, she told herself. *I'm Vermillion. I'm not afraid of any man, and especially not Caleb Tanner.*

She tossed her head, wishing her hair was fashionably done up and she was wearing rice powder and rouge, wishing she felt more like Vermillion and less like Lee. "Don't be silly. I wasn't afraid. I was enjoying a bit of sport, is all. I wanted to see what it might be like to kiss you."

He stiffened and a muscle tightened in his cheek. "That's what you were doing? Having a bit of sport?"

She glanced away, then turned back and forced herself to smile. "I didn't see any harm in it."

Caleb stalked her, looking hard, even dangerous. "Then tell me, Miss Durant, did my kisses meet with your approval?"

She shrugged her shoulders, feeling not at all like Vermillion and trying so very hard to pretend. "I suppose so. Andrew's kisses are a bit more forceful. Yours were—"

Caleb jerked her hard against him, cutting off her words. "So you like things rough—is that it? Then rough is what you'll get."

She tried to turn away, but he caught her jaw, holding her immobile, and his mouth crushed down with brutal force.

It was a hard, taking kiss. A fierce, plundering kiss with none of the gentleness he had shown her before and yet her whole body went liquid with heat. Her fingers dug into the front of his shirt and she wasn't sure if she were trying to pull him closer or push him away. It took sheer force of will to tear herself free and step away from him.

Once she did, for an instant she just stood there, staring into his face, amazed that even his rough, brutal kisses had the power to move her, trying not to flinch beneath his cold regard. Something burned at the back of her eyes, though she wasn't quite sure why. Afraid she was about to embarrass herself, she turned and grabbed the reins of her horse.

There was a rock not far away. She tugged Grand Coeur in that direction, settled herself in the sidesaddle, whirled the gray, and urged the horse into a gallop, bolting out of the trees and riding like fury back to the house.

She would be safe there, she told herself. Safe from Caleb Tanner. Safe from herself.

It was the latter that Lee feared the most.

Caleb watched the small figure riding off down the hill. He was hard and throbbing, aching with unspent desire, but it was the tightness in his chest he couldn't ignore. If he closed his eyes, he could still see Vermillion's face when she had looked up at him, see the moisture in her beautiful aqua eyes. She had stared at him as if he had wounded her in some way, as if she had given him a measure of her trust and he had betrayed her.

Damn it to hell, it was madness. The woman was one of the most notorious courtesans in England. She might be young, but already she'd had countless lovers. Stories of her exploits circulated with regularity in gentlemen's clubs all over London. Even now, the betting books laid odds as to which of her lovers she would choose as her protector.

So how was it her soft mouth had trembled under his as if she were an innocent? As if she had rarely been kissed before and certainly never in a way that had stirred her to passion?

It was insane to have kissed her at all, he knew, but ever since his meeting with Colonel Cox, visions of her full lips and ripe body had haunted him. He couldn't seem to think of anything else.

An intimate relationship, Major Sutton believed, might prove highly useful. *Seduce the seductress.* Why not? Even Colonel Cox believed the notion might have merit. Who knew what might be discovered?

But he hadn't expected her kisses to be so sweet. Hadn't expected her to behave like the innocent she often appeared. He hadn't expected the wild surge of jealousy he had felt when she mentioned her lover.

Or the tears in her eyes when she turned and rode away.

Dammit to bloody hell!

Caleb cursed himself as he swung up onto the back of the bay. He was an officer in the British Army, a man with an important assignment. What was he going to say to Colonel Cox if Vermillion sent him packing? If she dismissed him because he couldn't control his lust? God's teeth, it didn't bear thinking about.

He would have to apologize. There was no way around it. He just prayed it would be enough.

Sitting across from her friend, Elizabeth Sorenson, Lady Rotham, Gabriella Durant heard the sound of a door slamming closed at the rear of the house. A few minutes later, she recognized Vermillion's footsteps in the hall, then the thump of her kidskin boots racing up the stairs.

Gabriella rose from the sofa in the drawing room and made her way into the entry. "Vermillion? Darling, you mustn't be too long. Lord Nash is coming over this afternoon. I hope you haven't forgotten. He's promised to drive us into town to see the latest addition to Madame Tussaud's waxworks."

But Vermillion didn't answer. Gabriella sighed as she returned to the drawing room, an impressive salon done in cream and pale blue with ivory and gilt furniture and blue-and-gold damask curtains. A Chinese cloisonné vase overflowing with tulips sat on the marble mantel.

"I hope she's all right. I've been worried about her lately."

Elizabeth picked up her gold-rimmed porcelain teacup and took a sip of tea. "Why on earth would you be worried?"

"I don't exactly know. She's been behaving a little bit strangely. Perhaps she is nervous. Her birthday is coming up soon. She has promised to choose a protector. Perhaps she is having second thoughts."

"It was her idea, wasn't it?"

"For the most part, though I thought it well past time. Perhaps I pressed her a bit more than I should have."

"Nonsense. Vermillion is a vibrant, intelligent young woman—one who is currently being wooed by the some of the wealthiest, most sought after men in England. It's time she started living, made a place for herself in the world."

"That is what I always believed. From the day I brought her home from the orphanage, I began to think of her future. Marriage, of course, was never a consideration." She flicked a glance at her friend. "You and I both know being a wife is nothing more than a lifetime of discontent. Being shut away in the country, little more than a broodmare for one's husband." She shuddered dramatically. "It is hardly something I would wish for my niece, even were it possible to find a suitable match— which of course is out of the question."

"Choosing a lover is the only solution," Elizabeth agreed, one of the few who knew the truth of Vermillion's virginity. "We must simply be certain she picks the right man."

Gabby smoothed a wrinkle from the front of her

bright blue muslin gown. "She seems to have narrowed it down to three."

Elizabeth nodded. "Lord Nash, Colonel Wingate, and Lord Andrew Mondale. I think she would probably be better off with Nash, but Mondale is terribly dashing and he carries a desperate *tendre* for her. If I were to choose, I would pick someone young and passionate for my first lover." She studied the leaves in the bottom of her cup. "Charles was that way when we were first wed. Unfortunately, the passion he felt was not for me."

"Charles was a fool," Gabriella snapped, setting her cup and saucer down with a clatter. "Moll Cinders was little more than a prostitute off the streets. She had no style, no sense of class."

Elizabeth laughed bitterly. "That is scarcely a consolation, Gabriella."

"The man was an idiot. You are beautiful and talented, intelligent and kind." She sighed. "But then, husbands all seem to carry the singular trait of being enamored of any woman other than the one they married."

Elizabeth made no reply, just returned her cup and saucer to the Hepplewhite table beside her chair. "At least I was smart enough to find a way out." She grinned, a look of remembrance creeping into her bright blue eyes. "I shall always think of Lord Halford with genuine fondness. Lucas is as talented in bed as he is at the gaming tables. He was younger then, of course, not so jaded. But he was a wonderful lover."

Elizabeth gazed upward, toward Vermillion's room on the second floor. "Yes . . . if I were your niece, I would definitely choose a young man for my first time."

"And gossip has it Mondale is nearly insatiable in bed." Gabriella gave up a wistful sigh. "Oh, to be that young again."

Elizabeth just laughed. "You needn't mourn your lost youth, Gabby, certainly not as long as Claymont continues to share your bed."

Gabriella thought of the handsome man who was her longtime lover and her worry for Vermillion faded. It was a good life for a woman, a life of excitement and freedom, living as you pleased, under no man's thumb.

Yes, she was doing exactly the right thing.

Two days passed. Vermillion was avoiding him, and knowing how much pleasure she took in her horses only made Caleb feel worse. It was late in the afternoon when he passed behind the house and chanced to see her slipping out the back door. Determined to head her off, he watched her descend the terrace steps and make her way to the spot she liked at the rear of the garden.

Caleb glanced around, checking to be certain no one saw him, then entered the garden and started walking quietly through the foliage, emerging a few minutes later in front of the bench next to the fountain. The moment she saw him, Vermillion surged to her feet.

"I told you before—you're not welcome here."

"I know," he said softly. "I came to apologize."

Vermillion glanced away. She looked paler than she should have, less vibrant, and he wondered if he were the cause. "You have nothing to apologize for. The fault was mine. I shouldn't have let you kiss me."

He eased a little closer, caught a whiff of her soft

perfume, and his groin subtly tightened. "You didn't really let me. Things just got a little out of hand. I work for you. I shouldn't have forgotten that. I'm sorry. I didn't mean to hurt you and I know that I did."

She swallowed. She didn't look much like Vermillion today, in her pale green muslin gown sprigged with little pink roses. She looked softer, more vulnerable. More like Lee. He found himself saying things he hadn't intended.

"I just . . . you just looked so pretty that day and I . . . I wanted to kiss you. If you hadn't mentioned Mondale—"

Her head came up. "What does Andrew have to do with it?"

He cleared his throat, embarrassed that he had reacted as strongly as he had. "You said you preferred the way Mondale kissed and—"

"I never said that." She looked down at her slippers, studied the leaves on the path beside her toes. She lifted her gaze to his face. "I liked your kisses, Caleb. No one's ever kissed me quite that way. I liked it very much."

Whatever he was feeling, the pressure in his chest began to ease. "As I said, I'm sorry. It won't happen again."

She nodded, but instead of looking pleased she looked regretful and thoughts of seduction slithered like a serpent back into his head. His body clenched and his loins began to fill. Caleb silently cursed.

"Thank you for the apology," Vermillion said, pulling his thoughts in a safer direction. "You didn't really have to. I wouldn't have fired you. Not for that."

Caleb gazed off toward the stable, wondering if he really had come just to keep his job. "I could use your help with the foal. His mother will be weaning him soon. It would be easier if there were someone he was attached to, someone who could take his mother's place for a while until he gets adjusted to being on his own."

Her features seemed to brighten. The sparkle returned to her eyes, but perhaps he had only imagined it had been gone. "I suppose I could come out early in the morning."

He nodded, tried not to feel quite so pleased. "I would really appreciate it if you would. I know it will be good for the foal."

"All right, then, yes. I'll come on the morrow." She was smiling when he left the garden. For the first time in the last two days, Caleb found himself smiling, too.

He told himself it was relief that his job was secure, that he could continue working to discover what was going on at Parklands, trying to ferret out a traitor. But he wasn't convinced it was entirely the truth. He reminded himself that the traitor might be the very female who had begun to haunt his thoughts, but convincing himself of that, he found, was even harder to do.

7

〜⚭〜

From the doorway of the small room she occupied on the bottom floor of the house in Buford Street, Mary Goodhouse waited in the darkness as Annie kissed baby Jillian good night. She smoothed back the infant's fine, light brown hair, then tucked the child into the cradle Miss Durant had provided each of the newborns at birth.

"Sleep tight, sweet luv," Annie whispered.

As soon as Annie disappeared upstairs to the bedchamber she shared with Rose, Mary drew her shawl around her shoulders and slipped quietly out of her room. The floors creaked in the hall and so did the hinges on the door at the back of the house, but none of the lamps came on inside as she slipped out into the darkness.

It was cold this late in the evening, the stars like crystal specks in the black expanse of sky above her head. Mary shivered as she walked the deserted streets, unnerved by the echo of her worn soles on the cobbles. An occasional hackney rumbled past. She spotted a ladybird talking to a group of sailors and kept on walking.

There was something important she had to do, a matter that would secure a future for herself and her babe and provide the money she needed to make the long sea voyage to the Colonies.

Freddie would be waiting. He had sailed for a town named Charleston in a place called South Carolina and she intended to find him. But she had to leave soon, before it was too near her time to make the journey.

Mary pulled her shawl a little tighter and kept on walking. She had sent a message with one of the local chimney sweeps, a note she had hired a scribe to write that simply read *I know everything. Meet me at the Cock and Thistle Tuesday at midnight.*

Mary was certain he would come. He had too much to lose not to answer her summons.

It was a bit of a walk to the tavern, but she didn't have much money, not enough for a hackney, at any rate. She had picked the Cock and Thistle because it was far enough away that she wouldn't be recognized but not so far that she couldn't make it afoot.

She glanced at her surroundings. In the daytime, she hadn't really noticed the dilapidated buildings with their boarded-up windows or the scraps of paper and trash lying in the gutters. She hadn't smelled the odor of sewage or seen the darkened alleys where drunken men slept off their stupor against the rough brick walls.

Mary ignored a trickle of fear and told herself not to worry; she was almost to the tavern. In the distance, she could see the glow of lamplight shining through the letters on the glass in the wide front window, hear the muted laughter of the patrons inside.

Still, as she passed the entrance to a deserted alley and a man stepped out of the shadows, a chill swept through her. His clothes were worn and a battered brown slouch hat covered most of his greasy hair. She would simply cross the street, she told herself, put herself a safe distance away from him. She turned and started walking in that direction when a second man appeared, this one wearing a woolen hat, tattered greatcoat, and old knit gloves with his fingers poking out through the ends.

The men were on her before she had time to run. Mary tried to scream but a dirty hand clamped over her mouth and an arm tightened viciously around her belly. She thought of the babe and kicked backward, connecting with the man's shin as he dragged her off the street and into the darkness of the alley. Mary struggled but his arms were like steel, his hold so tight she could barely breathe. Her heels bumped over the cobbles, then slid into the mud and dirt of the alley, and fear unlike anything she had known welled up inside her.

" 'Urry up, Shamus," the first man said. "We 'aven't got all night."

"Od's teeth! The bawd is heavier than she looks," the second man grumbled. "Got a bun in the oven, can't ye see?"

The first man moved closer, and in a thin ray of moonlight she could see the blackened stumps of his teeth, the perspiration glistening in the deep grooves and lines in his forehead.

"Ye shouldna' tried ta bargain with the devil, luv. 'Tis only gonna buy ye a ticket straight ta hell."

Fresh fear shot through her. Mary looked into the man's grizzled face and knew in that instant the message she had sent was a warrant for her death. She would never see her Freddie again, never live to birth her babe. Trying to get money from the man she had overheard that night at Parklands was the maddest, most dangerous thing she had ever done.

As Mary stared into the brooding dark eyes of her attacker, felt his fingers wrap around her neck and begin to squeeze, they were the last thoughts she ever had.

Dressed in breeches and boots, standing next to Arlie in the middle of the barn, Lee watched Caleb Tanner shoveling manure from one of the open stalls. His week was over. When he finished today, the wager he had lost would be paid.

Arlie chuckled softly. " 'E won, ye know."

She dragged her attention from Caleb back to her ancient groom. "What are you talking about? I won the race. That is why he is paying the forfeit."

His thin lips curved, showing a couple of missing teeth. "Pulled up, 'e did. Just at the last. Seen it plain. Standin' right outside when 'e did it."

Disbelief widened her eyes. "What are you talking about? Are you telling me Caleb Tanner *let* me win that race?"

"I'm sayin' the man 'ad ye beat. Behaved like a real gen'l'man, 'e did."

Lee shook her head. "I don't believe it. Caleb Tanner would have liked nothing better than to see me out here mucking out those stalls." She cast him a look. "If he won the race, why didn't you say something sooner?"

Arlie shrugged a pair of bony shoulders. "Couldn't do that now, could I? Ain't fittin' fer a lady ta be doin' that sorta' work. Figured better 'im doin' the shovelin' than ye doin' it yerself."

Lee fixed her gaze on Caleb, who bent to his task down at the end of the barn. His shirt was gone, draped over the side of the stall. The muscles in his broad back gleamed with sweat, flexing every time he hefted the shovel. His skin was smooth and tanned dark from the sun, his hair damp with sweat and curling at the back of his neck. For a moment, she just stood there, mesmerized by the sight of him, trying to ignore an odd sort of breathlessness and a funny little flutter in the pit of her stomach.

Arlie shuffled away, still chuckling, and Lee's temper heated. Jerking a pitchfork off the wall, she stormed down to the end of the barn.

"Get out! You're finished in here." Ignoring the astonished look on his face, she bent over and started forking the wet straw and manure out of the stall.

Caleb jerked the pitchfork out of her hand. "What the hell do you think you're doing?"

Lee whirled toward him, clamping her hands on her hips. "You won that race! Arlie said so! Now get out of this stall and let me go to work!"

Caleb started to smile, then he grinned. "You actually would have done it? You would have cleaned out the stalls?"

"What did you think? That I wouldn't stand by my wager? You figured you might as well let me win because it really wouldn't matter?" She reached out, grabbed the pitchfork out of his hands, and started furiously filling the wheelbarrow.

Caleb frowned. Stalking toward her, he reached over and jerked the pitchfork away. "Arlie's mistaken. You won the race."

She eyed him skeptically. "You're lying—I can see it in your eyes. What I can't figure out is why. Arlie says you were playing the gentleman. But you aren't a gentleman, are you, Caleb Tanner?"

His gaze ran over her, skimming the fullness of her breasts, the swell of her hips, outlined so clearly by the breeches. He reached out and caught the tops of her arms, and she didn't resist when he drew her toward him. His eyes were a darker shade of brown and there was a glint in them that hadn't been there before. Unconsciously, her palms came to rest on his naked, sweat-slick chest.

"No . . . ," he said softly, "I'm no gentleman." Their eyes locked for an instant, then his mouth came down over hers.

Lee staggered at the jolt of unexpected heat. Beneath her palms, his skin felt hot and slick. He smelled of sweat and horses, and the powerful muscles across his chest flexed each time he moved. He took what he wanted, but his lips felt softer than they should have and heat spiraled out through her limbs. His tongue slid into her mouth as he deepened the kiss and she started to tremble.

All too soon, Caleb ended the kiss. He let her go and when he stepped away, she could see the heavy ridge of his sex pressing against the front of his breeches. Instead of fear or repulsion, she felt a strange blend of curiosity and excitement.

"The week is over," Caleb said as if the kiss had never occurred. "Which of us won no longer matters. With your permission, now that Jimmy will be busy riding for you, I'll hire one of the village lads to help Billy do the dirty work in here."

Lee swallowed and nodded, tried to sound as nonchalant as he. "All right, that will be fine." She turned and started walking, her heart still beating madly, her legs like India rubber. Outside the stall, she stopped and turned. "I want a rematch. You owe me at least that much."

Caleb's lips curved. She remembered the heat of them moving over hers. "Anytime, Miss Durant." But the hunger in his eyes warned that racing him today could have dangerous consequences. Lee ignored the little voice daring her to accept the unspoken challenge; she turned and walked away.

It was later that same night that Vermillion joined her aunt Gabriella and a small party for a night at the theater. Jonathan Parker, Lord Nash, was their escort, handsome with his silver-touched brown hair, impeccably dressed in a blue, velvet-collared tailcoat, blue-and-silver waistcoat, and dove gray breeches.

"I'm glad you and your aunt accepted my invitation," he said as he escorted Vermillion into the Theatre Royale in Haymarket for a production of *Richard III*. "It seems eons since we've enjoyed a moment to ourselves."

Which was true, of course, with Wingate and Mondale hovering over her every moment, to say nothing of Aunt Gabby's usual throng of hangers-on. But she had purposely excluded the others tonight. If she were going to make the right choice, she needed to get to know each of the men a little better.

And Nash was certainly charming. He smiled as he offered his arm and led her through the lobby, which blazed with the light of a dozen crystal chandeliers. Candles gleamed against the deep-red velvet draperies, and gilt-framed paintings hung on the walls. Nash guided them up the sweeping staircase to his private box on the second floor and they sat down in small, round, velvet-covered chairs.

He leaned toward her and she felt the brush of his coat. "I hear Noir will be racing at Newmarket come week's end. I imagine he'll sweep the field."

"It's going to be a difficult race, but I believe Noir will win."

The red velvet curtains moved just then and Aunt Gabby, dressed to kill in an exquisite gown of black and silver, turned to see Lord Claymont walk in.

"Sorry I'm late," he said, smiling at Gabriella. "Though it doesn't appear I've missed anything yet." The earl was average in height and build, with lightly graying black hair and intense blue eyes. He was attractive and intelligent, a generous, kind-hearted man, and Vermillion had grown extremely fond of him.

"We've been invited to a party in honor of Michael Cutberth, darling. Isn't that exciting?" The actor was one of England's most renowned thespians and Gabriella was wild to meet him.

Not surprising. Aunt Gabby lived for nights like this.

The earl whispered something in Gabriella's ear and she laughed.

The viscount moved a little closer. "You must be looking forward to the race," he said. "When will you be leaving?"

"On the seventh. The horses have already departed."

He flashed her one of his charming smiles. He really was a handsome man. "I'm sure they'll all do very well."

Aunt Gabby tapped his sleeve with her painted fan. "It's going to be great fun, Jon. I've taken a house for the occasion—quite a lovely place, actually. I plan to do a little entertaining. Why don't you come with us?"

He flicked a glance at Vermillion, but regretfully shook his head. "I should like nothing better, believe me. Unfortunately, I've a ministers' meeting I cannot escape." He smiled. "I promise, however, I shall find a way to make amends." His eyes were warm on her face and Vermillion felt a smile of her own appearing.

They talked more of racing and a little of the war, the threat of invasion a constant worry on everyone's mind.

"Some say the little corporal will try to make the crossing with an armada of steam-powered airships," Nash told her.

Vermillion toyed with the diamond and ruby necklace at her throat. "Airships? I should think if Napoleon has been building steam-powered engines, using them on real ships would be far more efficient."

"I agree," Nash said. "But who can know the mind of the enemy?"

"I've heard rumors he is amassing more troops in Spain, which I suppose makes sense, in light of what happened at Oporto."

Jonathan turned toward her. "I'm certain General Wellesley has the matter well in hand. At least we must pray that he does."

Amazingly, the viscount actually spoke to her as if she had a brain. It was one of the things she liked about him. They didn't discuss the latest *on dit*, but matters of importance.

"They'll be starting the play any moment," Nash said as the candles at the foot of the stage were doused. A few minutes later, the red velvet curtain went up and Vermillion settled back to enjoy the performance.

It was late when Lord Nash's carriage returned them to the house at the edge of the city. Aunt Gabriella excused herself and retired upstairs, allowing Vermillion and the viscount a moment in the salon. Claymont would be waiting for Aunt Gabby in her bedchamber, having used the stairs at the rear of the house. It was a silly pretense, done mainly for the servants, but Claymont insisted, and occasionally even Aunt Gabby demurred to certain of Society's dictates.

"I hope you enjoyed the evening, Vermillion." The viscount's deep voice drew her attention. His gaze took in her low-cut sapphire gown with its black lace trim and nearly unobstructed view of her breasts, but didn't linger as another man's would have. "I know I certainly did."

Lee glanced away, finding it harder and harder to maintain her façade when she was with the viscount, a man she considered a friend. She forced her chin up and smiled her Vermillion smile.

"It was a wonderful evening. Mr. Cutberth did a marvelous job as Richard the Third."

"I hope you enjoyed the company, as well."

She thought she caught a glimpse of the desire he usually kept well-hidden. "I enjoy your company very much, Jonathan. I've come to consider you a very dear friend."

Nash drew her closer. Raising one of her black-gloved hands, he pressed a kiss into her palm. "I am hoping for more than mere friendship, Vermillion. In that regard, I've made my intentions perfectly clear. I wish to provide for you, dearest, to see to your pleasure in any way I can."

She didn't miss the faint roughening of his voice. She wished she felt at least some measure of passion for him, this man whose friendship she valued so highly.

Jonathan bent and brushed a kiss over her lips, then kissed her more deeply. A memory arose of Caleb Tanner's kisses and inwardly she prayed to feel some of the fire he stirred. Instead, when the viscount touched his tongue to her lips, she turned away.

"Thank you for a very lovely evening, my lord."

Nash stood rigid, a frown on his face. "I realize you are enjoying the chase, my dear, but I won't wait longer than your birthday. Think what a man of my position can do for you. Think of your future. I pray you choose well, Vermillion."

She moistened her lips, which suddenly felt dry. "I promise to do my best, your lordship."

Turning away, he strode out of the drawing room and Vermillion released the breath she hadn't realized she was holding. Her aunt had made choosing a lover sound simple, as if it were some kind of a game that could be played with the veriest ease. Instead, her nights grew more and more restless and images of Caleb Tanner continued to creep in.

She dreamt of him that night, though in the morning she only vaguely recalled. She thought of him again as she dressed in her comfortable men's clothing and made her way out to the stable to check on the foal. The gangly little colt with the fuzzy, sandy coat grew bigger every day. She smiled as she watched the tiny horse nursing, then laughed when he tugged with determination at his mother's swollen teat.

She was so engrossed in the foal she didn't hear Caleb approaching until he stood directly behind her.

"Up early this morning, aren't you? . . . Considering the lateness of the hour you returned home last night."

She stiffened at the sarcasm in his voice and turned to face him. He stood so close she could feel the heat of his body, look into his penetrating dark eyes. Even dressed in the simple garments of a servant, he looked big and strong, and more handsome than any other man of her acquaintance.

"What business is it of yours what time I returned?"

"Why, it's none of my business in the least," he said blandly, but disapproval formed a tight line around his lips. "It isn't my business where you go or when you return or whom you decide to kiss, though I would refrain from doing so in front of the windows if I were you. Might upset one of your other admirers."

Her temper inched up. "And if I were you, I would refrain from playing the role of Peeping Tom. It scarcely suits you, Caleb Tanner."

"You want to know what suits me?" His gaze raked her from head to foot. "Dragging you down in that nice clean pile of straw, tossing up your skirts, and doing what every other man you know wants to do—that is what would suit me. I shall, however, restrain from doing so, since I can hardly afford to lose my position."

Her face must have been scarlet. "You are rude and ill-mannered. I should have dismissed you for your insolence long ago." She glanced down at her breeches. "And if you haven't noticed, I am not wearing a skirt!"

Dark eyes slid over her hips and down her legs, and the edge of his mouth barely curved. "So I see. But if you're interested, I'm willing to make the adjustment. I find the notion of making love to a woman in breeches in some ways even more exciting."

For a heartbeat, she didn't move. Images of lying naked in the straw with Caleb Tanner floated round in her head. All of her suitors went out of their way to play the gallant, yet none of them could excite her with a single word, a single hot glance, the way Caleb could.

What would it be like if instead of Andrew or Jonathan, Caleb were her lover?

She let her gaze roam over his tall, broad-shouldered frame, the narrow hips, and long legs. Trying to gain control of the moment, she cast him the sort of seductive smile Vermillion would use on one of her admirers.

"If you're serious, perhaps I'll give it some thought. It might be amusing to consort in that fashion with a groom."

Those dark eyes glinted. "Make no mistake, Vermillion. The role you play for the others holds no appeal for me. The woman I want helps to birth kittens and rides like the wind. And I don't give a damn what she's wearing."

Then he bent his head and kissed her.

Oh, dear God! It was a searing, reckless, soul-stealing kiss and it set her on fire. She swayed toward him and her hands trembled as she reached up to grip his shoulders. They felt like steel beneath her fingers. He teased her lips apart and she felt the hot, damp slickness of his tongue. Caleb's arms came hard around her. He hauled her against his chest and deepened the kiss, claiming her mouth until she was utterly breathless. Then as suddenly as he had started, he stepped away.

Lee swayed unsteadily, reached out and gripped the top rail of the stall for support.

A corner of Caleb's mouth faintly lifted. "Shall I saddle your horse, Miss Durant?" Though his voice was cool, his eyes remained hot, filled with promises of the pleasure he could give her.

Lee swallowed, tried to calm the tremors coursing through her. "Yes . . . thank you. I believe I'm in need of a little fresh air."

One of his dark eyebrows went up. "Perhaps you would like some company. I could also saddle the—"

"No! I mean . . . no, I should rather go by myself, thank you." She tossed her head as Vermillion would have done, determined to put some distance between them. "The sun is shining and I need some time to myself." Careful not to look at Caleb, she walked out of the barn and into the cooling breeze, hoping it would sweep away the unsettling emotions his scorching kiss had stirred.

Knowing deep down even a North Sea storm could not succeed.

As Lee had feared, the ride through the fields gave her plenty of time to think, but she wound up feeling even more confused. Sitting in her bedchamber later that afternoon, she watched Jeannie fussing over the gowns spread out on the big four-poster bed and thought of Caleb and the way he made her feel. Even Andrew couldn't stir her to passion the way Caleb could.

"I think you should wear zee turquoise silk," Jeannie said in her thickly accented English. "It will bring out the color of your eyes." Jeannie Fontenelle was ten years older than Lee. During her years as lady's maid to the Countess of Essex, she had been married to a footman, but he had died of an influenza just months after the two were wed. Jeannie had been summarily dismissed, too tempting a morsel to dangle before the countess's roving-eyed husband.

For the last six years, Jeannie had worked for Aunt Gabby, the past two as Lee's personal maid. The relationship had turned into a friendship that Lee had come to cherish.

"I like the turquoise, as well," Lee agreed, not really caring what she wore to General Stevens's military ball she and her aunt would be attending with Colonel Wingate that night.

Lee flicked a glance at her maid. "I was wondering, Jeannie, if I could ask you something."

Jeannie stopped fussing with the gown. "Of course, *chérie.* What is it you wish to know?"

"There is a man I have met . . ."

Jeannie rolled her eyes. "A man? You meet legions of men every night, *n'est-ce pas?*"

"Yes, but this one is different. He has no wealth, no social position, nothing to recommend him, and yet I find him infinitely attractive. I wondered if . . . well, what you would think about taking such a man for a lover."

One of Jeannie's brown eyebrows shot up. "Your aunt Gabriella . . . you know she would not approve."

"I'm well aware of that. She wants me to choose a man of distinction, someone with money, perhaps even a title. She thinks that will make me happy."

"What do you think, *chérie?*"

"I don't really care about those things."

Jeannie reached over and squeezed her hand. "I believe in the end, you will 'ave to choose a man who can provide certain things for you, a man who moves among those with the same kind of wealth that you have been raised with. But you are young yet. Though your aunt has kept the secret well guarded, you are an innocent where men are concerned. If you want this man—if 'e can lead you into the world of passion that will be so big a part of your future, then I think you should 'ave 'im." Jeannie smiled. "Every woman deserves one man who can give 'er the dreams of 'er heart."

"Even if those dreams can't last?"

The older woman nodded. "*Oui, chérie.* Especially if those dreams cannot last."

Lee turned to stare out the window, her mind swollen with turbulent thoughts. "I shall think about it, Jeannie. My birthday is only a few weeks away. It is past time I began to make a life of my own. It seems the only way a woman my age is allowed to do that is either to marry or choose a man who will act as a protector. I've promised my aunt and I intend to keep my word. But perhaps between now and then, I can choose something for myself."

Jeannie smiled. "Do whatever it is your 'eart tells you. I lost my Robert, but for a time I loved him and 'e loved me. I would not trade the short time we 'ad together."

Lee thought of Caleb Tanner. Jacob would be returning soon and Caleb would be moving on.

Perhaps in a way, he would make the perfect lover.

8

❧

I am terribly sorry to disturb you, miss, but there is a Mrs. Hickam here to see you." Jones, the butler, stood perfectly erect, pale skin showing in the part through the middle of his hair.

"Thank you, Mr. Jones. I'll speak to her in here, if you please." Annie Hickam was here? Had the poor thing walked all the way from Buford Street? If she had, the matter must be important. Lee's heart kicked worriedly into gear.

Jones made an elegant bow, making the curls bob next to his ears. Departing the Cirrus Room, he returned a few minutes later with "Mrs." Annie Hickam in tow. She was staring upward as she walked in, awed by the chandeliers and the scene of cherub-filled clouds in a blue sky painted on the ceiling.

"Gor—ain't this bloomin' grand!" She spun herself around to look at the room from different angles, her simple brown skirt belling out around the scuffed brown shoes on her feet.

"Hello, Annie. It's good to see you." Lee greeted

her with a smile and reached for her hand and for the first time Annie seemed to realize where she was.

"Afternoon, Miss," she said, looking a little embarrassed. "Thanks for lettin' me in."

"I'll admit I'm a little surprised you have traveled so far from the city. Is everything all right?"

Annie released a weary breath. "I don't know, Miss. That's why I come."

"Why don't we sit down and I'll have Mr. Jones bring us some tea."

Annie shook her head, self-consciously toying with the cuff on her plain white blouse. "Oh, no, Miss, I wouldn't want to be a bother."

"It's all right. I promise it's no trouble at all." She motioned to the butler, who still stood guard at the door, and he turned and disappeared down the hall. As soon as Jones slipped out of sight, Lee urged Annie over to one of the cream brocade sofas. The tall woman sank down wearily onto the seat.

"All right," Lee said. "Now tell me what has upset you enough to travel all the way across London."

"It's Mary, Miss. She's gone."

"Gone? What do you mean? Gone where?"

"That's just it. None of us has the slightest notion. The last time we seen her was three nights past. Mary went to bed like the rest of us. She was already in her room when I doused the lamp next to little Jilly's cradle. Next mornin', Mary wasn't there. We thought maybe she got up early and left to visit friends, but if she did, she never come back."

"Have you spoken to the authorities?"

"Yes, Miss. Only just this mornin' before I left town. The night watch promised to keep an eye out, but I can tell ya, Miss, I am fearful. This ain't like our Mary . . . not a'tall."

A noise in the hall diverted Lee's worry for an instant. She watched Jones roll the tea cart into the salon, thinking *no, this isn't like Mary at all.* She was a sweet girl, rather shy, and not one to go off on her own. She had been easy prey for young Freddie Hully—and she was still desperately in love with him.

"I can't imagine where she might have gone," Lee said, walking toward the tea cart. "If she'd had enough money, she might have followed Freddie—not that it would have done her any good."

"No, Miss. The boy was up to no good where poor Mary was concerned."

Lee began to pour the tea, catching the flowerlike scent of the chamomile. "I'll take you back to the city and speak to the authorities myself. My aunt can consult Lord Claymont. Perhaps he'll be able to help."

"Thank ya, Miss. Rose, Sarah, Helen, and me—we knew ya would help us."

It was several hours later that Vermillion returned to Parklands from her trip into town, no less frustrated than Annie had been. The Magistrates' Office refused to believe anything untoward had occurred. They had found no sign of Mary, neither dead nor injured. No body meant no crime. In a way, Lee was grateful for the hope that provided.

She had spoken to Aunt Gabby, of course, who had little interest in the house in Buford Street but had always been supportive. Gabriella was sad to think that one of the poor girls might have fallen into even worse trouble than she had faced already.

Her aunt's concern only heightened Lee's worry.

Restless and unable to clear her disturbing

thoughts, she dressed in a cinnamon serge riding habit and made her way out to the stables. Noir and two other of Parklands's Thoroughbreds were already on the road to Newmarket. They'd had to hire a walker, a big man named Jack Johnson, to get the horses there, but the three racing days were important and the stakes were high, a prize that would be poured back into the development of the stable.

Parklands didn't race many horses, but Lee was proud to say the few they owned were winners.

Tomorrow morning, Caleb Tanner and Jimmy Murphy would be leaving for the event and the following day she and her aunt would make the journey.

The sun was high as Lee stood next to the fence, watching the mares and colts romp playfully in the field, but her mind kept returning to Mary and her worry that something dreadful might have occurred.

"What's the matter? You look like you lost your best friend."

She turned at the sound of Caleb Tanner's deep voice, looked up at him and sighed. "One of them, at any rate." She told him about Mary and the house in Buford Street, explained that the girl was five months gone with child, and that she had disappeared. Why she confided in Caleb she couldn't say, but she felt better once she had.

"I'm so worried about her. I wish I knew for certain that she is safe."

"You say the girl was a chambermaid here at Parklands?"

"Yes. That is how she met Freddie Hully, the boy who fathered her babe. He worked for the blacksmith in the village."

"What do you think could have happened to her?"

There was something in his tone that made her glance up at him. "I don't know. She had very little money. I can't imagine why she would have gone off the way she did."

"Perhaps Freddie came back and she simply ran away with him."

Lee pondered that, a thought that had also occurred to her. "I suppose it's possible." She gazed off toward the horses galloping across the field. The little sand-colored colt she called Loch kicked up its heels, then sprinted like fury across the meadow.

"Perhaps we'll hear from her," Lee said, her thoughts still on Mary. "I suppose it doesn't do the least bit of good to worry."

"No, not the least. Why don't I saddle Grand Coeur for you? A nice long ride ought to help clear your head."

"Yes, that's what I was hoping when I came out here."

His eyes remained on her face. "Perhaps today I could join you."

Even from a distance, she could see the hunger in his eyes, the heat he made no attempt to hide. She knew what he wanted. He had made himself more than clear. But she wasn't afraid of him and she was tired and worried and riding with Caleb would certainly turn her thoughts away from poor Mary.

"All right. I would be pleased if you would join me."

Caleb walked into the shadows of the barn, thinking of Vermillion and the invitation he had just received. She knew he wanted her. His imagination conjured images of her lush breasts and small waist, and how it would feel to have her naked and writhing beneath him. Desire for her clenched in his loins and he went painfully hard.

Caleb ignored a sweep of lust and forced the images away. He had other, more important matters to consider and he would do well to remember that. He thought of the woman, Mary Goodhouse, one of those he had seen through the window the day he had journeyed to London.

Had something really happened to the girl? Or had she simply slipped away with the lad who had got her with child?

Caleb thought of the secrets his superiors believed were being collected at Parklands and passed to the French. The girl had worked here as a chambermaid. Could there be some connection to her sudden disappearance? Tonight, he would send word of the missing girl to Colonel Cox through the contact that had been set up for him in the village. A silversmith named Cyrus Swift would see it done.

Caleb tightened the cinch of Lee's sidesaddle and checked the stirrup. In the meantime, Vermillion had invited him to accompany her. He went hard again and shifted to relieve the pressure against the front of his breeches.

His arousal remained as he finished saddling Grand Coeur and set to work on the bay, brushing the animal's coat, then setting the flat-seated saddle in place. Coeur nickered softly as he led both animals out into the courtyard.

The sun shone brightly overhead and thick white clouds floated in an azure sky. With the fields turned a brilliant emerald green and the trees leafed out along the hedgerows, it was the perfect day for riding.

The perfect afternoon for seduction.

Caleb lifted Vermillion into the sidesaddle, letting his hands linger at her waist, letting her see the desire in his eyes, making her wonder at his intentions. His heart was beating faster but so was hers—he could see the rapid flutter in the hollow at the base of her throat.

Since the morning in the stable when he had kissed her, every time he watched her ride out across the fields, it was all he could do not to follow. He knew she wanted him. Whenever they were together, the air around them seemed hotter, the distance between them smoldered with heat.

He couldn't help wondering, once they had reached the shelter of the trees, how she would respond if he dragged her down from her horse and into his arms, if he kissed her with the same unleashed passion he had shown her before.

Caleb cast her a glance that took in the heightened color of her cheeks. He meant to find out exactly what the lady would do and now seemed exactly the time. In the morning he would be off to Newmarket, there for the racing meet. Tonight he would send word of Mary's disappearance to Colonel Cox. In the meantime, seducing Vermillion into an afternoon's pleasure occupied the majority of his thoughts.

She looked over at him and smiled, and he thought that she looked almost shy. "I'm ready if you are."

It was a ruse, he knew, and yet he found her feigned innocence appealing. He nodded, thinking how pretty she looked in her cinnamon-colored riding skirt.

Wanting her.

Thinking that today he meant to have her.

She hadn't bothered putting her hair up today, just

left it loose down her back and swept it up on the sides with small, tortoiseshell combs. Ruby strands teased his cheek as he lifted her into the sidesaddle and the pressure in his groin grew more painful. Wondering if she had noticed his obvious arousal, he walked over to the bay, shoved his boot into the metal stirrup, and swung up on the horse's back.

"Let's ride toward the north end of the field," he said. *Toward the old shepherd's cabin.* The building was a ruin, he had recently discovered, too far gone to serve his purpose, but there was a tiny secluded meadow just beyond the cabin that perfectly fit his plans.

"All right." Vermillion rode out first and Caleb followed, enjoying the sight of her mounted on the gray, admiring her control of the horse. She was a splendid rider. He smiled to think he intended to put the talent to a far more intimate use.

Ahead of him, Vermillion set a leisurely pace, taking a hedgerow here and there, guiding Grand Coeur over a stream with ease. When she started to turn in the wrong direction, he moved a little in front of her, blocking the way, turning them casually toward the place he had in mind.

"Let's go this way," he said and she smiled and followed.

It didn't take long to reach the shepherd's cabin. Vermillion rode on past and so did he. As soon as they reached the meadow, he drew rein on the bay and whirled the horse to face her.

"Why don't we give them a rest? It looks as if there's a spring just over there." He pointed in that direction. "And there's grass enough to keep them content."

"I could use a stretch myself."

He swung down from his mount, then swung her down off the sidesaddle, holding her a little closer than needed, letting her absorb the heat of him, letting her know what she did to his body. When a faint tremor ran through her, he let her go and walked away. Making his way back to his horse, he untied the blanket behind his saddle and drew two sets of hobbles out of the saddlebags. Placing a pair on each horse, he removed their headstalls, and sent them off to graze.

She watched him start walking toward her. He heard a little gasp of surprise as he tossed the blanket aside, reached out and hauled her into his arms. He didn't give her time to protest, just bent his head and took her lips. They were soft as silk, smooth and sweet as honey, and beneath his determined assault, he thought that they trembled.

It was a clever act, one he was beginning to enjoy. He teased the corners of her mouth, coaxing her to open for him, then took her deeply with his tongue. He'd been hard off and on all day, his groin heavy with need and pulsing with heat, his blood running thick and hot.

His hands slid down, over the soft sun-warmed velvet of her riding skirt. He cupped the globes of her bottom, tested the firmness, and lifted her against him, letting her feel how hard he was, letting her know what he meant to do.

For an instant her body stiffened and she drew a little away. Caleb claimed her lips again and very softly kissed her. He nibbled the corners of her mouth, enjoying the game, sliding his tongue into the sweet, moist cavern. He deepened the kiss and felt her tremble, coaxed her with each caress to give him what he wanted, and Vermillion responded, melting against him, sliding her arms up around his neck.

He wanted to drag her down in the grass and lift her skirts, wanted to cover her small, lush body and drive himself inside her. Instead he forced himself to go slow. He wanted this to be good for her, good for both of them. He didn't know how many men she'd had but he wanted to be among those she remembered. He didn't know why it was important, only that it was.

Caleb felt her fingers digging into his shoulders and deepened the kiss, claiming her lips first one way and then another, his hands working the black satin loops on the front of her jacket. He eased the fabric off her shoulders and let it fall to the ground at her feet. Vermillion seemed not to notice. The bodice of the gown was cut indecently low and it was easy to slide his fingers inside, to cup one of her pale, full breasts.

They were round and firmer than he had imagined, heavy and warm in his hand. His pulse took a leap and fire sank into his loins. The blood pounding in his ears made his pulse feel thick and sluggish. Vermillion made a soft little mewling sound as he began to knead the fullness, to pebble the peak, then gently pinch the ends. He felt her go lax, as if her knees refused to support her. His fingers cupped the sweet curve of her bottom to lift and hold her against him and her hold tightened on his neck.

"Caleb," she whispered, the words faint and breathy, edged with her growing desire.

"Easy," he whispered, trying to control his raging lust, determined to make the experience last. He began to work the tiny jet buttons at the back of her gown, felt them part one by one, skimmed his fingers over the smooth skin beneath. He slid the bodice of the dress off her shoulders, leaving her naked to the waist, and eased back a little to enjoy the view.

Her breasts were high and full and tipped with big pink nipples, and as he gazed down at them, they quivered. Desire expanded inside him. His loins tightened painfully and he wondered how much longer he could resist the incredible temptation she made.

Reaching down, he cupped the heavy fullness, lowered his head and took the diamond-hard tip into his mouth. Vermillion whimpered and arched her back, giving him better access, and her fingers slid into his hair. She tasted like rose petals or silk or perhaps a little of both. She was trembling, clinging to him, making soft little sounds in her throat, and his arousal throbbed, grew even harder, pressed painfully against the front of his breeches.

He had to have her—and soon.

He took a breath and tried to slow things down, broke away for a moment, leaned over and picked up the blanket, spread it out on the grass at her feet. But when he turned to reach for her, Vermillion was backing away.

She had pulled the bodice of her gown back into place and was holding the jacket up in front of her breasts. "I-I have to get back," she said, her aqua eyes huge and liquid, looking for all the world like the innocent she often appeared.

"This is what you want," he said, his annoyance building, tired of playing the game. "We both know it. There's no need to pretend any longer."

Vermillion nervously moistened her lips, her gaze

still wary. "Perhaps when the time is right but . . . not yet. Not today." Turning, she fled toward her horse, reaching down to pick up her bridle along the way.

Two long strides and Caleb caught up with her. Frustrated and furious, he snatched the bridle out of her hand. "Give me the damned thing. If you're determined to leave, I'll be happy to do it for you. That's what you pay me for, isn't it?"

Vermillion said nothing as he bridled the horse and knelt to remove the hobbles. But she pulled her jacket back on and began to button the front.

"I'll tell you what I ought to do," he said, turning to face her, his eyes hard and dark. "I ought to strip you out of those clothes and haul you down on that blanket. I ought to give you exactly what you've been asking me for, practically since the moment I got here."

Her eyes widened. Then her chin shot up. "I didn't ask you for anything, Caleb Tanner. You're a clod and a boor, and I was a fool for thinking you were anything else!" She grabbed the reins out of his hands and started leading her horse over to a fallen log.

She never quite got there. Caleb caught her around the waist and swung her up on the gray, slamming her bottom down hard on the saddle.

Her aqua eyes blazed. "You are . . . you are . . . the most infuriating man I have ever met!"

A corner of his mouth curved up. "I'm going to have you, Vermillion, and we both know it. The only question is how long you want to play the game."

An angry growl slipped from her throat. Whirling the gray, she set her small heels into the animal's ribs, jolting the horse into action, and started racing away.

Caleb watched her ride over the hill, velvet skirts

rippling in the wind, red hair flying, thinking what a magnificent picture she made.

Wanting her more than ever.

He was still hard and aching. He reminded himself it was only a matter of time until he found relief. As he had said, he meant to have her.

Caleb felt the pull of a smile as she disappeared over a distant hill. Perhaps Newmarket would prove more interesting than he had imagined.

With renewed determination, he swung up on the back of the bay. Newmarket would come. In the meantime, he had other, more pressing matters to attend. As soon as he got back to the house, he would pen a note and ride to the village. He needed to send word to Colonel Cox.

He needed to discover what had happened to Mary Goodhouse.

9

_{✐✐✐}

The races at Newmarket were different from those at Epsom, where the racecourse was closer to London and attended in great numbers by the social elite.

The town of Newmarket was far more rural and though it was a major center for the sport, there were no grandstands and not nearly the fanfare that Epsom offered—though the populace of turfites, thimbleriggers, card sellers, and prostitutes was at least as large.

Men were the main spectators here, and a few women less concerned with creature comforts than the ladies in the city. In Newmarket, the races were viewed mostly from carriages parked along the perimeter of the course. They were lined up there already, some of the occupants wandering about, others spreading blankets on the grass beside their vehicles, where they laid out baskets of food and flagons of wine. It wouldn't be long before Aunt Gabriella and her party arrived to begin the day's festivities.

But Lee had come far earlier. Knowing Caleb would be there and considering what had transpired between them the last time they were together, it had taken all of her will to come to Newmarket. But Parklands' Thoroughbreds were her responsibility. Jimmy Murphy and the rest of the grooms would be expecting to see her and she didn't intend to disappoint them, certainly not because of Caleb Tanner.

She tried not to think of his hot kisses and arousing caresses in the meadow. If she did, she wouldn't be able to face him. In truth, instead of being embarrassed, she should be grateful. Caleb had provided her with her first real taste of passion.

Unfortunately, now that she'd had a glimpse of the world of pleasure she would be entering on her nineteenth birthday, she was more uncertain than ever. She had let Caleb kiss her, touch her as no man ever had, but the thought of another man taking those same liberties seemed completely repulsive.

She didn't understand it. None of the women of her acquaintance seemed to feel that way. They took their pleasure with whomever they wished and exclusivity wasn't a consideration.

Of course, Aunt Gabby was committed to Lord Claymont, but it hadn't always been so. In her wilder years, she had taken any number of lovers. Perhaps in some way Lee was different. Inwardly she worried it might be so. Even if it were, there was nothing she could do to change things or alter the course of her fate.

The stable loomed ahead, a large stone building surrounded by paddocks and stalls, humming with the hustle of grooms rushing to complete their tasks and the nicker and whinny of horses. Vermillion steeled herself for her inevitable encounter with Caleb and walked inside.

He was there in one of the stalls, brushing a big black gelding named Sentinel. He turned at her approach and her pulse surged with awareness. Dear Lord, the man could make her heart pound with merely a glance.

"Good morning," he said casually. "I see you've arrived safely."

She studied his face, trying to spot any trace of anger. She had worried that he would mock her in some way, but his expression was mild, even friendly, she noted with no little relief, and there was nothing in his manner that hinted at the intimacy they had shared.

"The journey passed quite pleasantly, thank you." She made a quick assessment of the black and a sorrel named Hannibal's Prize that would also be running. "It looks as if the horses also fared well."

Caleb slid the brush over Sentinel's glossy black coat. "According to Jack Johnson, the walker, they managed without a hitch."

They talked for a while of the race the animals would be running later that day, then she left to speak to each of the grooms. She praised Jack Johnson for taking such good care of the horses, then walked over to the jockey, Jimmy Murphy.

"What do you think, Jimmy? You and Noir seem to have been working well together. How do you assess his chances of winning against such a difficult field?"

Jimmy realized he still wore his flat felt cap and jerked it hurriedly off his head, exposing his rumpled bright red hair. "Noir's the best, ma'am. He's gonna win for sure and certain."

"What of Sentinel and Hannibal's Prize? Are they ready for this, do you think?"

"They don't have Noir's experience, o' course, but they're fast, ma'am. And they surely do like to win."

"Then let them," she said with a smile. "Sentinel runs best if he stays in the field until the last leg of the race. Hold him back until then." She flicked a glance at Caleb, who had walked up beside her. It felt a little harder to breathe with him standing so near.

"Just don't bury him," Caleb told Jimmy. "Keep him somewhere toward the front or outside of the pack. When you make the last turn, cut him loose. Sentinel will do the rest."

"And with Hannibal," Lee added, "don't go to the whip. He hates it. He'll draw back rather than move ahead. I imagine you've figured that out already."

"Yes, ma'am. Mr. Tanner done cautioned me on that."

"Good. As to the rest of it, listen to Mr. Tanner. He knows what he's doing." She didn't look at Caleb this time, but a blush crept into her cheeks. Caleb had known only too well what he was doing that afternoon in the meadow.

"Yes, ma'am," Jimmy said. "I surely will."

Jimmy left but Caleb remained where he was, just a few inches behind her. She could feel his solid presence and her pulse kicked up.

"He'll do a good job. Jimmy wants to please you." His voice softened into the same tone he used to gentle the horses. "I'd like to please you, too, Vermillion. I think we both know exactly the way I might do that."

Her cheeks burned. Her skin was tingling, her heart thumping. He wanted to please her and he knew exactly the way. *Sweet God in heaven*. She remembered the way he had feasted on her breasts, the fierce, searing pleasure, and suddenly felt hot all over.

"M-my aunt will be waiting," she said. "I have to go."

His mouth edged up. "Perhaps you'll need to come back a little later. This evening, perhaps . . . to talk about tomorrow's race?"

Oh, God. Her legs felt shaky, her mouth dry. "No, I . . . I don't think so. I have to go." She turned away from him and practically ran from the barn. Her heart was still hammering when she spotted Aunt Gabby's carriage. Wingate's vehicle sat behind it, and one belonging to Elizabeth Sorenson.

She took a deep breath and walked toward them, trying not to think of Caleb and hoping they wouldn't notice the heightened color in her cheeks. *Lord, the man was a menace to the female population.*

She forced a smile to her face and headed for the group ahead. Lord Claymont had not yet arrived, but he would get there soon. Women were mostly excluded from the masculine world of horseracing, the reason Parklands' Thoroughbreds raced under the earl's blue-and-gold colors, a ruse that fooled no one but satisfied the rigid lines of conduct established by the powerful Jockey Club.

She joined the group in Aunt Gabby's carriage, but her thoughts remained on Caleb and the heat in his eyes and what it did to her when he looked at her the way he had in the barn. Thank God, the races were getting ready to start, a match race, first, between two rival owners, then heat-racing, where the horses that won each heat then raced against each other. Several sweepstakes races were to follow, events that would include Sentinel and Hannibal's Prize. Noir wouldn't be racing until day after the morrow, when the Newmarket Gold Cup was scheduled to be run.

By the end of the afternoon, Sentinel had won his race and Journey had finished third in another. Parklands' Thoroughbreds had made a very good showing thus far and the big race was yet to come.

"My, what a day," Aunt Gabby said laughing. "You can be proud of yourself, darling. Whether you get credit or not, you have proved yourself a worthy opponent."

Vermillion didn't care whether her name appeared on a sweepstakes' cup. She cared about the horses and watching them run. "It isn't the most important thing, but it does feel good to win. I cannot deny it."

Later that night, she attended the party Aunt Gabby threw to celebrate the day and didn't get to bed until nearly dawn. She was exhausted. Her feet ached from dancing for so many hours and her head hurt from too much champagne. She slept far longer than she intended and woke up grumpy and out of sorts.

"I hate being late," she grumbled as she traveled with Jeannie to the racecourse later that morning in one of the open carriages. "It makes a bad impression on the grooms." Since none of their horses would be racing today, the rest of their party remained at the house her aunt had rented—most of them still abed.

"I need to speak to Jimmy Murphy," she said. "Go over a few things concerning tomorrow's race."

"The boy will be 'ere—'e adores you for letting 'im race. And that new trainer will be here as well. What was 'is name?"

Vermillion ignored a faint leap of her heart. "Tanner. Caleb Tanner."

"*Oui* . . . now I recall. 'E is very handsome, *n'est-ce pas?*" Jeannie cast her a glance. The woman had been her maid and her companion for years. Jeannie knew her well, better even than her aunt. Lee prayed Jeannie didn't suspect that Caleb was the man she thought to take as her first lover.

"I suppose he is attractive . . . in a rather basic fashion."

"The man is built like a stallion, no? I have seen him working. All those beautiful muscles and those eyes . . . so dark and hot."

"I'm afraid I haven't noticed."

Jeannie said no more, but her lips curved in a knowing smile Lee purposely ignored. There was no way her friend could know for certain and this was one subject Lee didn't intend to discuss any further.

Fortunately they were nearing the racecourse and Jeannie's attention fixed on the colorful sights and sounds. The coachman parked the carriage in the shade of a plane tree and Lee set off to make a check of the horses.

As she had expected, the animals were being well cared for. Caleb was a conscientious head groom, as capable as Jacob had been, perhaps even more so. But as she wandered through the barn, stirring up dust motes and inhaling the scent of new-mown hay and freshly oiled leather, she saw no sign of him.

She spoke to Jack Johnson and a small blond boy named Howie Pocock, now the youngest of Parklands' grooms.

"I'm looking for Jimmy. Do you know where he might have gone?"

'E went off wi' Mr. Tanner," Howie said. "I ain't exactly sure where they went, ma'am."

"Thank you, Howie. I'll just have a quick look round." With the races yet to start, she wandered out of the barn in search of them, wanting to be certain everything was in place for tomorrow's all-important Gold Cup Race.

Perhaps they're in another one of the buildings, she thought, not seeing Jimmy or Caleb among the grooms or trainers milling about.

Deciding to take a shortcut between two low-roofed wooden structures that housed other owners' horses, she was halfway down the narrow path when a man stepped out of the shadows along the wall. She hadn't noticed him when she entered the path. If she had, she would have gone the longer way round.

"Top o' the mornin', luv." He smiled down at her and she wished she hadn't left her bonnet in the carriage. She wasn't wearing one of her low-cut gowns, but his hazel eyes slid over her as if she were. "Looks like today's me lucky day."

There was something in that too-bold glance that set warning bells off in her head. "Excuse me. I'm afraid I've made a wrong turn somewhere." Turning round on the path, she started back the way she had come. At the sound of his footfalls in the grass behind her, she quickened her pace, but a big hand closed over her wrist and he spun her back to face him.

"What's yer hurry, luv?" His eyes wandered again, fixed on the roundness of her bosom. "Surely, ye've a minute or two ta spare." He was a young man, blond, big through the shoulders, not unpleasant to look at, though his clothes were badly worn, his hair shaggy at the nape of his neck, and he badly needed a shave.

"I'm sorry, sir, I have business to attend. Please let go of my hand." Angry at herself for wandering off on such a deserted path, knowing there were blacklegs and sharpers about, she tried to pry lose her hand.

"Me name's Danny," he said, his hold going tighter. "I'm pleased ta make yer acquaintance." A glance up and down the narrow space between the buildings confirmed that she was alone and he started hauling her toward him. "Yer a fetchin' little baggage and no mistake. I can see ye don't come cheap, luv, but me blunts as good as the next man's." He held up two pieces of silver. "What ye say, lass? A quick tumble before ye go on yer way?"

Lee swallowed as realization dawned. *Good Lord, he thinks I'm a doxy!* She was hardly that and she never would be. What a courtesan did was different, her aunt had always said. She was the one in control, the one who did the choosing. It meant both pleasure and freedom. It was not in the least the same.

"My friends are waiting." She tugged on her wrist. "I have to go." She jerked harder, but he didn't release her.

Instead, he stuffed his free hand into the pocket of a pair of worn breeches and pulled out another coin. "Ye drive a hard bargain, luv, but I wager yer worth it."

She started to tell him she wasn't interested in his money but he moved so quickly, she only got out a squeak before she was flat on her back beneath him, his heavy weight pressing her into the grass between the buildings.

"Let . . . me . . . go," she said between panting breaths, truly angry now, shoving against his chest to dislodge him, trying to suck in a breath of air. "I'm not a . . . doxy . . . you fool! I don't want your money!"

Still gripping her wrist, which he dragged above her head, he dropped the coins into her palm and closed her fingers around them, then started to shove up her skirt. For the first time, real fear shot through her.

"Let ... me ... go!"

Instead she felt one of his hands groping her breast. She could feel his hardness pressing into her stomach and the edge of fear blossomed into full-blown panic. She tried to scream, but he muffled the sound with a wet, sticky kiss. She gagged, tried to turn her head away, and the bristles on his face roughly abraded her cheek. She struggled harder, tried to dislodge him as one of his callused hands slid up her thigh; then he started working the buttons on the front of his breeches.

Desperate now, she bit down hard on his lip and tasted the coppery flavor of blood.

"Ouch!" The jovial expression faded from his face. He wiped the blood away with the back of his hand. "Lit'le tart. I'll swive ye now and keep the blunt. I'll learn ye ta toy with Danny Cheek."

The sounds she made were muffled by the hand that covered her mouth and another of his breeches' button's popped free. She started fighting again, tried to bite him, tried to twist free, but he was big and strong and his heavy weight pinned her in the grass.

"Let her go." The familiar voice was soft with deadly warning, and hearing it now sent a wave of relief rushing through her so strong she felt dizzy. She turned her head enough to see him, standing a few feet away, his legs braced apart and his hands balled into fists. "I said, let her go."

Danny Cheek's big body tightened. Then his heavy weight lifted away as he slowly gained his feet. Tears of relief clogged her throat. Caleb was here. Everything was going to be all right. With shaking hands, she sat up and pulled her dress down, covering her garters and stockings. Using the wall of the building for support, she pushed herself unsteadily to her feet.

A short distance away, the two men faced each other as if they meant to tear each other limb from limb. The blond man's face was a fiery shade of red and she had never seen such fury in Caleb's dark eyes before.

Something shifted in the blond man's expression. He cast her a glance, then shrugged as if the matter were no longer important. "Ye want her that bad, me friend, ye can have her." Reaching down, he picked up the coins she had left in the grass and turned to leave, but at the very last instant he spun back.

Lee screamed at the powerful blow he unleashed at Caleb, who ducked the impact as if he had known it was coming and threw a hard punch in return. A trickle of blood appeared at the corner of the blond man's mouth. Caleb's second blow landed with such force it knocked Danny Cheek clear off his feet. He hit the ground with a grunt and his head whacked hard against the wooden wall of the building. His eyes rolled up inside his head and his face went slack. He didn't move so much as a muscle.

The last of her fear disappeared, leaving her limp and shaken. Caleb remained exactly where he was, feet still braced and his hands still fisted. A slow breath whispered from his lungs and he lifted his gaze to her face.

Caleb frowned as he started walking toward her. She didn't realize she was crying until he hauled her into his arms.

"It's all right. I've got you."

She leaned into the heat of him, the solid feel of his body. "I'm sorry. I just—"

"It's all right," he repeated, smoothing back a curl that had come loose from its pins and drooped beside her ear. "He's not going to bother you again."

Her fingers curled into the front of his homespun shirt. She tried to stop shaking but she kept thinking of what might have happened and fresh tears stung her eyes. Caleb just held her, pressing her into the warmth of his chest.

"I wasn't . . . I wasn't frightened at first, but then . . . then I couldn't make him stop and I couldn't get away." She dragged in a shaky breath, but she didn't let go and neither did he.

Instead his hold seemed to tighten. "It's over." She felt his lips against her hair. "It was just a mistake. There's nothing more to be afraid of."

She nodded, hung on to him a few moments more, absorbing the feeling of safety that was unlike anything she had felt before. Caleb was different. She knew that in some deep, elemental part of herself. He was nothing at all like the other men of her acquaintance. As maddening as he could be, he always seemed to be there when she needed him.

She took another deep breath and straightened away from him, forced herself to move away. "Thank you, Caleb. I don't know what would have happened if—"

"The man was an idiot. It's over and you're safe. That's all that matters." He flicked a glance at the figure crumpled against the wall, then settled a hand protectively at her waist and started leading her away. Behind them, she heard the blond man groan and begin to move in the grass, but she didn't think he would follow. The murderous look in Caleb's eyes had warned what would happen if he did.

Caleb stopped in a spot out of sight behind a hedgerow and turned her to face him. He caught her chin to examine the beard scratches on her cheek, then took out a handkerchief and wiped away a smudge of dirt beneath her ear. With a softly muttered curse, he stuffed the handkerchief back into his pocket and she realized he was still angry.

"I can't believe you went off by yourself that way. You know the sort of men who frequent places like this. What the hell were you thinking?"

She swallowed, tried not to be intimidated by the hard look in his eyes now directed at her. "I was looking for Jimmy. I wanted to make certain everything was set for tomorrow's race. I knew I had made a mistake the moment I saw the man on the path but by then it was too late."

His features didn't soften. "You're still shaking, dammit. I would think in your line of work, you'd be used to dealing with a man's unwanted advances."

He was speaking to Vermillion, but it was Lee who had nearly been ravished—mistake or not. Her chin went up. She hoped it didn't tremble. "Sleeping with one's lover is scarcely the same as being forced to the will of some low-moraled gutter rat. I should think even a man like you would understand that."

She turned away from him, trying not to think what had almost happened, determined not to let him see how upset she really was. She started hurrying along the hedgerow, desperate for a moment to compose herself, to become Vermillion again, but the sound of Caleb's boots, pounding through the grass behind her, told her she wasn't going to escape.

Lee whirled to face him and he must have noticed how pale she was, for he hesitated only an instant before he pulled her into his arms.

"I'm sorry, dammit. When I saw you struggling with that big blond oaf, something inside me just snapped." She felt his chin on the top of her head. "Howie told me you'd gone off to look for Jimmy. When he showed me which way you went, I was afraid you were in for trouble." He held her away from him. "Don't ever do that again, you hear me?"

Lee looked up, caught his fierce black scowl, and began to smile. She was his employer, the woman who paid his wages. Only Caleb Tanner would have the cheek to give her orders. And yet she found his concern oddly endearing.

His scowl went even blacker. "You think it's funny? You were manhandled and very nearly raped and you think it's funny?"

She shook her head, fighting a grin. "I don't think it is the least bit funny. I do, however, find your audacity amusing—considering I am the one who is supposed to be giving the orders. And I am extremely touched by your concern. Thank you again, Caleb. I shall not forget what you did for me today. And I will remember to be more careful in the future."

The scowl slid away, but the worry remained. "This isn't a place for a woman alone, Vermillion."

The smile she wore softened. "Lee," she said to him gently. "My friends call me Lee." Then she turned and walked away.

The day of the Gold Cup arrived and Vermillion, along with her aunt and several carriages filled with gaily dressed members of their party, left the house and headed for the racecourse. Though a bright sun beat down on the row of coaches lining the course, a stiff wind rattled the flags and banners set out along the distance the horses were set to run.

Seated in the carriage today, next to Colonel Wingate, Vermillion watched the colorful spectacle and the jockeys milling about in the bright silks of their owners' stable: the scarlet and blue of the Earl of Winston, the impressive green and gold that signified the Duke of Chester, the familiar purple-and-white silk of the Earl of Rotham.

Vermillion could see the countess in a coach farther down, seated across from the earl, their attendance together done occasionally for the sake of propriety. Next to Vermillion, across from her aunt, Colonel Wingate leaned toward her.

"It's nearly time, dear one. With your permission, I'd like to place a wager in your name." The colonel looked splendid in the full regimental uniform of the Life Guards, gold epaulets sparkling on his scarlet coat. "I've spoken to your aunt," he said, smoothing his black mustache. "If Noir wins the race, I intend to host a party tonight in celebration."

She smiled. "That would be lovely, Colonel." Sometime over the past few days, she had eliminated Wingate as a candidate for protector, but in typical military fashion, the colonel refused to concede the battle.

"And the wager?" he pressed.

"I should be pleased to accept." Wingate was a favorite of Aunt Gabby's, a close chum of Lord Claymont's since boarding school. Perhaps that was the reason Aunt Gabby had spoken on the colonel's behalf in regard to his suit as her protector.

"The man is a well-respected officer, darling. Oliver is intelligent and kind, if a bit stuffy at times. And you can see the man adores you."

He adored the notion of bedding her, Vermillion thought, besting men years younger and thereby proving his virility. But she was no longer interested in the colonel and she didn't think that would change. Like the horserace soon to start, she had narrowed the field to Mondale and Nash, and as her birthday neared, it was a neck and neck drive to the finish.

Wingate's aide, Lieutenant Oxley, spoke up as the colonel rose to leave. "Shall I take that for you, Colonel? The betting post is just there, beyond the trees." The lieutenant, a young man in his twenties with sandy hair and hazel eyes, also wore his very impressive scarlet uniform. Though the lieutenant wasn't particularly good-looking, there was a sweet sort of shyness about him that somehow made him attractive.

"Thank you, Lieutenant." Wingate handed him a pouch of coins and instructions on how much of a wager to place for each of them.

Oxley departed and Vermillion fidgeted on the seat, eager for the race to begin.

Caleb Tanner appeared at the edge of her vision, walking toward her with the same erect bearing as the colonel, a fact she had noticed before. Beside him, a shorter man in a dark gray tailcoat and light gray trousers tried to match Caleb's long-legged strides.

Both men stopped in front of her and the grim look on Caleb's face put her on alert. "I'm sorry to bother you, Miss Durant, but this is Constable Shaw. He's here on a matter of some importance."

He was a lean-faced man beneath the high beaver hat he removed and clutched in one hand, his features tight and drawn. She whipped her eyes back to Caleb for some sign of why the man had come, but his expression remained unreadable and suddenly she knew.

Her insides drew into a painful knot and her hands started shaking. Lee rose unsteadily to her feet, praying she was wrong. "If you all will excuse me . . ."

"What is it, darling?" Aunt Gabby asked worriedly.

"I-I'm not yet certain."

The colonel stood up beside her. "I shall accompany you, dearest. We'll discover what this is about."

Lee stopped him with a hand on his shoulder. "Thank you, Colonel, but I would prefer to speak to the constable in private."

Wingate flicked a glance at Gabriella, who simply nodded, accustomed to her niece's independence, having encouraged it for as long as Lee could recall.

Wingate made a stiff inclination of his head. "As you wish, my dear."

Turning away from him, Lee descended the carriage stairs and walked to where Caleb and Constable Shaw stood waiting beneath the shade of a tree far enough away so they wouldn't be overheard. It occurred to her that she should send Caleb away, as she had done the colonel, but her heart was beating with fear and she wanted him to stay.

"I am sorry to be the bearer of bad news, Miss Durant," the constable said, "but this concerns the matter of a Miss Mary Goodhouse."

She steeled herself and tried to remember to breathe. "Have they . . . have they found Mary then?"

"I'm afraid so, Miss. Unfortunately, late in the evening on the night before last, Miss Goodhouse was found floating in the Thames."

Lee swayed on her feet, suddenly light-headed. She clenched her teeth as a wave of nausea hit her. Caleb's big hand settled at her waist and she held on to his arm until the spots dancing before her eyes disappeared.

"Take a deep breath," he said softly. She took several, in fact, and the nausea began to recede. "Better?"

She nodded. "Yes . . . thank you." She tried to smile but her lips refused to curve and she had to force back tears. "It is just such a shock, is all. I had hoped . . . prayed that Mary had simply gone off with a friend, or perhaps was trying to reach Freddie Hully, the man she loved."

The constable turned the brim of his hat in his hand. "It appears that wasn't the case. I hate to be indelicate, Miss Durant, but the fact is a murder has been committed and we were hoping you might be able to shed some light on the crime."

Murder. The word swirled through her head with all of its horrible implications and the nausea returned. "I'll help in any way I can."

He cast a glance at Caleb, whose jaw looked hard, then started speaking again. "Her body appeared to have been in the water for some time, which leads us to believe she may have been killed the night she went missing."

Lee's fingers tightened around Caleb's arm. "You are . . . you are absolutely certain it was murder? It couldn't have been some sort of accident?"

"As I said, she was in the water for quite some time, but the marks on her throat were clear to see. We believe she was strangled, then thrown into the river in the hope she would simply disappear."

Lee trembled, but Caleb was there and his close-ness became her anchor. "Dear God, poor Mary."

"Is there anyone you can think of, Miss Durant, who might have wished to do her harm?"

Lee shook her head. "No, I-I can't imagine anyone wanting to hurt dear Mary."

Caleb turned her to face him. "You told me she had previously worked at Parklands. Did she have any sort of disagreement with anyone there? Another member of the staff, or perhaps even one of the guests?"

"No. Everyone liked Mary. The housekeeper came to me in her behalf when she found out Mary was with child." Lee glanced up, her stomach roiling again. "Oh, God, the babe." Tears came then, a sudden rush of them that clogged her throat and spilled onto her cheeks.

"That's enough for now," Caleb said to the constable, keeping her close at his side. "Once she's had time to think things over, perhaps she'll be able to come up with something that will be useful."

Like everyone else, the constable did as Caleb commanded.

"I shall speak to you again after your return to Parklands," said Constable Shaw. "Again, I am sorry for your loss."

She nodded, dashed the tears from her cheeks with the tip of her glove, and looked up at Caleb. "I can't go back to the carriage just yet." She gazed in that di-rection, saw the others laughing. "I can't simply forget poor Mary and pretend the death of a servant is unimportant." She looked up at him, hoping he would understand. "I can't be Vermillion—not today."

Caleb nodded. "I'll tell your aunt you are feeling

unwell and need to return to the house. It isn't that far. There's a wagon parked behind the stalls—I can take you there myself. The Gold Cup won't be run until later in the day. I can be back here before it begins."

She swallowed past the tightness in her throat. "Thank you."

They spoke little as the wagon rumbled along the dirt road leading to the big Tudor mansion her aunt had rented. Lee tried not to think of Mary and the babe, but in the end, she couldn't help it.

"What could have happened?" she asked softly. "Why would she go off like that in the middle of the night? Why would she risk herself and her unborn child that way?"

On the wooden seat beside her, Caleb flicked the reins, setting the horse into a trot and jolting the wagon forward. "Whatever the reason, it must have been important."

"Yes . . ." Lee agreed. "Very important to Mary."

10

Be at ease, Captain Tanner."

"Thank you, sir." Caleb relaxed a little, though his back remained straight, his feet braced slightly apart. Standing in front of the colonel's desk, he waited as Cox reviewed the latest report Caleb had sent him in regard to the death of the maid, Mary Goodhouse.

Cox set the letter aside. "Since your return from Newmarket, have you spoken to the girl, Vermillion, in this regard?"

"I've questioned her as much as I dared. She says Mary was well-liked and had no enemies she knew of. She believes the boy, Freddie Hully, the father of Mary's unborn child, is no longer in England and that even if he were, he wasn't the sort to commit a violent crime."

Cox leaned back in his chair, silver hair freshly barbered and shining. "So tell me, Captain, what do you think happened to the girl?"

"I wish I knew. No one saw her leave that night and no one knows where she went. It could have been simple bad luck, being in the wrong place at the wrong time. Walking up on a crime, perhaps, something like that."

"It could be, but you don't really think it was."

"No sir, I don't. There had to be a reason she left the house at that hour in the first place."

"So you believe there is a chance she was somehow involved in the spy ring working out of Parklands."

Caleb clasped his hands behind his back, trying to appear nonchalant. "So far we have yet to prove there *is* a spy ring working out of Parklands."

The colonel opened a file on top of his desk. "Actually, it would seem we have recently managed to do so." He lifted out a sheet of foolscap and handed the paper to Caleb. "Three days ago, a man was apprehended near Folkstone on the coast. The sheriff had heard rumors of smuggling in the area and he was on alert. When he took the suspect into custody, he found a satchel containing a number of letters. Those letters carried information about General Wellesley's troop movements in Spain."

A knot of tension coiled in Caleb's stomach. He finished scanning the page and handed it back to Cox, who returned it to the file.

"I don't believe it is necessary to discuss the methods we employed," Cox said. "It is enough to say the courier was convinced to divulge his sources. He said he knew only one thing—the documents he was transporting were originally picked up in a small village near Kensington on the outskirts of London. The name of the village was Parkwood."

Parkwood. The knot in Caleb's stomach went tighter. It was the tiny village closest to Parklands. Just a few shops, a market square, a church, and a tavern called the Red Boar Inn. Inwardly, he cursed. He had been hoping . . .

"We'll send a man to keep watch in the village," Cox said, "but trying to keep track of every servant and guest coming and going from the Durant house is a nearly impossible task."

Cox leaned back in his chair. "So what of the girl and her aunt? Are they behind this, do you think?"

Caleb straightened a little beneath the colonel's regard. "As much as it now appears that Parklands is somehow involved, I don't believe the younger Durant is the traitor we're looking for."

"Based on what, Captain Tanner? The time you've spent in the woman's bed?"

His mouth edged up. "Sorry, sir. So far I've failed my duties in that regard. I speak merely from observation, Colonel. And from instinct. It has served me well in the past."

"Based on your outstanding service record, I would have to agree. What about the aunt? Gabriella Durant has any number of connections with the French."

"Unfortunately, I've only been in her company a couple of times and we've yet to have any sort of conversation. She doesn't ride and rarely comes out to the stable. If I had access to the house, perhaps—"

"Actually, we're working on that now. Until we find a way to bring you in closer contact, you'll have to do the best you can from your position as trainer and groom."

"Yes, sir." At least in that he had been successful. At Newmarket, Noir had won again.

The colonel rose from behind his desk. "Keep a sharp watch, Captain."

"I will, sir."

"I'll let you know if we turn up anything new on Mary Goodhouse."

"Thank you, sir."

Leaving by the rear entrance through which he had entered, Caleb walked out of the colonel's Whitehall office and into a dismal London day. Inwardly, he replayed the conversation he'd had with Cox, including the confirmation that Parklands was likely involved in passing information to the French.

Thoughts of Vermillion rested heavily on his mind. He tried to imagine her a traitor who slept with men to gather information, but the picture wouldn't gel. He hoped his instincts, always reliable in the past, were on track again in this.

"So how'd it go in there?" Major Mark Sutton, his helmet clamped beneath one arm, walked up as Caleb headed away from Whitehall.

"The news about Parklands wasn't good. Looks like something is definitely going on, but I imagine you already know that."

He nodded. "Cox called me in as soon as the report on the courier arrived. Looks like the Durant women are in it up to their pretty little necks."

Caleb shook his head. "Not necessarily. My instincts tell me the younger Durant has no idea what's going on, but of course I can't be sure. I'll keep after it. Maybe something will turn up."

"I gather you haven't bedded the wench yet."

Caleb felt a flicker of annoyance. He could have told Sutton he intended to do just that. All he had to do was wait till the time was right. But for reasons he couldn't completely fathom, he didn't want the major or anyone else to know what went on between the two of them.

"As far as I know, Vermillion isn't involved with anyone at present—and that includes me."

Sutton paused on the paving stones. "I suppose that's going to change on the night of her birthday."

Caleb stopped, too, an odd heaviness creeping into his chest. "Yes, I suppose it is."

Sutton pulled a watch fob from the pocket of his jacket. "I've got to run. Got a meeting with one of my contacts."

"Is that how we caught the courier? One of your contacts told you the man was coming through that night and you fed the sheriff some cock-and-bull story about smugglers?"

Sutton smiled. "Let's just say, I'm a handy fellow to have around."

Caleb watched the major walk away and wondered what the man would turn up next. Whatever it was, he hoped it didn't involve Vermillion.

He thought of her as he made his way out of the city, riding along a back road toward Parklands. Trying to figure her out was frustrating, to say the least. The more he was around her, the less he understood her. It was almost as if she were two different people: the mysterious courtesan Vermillion he rarely saw in the stable but half the wealthy men in London spoke of with a kind of awe and a number claimed to have bedded; the other a pretty young woman with a generous nature and an air of innocence and lack of guile Caleb found wildly appealing.

It had to be some kind of game he didn't yet understand, though something told him it was crucial that he did. He needed to discover the woman she really was, to slip past her defenses and see inside her head. Seduction seemed the answer.

Caleb wished he didn't look forward to the notion with quite so much relish.

Dark clouds rolled overhead and the air smelled of mud and damp leaves. The rhythmic clop of the horses' hooves disappeared beneath the low groan of thunder. A storm was moving in. Seated inside the elegant Durant barouche next to Jeannie, Lee straightened the skirt of the black bombazine gown she had worn to Mary's funeral and removed the matching black bonnet, hoping they arrived back at Parklands before the sky opened up and the deluge began in earnest.

She set the bonnet on the seat between her and her maid and perhaps she sighed, for her aunt's silver-blond head came up from the book she had been reading.

"My poor darling." She closed the book and set it on the seat beside her. "I know how terrible all of this has been for you, but it wasn't your fault. You did everything you could to help poor Mary."

Lee stared out the window, saw a distant flash of lightning. "I suppose I did. I just wish it had been enough." Both Aunt Gabby and Jeannie had accompanied her to the simple graveside service at the parish church near the house in Buford Street. Helen, Annie, Rose, and Sarah were there, and yet she had felt unbearably alone. Insanely she wished that Caleb could have been there, but the thought was so absurd she pushed it out of her head.

"I keep thinking about her. I don't understand it. Why would she leave the house in the middle of the night? Why would someone want to kill her?"

"Whatever the reason, it had nothing to do with

you. You need to put it behind you, darling. In time, perhaps the constable will be able to apprehend the man who killed her. Until then, there is no use torturing yourself."

Jeannie sat up straighter on the seat beside her. "*Oui*, I 'ope they catch 'im. I would like nothing so much as to watch 'im 'ang."

"I wish I could tell them something useful, something that would help." But she couldn't. She had no idea why Mary had left the safety of her home, whom she might have been meeting, or why.

"The matter is in the hands of the authorities," Aunt Gabby said. "It's their responsibility to see Mary's killer brought to justice."

But no matter how many times her aunt continued to remind her Mary's death was not her concern, the questions kept whirling round in her mind. By supper she had a pounding headache. She ordered a tray sent up to her room and stayed awake thinking about Mary until late into the evening.

It was well past midnight and still she couldn't fall asleep. Finally giving in to the restless energy she couldn't seem to shake, Lee shoved back the rose silk counterpane and climbed down from her big four-poster bed. Pulling a yellow quilted wrapper on over her night rail, she paused to light a candle, then headed downstairs, thinking that perhaps a glass of milk would help her to fall asleep.

The house was quiet, the kitchen empty. As she walked toward the windows at the rear of the kitchen, she caught the glow of a lantern burning at the far end of the stable. Old Arlie and the rest of the grooms would be asleep in their quarters in the opposite end. She hesitated only an instant before she blew out the candle, set it down on a long wooden table, and turned toward the door.

She knew what drew her, knew that it was Caleb she needed to see. She wanted him to hold her as he had done before, to speak to her in that soft way of his and ease her troubled thoughts.

As she walked toward the yellow glow of the lantern, drawn like a moth to a flame, she knew she faced that same kind of danger. Caleb wanted her. He had made his desire more than clear. But when she thought of Mary and how short life could be, thought of her birthday little more than two weeks away, she no longer cared.

She had almost reached the far end of the barn when she saw a man's tall figure move out of the shadows beside the lantern and snuff out the flame.

"Caleb . . . ?"

The man turned at the sound of her voice, but did not speak. For several long moments, he said nothing and she thought that she was mistaken and the man was someone else, a traveler, perhaps, who had wandered in off the road seeking shelter from the approaching storm.

"It's late," he said softly. "You should be in bed."

Relief and a warm sort of awareness trickled through her. She walked quietly toward him, close enough to look into his face. For a moment, the dark clouds parted. In a sliver of moonlight slanting in through the window she could see the faint roughness of his late-evening beard, the hard line of his jaw, the reflection of lamplight in the centers of his eyes.

She stopped in front of him, the ache inside her growing, the need, the yearning for him to open his arms as he had before and pull her protectively against him.

"I couldn't sleep. I saw the lantern burning. I thought..."

She saw him move in the darkness, closing the short space between them. "I'm glad you came." She felt his fingers encircling her wrist and then he was leading her forward, down to the far end of the barn and into the small room he occupied, opening the narrow wooden door and drawing her in.

He closed the door and left her for a moment. She heard him moving in the darkness, the sound of flint striking tinder, then a candle flared and his shadow appeared on the wall. The room, she saw, was tidy, the narrow bed perfectly made, the blanket on top carefully tucked in. A bowl and pitcher perched on top of the bureau at the side of the room and a ladder-backed chair rested in the corner. A pair of brown breeches were neatly folded on the seat and a pair of worn, high-topped leather riding boots sat on the floor beside the chair.

"Welcome to my humble abode." His smile was faint, his dark eyes intent. The slight curve of his mouth slipped away altogether as he looked at her standing there in her nightclothes.

She glanced down at her yellow quilted wrapper and tried not to feel self-conscious. "I know I shouldn't have come but I . . ." She shook her head, her voice trailing off a second time. What could she tell him? That she needed him? That somehow he had become important to her? That Mary's death continued to haunt her and he was the only one who might understand.

"But you what?" he pressed, standing close again,

moving so quietly she hadn't heard his footsteps on the rough wooden floor.

She glanced away, uncertain now, thinking that perhaps she should simply turn and leave, go back to the house and her empty room.

She felt his fingers on her chin, turning her to face him. "I know why you came, Vermillion—we both know—even if you aren't ready to admit it."

Framing her face between his palms, he lowered his head and his mouth came down over hers. It was the gentleness that surprised her, the unhurried claiming, little more than a brush of lips. There was mastery in the kiss, a promise of things to come, yet his lips were so soft they seemed to melt into her own, to blend and sink into a perfect union.

Slow heat enveloped her. Warmth slid into her stomach, seeped out through her limbs, seemed to wrap around her. The kiss went on and on, a coaxing, lingering, mind-numbing kiss that took and gave and seemed to have no end. He teased her lips apart and his tongue slid in, and the bottom dropped out of her stomach. Her breasts swelled beneath the heavy quilted wrapper and her nipples tightened, turned sensitive where they rubbed against her cotton nightgown.

Caleb's tongue entwined with hers and heat washed over her. He kissed her one way and then another and her legs began to tremble. She clutched the front of his full-sleeved shirt and kissed him back, wanting to please him, using her own tongue as he had done. Caleb groaned into her mouth and his arms came around her. He kissed her even more deeply and the trembling in her legs moved through the rest of her body.

She had tied back her hair before retiring. Caleb slipped the ribbon from the end, then combed his fingers through the heavy dark red curls, spreading them around her shoulders. The quilted wrapper magically slipped away. The little pink bow closing the drawstring at the top of her nightgown fell beneath the skill of his hands. The opening parted and he slid the garment off her shoulders and down over her breasts. Caleb kissed her as it pooled in a soft heap at her feet.

He drew back to look at her and she could feel the heat of his eyes burning into her. She resisted the urge to cover herself but only just barely. Caleb leaned over and kissed her again. He trailed kisses along her jaw and she felt the warmth of his mouth on the skin beneath her ear, the glide of hot, open-mouthed kisses along her neck and shoulder. One of his big hands cupped a breast and he started to knead the fullness, to shape it into his palm.

A wave of pleasure washed through her. Goosebumps raced over her skin. He kissed his way to her breasts, bent his head and took one into his mouth, and the fire he had kindled roared into a blaze. His mouth was like hot, wet, silk and everywhere he touched her seemed to burn.

Lee clung to his powerful shoulders, feeling the tension there, no longer able to think, no longer caring, filled with desire and every moment sinking deeper under the spell he wove around her. She slid her fingers into the silky dark hair curling at the nape of his neck, and her head fell back, giving him better access to her breasts. Caleb tended one and then the other, sucking them into his mouth, laving and tasting, tugging on the ends. He left them swollen and aching, her heart pounding savagely and her body filled with a longing unlike anything she had known.

"Caleb . . ." she whispered, her hands trembling as she slid them beneath his shirt, desperate to touch him as he was touching her. Reaching down, he dragged the garment over his head and tossed it away, and in the flickering light of the candle she could measure the breadth of his shoulders, see the indentations that marked his ribs, the deep contours of muscle shadowed by the flickering candlelight. A thatch of curly brown hair spread over his chest and arrowed down to his waist and her fingers inched to know the texture, to discover the feel of it against her skin.

Caleb pulled her back into his arms and kissed her again. As he had rightly guessed and she had only suspected, she had come to him for this, come so that he could guide her in this joining of a man and woman that was destined to become part of her future.

His hands skimmed over her body, moving lower, cupping the womanly place made to receive him. She was wet, she realized as he began to touch her there, slick and hot and ready to accept him inside her. She thought that he would move to take her, but instead he began to stroke her, parting the folds of her sex, caressing her lightly, slowly, then penetrating more deeply, his fingers sliding into her again and again.

The flames returned, hotter than before, the craving so strong it was nearly pain. She hadn't known, though she should have suspected. Should have guessed from the women's whispered words and knowing glances, but until now, until Caleb, she hadn't imagined the clawing need, the scorching desire a man could ignite in a woman.

She made no protest when he lifted her into his

arms and carried her over to his narrow bed, just slid her arms around his neck and rested her head against his shoulder, trusting him to guide her. As he settled her on the blanket and began to remove his breeches, her eyes widened at the heavy part of him straining upward against his belly. He was long and thick, like the stallion she had seen with the mares. But she knew that a woman was made to accept this part of a man, and that a man was often measured by the length, breadth, and hardness of his shaft. If that were so, Caleb was quite a man.

She closed her eyes as he came up over her, parted her thighs with his knee and settled himself between her legs. He could feel her trembling, she knew, but he wouldn't guess her secret, not yet. Aunt Gabby had woven the web of deceit too well, sparing her the boundaries she would have faced if her innocence had been suspected, protecting her behind a curtain of mystery that had made her one of the most sought after women in London.

He was kissing her breasts again, laving the tips with his tongue, making them quiver and tighten. A faint whimper came from her throat and she tangled her fingers in his hair.

"I want you," he said. "God, Vermillion, I want you so much." He covered her mouth with his, kissed the side of her neck. When he started to repeat her name, she pressed her trembling fingers over his lips to stop the words.

"Not tonight, Caleb, please. Tonight, won't you please call me Lee?"

Something shifted in his features. She wasn't sure what it was, but when he kissed her again, the gentleness was gone. It was a fierce, claiming kiss, a wild, possessive kiss, and pleasure streaked through her, hot and wet and almost painful in its intensity. She clung to his shoulders as he eased her legs even farther apart and she felt his hardness begin to slide inside her.

She thought she would be afraid, but she felt no fear, only a sense of joy and an odd feeling of pressure that continued to expand, filling her with a powerful need to join with him. He pressed himself deeper, but as slick and wet as she was, he couldn't seem to fit.

For the first time, worry struck. Dear Lord, perhaps she was too small. Perhaps something was wrong with her. Perhaps she truly was different from the rest of the women.

"Caleb . . . ?"

"You're so damned tight." Beads of perspiration broke out on his forehead. "I didn't expect . . ." He kissed her hard. Kissed her deeply and thoroughly until she was wetter still and desperate for him to take her. He thrust his tongue into her mouth at the same instant he drove himself hard inside her.

Her body spasmed, tightened in pain, and a cry tore from her throat.

Caleb went utterly still. He looked down at her and she saw the confusion, saw the instant he realized what had just occurred. "It can't be. No." He shook his head. "It isn't possible."

Lee barely heard him with the little sobs creeping out and her eyes filling with tears.

"Goddammit! What the hell is going on?" He wrenched himself so violently out of her body, pain shot through her again.

She tried to struggle free of his heavy weight, but Caleb pinned her to the bed. He propped himself on his elbows and held on to her wrists. "You can't be a virgin. It's impossible. You're Vermillion. You've had countless lovers."

"I'm Lee," she whispered, hating herself for the mess she had made of this. "I won't be . . . won't be Vermillion till the night of my birthday."

Caleb stared down at her, his dark gaze turbulent. "I don't believe this." Swearing a silent oath, he released her wrists, rolled onto his side, and gathered her into his arms. "God, why didn't you tell me?"

Lee hung on to him, wishing she had done just that. "I was afraid to. I didn't know what you would think."

He clenched his jaw and said something she couldn't quite hear. "How badly did I hurt you?"

She loved the feel of his arms around her, felt grateful for them. She shook her head, tried to smile. "The pain is gone. I'm told it only hurts the first time."

He took a deep breath, slowly exhaled it. "I thought I knew why you came here tonight. Now I'm not so sure."

She rested her head on his chest, comforted by the steady rhythm of his heart. "You were right. I came for this. I wanted a man of my own choosing. I wish I had pleased you, Caleb, and I know that I did not."

He caught her chin with his fingers. "You pleased me. Just by coming here, you pleased me. By choosing me as that man. I only wish I'd known. Now that I do, I'm not sure—"

"Please, Caleb. I want this."

He sighed into the dimly lit room, raked his damp hair back from his forehead. "We'll just have to take things slower. I'll make it good for you, Lee, I promise." Bending his head, Caleb leaned over and very softly settled his mouth over hers. It was another of his slow, languid, unhurried kisses and the heat he had stirred before flamed up and licked through her limbs.

He touched her as he had before, his fingers sliding inside her, stretching her and preparing her to accept him. He didn't stop until she was writhing on the bed, flushed with desire, and begging him to take her. He slid into her more easily this time, filling her completely, yet the pain never surfaced, only the craving, the wild, uncontrollable yearning.

Beneath him on the narrow bed, her restlessness grew and her body shifted against the heavy fullness inside her. Unconsciously, her back arched upward, thrusting her breasts into his chest. She pressed her mouth against his skin, felt the heat, tasted the slick, damp, saltiness of it, circled his flat copper nipple with her tongue, and heard him groan.

He went still for a moment, trying to hold himself in check, working to regain his control. Then he started moving again, easing himself out, then driving deep once more. Slow and easy, muscles straining, drawing out the pleasure. His movements grew faster, his hips flexing, driving him deeper still. The rhythm increased, enveloped her, the heavy thrust and drag, the fullness, the pressure against her womb, the heat and the need and the overwhelming sense of urgency.

Then her body suddenly tightened and a wave of pleasure tore through her. Little shivers rushed over her skin. Tiny pinpricks of light seemed to burst behind her eyes. Her insides tingled and she cried out Caleb's name.

"That's right, love. Let yourself go."

She heard a roaring in her ears like the wind through the trees and her body seemed to fly apart. "Caleb!" She bit down on her lip as pleasure speared through her, sweeter than anything she could have imagined. She clung to Caleb's neck as he pounded into her, taking her hard, unable to stop himself. An instant later, his body went rigid, his muscles tightening. He tried to withdraw, but she wasn't ready for that and she gripped his hips, felt the wetness of his seed spilling inside her. His head fell back and a low guttural groan filled the quiet of the room.

For long moments, neither of them spoke. Eventually their heartbeats slowed and Caleb shifted a little on the mattress, then lay down on the blanket beside her, fitting her back to his chest spoon-fashion in the narrow bed.

He toyed with a lock of her hair. "I can't believe it. You were a virgin." He smoothed the strand between his thumb and forefinger. "In God's name, why did you pretend to be something you were not?"

Lee sighed into the darkness. "It's hard to explain, Caleb." She turned onto her back so that she could look up at him, into the dark eyes he fixed on her face. "I told you once before—I'm a Durant. It's my destiny to follow in the footsteps of my grandmother and aunt."

In the moonlight, she saw a muscle tighten along his jaw. "You were a virgin," he stubbornly repeated. "Why would you choose that sort of life?"

Lee turned toward him, wound her arms around his neck. "Please . . . I don't want to talk about this now." She pulled his head down and gave him a feather-soft kiss. "You want me," she whispered. "I can feel how hard you are."

"I get hard every time I look at you. If you hadn't been so innocent you would have figured that out long before this."

She flushed but didn't look away. "My birthday

isn't that far off. We won't have much time together. I want you to make love to me again."

Several emotions flickered in his eyes, but the heat was clear to see. He kissed her deeply, then a corner of his mouth edged up. "I suppose, since you're my employer, I'm compelled to do as you say."

Lee closed her eyes as he came up over her, filling her again. Very slowly, he started to move inside her. Clinging to the muscles across his shoulders, she let him sweep her into the world of pleasure that he had shown her before.

She didn't linger when they finished this time, just got up from the narrow mattress, walked over and silently began to pull on her clothes. She could feel Caleb's eyes on her, watching her from the bed.

"Make me understand, Lee." His deep voice drifted across the small, low-ceilinged room. "Tell me why you would sacrifice your life, your future, as you are planning to do."

She only shook her head. "You wouldn't understand."

She heard the rustle of fabric as he sat up on the edge of the bed and wrapped the blanket around his waist. "It wouldn't have anything to do with loyalty, would it? Some sort of patriotic sentiment you still feel toward France? I know your family came from there."

She frowned as she pushed her arms into the sleeves of her nightgown and tied the drawstring at the neck. "I don't know what you mean."

Caleb shrugged. Bare-chested, he tucked the top of the blanket in to hold it up and started walking toward her. In the moonlight, she noticed a fine tension in the muscles across his shoulders.

"I've heard rumors," he said. "There are people who say you and your aunt hold certain loyalties toward the French. It would certainly be understandable if you were willing to sacrifice yourself in order to collect information that might be helpful—"

"If you are saying what I think you are, that is completely insane. I was born in this country—so was my aunt. We both love England. This is our home. Every time we read in the papers how many of our men have died, how many have suffered at Napoleon's hands, we are heartsick. As for any loyalty I might feel toward the French—for God's sake, Caleb, a number of my family died by the guillotine. England gave us refuge. How can you possibly doubt our loyalty?"

Caleb said nothing for several long moments, but his eyes ran over her, taking in her defiant stance, the way her small hands fisted, the flush of color in her cheeks, and the tension slowly ebbed from his shoulders. He stood in front of her, barefoot and barechested and so handsome it made an ache rise in her throat.

"Why then?" he said softly.

Lee glanced away, unable to hold his penetrating gaze a moment more. "Because it's what Aunt Gabby wants. Because I owe her and I can't repay her in any other way. Because she loves the life she lives and through me she can continue to live it. Because I don't want to return her years of kindness by making her believe I feel disdain in any way for the life she has chosen."

Caleb said nothing. He stood so close she could see the dark centers of his eyes, read the turbulence there. Then his big hands framed her face and he bent his head and very softly kissed her.

"Don't go yet," he said. "There are hours before dawn. I'll make sure you're back in the house before anyone wakes up and finds you missing."

She knew she should go. Every moment she spent with Caleb put her in peril. *Love.* It was the greatest danger a woman could face. Mary had suffered for it. Her mother had suffered for years and died with a broken heart that had never mended.

Lee looked up at Caleb, knowing the risk, knowing part of her heart already belonged to him. Willing to accept the risk, even if it meant losing an even bigger portion during the short time they had together.

Caleb took her hand and carried it to his lips. She didn't resist when he lifted her up and carried her across the room, back to his narrow bed.

11

Mounted on the big bay gelding named Duke, Caleb rode toward the village of Parkwood. It was early afternoon, the first chance he'd had to get away. The village wasn't far. As he approached from the south, he could see roofs and chimneys in the distance. He passed a wagonload of hay and the driver waved a greeting. A pot-seller's wagon rumbled along ahead of him, its cargo clanging and clattering as the vehicle dipped and swayed behind the donkey struggling to pull its heavy load. Caleb barely noticed.

He was on his way to the house on the opposite side of town that belonged to Cyrus Swift, the silversmith who carried messages for him to London. The one he needed delivered today concerned Vermillion.

Since he had awakened her from a deep sleep snuggled beside him, Caleb hadn't been able to stop thinking about her. Over and over, he replayed the night they had shared, which was nothing at all as he had imagined and one he would never forget. As he reined the horse off the road onto the lane leading to the silversmith's house, one thing was clear: Vermillion hadn't been selling her body to gain information.

Until last night, she had been a virgin.

Several different emotions filtered through him at the thought, none of which he completely understood. His desire for her hadn't lessened as he had believed it would. Instead, every time he recalled her small body sweetly gloving his shaft, he got hard all over again. He wanted her even more than he had before, and thoughts of her upcoming birthday, knowing she planned to give herself to another man, sat like a crushing weight on his chest.

He wasn't sure what he meant to do, but letting another man touch her, make love to her as he had done was something he refused to let happen. He had to do something to change the tide of events about to be set in motion and Caleb believed he might have found a way.

Riding into the yard of the silversmith's white-washed, thatched-roof house, he swung down from the bay. The place looked a little forlorn with its window boxes untended and weeds growing up between the bricks in the walkway leading to the entrance. He banged on the wooden door, considering his plan, praying his instincts were right about Lee Durant and knowing how much he had to lose if he were wrong.

Knowing how much England had to lose.

"Captain Tanner! Please, come in." Cyrus Swift was a slight man with fine bones and refined features. His hair was as silver as the craft he had perfected and his smile was genuine and always exceedingly warm. "Its good to see you. Could I offer you a glass of cider or perhaps some elderberry wine?"

Caleb shook his head. "No, thank you, sir. I can't

stay long. I said I had an errand in the village but they'll expect my immediate return."

Swift nodded, though Caleb could see he would have liked the company. "Come then." Swift motioned him into the parlor, a room that had once been cozy and well-cared for, with bright floral slipcovers on the sofas and ruffled curtains at the windows. But Mrs. Swift had passed on last year and the signs of a bachelor household had begun to surface.

A stack of old newspapers sat in a haphazard pile on a piecrust table near the hearth. The curtains drooped and the rugs could have used a good beating. A Swift-made silver tea service sat on a tea cart near the door, but the pieces were tarnished.

"There's pen and ink on the desk. I believe you know the way."

"Yes, sir." Caleb had been to the house on several occasions to send or retrieve a message.

Following Cyrus farther into the parlor, he went over to the small oak writing desk along the wall, drew out a piece of foolscap, and plucked the quill pen out of its silver holder. He scratched out a note requesting a meeting with Colonel Cox as soon it could be arranged, then signed it, *Respectfully, Captain Caleb Tanner.*

"I shall see it delivered today," Swift promised.

"If it's at all possible, I'd like you to wait for a reply."

He nodded. "As you wish."

"Thank you, Mr. Swift. Your help in this has been invaluable."

"It is the very least I can do, Captain Tanner. I lost my eldest son, James—God rest his soul—ten years ago in the Netherlands Campaign. My youngest boy is a corporal in the 95th Infantry. I have no wish to lose him, as well."

"No, sir. With the help of people like you he'll have a far greater chance of staying safe."

Swift walked Caleb to the door. "I'll leave the reply in the usual spot in the barn, Captain."

"Thank you again for your help, Mr. Swift." And then he was gone.

Caleb had no idea what Colonel Cox would say when he heard the idea Caleb had come up with, but the army needed someone inside the house, someone close to the occupants, someone they could trust. Caleb prayed the colonel would see the merit in his plan.

Laughter echoed through the house. Servants hurried about beneath the weight of heavily laden silver trays. Food and drink sat on linen-draped tables and champagne flowed like water. The guests were all enjoying themselves but to Vermillion, the house party seemed endless.

In a gown of emerald silk, daringly low-cut and embroidered in fine gold thread across the bodice, she wandered from room to room, smiling and nodding and pretending an interest in the various conversations around her. In truth, all she could think of was Caleb and that she had gone to him last night and the two of them had made love.

She wasn't an innocent anymore. She had given herself to a man and not one of those she had vowed to choose as a lover, but Caleb Tanner, Parklands' head groom.

Her pulse leaped just thinking about it. She remembered the way he looked standing there naked, his hard body bathed in a shaft of moonlight streaming in through the window of his tiny room. She could see the wide bands of muscle across his chest and the sinews in his legs, remember the power and strength of him, pressing her down into the mattress.

Warm color rose in her cheeks as she thought of her response to his ardent lovemaking, like some wild creature freed at last from its bonds by the skill of his hands.

More disturbed than she wanted to be, Lee left the drawing room, escaping into the library for a moment's respite from the crowd, closing the tall, ornate doors behind her. She was sitting in the window seat, staring out at the garden when she heard a sound across the room.

"Vermillion?" The familiar voice drew her attention to the doorway. "What on earth are you doing in here by yourself? Everyone is looking for you." Her friend, Elizabeth Sorenson, stood framed in the opening.

"It's all right, Elizabeth. I just needed a moment alone. I'll return to the party in a moment."

Elizabeth surprised her by closing the tall doors behind her, the sound echoing into the quiet as the countess began to walk toward her.

"What is it, Lee?" she asked. "You haven't seemed yourself lately. Your aunt has been worried and so have I." With her short, curly black hair, slender build and long legs, Elizabeth's timeless beauty was marred only by the worry on her face.

Lee forced herself to smile. "Why in heaven's name would you be worried, Beth? I am perfectly fine."

"I realize your birthday is very near," Elizabeth said gently. "You've promised to choose a lover, but perhaps you are simply not ready."

Not ready? She wondered what the countess would say if she knew Lee had already chosen a lover, that even now she yearned for him, that she wanted him to make love to her again.

"It has to happen sooner or later," Lee said. "You know as well as I, marriage lies nowhere in my future. I said that I would choose and so I shall."

Elizabeth's frown only deepened. "There is certainly no rush. Aside from the fact you could start to live your life on your own terms, there is no real urgency. Gabriella knows how independent you are. She thought you would appreciate the chance to truly become your own person, but perhaps it would be better if—"

"If what, Beth?" She got up from the window seat and walked toward her friend. "Perhaps it would be better if I waded through another dozen men? If I attended another hundred of my aunt's tedious parties? In the end, the result would be the same."

"But surely—"

"I appreciate your concern, Beth, I truly do, but my aunt is right. It is time I made a life for myself and that is what I am going to do." She managed to muster a smile. "And it is also time I joined Aunt Gabriella and the rest of her guests."

"They are your guests, too, Lee. They are your friends as well as your aunt's."

"Are they?" She lifted her gaze to Elizabeth's lovely face. "Aside from you and a handful of others, most of them are people I scarcely know. They are here to be charmed by La Belle. As for Vermillion, she is merely a curiosity. They are fascinated by the mysterious persona my aunt has created. They have no desire to know the woman inside, the woman behind the mask she wears." Turning away, she started once more for the door.

"Dearest, wait—"

But Lee kept walking, out of the library and down the hall. She meant to return to the others—she truly did—but as she spotted Colonel Wingate striding down the hall in her direction, saw Andrew Mondale walking toward her the opposite way, she turned instead and hurried up the stairs.

"Vermillion, my beauty—where are you going?" Mondale's voice floated up behind her. "Come down and join the party."

Vermillion turned and smiled. "Shortly, Andrew, I promise." And she would, she told herself, in just a little while. Reaching the safety of her room, she closed the door and leaned against it. Her chest felt as if a boulder pressed upon it and her stomach felt queasy.

For the first time, she realized exactly how much trouble she had brought upon herself. "Oh, dear God—what am I going to do?" Tears burned her eyes. She had to go back downstairs, had to continue her charade—for her aunt and perhaps, as Aunt Gabby believed, for herself. But after making love with Caleb, she was no longer certain she could continue in the role she so desperately needed to play.

Turning away from the door, she walked over to her rosewood dresser, poured water from the porcelain pitcher into the basin, and washed the rouge and rice powder from her cheeks. She wiped away the color on her lips and rang for Jeannie, who appeared in her bedchamber a few minutes later.

"*Mon Dieu!* What are you doing?"

"Help me get out of this, will you? I'm having trouble with the buttons."

Jeannie looked at her aghast, stunned by her freshly washed face and half-undressed appearance. "You cannot possibly mean to disrobe. The party . . . it is not yet midnight!"

"I don't care what time it is." She tried to reach the buttons at the back of the gown, determined now, desperate to escape. "I have to get out of here."

"*Dieu du Ciel*—you 'ave gone completely mad." But the slender woman stepped in and took charge, quickly dispatching the buttons and helping her slide out of the emerald silk gown. As soon as Lee was free of her garments, she went over to her armoire and pulled open the bottom drawer. A pair of men's breeches and a white linen shirt, carefully folded, lay on top. In minutes she was dressed and dragging on her riding boots.

"I cannot believe this," Jeannie grumbled as Lee pulled the pins from her hair and shook her head, unseating the heavy red curls. She quickly brushed them out, then clipped the curly mass back on the sides with little mother-of-pearl inlaid combs.

"Look at you. What if someone sees you?"

"No one is going to see me. I'm going down the back stairs." She turned, caught her friend's hand. "I need this, Jeannie. I have to get out of this place—just for a little while."

Her friend looked into her face. Whatever she saw made her eyes go wide. "*Nom de Dieu!* It is the man you spoke of. You 'ave given yourself to 'im!"

Lee glanced away, embarrassment only one of the dozen emotions she felt. "It doesn't matter. Nothing can change what's going to happen the night of my birthday."

"Oh, *chérie,* if I had believed making love with this

man would make you so unhappy, I would 'ave begged you not to do it."

"I'll be all right, Jeannie. Women make love to men every day—no one knows that better than we do. I just need a little time to straighten things out in my head. The party will go on most of the night. I'll be back before it's over."

Jeannie said nothing and Lee turned away. Pausing at the bedchamber door, she checked to be certain no one was about, then hurried down the hall to the servants' stairs. Making her way out a little-used door leading into the garden, she raced off toward the stables.

The night was warm and clear, the moon shining down and lighting her way. Caleb would likely be in the stable and part of her desperately wanted to see him. Another, saner part never wanted to see him again.

A soft wind blew through the branches of the trees as she followed the path to the big stone building that housed Parklands' valuable Thoroughbreds. The lanterns had all been snuffed out, the grooms retired for the night.

Moving quietly, she disappeared into the darkness inside the barn and made her way along the row of stalls. Spotting Grand Coeur's gray head watching her over the top of stall, she grabbed a bridle off the rack and moved in the horse's direction. Coeur made a soft, nickering sound as she slipped the bridle over his ears and led him from his box.

The open fields beckoned. No one had seen her leave the house or discovered her in the stable. Not quite sure whether she was disappointed or relieved that Caleb hadn't appeared, she urged the horse out of the barn and into the pasture. As soon as they had traveled a safe distance away, she nudged Grand Coeur into a gallop.

In need of an outing as much as she, the stallion stretched out beneath her and together they raced off toward the freedom of the open fields.

Beneath a waning moon, Caleb rode the big bay gelding back toward Parklands. He was returning from a trip to the village. The reply Cyrus Swift had received from Colonel Cox rested in his saddlebags.

Caleb shifted on the flat leather saddle, thinking of the words scrolled on the note. Before dawn on the morrow, he had been ordered to collect his belongings, leave Parklands, and return to London. Jacob Boswell would be resuming his job as trainer and groom. Caleb was instructed to say nothing of his departure to anyone—including and especially not Vermillion or Gabriella Durant.

It wasn't the answer he had expected. He wasn't sure why Cox had ordered his immediate return, but he still held hope the colonel would at least consider his plan. Caleb's message had only made very brief mention of what he had in mind. Tomorrow in London he would fill in the missing details.

It was clear and warm, a soft breeze ruffling through his hair as he rode at an easy gallop back to collect his things. He tried not to think of that same breeze drifting through his window last night, cooling his heated skin as he made love to Vermillion, but thoughts of her haunted him. She was there in his mind when he crested the top of a hill and spotted a rider on the grassy slope below.

Caleb pulled rein, drawing the bay to a halt in the

shadow of a wide-spreading yew tree. Below him, first running hard, then slowing to a leisurely gallop, Grand Coeur's dappled coat glistened like silver in the moonlight.

He recognized the petite, confident rider.

Caleb felt an instant leap of his pulse. Last night he had taken her innocence. He had made love to her three times in the small room he occupied in the stable and would have had her again if they had awakened in time. Just thinking about her made him hard, made him want to ride off the hill and drag her down from her horse, made him want to strip away her clothes, haul her down on the grass, and bury himself inside her.

He watched her from his place on the knoll, wondering where she might be heading, suspicious for a time, worried that he had been wrong about her. But it soon became apparent she had no destination, that her meandering course led mostly in circles and her moonlight ride was nothing more than that.

He thought about the hours he had spent with her last night and the fact that she had been a virgin. There was no denying the truth, no way to pretend the blood on her lovely pale thighs hadn't been a result of what he had taken from her.

Perhaps it wouldn't have happened if he had known the truth.

Or perhaps he was lying to himself and the desire to have her would have been so strong he would have taken her just the same.

As he watched her turn the gray and ride into a copse of trees, Caleb nudged Duke into a gallop and rode off down the hill. As soon as she saw him, she drew rein, pulling Grand Coeur to a halt beneath the overhanging branches of a tree.

"Caleb! What . . . what are you doing out here?"

He shrugged, hoping to appear nonchalant, feeling not the least that way. "The same as you." He swung down from the bay and looped the reins around the trunk of the tree. "I couldn't sleep. I thought maybe a ride would help."

Reaching up, he lifted Vermillion down from the gray and tied the stallion's reins to a tree a few feet away. "You've a house full of guests. There were so many candles blazing it looked like the place was on fire. I figured you'd be busy entertaining." Busy with Mondale or Nash or one of the other men who danced to her tune. He tried to keep the irritation out of his voice, but didn't quite succeed.

Lee seemed not to notice.

"I was there for a while." She sat down on a fallen log and Caleb sat down beside her. She looked beautiful tonight in her simple white lawn shirt and brown breeches. She had left her fiery hair unbound and the thick curls glowed like burning coals in the moonlight. The powder was gone from her face and he thought he caught the faint track of tears.

"What is it, Lee? Why did you come out here?"

She gazed off toward the low grass fluttering in the wind, forming patterns in the fields. "I don't know if I can go through with it, Caleb. I know I have to, but I don't know if I can."

His chest felt heavy. He knew exactly what she meant. He wasn't sure he could let her, even if it was what she wanted. "You're talking about the decision you're supposed to make the night of your birthday."

She nodded.

"Because of what happened between us last night?"

She looked up at him. A hint of kohl still outlined her eyes and they looked huge and blue-green in the moonlight. "In a way, I suppose. Until last night, I never understood what it would be like to make love . . . how much of yourself you give to a man. I never realized that every touch brands you, steals something from you. That when you take a man inside you, it's like . . . it's like giving him a piece of your soul."

She stared past him over the rolling hills and he thought how beautiful she was and how her words touched him.

"I don't suppose you would understand," she said, looking back at him. "I'm sure it's different for a man."

Was it different? In the past, he had bedded any number of women, all of them more than willing and almost none of them worth remembering. Some he paid for their trouble, nameless, faceless women he left behind in alehouses and far-off military encampments.

But what of the woman who sat beside him? Lee was different from the others he had known, a combination of innocence and sensuality that made him want her as he never had another. She was more independent than any woman he had ever met and at the same time helplessly trapped in a life she couldn't seem to escape. He thought of her day and night and wanted her endlessly. Just sitting so close had him hard and aching to be inside her.

Perhaps he had given Lee Durant a piece of his soul as well.

Caleb didn't much like the thought.

"What happened between us, Lee, it was special. Never doubt that."

She made no reply. Perhaps she didn't believe him. If he didn't come back, it was probably better that way.

"In less than two weeks," she said, "everything in my life is going to change."

On her nineteenth birthday. The thought squeezed something inside his chest. "Listen to me, Lee. There's no law, no commandment that says you have to choose a protector that night or any other. You don't need the money. You don't have to invite Mondale, or Nash, or anyone else into your bed. You don't have to become Vermillion. You could stay the way you are. You could just be Lee."

She raised her eyes to his and he could see regret reflected there. "I have to do it. It's the only way. My aunt loves her life, Caleb. She loves the parties and the endless attention. She's getting older. Her beauty is fading. I know how much it bothers her, how much she wants things to stay the same. If I become Vermillion, Aunt Gabriella can live on through me."

"You don't owe her that, Lee. No one owes anyone that much."

"You're wrong. I owe her everything. When my mother died, I was left completely alone. I was four years old when the lady who owned the cottage we lived in left me at the orphanage. She didn't know how terrible that place was—no one knew. They beat us, Caleb, for the slightest infraction. They locked us in the cellar with the rats if we did something wrong. There weren't enough blankets and not enough food. If Aunt Gabby hadn't come . . . if she hadn't taken me home with her, I would have died in that place, I know I would have. I loved her the moment she lifted me into her arms and she loved me. I would do anything for her, Caleb. Anything to see that she is happy."

"Tell her, Lee. Tell her the way you feel."

"How can I? I'm not even sure myself. Perhaps she is right, perhaps the freedom of a life like hers is worth whatever it costs."

He didn't believe it. Not for an instant. "You could have a husband, Lee, a family. That's something every woman wants. It isn't fair that you should have to give those things up."

Her eyes locked with his and there was something in them he had never seen before.

"Is that a proposal, Caleb? Are you asking me to marry you?"

His stomach instantly knotted. For several long moments he simply sat there. The thought of marriage had never entered his mind. She was Vermillion, a courtesan. But after last night, he, more than anyone, knew it wasn't the truth.

He cleared his throat, needing time, groping for something to say. "What kind of a life would you have with a man like me?" He knew she was thinking he meant as the wife of a groom, but he was thinking of a man dedicated to war, one who would soon be returning to Spain.

Her features shifted, seemed to close up. She tossed her head and a brittle little laugh came from her throat. "What sort of life, indeed. Not the sort I am used to, that is for certain. You're a groom. A groom doesn't ask his employer to marry him and even if he did, it would hardly be seemly to wed one of the servants."

A muscle tightened in his cheek, though why he should be angry eluded him. He wasn't proposing, and even if he were, Vermillion would never marry the groom he pretended to be. She wouldn't give up her luxurious way of life for a man so far beneath her.

His mouth curved up, but his smile held no warmth. "You're right. A man like me is only good enough for a tumble or two before it's time to move on to someone more suitable. Was that it, Vermillion? You needed some instruction before you sold yourself to Mondale or Nash?"

Color washed into her cheeks. "That isn't true."

"Isn't it?"

She leaped up from the log and whirled toward her horse, but Caleb stepped in front of her, blocking her escape.

"Get out of my way."

"Are you sure that's what you want? We've time for another quick tumble. Perhaps you'll learn something new that might prove useful."

She jerked her small hand free and drew back to slap him, but Caleb caught her wrist. "You managed that trick before. You don't want to do it again."

"Let me go." She struggled as he hauled her against him.

"I don't think you want that any more than I do."

She pressed her palms against his chest but she was half his size and she hadn't a prayer of dislodging him. Bending his head, he captured her mouth in a rough, demanding kiss, anger riding him hard. Lee fought him for a moment, but he just kept kissing her and slowly the kiss began to gentle. He kissed her the way he had last night and little by little her struggles slowly ceased. Her hands moved over his chest, up around his neck, and her fingers tangled in his hair.

Leaning into him, she kissed him back as wildly as he was kissing her. Caleb groaned. He was achingly hard, hungry for her, ready to take what she now wanted to give him.

Instead, she eased a little away. "I gave myself to you because it was you that I wanted, Caleb. I care nothing for Mondale or Nash, or anyone else—surely you know that by now. I can't bear the thought of them touching me, making love to me as you have. I can't imagine giving myself to another man the way I have given myself to you."

Caleb read the pain in her eyes and his chest constricted. *Damn them. Damn them all to bloody hell.*

He cursed her aunt and the others for what they were doing to her even as he cursed himself for what he had already done. Reaching out, he framed her face between his hands, settled his mouth over hers, and very softly kissed her. She tasted like expensive champagne and smelled like night-blooming flowers, and heat slid into his groin. His shaft lengthened, thickened, hardened till it was painful. His pulse ricocheted skyward and desire exploded in his blood.

They made love on the soft green grasses behind the trees. Spreading his shirt beneath them, he lay down on his back and settled her above him. At first she seemed surprised that they could make love in this way. He watched her teeth sink into her bottom lip as he lifted her a little and eased her down on his shaft, her body gloving him so perfectly he groaned. It didn't take her long to realize the power he had given her and soon she began to ride him, gently at first, then moving faster, taking him more deeply, absorbing the pleasure.

His own pleasure swelled with each of her movements. As she bent her head and kissed him, lifted herself then took him fully again, he palmed her bare breasts. Silky red hair teased his chest and he fought not to lose control.

They reached their peak together, her soft cry filling the night. A few minutes later, he rolled her onto her back and took her again, more gently this time, determined to make it good for her.

Afterward, spent and sated, they lay together in the grass, watching the moon drift by overhead. Tomorrow he would be leaving, but he could not tell her. He thought how much he had come to care for her, this innocent, free-spirited young woman, and wished that he could change things, wished there weren't so many secrets swirling around them.

It was essential that someone get inside the house.

Caleb prayed his plan would work and he could return.

And that Lee would forgive him if he did.

12

Dear Lord, she had spent another night making love with him! It was late morning now. She had only been away from him a few hours and yet she longed to see him again. It was madness, insanity, but she could not seem to help herself.

Lee thought of Caleb and her growing feelings for him and nervously bit her lip. When a knock sounded at the door, she was grateful for the distraction.

"I am sorry to disturb you," Jeannie said, "but your aunt wishes to see you. She is worried that you are unwell."

Suffering a hint of madness, undoubtedly, but otherwise very well indeed. "Tell her I am fine. I had a bit of a headache last night, but it is gone this morning."

Instead of leaving, Jeannie stepped into the room and quietly closed the door. "You said that you would return last night, but you did not come back until early this morning. It is not safe for you to be out there by yourself."

And even less safe to be with Caleb. Lee glanced

away. "I wasn't in any danger and even if I were, I can take care of myself."

One of Jeannie's brown eyebrows went up. "Ah, no—you were with 'im! Oh, *chérie,* do you know what you risk?"

"As I said, I can take care of myself."

"Are you certain of that?"

Was she certain? She had never been less certain of anything in her life. And yet she knew she was doing exactly what she wanted.

She reached over and caught her friend's hand. "Listen to me, Jeannie. There isn't much time left before my birthday. I want these last two weeks for myself."

Jeannie sighed. "It is my fault this 'as 'appened. I never should 'ave encouraged you. I do not know what I was thinking."

"No, Jeannie, you were right. I don't believe I shall ever feel this way about another man. I might never have understood what it is like to truly experience passion." *And love.* As much as she wished to deny it, she knew she was more than half in love with him.

"Be careful, *chérie.* You know this cannot continue. I do not wish to see you hurt."

But that was bound to happen and Lee knew it. Once she had chosen a protector, she would be leaving Parklands, bidding a last farewell to Caleb Tanner.

Then again, perhaps Caleb would be the first to leave.

An uneasy feeling settled over her. There was something in his manner last night as he bade her farewell. She wasn't sure what it was but even now the uneasy feeling remained.

It stayed with her all through the morning, and

after a light breakfast of cocoa and biscuits with her aunt, she headed straight for the stable.

"Good day ta ye, Miss Lee." Arlie shuffled toward her down the corridor in the middle of the barn, his spine bent but a smile on his wrinkled face.

"Good morning, Arlie." She glanced around for Caleb, but didn't see him.

"'E's gone, Miss. Took off sometime afore dawn. Left ye this note, 'e did. Found it on a nail in front of Grand Coeur's stall." Arlie dragged a folded piece of paper from the pocket of his breeches and held it out to her.

Her heart was thundering. She could hear the pounding in her ears. Reaching out, she took the note and broke the drop of candle wax he had used for a seal.

> *Lee,*
> *A problem has arisen and I am called away. Jacob will be returning to resume his duties on the morrow. Perhaps we shall meet again.*
> *Your servant, Caleb Tanner*

Her heart beat painfully as she read the note again, searching for some hidden meaning, some small word that told her what they had shared had meant something to him, that leaving her wasn't what he wished to do. But there was nothing of comfort in the message.

She surveyed his parting words, *Your servant, Caleb Tanner.* No man had ever been less of a servant and of course Caleb knew it. It was the sort of closing a gentleman might use, but Caleb wasn't a gentleman.

Or was he?

There had always been things about him that simply did not fit. His speech was that of an educated man, his manners those of the upper classes—along with his arrogance. Perhaps he was a highborn man, fallen heavily into debt and running to avoid debtors' prison. Perhaps he had done something worse. Whoever he was, she had cared for him greatly and now he was gone, casting her aside as if she had meant nothing to him at all, leaving only a brief note of farewell.

Lee's heart filled with a weighty despair. She had tried so hard not to love him, but part of her was deeply in love and that part would never forgive him. She told herself it was better this way, better he was gone and she could go on with the life laid out for her.

Crumbling the note in her hand, she swallowed past the tight knot in her throat and ignored the sting of tears. Caleb was gone. That part of her life was over.

Vermillion tossed the paper into the waste bin and vowed not to think of Caleb Tanner again.

The afternoon slipped past and the hour grew late. The moon slid away, disappearing behind a cover of dense black clouds that boded rain. A heavy mist hung over the earth, dampening the long black woolen cloak draped over the woman's shoulders. Beneath the hood, her hair was damp, and fine strands clung to the nape of her slender neck.

She didn't like being out on a night like this. As she walked the narrow path toward the village, every shadow seemed a villainous creature ready to spring out of the darkness, and the damp, spongy ground distorted the sounds in the inky night.

It didn't matter. She had to see him. He would expect her to have something for him by now and she didn't want to fail him.

They were meeting at their usual place in the village, a small attic room above the Red Boar Inn. They never spoke at the house. It was too dangerous, he said, people might see them. It didn't matter. She didn't mind slipping away, even on a night like this. Not for him. And here she didn't have to share him.

He was waiting as she climbed the outside stairs along a shadowy wall protected by dense gray-green ivy. Standing in the darkness lit only by a single tallow candle, he was as attractive as he had been the first time she had seen him, more so with each passing year. His eyes ran over her, surveying her from head to foot, and she smiled at the gleam of interest that appeared in his eyes.

"You look extremely fetching tonight, my sweet."

She blushed and smiled, pleased that he seemed to approve of the new blue muslin gown she'd had made with the money he had given her the last time they were together.

He eased back the hood of her cloak, then pulled the drawstring and removed the wet garment, draped it over the back of a wooden chair.

"The gown suits you. It brings out the color of your eyes." The room was small and stark, with only a slatted bed and nightstand, a dresser with a chipped basin and pitcher, and the lone wooden chair. Perhaps that was the reason his elegant figure seemed such a powerful force.

"I 'ave learned something," she said with her soft French accent. "It may be important. I knew you would wish to 'ear it as soon as it could be arranged."

He moved closer, till she could smell a hint of brandy on his breath and his expensive cologne. "I thought perhaps you had simply missed me." His hands were encased in butter soft kidskin. He tugged on the end of each finger, slowly removing the gloves, then he tossed them onto the seat of the chair. "I was hoping you might wish to continue where we left off the last time we were here."

The last time they were there. A little thrill went through her. She hadn't forgotten. She never forgot the brief hours she'd spent with him. "I always wish to be with you. It 'as been far too long since we are together."

He reached up and stroked her cheek and her insides trembled. All he had to do was look at her and she melted a little inside. His hand encircled the nape of her neck, drew her toward him. He reached out, cupped one of her breasts, squeezed it, gently at first, then harder, just to the point of pleasure-pain.

She sucked in a breath, unconsciously tried to draw away, but he pulled her back and his touch turned gentle. He stroked her nipple through the bodice of her gown and pleasure washed over her again.

"What have you brought me?"

She told him what she had learned, knew by the slight curl of his lips that she had pleased him. She knew the taste of those lips, knew the feel of them moving over her body, knew the sweet, unbearable excitement they could bring.

But first she would give to him. He had come to expect that now and she would never disappoint him. When he rested his hands on her shoulders and gently urged her down, she knelt in front of him. She waited while he opened the front of his breeches and freed himself, admired the length of him, the hardness that would soon be inside her.

She knew exactly how to please him. She felt his fingers on the back of her neck, holding her immobile as she took him into her mouth. She had told him something of value and in return for her loyalty, soon he would make her his.

Once this was over and his job was complete, they would go away together, leave this country, travel to a place they could live together in luxury and peace.

She thought of those things as his body tightened and he spilled his seed, then drew her to her feet. He brought her hand to his lips, then led her over to the bed. Soon he would be ready to make love again and if he used her a little roughly she didn't care. As long as she could be with him, she would give him anything he wanted.

And he would see to her pleasure as well.

"Tell me," he commanded. "Say it." Reaching out, he cupped her breast, massaged the fullness, pinched the end.

She told him what every man wanted to hear and especially this one, that *he* was what she needed, fully aroused and embedded deeply inside her. The words seemed to please him. It was always better when she pleased him, and it seemed she had done so tonight.

He took her hand, pressed it against the front of his breeches, and she could tell that he was hard. A little shiver went through her as she turned her back so that he could help her remove her gown, then he paused to remove his own clothes.

Soon you will be mine, she thought, enjoying the sight of him naked. *Soon I will have you all to myself.* She smiled as he drew her down on the bed, leaned over, and kissed her. Sliding himself inside her, he slowly began to move.

Four days had passed since Caleb had left. As he had promised in his emotionless note, Jacob Boswell had returned that same day to resume his job as trainer and groom. In the time that had passed, Lee had become surprisingly adept at banning Caleb Tanner from her thoughts.

As angry as she was at his callous departure, she could scarcely fault him for his lack of feelings. He had never spoken of love nor even mere affection. He had wanted her, nothing more. It was a simple case of lust.

Lee wished she had been able to keep her own emotions as carefully contained. Instead, on the rare occasion she allowed herself to think of him, she felt a sharp sting of longing. She reminded herself she had known from the start her time with Caleb would be brief. If the unlikely circumstance occurred that she found herself with child, she would manage without him. That also, she had known.

At least he hadn't lied to her.

She thought of the women in the house on Buford Street, all of them abandoned by men who professed to love them. And, of course, there was her mother.

Though Vermillion could barely recall her face, she knew her mother had suffered from abandonment and shame. Angelique Durant, the daughter of a courtesan, had fallen hopelessly in love with a nobleman. The man, heir to one of the most powerful titles in England, had rashly spoken of marriage, and Angelique had been foolish enough to believe him. When she learned of his betrothal to another woman, she had been devastated.

One of Lee's few early memories was of her mother sitting on a bench in the garden, sobbing uncontrollably. Years later, Aunt Gabby had explained that an article had appeared in the *Times* that day, announcing the birth of a son to Robert Leland Montague, Marquess of Kinleigh.

Kinleigh. The man who was Vermillion's father.

Seated on a stool in the music room, Lee lovingly plucked the strings of a gilded harp, evoking the chords of a melancholy song. As she rested her cheek against the finely curved wood, she thought of her mother and began to feel grateful that Caleb was gone.

It was over between them. She had lost a piece of her heart, but not all. She wasn't an innocent any longer and making it known to Lord Nash that it was he she intended to choose the night of her birthday would be far easier now.

"Excuse me, Miss."

Her hands went still. She looked up to see the butler in the doorway.

"Terribly sorry to disturb you, Miss, but your Aunt Gabriella wishes to see you in the Green Drawing Room."

"Thank you, Jones." Tilting the harp back onto its base, Vermillion rose from her stool and started across the library toward the door. In a simple apricot muslin gown and wearing only a hint of rouge, she wasn't dressed for visitors and there was every chance her aunt would be in company with someone.

Then again, it was the middle of the day. Surely, her appearance would be suitable enough.

Making her way along the hall, she heard the husky ring of male voices and again considered a change of attire. But something had happened to her in the past few weeks since she had met Caleb, and she was beginning to feel more comfortable in her own clothes, her own skin. She waited while Jones slid open the drawing-room door, then drew in a steadying breath, pasted on a smile, and walked in.

As she had guessed, her aunt was not alone. There were two uniformed British officers seated across from her, men in scarlet tunics laden with heavy gold braid. Their breeches were navy blue, as well as the cuffs on their immaculate, perfectly tailored scarlet jackets, and tall Hessian boots gleamed in the sunlight coming through the mullioned windows.

They came to their feet the moment she stepped into the drawing room. She summoned her practiced smile, but the smile froze on her lips.

She didn't know the man on the left, but the other one, slightly taller, dark-haired and dark-eyed, was a man she knew only too well. She had spent two nights making love to him. That man was Caleb Tanner.

"Come in, darling." Aunt Gabby motioned her forward. She must have seen the stunned expression on Lee's face for she smiled. "I realize it must be a bit of a shock to find one's groom in full military dress and standing in the drawing room, but it is rather exciting as well. Do join us, dear."

She made her way toward them, walking on legs that felt encased in lead.

"Allow me to introduce Major Mark Sutton and Captain Caleb Tanner." Her eyes twinkled merrily, as if she had stumbled upon some rare bit of news. "I believe you have already made Captain Tanner's acquaintance—as he was recently employed as Parklands' head groom."

Lee wanted to sink into the floor. She wanted to close the distance between them and slap his handsome face. She had known something was wrong, that he was no ordinary servant, but she never would have guessed anything close to this.

In the end, she simply did what she had been trained to do and smiled at him pleasantly. "I'm afraid I don't understand, Captain Tanner. Why has an officer of the British Army been working in our stable?"

Gabriella answered before he could speak, her eyes bright with excitement. "It was a matter of intrigue, it seems. Until today, Captain Tanner was under orders not to reveal his true identity. Perhaps Major Sutton can explain it to you, as he did to me."

Sutton cast her a glance, a taller than average man with curly black hair and a disarming smile. "Let me begin by apologizing for the deceit we have perpetrated upon you and your most charming aunt. I assure you it was necessary."

"Is that so?" She tried not to look at Caleb, but her gaze kept slipping toward him. His face was set, his features grim. She tried not to notice how handsome he looked in his perfectly fitted uniform, his hair cut short, and his face recently shaved. She tried to still the too rapid beating of her heart.

"I'm afraid we believed the deception to be necessary at the time. You see, we were trying to capture a deserter, a cavalryman in Captain Tanner's regiment who had killed an officer during his tenure in Spain. We had reason to believe the man had returned to England and was involved in the business of racing horses. As you know, Captain Tanner has a good deal of expertise in that area and it was believed he could be of assistance."

"I see." She didn't, of course. She couldn't seem to concentrate on the major's words.

"Five days ago, the man we were seeking was apprehended near the racecourse in York, and Captain Tanner was recalled to his duties. Both the Captain and I wished to personally apologize for any inconvenience you might have suffered."

She stared hard at Caleb, who hadn't yet said a word. "This man ... did he ... did he have anything to do with the murder of Mary Goodhouse?"

Caleb shook his head, his eyes dark and fixed on her face. "No. I'm afraid this was a completely separate matter."

"Smile, darling. Jacob has returned and all is well. And in a roundabout manner, we have been instrumental in capturing a fugitive from justice."

Smile. She thought she already was.

"In celebration," Aunt Gabby went on, "I've invited Major Sutton and Captain Tanner to join us for supper. Perhaps if we are lucky, they will share a few of their adventures in Spain."

She could feel the muscles tightening around her mouth as she forced her lips to curve. "How delightful. I'm sure that will make for a fascinating evening. For now, however, I'm afraid I shall have to leave you. There are several matters of importance I need to attend. If you gentlemen will excuse me ... ?"

"Of course." Major Sutton made her a very gallant bow and Caleb made a polite nod of his head.

As she turned toward the door, his eyes caught hers one last time. There was turmoil there and something else she could not name. She hoped he could read the seething anger in her own and that he would be wise enough to stay away from her as long as he was there.

Of course Caleb didn't stay away. Though supper was an intimate affair by Aunt Gabby's standards, Lee dressed in a midnight blue silk gown trimmed with blue lace, seated herself at her dressing table, and waited while Jeannie pinned up her hair, coiffing it in soft curls over a narrow diamond headband.

Diamonds encircled her throat and glittered in her ears. Though the gown was daringly low-cut, she wore a little less powder tonight and only a dash of rouge on her lips and cheeks. She told herself it had nothing to do with Caleb, but she knew it wasn't the truth.

For all his deceit, Caleb had shown her that a man could be attracted to her just as she was. Since she had met him, she had become more her own person. She liked herself better this way—allowing some of Lee to shine through. She tried not to wonder if Caleb would approve, since it really didn't matter.

It also didn't matter that she still found him attractive or that making love with him had been one of the most incredible experiences of her life.

All that mattered was that he wasn't the man she had believed him to be. The trust she had felt for him, the admiration that had led her to give herself to him, none of it was real. There was no Caleb Tanner, not as she had known him, at any rate. This other man was someone she barely recognized—a man who meant nothing to her in the least.

" 'E is quite something, your Captain Tanner." Jeannie stuck another pin into Lee's upswept hair.

"The servants, they gossip about 'im. Already, they 'ave heard the story of why 'e was working in the stable."

"Yes, I'm sure they have." Sometimes she thought they knew more about what happened at Parklands than she did.

" 'E is even more 'andsome in 'is uniform, *n'est-ce pas?*"

A fresh rush of anger slid through her. "He is also a liar."

" 'E was ordered to keep 'is silence. I do not think 'e had a choice."

Lee looked at Jeannie over her shoulder. She had long ago given up denying her involvement with Caleb, but she didn't intend to discuss him any further. "I don't want to talk about Captain Tanner."

Jeannie arranged another curl. " 'E came back for you, I think."

"If he did, it was only for one reason, and if he thinks for a moment he is going to take up where he left off, he had better think again."

Jeannie said nothing to that, just finished dressing Lee's hair and held up a mirror so she could see the back. She took a quick glimpse, nodded, and rose from the stool in front of the bureau. A few minutes later, she left the bedchamber, prepared to face the evening ahead.

At the top of the stairs, she took a long, courage-building breath. She shook out her dark blue silk skirt and descended to the foyer.

The gentlemen were waiting.

She amended that. The gentlemen—and Caleb—were waiting, prepared to escort the ladies into the dining room, an extravagant salon decorated in a Grecian motif with paintings of ancient temples supported by artificial columns along the walls.

She was only a little surprised to see Lord Claymont in company with the two uniformed men, looking, though several years older, equally as handsome as they.

"Good evening, Vermillion, dear." Leaning over, the earl brushed a kiss on her cheek. "You're looking quite fetching this evening."

"Thank you, my lord." She turned to the other two men. "I presume you all have met."

Claymont smiled. "Actually, I've known Major Sutton for the past several years. And of course I'm well acquainted with Captain Tanner's father."

Her eyes cut briefly to Caleb and she wondered what other secrets he had kept from her. "I'm sorry . . . I don't believe I know who that is."

"Why, the Earl of Selhurst, my dear. William and I have been friends for a number of years."

Her eyes must have reflected the betrayal she felt for a muscle tightened along his jaw. Not only a captain of the cavalry, but also the son of an earl.

She gave him an insipid smile. "I'm impressed, Captain Tanner. Just think, a member of the aristocracy, son of a high-ranking member of the *ton*—shoveling horse manure out in our stable. Imagine how that will heighten our somewhat dubious standing in Society."

Her aunt's silver-blond eyebrows shot up. "Darling, really. I doubt Captain Tanner wishes to be reminded of the tasks he was forced to perform in the line of duty."

Instead of getting angry, Caleb's mouth curved with amusement. "There are worse jobs, I promise you. Believe it or not, I enjoyed my brief tenure working with the horses." His eyes moved down to her breasts. "I found the riding especially . . . pleasurable."

She flushed; she couldn't help it. She knew he wasn't talking about horses and the anger she was feeling heated up another notch.

There was nothing she could do—at least not here.

"I think it's time we went in to dinner," her aunt said, breaking the tension between them. She captured Lord Claymont's arm and led him off toward the dining room.

"Shall we?" Major Sutton, as senior officer, offered to escort Vermillion and she rested her hand on the sleeve of his scarlet coat.

"I am honored, Major." She flicked a glance at Caleb, then gave the major a smile so bright it could have lit up a darkened room.

Caleb's bland expression turned into a scowl that made her smile go even wider. As she walked into the dining room, clinging rather tightly to Major Sutton's arm, she could feel Caleb's eyes on her. They burned with an inner fire and for the first time since she had seen him standing in the drawing room, Lee felt a wave of satisfaction.

13

❧

Supper was an endless affair. Seated at the head of the long mahogany table, Aunt Gabby sat smiling and laughing with her guests. Still a lovely woman in the glow of the candles burning in the silver candelabra, Gabriella was in rare form tonight, charming the men as she always did, regaling them with tales of her travels as a young girl visiting Paris. By the end of the evening, she had even managed a few rare smiles from Caleb.

Major Sutton entertained them with stories of the war, though he was careful not to say anything inappropriate in the presence of ladies. Caleb was mostly quiet, his gaze finding hers time and again throughout the lengthy evening.

She was glad when the men retired for brandy and cigars and she was finally able to slip away. While Aunt Gabby went upstairs to refresh herself, Vermillion quietly made her way out to the garden. A warm wind ruffled the leaves and an owl hooted somewhere in the distance. The sky was nearly black and bright stars glittered overhead. It was an evening much like the last night she had spent with Caleb.

Thinking about that night seemed to conjure him out of the shadows. How he managed to appear so soundlessly she wasn't really sure. He had always moved with a sort of quiet grace and he did so now, stepping out of the darkness just a few feet away from where she sat.

"I saw you come out here," he said. "I've been hoping to get you alone since I arrived. We need to talk, Lee."

She came up off the wrought-iron bench, anger warring with hurt, disappointment, and feelings of betrayal. "My name is Vermillion and there is nothing to talk about. I don't even know you. Therefore there is nothing to say." She meant to walk past him, but Caleb caught her arm.

"My name is Caleb Tanner. I'm twenty-eight years old. My father is the Earl of Selhurst. My mother, God rest her soul, died when I was born. I have three brothers, Lucas, Christian, and Ethan. I joined the army eight years ago. I've served in the Netherlands, India, and also in Spain. Currently, I'm on special assignment to General Wellesley. Now you know who I am. As I said, we need to talk."

Instead of a reply, she ignored him and simply started walking.

"Running away isn't going to change what happened."

She stopped and turned to face him. "I am not running away. I am leaving, as I find present company fatiguing in the extreme. Now if you will excuse me . . ."

Apparently he wouldn't, since he stepped into the path in front of her, blocking her escape. "I would have told you the truth if I could have. I was under orders from my superior, Colonel Cox, making that impossible."

"What about the other, Caleb? Was making love to me part of your assignment, too?"

Caleb stiffened a little and she noticed the way the gold buttons glittered on his scarlet coat. "I apologize for what happened between us. I wanted you. It's as simple as that. Perhaps it wouldn't have happened if you hadn't been pretending to be something you were not."

Her chin went up. "Need I remind you—I wasn't the only one pretending?"

"As I said, it was necessary at the time."

She tilted her head back and looked him straight in the face. "Why did you come back here?"

Caleb's eyes remained locked with hers, but there was something in them. She wished she knew what it was.

"Because I wanted to explain. I was hoping I could make you understand." In the light of the torches he looked impossibly handsome and her heart continued its ridiculously uncomfortable patter.

"Fine. So now you've explained and I understand and you can leave." She tried to brush past him, but he caught her arm and turned her once more to face him.

"And I wanted you to know that if there were . . . consequences . . . to what happened between us, I would not shirk my duties."

Her lips tightened. She jerked free of his hold and settled a hand on her hip. "And just what, exactly, does that mean?"

"It means I would accept my responsibilities. I would provide for you and the child."

She laughed. It rang with bitterness through the garden. "I have plenty of money, Caleb. I don't need any of yours. If there is a babe, I am perfectly capable of caring for it myself."

"The child would be mine as well, Lee. I would want him to know his father."

It was a worry she had considered in regard to choosing a protector. An image of Caleb in that role popped into her head, but she ruthlessly forced it away.

"Then I shall be happy to keep you informed. However, I don't believe you need worry on that account." She flushed, unwilling to discuss her monthly curses with a man who was still a virtual stranger. "In the meantime, I suppose this is farewell. Good night, Captain Tanner. Have a pleasant journey back to London or Spain or wherever it is you are going."

She pushed against his chest, trying to shove him out of her way, but she might as well have been trying to move a block of stone.

"Eventually, I'll be returning to Spain. Not yet. And as for my immediate departure from Parklands, your aunt has been kind enough to invite Major Sutton and me to the weeklong house party she is giving. I believe the festivities begin on the morrow and end with the celebration of your nineteenth birthday."

For the first time, her aplomb deserted her and a knot of dread tightened in the pit of her stomach. "Surely you . . . you don't intend to be here for that."

His eyes went dark and his smile turned feral. "I wouldn't miss it for the world."

Lee stood frozen as Caleb caught her hand and brought it mockingly to his lips. He pressed a soft kiss against her fingers and a little tendril of heat curled in the bottom of her stomach.

"So you see, sweeting, for now it is adieu and not farewell."

Lee said nothing. She was thinking about the heat of his mouth against her hand and trying not to remember the way it had felt when he had kissed her.

"It's getting late," he said. "Unless you wish me to do exactly what you are thinking, I believe it's time I escorted you back inside."

She flushed as he offered her his arm, as if he had done it a thousand times—as if it were his right. Anger dissolved her embarrassment and stiffened her spine.

"Go to bloody hell, *Captain* Tanner."

This time she shoved hard enough to catch him off balance and he took a step backward, barely able to stop himself from toppling into the shrubbery. Blue silk rustled against the legs of his navy blue breeches as she brushed past him. She wasn't ready to forgive him, not yet. If she did, she might wind up back in his bed and she wasn't about to let that happen. Not with her birthday only a week away.

Slippers crunching on the gravel path, she cast a last glance over her shoulder. She thought she caught a glint of amusement and what might have been determination in Caleb's dark eyes before he turned and walked away.

"So how did it go?" Major Sutton rode beside him on the trip back to London. It was late, well past midnight. Ever the gracious hostess, Gabriella Durant had invited them to spend the night, but the journey wasn't overly long and they needed to pack the appropriate clothing for their return. Caleb felt a shot of satisfaction that he had managed an invitation—or at least Sutton had. A big four-poster bed in a guest room upstairs would be far more comfortable than the bunk he had slept on in the stables.

He flicked a glance at the major, who had so expertly won the Durant woman's confidence. "I thought the day went extremely well, considering...."

One of Sutton's black eyebrows went up. "Considering that you've obviously bedded the younger of the women. I don't imagine Vermillion was particularly happy to discover your deception."

Caleb's mouth barely curved. "You might say that." He didn't confirm or deny the major's assumption, but one of Sutton's talents was reading people and apparently he had seen enough looks passing between them to believe they had been intimately involved. "I think if she'd had a gun, she would have shot me."

"Yes, well, better to discover one's lover is not a groom but the son of an earl, than the other way round."

Caleb made no reply. He wasn't all that certain Lee would agree.

"At any rate, we've gained the access we need. What you do with the girl from now on is your business, but I would suggest if you can find your way back into her bed, you should do so. It would certainly better our chances of gaining information."

He smiled and Caleb caught a flash of white teeth in the darkness. "Besides, she is a fetching little baggage. My God, the girl has breasts like ripe melons. I thought on several occasions tonight they were going to spill out the top of that dress. I daresay I was hard beneath the table for the better part of the evening."

Caleb's gloved hand fisted on his horse's reins. He drew the animal to a halt in the middle of the lane. "I realize you're my superior, Major Sutton, but when it comes to Vermillion, I suggest you keep your thoughts to yourself. There is a line, sir, and you have just crossed it."

Sutton eyed him in the darkness. "I see."

"I don't think you do. The girl is not the woman she appears. In truth, until I took her innocence, she was a virgin."

"That's impossible."

"I wouldn't have believed it either, but I can tell you with all certainty that it is exactly the truth."

"But why would she pretend—"

"She has her reasons. They have to do with being a Durant and the loyalty she feels to her aunt. Whether they are valid or not is another matter."

"Interesting . . ." Sutton nudged his horse forward and they started riding again along the lane. "On the other hand, thanks to you, Vermillion is now exactly what she has always seemed. All in all, I don't suppose it matters which man among us was the first."

Caleb clamped down on his jaw, fighting to contain the fury that shot through him. He was coming to dislike Mark Sutton more and more. If the man hadn't been his superior, Caleb would have dragged him off his horse and given him a taste of the punishment he had doled out to the last man who had insulted Vermillion.

Instead, he forced himself to remain silent as they rode the rest of the way down the lane back to London. All the way there, he kept thinking of the hurt and betrayal he had seen in Lee's face.

And wondering what would happen when she found out he was betraying her trust again.

The weeklong house party began the following day. The first event was an evening of gaming, dancing, and entertainment designed so that guests could become better acquainted. Though most already knew each other, there were always a number of recent acquaintances Gabriella had made. Actresses and opera singers, poets and artists, men like Major Sutton and Captain Tanner.

Lord Nash was there for the week, as well as Colonel Wingate and, of course, Lord Andrew Mondale. Lee was chatting with the colonel when a flash of scarlet caught her eye and she turned to see Caleb walk into the drawing room.

The moment he spotted them, a scowl appeared on his face. He quickly smoothed it away.

"Captain Tanner," the colonel called out to him, drawing him in their direction though he was already walking that way. "I don't believe we've met."

"No, sir. Not formally."

"You know Miss Durant, I assume."

The edge of his mouth barely curved. "Yes, I've had the pleasure."

She colored. She prayed the colonel wouldn't notice.

"Good evening, Miss Durant."

"Captain Tanner."

The colonel seemed unaware of the tension in their exchange. "You're assigned to Wellesley, I hear. Some sort of special duty. All very hush-hush, I gather."

"I'm afraid I'm not at liberty to discuss it, sir."

"No, no, of course not. All the same, it's quite a

coup, I would say, career-wise. Wellesley has grand ambitions. If you're one of the chosen, you could go very far. I gather that is your intention."

"Yes, sir. The army's been my home for the past eight years. I don't see any reason for that to change." He flicked a glance in Lee's direction, but his expression didn't alter.

He would be returning to Spain. She knew it shouldn't bother her, told herself it didn't.

They spoke for a moment more, trivialities, talk of the war. All the while she continued to smile and tried not to look at Caleb. Every time she did, her gaze slid down to his mouth and she remembered the heat of it pressed against her skin.

As soon as she could politely escape, she excused herself and slipped away. She had made it as far as the gaming room when Andrew Mondale appeared, handsome, almost pretty with his gleaming golden hair, jonquil tailcoat, and dark green breeches.

"Where have you been, my heart? I was about to perish of loneliness without you."

She arched a brow. "Really? And here I thought Juliette Beauvoir was keeping you well entertained." Beautiful and black-haired, with a pouty mouth and big blue eyes, Juliette was an actress in Drury Lane. She had set her sights on Mondale some weeks back. As far as Lee was concerned, she could have him.

"Juliette is not you, my dove. Surely you can't think she interests me in the least."

She toyed with a wispy red curl next to her ear, a gesture unconsciously Vermillion. "Actually, I think you and Juliette would suit." She looked thoughtful. "Yes, I believe the two of you would suit very well."

Andrew slapped a hand over his heart. "You

wound me, my pet. You know there is only one woman for me." He caught her hand and brought it to his lips. "It is you and none other, my beauty."

Vermillion laughed. Andrew could often be charming. But it was Nash she would choose. After Caleb, she knew the deep sort of bonding that intimacy with a man could bring. She wouldn't risk those feelings again and especially not with a man as inconstant as Andrew.

"Behave yourself," she said. "I believe Juliette is watching. Besides, I need to find my aunt. Why don't you try your hand at whist while I am gone?"

"I suppose if you insist . . . but my heart shall bleed until your return."

She laughed again as she turned to leave—and bumped right into Caleb. He steadied her with a big hand at her waist and leaned to whisper in her ear.

"I could manage to make his heart bleed in earnest, if only you just say the word." There was the mere hint of a curve to his lips and she thought that he might have been only half in jest.

She managed a flirty smile. "Why, Captain Tanner—you aren't jealous, are you?"

His eyes darkened. "I am jealous of every man in this room and undoubtedly you know it."

But she hadn't. Not really. And she was stunned at the realization that Caleb still felt something for her. She didn't know quite what to say. Fortunately, at that moment, the three-piece orchestra in the corner struck up a waltz, filling the room with music and ending their brief exchange.

Caleb saved her from an embarrassingly lengthy silence by taking her hand and leading her out to the dance floor.

"I've seen you waltz," he said. "I watched you through the windows. I wondered how it would feel to hold you in my arms."

She rested a faintly trembling hand on the shoulder of his scarlet uniform jacket and felt the outline of his heavy gold epaulets. With a single long stride, he led her into the waltz.

That he was an excellent dancer came as no surprise. He had always been a graceful man and here he seemed completely at home, gliding her into each turn, sweeping her along with him as if they had danced together a thousand times. His hold was firm and steady, his shoulder warm and solid beneath her hand. The conversation in the room seemed to slowly fade. The faces of the guests blurred into little more than a haze of color and for this brief time there was only Caleb.

Her heart swelled, pounded. Her chest squeezed, and in that moment, the shocking realization hit her: She was in love with Caleb.

Not just a little in love, but passionately, dangerously in love.

"I need to talk to you," he said. "When can we meet?"

But Lee was so engrossed in her newfound knowledge that she barely heard him. "Wh-what did you say?"

"I said we need to meet. We need to talk. I'll come to your room tonight, a little after midnight."

She missed a step, thinking of Caleb in her bedchamber, thinking what would happen if she actually let him in. "Are you insane? You can't come to my room."

He smiled. He had the whitest, most wonderful

smile. "You might want to keep your voice down. One of your lapdogs might hear. I don't think they would appreciate knowing you were inviting a man to your room."

"I'm not inviting you to my room! I'm barely speaking to you!"

He stifled a grin, but amusement danced in his eyes. He led her into a turn, then pulled her back into his arms, holding her a little closer than he should have.

"Make some excuse and retire a little early. Don't forget to leave your door unlocked."

"Listen to me, Caleb Tanner. If you come to my room, I won't be there. You might be used to giving orders to your men, but I am not one of your soldiers."

Without missing a step, he drew her even closer. She could smell his cologne, feel the strength of the hand at her waist. There was something in his eyes. Dear Lord, if only she knew what it was.

"It's important, Lee."

The music abruptly ended. Caleb's hold lingered an instant longer, then he made a very formal bow and stepped away.

As soon as they reached the edge of the dance floor, Lee excused herself and left him. Caleb watched her until she disappeared from the drawing room.

I'm a fool. Completely insane. He had tried to talk himself out of it, known he was acting as ridiculous as the rest of her besotted swains, but still couldn't stop himself.

Returning to Parklands had been a mistake. He

should have stayed as far away from Lee as he could get. Unfortunately, he'd had no choice. Orders were orders and his were to find a traitor. Though he no longer believed that Vermillion was involved, someone at Parklands—a frequent guest, one of the servants, or even Gabriella Durant—was involved in a conspiracy to obtain information and convey it to the enemy. It was his job to discover who it was.

What he didn't need to do was to become even more involved with Lee.

Standing in the darkness at the edge of the terrace, Caleb cursed himself. Through the windows of the drawing room, he could see her in conversation with Jonathan Parker, Lord Nash. It made his insides tighten. He hadn't encountered Nash yet but undoubtedly he would. As much as he respected the viscount, he couldn't bear to think of him touching Lee as he had, spending time in her bed.

Through the tall windows of the drawing room, he could hear her smoky laughter, watch her smile at something Nash said, and his stomach clenched with jealousy. In some strange way she belonged to him.

He wanted her, had from the moment he had first seen her. He still did.

He thought how lovely she looked tonight in her high-waisted topaz gown. With her fiery hair swept up in curls, a few soft tendrils framing her face, she looked older, more sophisticated, yet now he noticed the innocence that sometimes crept into her expression, the charming naïveté that hid behind her practiced smile.

Perhaps those were the very things that made her so attractive to men, made her appear so mysterious and intriguing.

She was wearing very little face paint tonight, just enough kohl to make her eyes look huge and blue-green, enough rouge on her lips to remind him how soft and full they were, how sweet they tasted.

Caleb cursed as a shot of lust slid into his groin and his shaft went achingly hard. He was glad for the shadows on the terrace and annoyed at the heavy bulge straining against the front of his breeches.

Dammit to bloody hell. What was it about her that made her so different from the rest of the women he had known?

Cursing the unwelcome hold she had over him, Caleb walked away from the window. He couldn't afford to think of her and so he turned his attention to the task he had set for himself tonight.

The party was in full swing, guests drinking, gambling, dancing, some sneaking off to assignations in the rooms upstairs. The drawing rooms in this wing of the house echoed with laughter and gaiety, but the opposite wing was mostly dark. The library was there and the study. Both rooms opened onto the garden.

Careful to stay in the shadows, Caleb made his way in that direction.

14

❧

Gabriella Durant stood next to Elizabeth Sorenson beneath the extravagant cloud-painted ceiling of the Cirrus Room. It hummed with the laughter and conversation of guests, the busy hustle of liveried servants carrying silver trays heavy with hors d'oeuvres and champagne.

Elizabeth's blue eyes latched onto one of the men across the room. "My God—did you invite Charles?" Gowned in white satin glittering with brilliants, Elizabeth stared at her husband as if a ghost had appeared on the opposite side of the drawing room.

"He arrived with Lord Claymont. Dylan said Charles asked if he could come." It was very bad *ton*, Gabriella knew. A man could come to an affair like this with his mistress, but never his wife.

Years ago, after Charles had abandoned his bride for another woman, Elizabeth had shown her disdain for Society and done exactly as she pleased. She still did. But she rarely appeared at a function where her husband would be present and Charles did his best to avoid his errant wife.

Or at least he had done so in the past.

Lately, Gabriella had noticed, Charles had made an unexpected appearance on several occasions and much of his attention had focused on his beautiful wife.

"Perhaps he has come because you are here."

"Charles?" She laughed and Gabriella didn't miss the bitterness in her voice. "I am the last reason he would be here. Perhaps he has his eye on an actress or an opera singer . . . Juliette Beauvoir perhaps. I heard he has been without a mistress for some time."

"Now that you mention it, I had heard that as well." Gabriella looked at her friend, whose gaze kept straying across the room toward the lean, sandy-haired man she had married but with whom she no longer shared a bed.

"Have you seen much of Charles lately?" Gabriella asked.

Elizabeth turned. "It's funny you should ask. You know he has been living at Rotham Hall these last several months." It was the earl's estate not far from the city where Elizabeth lived with her sons Peter and Tom. "I told him if he wished to stay with the boys for a while, I would move into the town house, but he said there was plenty of room for all of us."

"Interesting."

"I was surprised, to say the least. I might have moved, but the boys seemed so happy to have the two of us there I decided to stay. I don't imagine he'll remain much longer."

"So the two of you have been spending time together."

She glanced away. "I see him at breakfast on occasion. I make it a point to stay out of his way."

And it probably broke her friend's heart. Gabriella might have cursed Charles Sorenson as she had more than once over the years if she hadn't spotted the earl just then, staring at his wife from across the room, his face wreathed in an expression that could only be described as longing.

Dear God, had the man finally realized what he had thrown away? Was it possible? Charles was older now, less of a rogue than he had been back then. Though Elizabeth's reputation had been in tatters for years, Charles had maintained a façade of respectability. At any rate, a man having a mistress was accepted among the *ton*. But Charles was risking a blow to that façade by being here tonight with Elizabeth.

Was it really Juliette Beauvoir or some other woman who tempted him? Or could it be his lovely, heartbroken wife?

"Have you seen Vermillion?" Elizabeth asked, drawing her thoughts in another direction.

"The last time I saw her, she was talking to Lord Nash." She turned a searching glance around the room, but her niece wasn't there.

"Perhaps she has returned to the gaming room. I saw her there earlier, in conversation with Lord Andrew."

Gabriella sighed. "More likely she has gone off somewhere by herself. The closer we get to her birthday, the more worried I become." She returned her attention to Elizabeth. "I may have made a mistake, Beth. I don't think she is ready."

"I've been thinking that myself."

"For me it was different. I was enamored of my first lover and at least half dozen other of my admirers. My only difficulty in choosing a protector came in knowing I would have to give up the rest—at least for a time. Most of my liaisons didn't last long, not in the beginning. Since Claymont, I haven't felt the restlessness I felt back then."

"I think he loves you."

"Claymont? Perhaps he does. He says so often enough."

"What about you? Do you love him?"

She shrugged her shoulders. "What would it matter? Dylan is an earl. We live in two different worlds."

Elizabeth gazed toward her sandy-haired husband across the drawing room. "Speak to Vermillion," she said. "Tell her she doesn't have to choose unless she wishes it. She's a woman now. Tell her whatever decision she makes should be her own."

Gabriella nodded. Once again, she scanned the room for her niece, but Vermillion wasn't there.

Closing the terrace door softly behind him, Caleb stepped into the darkened study. He slid the draperies closed behind him and went in search of illumination. A brass lamp sat on a Hepplewhite table. Lifting the chimney, he struck flint to tinder and lit the wick, and a soft yellow glow filled the room.

Caleb held up the lamp to survey his surroundings, found himself in a large, wood-paneled, book-lined room. A burgundy leather sofa and chairs clustered before the marble-manteled hearth. A rosewood desk sat in front of the windows, a comfortable leather chair resting on the polished wooden floor behind it. A crystal inkwell and a white plumed pen in a silver holder sat on a felt ink blotter on the desktop.

He didn't waste time, just carried the lamp to the desk, sat down in the chair, and began to pull open the drawers. Estate ledgers took up most of the bottom one. He drew out the heavy leather volume, cracked it open and scanned the pages, but didn't see anything of interest.

The second drawer was devoted to Parklands' Thoroughbred racing operation. Each horse the stable owned had been entered into a leather ledger but the handwriting was different from the other he had seen, the letters smaller, well formed, and precise. He imagined the writing must be Lee's and closed the book, refusing to let his mind be distracted by thoughts of her.

Instead he studied the contents of the rest of the drawers, then searched the desk for some sort of lever that might conceal a hiding place of some kind. Finding nothing, his frustration mounted. He was closing the top drawer, still seated in the chair, when the ornate door swung open and light spilled into the study.

He had been certain he would hear footfalls against the marble floor of the hall, but these had been light, the merest shuffle of small, feminine feet encased in butter-soft kidskin, and he had not noticed. Caleb silently cursed as Lee walked into the room and firmly closed the door.

"What are you doing in here?"

She was looking at him as if she had discovered a thief, which in a way, she had.

"I suppose I could ask that question of you, but it is, after all, your house. You have a right to be in here."

"That's right. And you don't."

He shrugged his shoulders. "Perhaps I needed a respite from the party."

"You were going through the desk." She walked toward him, her spine straight and anger snapping in her eyes. "What were you looking for, Caleb? What else haven't you told me?"

He thought of lying, but he had lied to her too many times already. And he trusted her. It was a good thing because the moment she had stepped into the room, he'd had no other choice.

"Lock the door. What I'm going to tell you can't go anywhere other than this room."

She hesitated for a moment, then went over and turned the key in the lock as he wished he had done. The narrow skirt of her topaz gown brushed her hips as she walked back to where he stood beside the desk.

"First I want you to know that by telling you this, I am disobeying orders."

"And why, pray tell, would you do that?"

He sighed, raked a hand through his hair, wished she wouldn't keep looking at him that way. "Because I've lied to you enough. Because, in the time I've known you, I've come to trust you. And because I could use your help."

Her features didn't soften. "Go on."

"There's a spy at Parklands. I'm here to catch him." Or *her*, but he didn't say that. Instead he told her what they had discovered so far, explained that General Wellesley believed that the casualties in Spain would have been considerably reduced if certain information hadn't reached the enemy—information that seemed to have come from Parklands.

"That's absurd. I don't believe a word of it—not for a moment. This is just another one of your lies."

"I'm through lying, Lee. If I could have told you the truth before, I would have done it. I shouldn't be telling you this now."

Her eyes looked troubled and such a deep shade of aqua he could have gotten lost in them. "If it's true, who do you think is responsible?" She glanced down at the desk, realized why he had been going through the drawers. "If you're confiding this information to me, then you don't think I am the traitor." Her head came up. "Tell me you don't believe the traitor is Aunt Gabby."

He wished he could. He wished he knew a lot more than he did. "I don't know who it is. That's what I'm trying to find out."

"Is Major Sutton also here for that reason?"

"Yes." But he hadn't told the major his intention to visit the study. He didn't like the man. In some strange way, he didn't trust him.

"My aunt is a loyal Englishwoman. She would never betray her country."

"Then help me prove it. Help me find out who is."

She said nothing for the longest time. "Is that the reason you wanted to talk to me tonight?"

"No. The matter I wish to discuss is personal."

She turned away before he could say anything more in that regard and he thought maybe it was better that he didn't. Not yet. She didn't trust him. Not anymore. She wasn't ready to hear what he had to say. Perhaps she never would be.

He watched her walk, stiff-backed to the door, then stop and turn. "Don't bother coming to my room. The door will be locked." She left the study as silently as she had entered. Though he never heard a sound, he knew she had escaped down the hall.

It was late. Lee couldn't sleep. The night was overly warm and though a breeze blew in through the open windows, the sheets felt warm and sticky against her skin. The gilded clock on the mantel chimed four. Downstairs, the last of the guests had finally succumbed to fatigue and wearily climbed the stairs to their beds. Not all of them slept alone.

Lee tried not to think about that. She tried not to think about Caleb and finding him there in the study. It was only by chance that she had. Her destination had been the library. She needed a moment, just a little time away from the laughter and gaiety that seemed to grate on her nerves. But when she reached the tall ornate doors and heard the moans and giggles coming from the opposite side, she continued down the hall to the study instead.

She hadn't expected to find Caleb there, searching through Parklands' private records, hadn't thought to catch him in another of his lies.

Lee punched her pillow and tried to get comfortable, but her nightgown wrapped around her legs and the cotton fabric stuck to her skin. She sat up in bed, defiantly pulled the garment off over her head, and tossed it across the room. She pulled the ribbon from the end of her braid and raked her fingers through her hair, let the breeze through the open balcony doors flow over her naked skin. Moonlight slanted in, giving the room a soft glow.

Her restlessness increased, became nearly unbearable. Wrapping the sheet around her, she slid out of the bed and started toward the balcony. A noise behind the filmy curtains drew her attention to the door and she paused. The curtains fluttered. She should have been surprised to see Caleb walk into the room but somehow she wasn't.

She pulled the sheet a little tighter around her and

wondered if he had watched her undress. "Do you ever take no for an answer?"

"Not very often." He was wearing dark brown breeches and a white lawn shirt, rather like the clothes he had worn as a groom, but the tall black Hessians were those of a soldier.

"I told you I'm not one of your men. I don't have to obey your commands."

"But you *will* keep silent about the things I told you in the study."

If he was telling the truth, men's lives were at stake. "I wouldn't want to see any more of our soldiers die unnecessarily. I won't repeat what you said."

He took a step toward her, but she took a step away. "Why are you here? Do you have another lie you wish to confess?"

Caleb shook his head. "I'm through lying. I told you that before."

"Then tell me why you've come." His eyes ran over her. She could feel the heat in them and little prickles ran over her skin.

"Why did you take off your clothes?"

Heat infused her cheeks. He *had* been watching. "Because it's a hot night and I thought I was alone."

"Or perhaps because it's a hot night and you were alone and you hoped that I would come. Perhaps you wanted the same thing I find myself wanting right now."

He took a step toward her. She turned to flee but one of his boots pinned the bottom of the sheet to the floor. To escape she would have to abandon the sheet and she refused to do that.

Instead she turned to face him. "Get out of my room, Caleb."

"Not yet. There's something I need to know before I leave."

He moved in that silent way he had and suddenly he was standing so close she could see the black centers of his eyes. He caught her waist and pulled her even closer. The protest she was about to make died in her throat as his mouth crushed down over hers.

There was nothing gentle about the kiss. It was fierce and demanding, ruthlessly possessive, and it made her hot all over. He kissed her until her knees felt weak, until her fingers curled into the front of his shirt and she was trembling, making little mewling sounds in her throat and whimpering his name.

"God, I've missed you." He kissed her throat, kissed her naked shoulder, shoved the sheet down and kissed her naked breasts. She swayed toward him as his mouth closed over a nipple and he sucked hard on the end. She didn't resist when he stripped away the sheet and ran his hands over her body, down over her hips. A hard thigh wedged between her legs and she moaned when he lifted her a little, rocked her against him, forced her to ride him.

She was wet. So hot and wet. She needed to touch him, feel the heat of his skin, the hardness of his chest. She tugged his shirt free of his breeches and he dragged it off over his head and tossed it away, then returned to kissing her again. His hands moved lower, cupping her bottom, his fingers sliding between the globes, lower, parting the folds of her sex and stroking her there. Heat and need washed over her, making her tremble, making her slick and hot and desperate to feel him inside her.

She didn't protest when he lifted her up and car-

ried her over to the bed, settled her on the edge of the
deep feather mattress.

He didn't take time to get rid of his clothes, just
opened the front of his breeches and freed himself,
guided his hardness to the entrance of her passage,
and drove himself home.

His head fell back and for a moment he paused.
"Sweet God, I've never known a woman who could
make me feel the way you do." The softly spoken
words sent a fine tremor through her. Caleb kissed
her again, as wildly as before, and she clung to his
neck. He filled her completely, eased out, then
drove hard inside, gripped her hips and began a
rhythmic thrusting that had her arching up from the
bed.

The heat in the room increased. Skin met skin, slick
and damp, until their bodies glistened with perspiration and the blood in her veins began to burn.

"Caleb," she whispered, her fingers digging into the
muscles across his shoulders. "Dear God, Caleb!"

He kissed her deeply, his mouth absorbing her soft
little cries of pleasure. The beating of sweat-slick flesh
matched the rhythm of his relentless thrusts, and her
nails scored the skin on his back. When her climax hit,
it came swift and hard. Pleasure washed over her,
thick and fierce and sweeter than ever before.

Caleb reached release an instant later, but she
barely noticed, was only faintly aware of his heavy
weight lifting off her. He scooped the sheet up off the
floor and floated it over her, then buttoned the front
of his breeches and sat down beside her, bare-chested,
on the edge of the bed.

She smiled up at him contentedly as he reached out
and ran a finger down her cheek.

"I found out what I needed to know."

The covers slipped. She yanked them up again and sat up in the bed, the fuzzy lethargy beginning to disappear from her head. "What . . . what are you talking about?"

"I wanted to know if it would be the same . . . if it was as good between us as I remembered."

Her chin inched up. "Was it?"

"Better." He reached out and caught her chin, leaned down, and lightly kissed her. "I know a lot has happened. If we had more time, I wouldn't press you. But your birthday's coming up. I know what I'm asking isn't fair. I know it won't be long before I'll have to go back to Spain, but . . ."

"But what?"

"But what we have together . . . when men and women make love, Lee, it isn't always the way it is with us."

She knew that. She was in love with him. It wouldn't be the same with anyone else.

"The night of your birthday, you've vowed to choose a protector. I was hoping . . . Lee, I want you to pick me."

She said nothing. For a fleeting moment, she had actually imagined he might offer marriage. It was impossible. No man of his station would marry so far beneath him, and in truth, she didn't want marriage either.

She knew what married life meant—at least for a woman. She only had to think of Elizabeth Sorenson. She only had to look at the dozens of men who came to Parklands—most of whom were married.

"I can't do that."

His soft look faded. "If you're worried about

money, I assure you I have more than enough. My grandfather left me a very tidy fortune. You won't want for anything—I can promise you that."

"I don't need your money. Surely you know that by now."

"Then why won't you agree?" The muscles went rigid across his bare shoulders. "Or perhaps you've decided to broaden your education? Perhaps you think Mondale or Colonel Wingate can teach you something I can't. If that is the case, rest assured, we have only just—"

"I won't agree because I'm not sure what I'm going to do." The moment the words were out of her mouth, she realized they were true.

She was a different person since she had met Caleb, more sure of the woman she was inside. Perhaps she wouldn't choose anyone at all. She had plenty of money. She could buy a house somewhere in the country, take her horses along, start a life of her own. It wouldn't be easy—a woman alone, particularly a young one. But if she changed her name, pretended to be a widow, perhaps, went somewhere she wasn't known . . .

Still, there was Aunt Gabby to think of. She owed her aunt so much and Gabriella would be wildly disappointed. Gabriella had imagined Vermillion taking a place beside her in the world of the demimonde, believed that the two of them would continue as the Durants had done for generations. But surely there was another way to ensure her aunt's future happiness—if only she could find it.

Caleb shifted on the bed. "Are you telling me you don't intend to choose any man at all?"

The more she thought about it, the more right it

seemed. She would speak to Aunt Gabby, make her understand. She would find another way to repay her. But Caleb didn't need to know that. After the way he had treated her, he deserved to think whatever he wished.

"As I said, I'm not sure what I'm going to do. I'll simply have to wait and see."

Caleb stood up from the bed. The cords in his neck stood out in anger. "If that's the way you want it." Reaching down, he grabbed his shirt and pulled it on over his head, his usually fluid movements stiff with tension. Stuffing the shirt into the waistband of his breeches, he stormed toward the open doors. "It's fine with me!"

Lee watched him cross the balcony and climb over the rail. A soft thud was all the noise he made in his nearly silent drop back to the ground below her room.

Inwardly, she smiled. *Let him think I want someone else—it will do him good.*

She stretched and plumped her pillow, thinking of the things he had said, how what happened between them was different than it was for other people. Then she thought of their earlier meeting, how she had found him in the study, searching through the big rosewood desk, and her smile slowly faded.

Was there really a traitor at Parklands?

Caleb had lied before, but somehow she didn't think he would lie about something as important as this. And according to him, her aunt was one of those under suspicion. A little shiver ran through her. She remembered the thousands of men killed and wounded in the terrible battle at Oporto. Aunt Gabby was innocent, she knew. Still, if there were a traitor

among the guests or servants at Parklands, it was her
duty to help catch him.

As she stared up at the ceiling above her bed, she
began making lists of possible suspects. She fell asleep
wondering which of them might be capable of betraying his country.

15

Another night of gaming and entertainment. Tonight the famous opera star, Isabella Bellini, would be singing. Afterward there would be dancing. Again. It was beginning to get on Caleb's nerves.

"Caleb! Caleb Tanner!" Across the drawing room, Jonathan Parker strode toward him, a smile of greeting on his face. "I heard you were here. It's good to see you."

"And you, as well, my lord."

"Jon, please. You're not a child anymore and we have known each other for what—nearly thirty years?"

Caleb smiled. "Close enough." But they hadn't seen each other for nearly ten, not since he had left Selhurst Manor to join the army.

Nash stepped back, surveyed Caleb's scarlet tunic and navy blue breeches and the way he had filled out since he had joined the cavalry. He nodded his approval. "The army suits you, Caleb. Your father thinks so, too. He and I have spoken of you often." Both men were active in the House of Lords, as had been Nash's father before him.

"I'm hoping to see the earl before my return to Spain."

"You had better." The viscount turned toward a passing waiter, lifted a glass off a silver tray. "Champagne?"

"Brandy." Nash reached over and picked up a crystal snifter. Caleb accepted the glass and both men took a drink.

"He follows your career, you know. He has every article that has been printed in the newspapers carefully pasted into a scrapbook. The earl is extremely proud of you, Caleb."

He shifted uncomfortably. With four boys in the family and being the most troublesome of the lot, he had often been overlooked—until he joined the army. After that the relationship between him and his father had changed, become what he had always hoped it would be.

"How is my father?" Caleb asked. "Well, I trust."

"Very well, I'm pleased to say. Still, I believe he would very much like to see you."

"He's at Selhurst, I gather."

He nodded. "You know how he loves his horses."

It was the single thing the two of them had in common. Funny, but until his job at Parklands, Caleb had never understood how much he had wanted that sort of life for himself. As he had worked each day with the horses, he found himself imagining a stableful of beautiful, blooded Thoroughbreds much like the ones at Selhurst Manor. The image of a wife and children had also popped into his head, but he had ruthlessly forced those thoughts away. His life was the army. It always would be.

"What about my brothers? Have you any news of them?"

Nash chuckled. "Christian is still in the blissful throes of the newly married. Ethan—well, you know what a wanderer he is. I doubt he'll succumb to the marriage trap for quite some years."

"And Lucas? I spoke to him once, but only briefly."

"Luc is still the rogue he always was." He smiled and looked over Caleb's shoulder. "As to how he fares . . . why don't you ask him yourself?"

Caleb turned, recognized the tall man striding toward him, a faintly arrogant smile on his face.

Lucas Tanner, Viscount Halford, came to a halt at his side. "Greetings, little brother."

"Luc! I can't believe you are here."

Nash stepped away from them. "I think I'll leave you two siblings to get reacquainted. Good to see you, Halford."

"You, as well, Nash." Luc looked as lean and fit as he had that day at the auction, as tall as Caleb, his hair so dark a brown it looked black. He was somberly dressed, his preference, in a dove gray tailcoat, silver waistcoat, and snug black breeches.

"I have to admit, you're the last person I expected to see at Parklands," Caleb said, "though perhaps I shouldn't be surprised."

"Believe it or not, I was invited. Besides, I heard you and Sutton were here. Damn, it's good to have you home." Bright blue eyes ran over his scarlet tunic. "I see you're back in uniform. Far more appealing to the ladies, I imagine, than the clothing of a groom."

"It was necessary at the time."

"I gather you've finished your mission. I'd like to have been a fly on the wall when Miss Durant discovered your deception."

"I think she wanted to take a bat to my head."

Luc chuckled softly. "I heard the gossip. Something about catching a murderer, I believe."

Caleb glanced away. "More or less."

Luc cut him a look. Caleb had never been able to lie to his brother. Apparently, he wasn't any better at it now than he'd been when he was a boy.

"More or less?"

"That's what I said."

"All right, we'll leave it at that for now." Luc stopped a waiter, plucked a snifter of brandy off the tray. He took a sip, then followed Caleb's gaze to the petite, red-haired woman sweeping into the drawing room.

"Ah, the lady of the evening. She's quite something, isn't she?"

"Who?" Caleb took a casual sip of his brandy.

"Don't be irritating. You know very well who I'm talking about. I didn't recognize her that day at Tattersall's though I had seen her a few times before." His gaze shifted back to Vermillion. "There is something different about her even now. Ah, yes. She isn't wearing rice powder and paint, just a little rouge on her lips and cheeks. I daresay, she doesn't need anything at all. Gad, the girl's a beauty. I wouldn't mind tapping into a little of that myself."

Luc gave her a slow perusal. "In fact, if you don't mind, I think I'll—" He took a step, but Caleb blocked his way.

"Not on your life."

Luc grinned up at him, a dimple notching his

cheek. "I had a feeling there was more going on here than the simple call of duty."

Caleb glanced at Vermillion. "It isn't what you think, Luc."

"Isn't it?"

"Not exactly."

"I don't suppose you'd care to elaborate."

"Let's just say, she isn't all she seems."

Luc drilled him with a glare that demanded an explanation and Caleb sighed in defeat. "I'm the only man who's touched her, Luc. And if I have my way, that's how it's going to stay."

His brother frowned. "I thought you were returning to Spain."

Caleb flicked a glance at the woman across the room. "That's the hell of it. I wish to God I'd never met her. Now that I have, I don't know what I'm going to do about it."

Luc didn't say anything more. Caleb watched Vermillion promenade the room on Colonel Wingate's arm and a spark of jealousy began to burn in his stomach.

Luc leaned toward him. "You may have been the only man who has touched her so far, but I wouldn't count on that exclusivity in the future."

Caleb set his brandy glass down on a Hepplewhite table. "Excuse me. There's something I need to do."

He ignored Luc's chuckle of mirth as he started across the drawing room, intent on hunting down his prey.

Lee spotted Caleb striding toward her, long legs eating up the distance between then, a black look on his face. God's teeth, he had said he needed her help.

Now that she was trying to give it, why couldn't he just stay out of her way?

She smiled up at the colonel. "Perhaps we could continue our discussion on the terrace? It's getting a little stuffy in here."

The colonel's eyes heated up. She hoped she could keep him in line long enough to ferret out any information he might have.

"Splendid idea, my dear." He started guiding her toward the French doors leading outside just as Caleb walked up.

"I'm sorry to disturb you, Colonel, but I believe your aide, Lieutenant Oxley, is looking for you. It seems to be a matter of some importance."

"Thank you, Captain." He turned to Vermillion. "I'm terribly sorry, my dear, but duty calls."

She gave him a smile of regret. "I understand completely. Perhaps a little later . . . ?"

"Certainly, my dear." The colonel made a very proper bow. "I shall return to you the first instant I am able."

The moment Wingate turned away, Caleb gripped her arm and propelled her none too gently through the French doors out onto the terrace.

"What the hell do you think you're doing?" Hard dark eyes bored into her. "Or have you already forgotten that I am the man who spent a portion of last night in your bed?"

She planted her hands on her hips, her irritation beginning to build. "I haven't forgot anything—more's the pity. What I'm doing—as it appears *you* have already forgot—is trying to help you."

"Help me? You think throwing yourself at Wingate is helping me?"

A sudden suspicion hit her. "Oxley isn't looking for the colonel, is he? You just made that up."

A satisfied smile curved his lips. "Maybe the walk will cool his ardor."

Lee rolled her eyes. *Men.* "Wingate knows a lot about the war, Caleb. I'm trying to discover if his loyalties are not what they seem. You did ask for my help, whether you remember it or not."

"Not that kind of help, dammit."

"Can't you see? I know these men. I might uncover something useful."

"Forget it. In case you haven't figured it out, there is every chance your friend Mary Goodhouse wound up dead because of something she learned while she worked at Parklands. I don't want that happening to you."

"Good Lord—you think that's what happened? That Mary was killed because she knew something about the traitor? You think the traitor killed her?"

"Him or someone he hired. She was working here before she moved to the city. She could have overheard something she shouldn't have."

Lee settled back against the rough brick wall, suddenly needing the support. "If that is the case, then you *must* let me help you. Mary was my friend. I want to see her murderer captured and brought to justice."

Caleb caught her shoulders. "Listen to me, Lee. This isn't a game we're playing. If we're going to catch whoever is in league with the French, we have to be very, very careful."

She thought of Mary, strangled and dumped into the river, and a shiver crept down her spine. "I can certainly see your point."

"Does that mean you'll stay out of this, let Major Sutton and me handle things?"

"Surely there is some way I can help."

"You can keep your eyes and ears open. Watch the servants. Listen to the household gossip. If you notice anything suspicious, come to me."

She nodded. "All right." But she wasn't about to abandon her quest. She had ways of getting information that Caleb Tanner simply did not have. She saw his eyes move down to the soft flesh swelling out the front of her gown.

You see, Caleb Tanner. This is one job you simply are not equipped to handle.

"You'd better go back in," he said, but his eyes said he wanted her to stay, that he would very much like to do something far more exciting than return to the stuffy drawing room, something like what they had done in her room the night before.

"I suppose I should." But she didn't want to leave. She wanted to do exactly what they had done last night and it made her recall the offer he had made to act as her protector. It wasn't going to happen. He would be leaving soon and she would be left alone, facing the same uncertain future that she was facing now.

Whatever she decided, at present she had more important problems. She needed to concentrate on how she was going to help catch a traitor.

Elizabeth stood in the shadows cast by the torches on the far end of the terrace. In the past ten years, she had attended so many parties like this one she had long ago lost count. In truth, tonight she would rather have stayed home with her boys, Peter and Tom, but

Charles hadn't been dressed to go out, so she thought he meant to stay at the house and that meant she was the one who had to leave.

Now he was here, looking so handsome it made her heart squeeze every time she happened to catch a glimpse of him. She told herself to leave, to return to Rotham Hall, forget Charles and his search for a new mistress, but some demon masochistic force seemed to hold her there.

"I thought I saw you walk out here."

She turned at the unexpected sound of his voice. "Charles . . ." She hadn't heard his approach, though she should have. She knew the rhythm of his footfalls as if they were her own, had listened for them returning up the stairs night after night for the past ten years.

"Beautiful evening, isn't it?"

She moistened her lips, which felt parchment dry. "Yes . . . yes, it's lovely."

"I thought perhaps you were going to stay home tonight. You mentioned something of the sort to Matilda." The housekeeper, a longtime family retainer who had become a confidant of sorts.

Her stomach tightened. He hadn't known she would be here, of course, or he wouldn't have come. "I'm sorry. I didn't mean to interfere with your evening. I had thought to stay home, but since it appeared that was your intention, I assumed it would be best if I went out."

"The house is quite large. As I said before, there is room enough for us both. You didn't have to leave just because I was there."

She frowned. This wasn't making any sense. "I'm afraid I don't understand. If you were planning to stay home, why are you here?"

"Because you are here, Beth."

The bottom dropped out of her stomach. "Wh-what are you talking about?"

"I know it's too soon, that I should wait, give you a chance to get to know me again, but it's agony, Beth. Watching you, wishing things were different. I'm talking about a reconciliation. I'm not the same man I was ten years ago. I don't believe you're the same woman. I want us to try again."

Disbelief mingled with fear and both of them coursed through her. It had taken years to get over the pain of losing the man she had fallen so deeply in love with. She couldn't survive that kind of pain again.

"I don't . . . I don't think that's a good idea."

"Why not?"

Because if we try, I'll start loving you again. Because if I lost you a second time, I couldn't bear it. "Because too many years have passed, Charles. There's too much water under the bridge."

"Is there someone else? I rather thought . . . you haven't seemed interested in anyone for quite some time. I imagined that perhaps . . ."

"Perhaps what, Charles?"

"That perhaps you might come to feel some affection for me. You did once . . . all those years ago. I was too arrogant, too wrapped up in myself to understand the gift you were offering me. I'm older now. I realize how precious that gift is. I wouldn't throw it away again."

Elizabeth swallowed. She couldn't stay out here with him a moment more. She couldn't bear to listen to another of his softly spoken words. If she did, she might weaken and she simply could not do that.

"I-I have to go in. Gabriella needs my help with the entertainment. If you'll excuse me, Charles—" She tried to walk past, but he caught her arm.

"Think about it, Beth. That's all I ask."

He let her go and she started walking, her legs trembling, hurrying as fast as she dared back to the safety of the house. She didn't look at Charles. Not once. She was afraid of what might happen if she did.

The party was winding down. Most of the servants had been dismissed or retired to their beds. In an intimate drawing room at the rear of the house, Gabriella Durant's laughter drifted through the hallways as she entertained her last few guests. Likely, she would keep them company for several more hours at least.

The house was mostly dark. The woman glanced around, stepped out of her third floor room and started down the hall. The servants' stairs were empty, most of the household asleep. She slipped out into the second-floor corridor, bare feet padding on the polished wooden floor. She knew which room was his, knew he would be there sleeping in the big room next to the mistress's extravagant suite, a quiet, airy room with a large, comfortable bed and a view out over the garden.

She shouldn't go to him here, she knew, but she wanted to see him. Needed to see him.

She knew he would be angry at first, but she would explain how careful she had been, that no one had seen her leave her room; and she would please him, give him the kind of pleasure that would make him forgive her small indiscretion.

She tapped on the door, then turned the knob, found it unlocked. She wouldn't need the skeleton key she had taken from the pantry. She slipped inside and closed the door, jumped a little when she heard the sound of his husky voice.

"What are you doing in here? You know better than to come here." The sheets rustled as he sat up in the wide, carved bed. "You know how disastrous it would be if we were discovered."

She moved silently toward the bed, saw him toss back the sheet, swing his legs to the side of the mattress, plant his feet on the floor.

"Please, *mon cher* . . . do not be angry. I 'ad to see you. I 'ave missed you. Let me show you 'ow much."

He tensed as she knelt on the floor in front of him but he didn't push her away. Reaching down, she caught the hem of his nightshirt, shoved it up over his legs. They were strong legs, nicely muscled. He was already hard, she saw, anticipating what she meant to do. She reached down and cupped his sex, pleased at how quickly he had responded.

"You can't be in here," he said, but the protest was weak. She caressed him, cupped him, took him into her mouth, and a few minutes later heard him groan.

She thought that afterward he would invite her into his bed, that he would make love to her, even if the loving would be brief, but it was not to be.

"You have to leave. Now. Before someone sees you. Never come to me again. Not here. If you have information, send word and I'll meet you at the inn."

Anger trickled through her. She didn't deserve to be treated this way. " 'Ow much longer? I am tired of hiding what I feel for you. You said you would take me away from here. You promised."

He caught her shoulders, squeezed until it hurt. "Listen to me. You will do as I say, do you understand me?" His hold gentled, turned into a caress. "It won't be that much longer. As soon as this is over, we'll go away together. I'll buy you a house, something expensive, a place in the country—perhaps another one in the city. I'll dress you in beautiful gowns, buy you jewelry. You'll have everything you ever wanted."

"All I want is you."

He bent his head and kissed her and the anger slowly faded.

"Do as I tell you," he said more gently. "Find out what you can. Leave word in the usual place and I'll meet you at the inn. Now be a good girl and go back to your bed. And be careful when you leave. Make sure no one sees you."

She didn't want to go. She wanted to climb up on the deep feather mattress and have him make love to her. But she had displeased him enough by coming to his room.

"Au revoir, mon coeur," she said. She left him there in the bedchamber and started toward her quarters on the floor above. One day soon, she would have the information he wanted. Then they could leave the country, go somewhere together. She smiled as she slipped back inside her room and closed the door, her head filled with pleasant dreams.

16

———❦———

Lee awakened early the following morning. She had work to do. Dressing in a simple skirt and blouse, she made her way out to the stable, spoke to Arlie, then talked to Jacob about plans for an upcoming race. Noir was ready, Jacob said, then went on and on about Caleb, praising him for the work he had done with the horses.

"There's a one-day race in Donneymead," she said. "That is only a few hours' walk from here. Take Noir and a couple of the younger horses. It will help get them ready for the meet at St. Leger."

"Aye, Miss. I'll see it done."

She left the older man and headed back toward the house, pausing as she passed by one of the stalls. Muffin was feeding her kittens, all of which appeared to be healthy and growing by leaps and bounds. Lee stroked the yellow cat's fur and left them, thinking of Caleb and the night the kittens had been born. She would have liked to take Grand Coeur for a ride, but Gabriella had planned a lavish picnic down by the stream and she didn't want to disappoint her.

By the time she returned to the house and Jeannie helped her into a gauzy white muslin gown and tucked her hair up beneath a wide-brimmed straw bonnet decorated with artificial roses, the group was assembled at the bottom of the stairs.

"All right, everyone." Gabriella clapped her hands and smiled like a little girl. "There are carriages waiting out front. It isn't that far. Those of you who prefer to walk may come with me."

Lee glanced around, searching for Caleb, but he wasn't anywhere in sight. Not everyone was in attendance. Some were still abed, others merely not inclined to a day in the sun. Lord Andrew was among those remaining behind, she noticed, as was Juliette Beauvoir.

Lee tried not to wonder what Caleb planned to do for the day, whether he might be bold enough to snoop through some of the guests' bedchambers or if he might be interested in whiling away the hours with the lovely Juliette. Lee swiftly buried the thought. She didn't have time for jealousy, though she was coming to dislike the conniving young woman in the extreme. She needed to continue her efforts to gain information and the picnic would perfectly suit.

As Gabriella had promised, it didn't take long to reach the grassy meadow. Walking next to Elizabeth Sorenson, they chatted pleasantly along the way, though Elizabeth seemed strangely quiet today.

"Come, darlings—join the party. Have a glass of champagne or perhaps some ratafia." Aunt Gabby stepped between the two women, linked arms with them, and led them toward linen-draped tables that had been arranged for the occasion. There were benches and chairs enough for all and each table was spread with fine porcelain plates and gleaming silver and crystal. Not exactly Lee's idea of a picnic, but the guests seemed excited about it.

A few feet away, another row of tables overflowed with food: roast partridge and pickled salmon, oysters in anchovy sauce, venison and mutton pasties, cold meats, jellies, candied fruits, and custards, and wine, of course, to accompany the meal. It was a lavish spread and guests lined up, plates in hand, ready to indulge themselves.

It was sometime later that Lee was finally able to escape her aunt and begin interviewing the guests, having earlier that morning mentally listed which of them might know something important, something that would help the French.

Sir Peter Peasley was a frequent visitor to Parklands and a close friend of Colin Streatham, who worked for the Secretary of State. He might be privy to inside information. Lisette Moreau was French and also often a visitor. Would Sir Peter tell her military secrets in order to please her? And even if he did, what role did Parklands play?

Caleb believed someone in the house might be involved in conveying the information. Another of the guests? One of the servants? Perhaps the house was simply a meeting place where information was exchanged before being passed on to the enemy.

She surveyed the group clustered on blankets beneath the trees or still seated at the tables. Charles Sorenson was a high-ranking member of the House of Lords. What might he know? Claymont was a man of equally high position, though she refused to believe the earl might be involved. She knew the earl, Dylan Sommers, had known him for years. He was the most trustworthy man she had ever met. He simply wasn't capable of that kind of deceit.

And there was Wingate, of course. The colonel was a high-ranking officer of the Life Guards, reporting directly to General Ulysses Stevens. He might have access to a great deal of valuable information. Even Lord Nash, advisor to the Chancellor, would have access to important documents and the like.

Lee sighed as she watched the people beneath the trees and thought how impossible a task it would be to ferret out the traitor.

Assuming there really was a traitor.

Assuming that person was actually there at Parklands.

"You look as if you are pondering the fate of the world." Major Sutton stood beside her, gold buttons gleaming, curly black hair ruffled by the breeze.

"Perhaps I am."

"I can think of something much more fun. Perhaps I could persuade you to walk with me. Yesterday I stumbled upon a wonderful old ruin . . . part of a medieval abbey, I believe. I'm sure you've seen it. Perhaps you would join me in exploring the place." He took her arm, started leading her away from the group toward a path that began at the edge of the trees.

She looked back over her shoulder, but her feet kept moving as he firmly led her away. "I-I think I had better go back and join the others. My aunt will be—"

"What's the matter?" One black eyebrow went up. "You're not afraid, are you? Tell me you wouldn't rather take a walk through the woods than sit round listening to a bunch of old fools gossip."

"Well, I—"

"Actually, the lady was looking for me." The voice sounded familiar, but when she turned, it wasn't Caleb. Lucas Tanner strode toward her, a hard look on his face. Fortunately, the warning in his intense blue eyes was not directed at her.

Major Sutton seemed not to notice. "Is that right, Miss Durant?" He must have recognized the lie for what it was, but Luc's look of warning had put her on alert.

"Yes, actually, I was." She stepped away from the major, reached over and took Luc's arm. "I didn't see you earlier. Have you eaten, my lord?"

"Yes, but I believe I could use something to drink. If you'll excuse us, Major . . . ?"

Sutton made a brief bow and a look passed between the two men. Lee let Lucas guide her back toward the others, stopping just out of earshot.

"Sutton has a reputation, love. When it comes to women, it isn't a good one."

"I believe you have a similar reputation, my lord."

His mouth edged up. "Perhaps that is so, but I've never forced a woman to do anything she didn't want to do."

Lee frowned, not liking the thought. "If that is the sort of man the major is, I appreciate your timely rescue."

"I was merely acting in my brother's stead. He seems to be quite protective of you."

"From what I know of Caleb . . . Captain Tanner, he is simply a protective sort of man."

"Perhaps. You should know, in that same way, I am equally protective of him. He's my brother, Vermillion. I don't want to see him hurt."

Her eyes widened. "How could I possibly hurt your brother?"

"I'm not entirely sure. Just make certain that you do not."

She might have argued, told him that what happened between her and Caleb was none of his concern, but there was something about Lucas Tanner that commanded people to do his bidding. It was a trait that seemed to run in the family. Or perhaps it was the glint in those hard blue eyes that promised retribution if she didn't heed his words.

Since the notion was preposterous and in all likelihood she was the one who was going to get hurt, she simply kept her silence.

"I thought your brother might join us. Where is he?"

"I'm afraid I haven't seen him. Caleb has an annoying habit of disappearing."

"Yes, so I've noticed."

Luc took her arm and started toward the punch bowl. "As I said, I think I could use something to drink."

Grateful for the distraction, Lee let him lead her away.

While the guests enjoyed the picnic, Caleb managed to slip into several of the rooms, but his brief search turned up nothing. Later, after Gabriella and her party returned to the house, he joined a small gathering in the music room where Lee entertained on the harp. He was surprised by her skill. She plucked the chords so beautifully it made his chest feel tight. He watched until she quit playing, hoping to speak to her, but as soon as she finished, her usual throng of panting men swarmed around her and he walked away in disgust.

Little by little, the afternoon slipped into evening and the night's entertainments began. He hadn't spoken to Lee all day and he was beginning to feel restless as he watched her bantering with her admirers. Earlier, from a distance, he had seen her talking to Colonel Wingate and Sir Peter Peasley, had watched her in conversation with Major Sutton and even his brother Luc.

Now supper was over and the dancing had begun. Mondale stood beside Lee in the drawing room and the next thing he knew the two of them were slipping outside onto the terrace.

Caleb's senses went on alert. Entering the terrace from the opposite end, he watched the two of them together, saw the damnable rake sweep her into his arms. Mondale kissed her, and anger shot through him. He wanted to tear the man apart, wanted to put Lee over his knee and paddle her until she saw Andrew Mondale for the womanizing rake he was.

The only thing that kept him standing in the shadows was knowing that he would be forced to leave Parklands if he did either of those things and he couldn't afford for that to happen.

He watched her break away from Mondale, ending the kiss. They talked a little while longer, then finally returned to the house.

Caleb's anger didn't lessen.

Dammit, he had always been a little hot-tempered, but Lee drove him nearly mad. He felt possessive of her as he never had another woman. He found himself thinking about her at the oddest times, remembering her in the stable smiling up at old Arlie or galloping over the fields, red hair flying behind her like a gleaming ruby flag.

He wanted her. Constantly. Ached with wanting her.

It was madness, he knew. His life was the army. It was what he did and he was good at it. He was, in fact, a hero of sorts, a soldier who had made his father proud.

Still, as the evening progressed and he saw Lee make her way alone out into the garden, he found himself following her into the darkness, remembering that he had seen her in the shadows kissing Mondale, wondering if she planned a secret tryst with him.

He told himself to hang on to his temper and hoped to hell he would succeed.

Lee tipped her head back, resting it against the pale knotted bark of a birch tree, staring up through the leafy branches. Thank God, she'd finally been able to escape. Every night, the evening seemed to grow longer, more tedious. The house was stuffy. The rooms smelled of candle wax and the cloying scent of women's perfume. Encouraging the colonel last night had been a mistake, and Mondale—dear Lord, the man must have at least three sets of hands!

Lee looked up through the branches, into the darkness broken by the glitter of stars, and inhaled a cleansing breath. Out here it was cool and the soft night beckoned. Here in the garden, she was at peace, able to absorb the sound of the crickets in the grass, the distant clink of crystal, and the faint notes of music coming from inside the house.

The week was slipping past. She had continued to dig for information and tonight she thought she might have come up with something at last. She needed to speak to Caleb, but all evening she had only caught an occasional glimpse of him.

She wondered where he was, thought of Juliette Beauvoir, and felt the sharp burn of jealousy. Or perhaps he had disappeared from Parklands as he had before. Her stomach knotted at the thought and because it did, her temper inched up. She relaxed when she spotted a shadowy figure moving along the path in her direction and realized it was Caleb. Her heart kicked up and she cursed him for the ease with which he could affect her.

He stopped when he reached her and the usual scowl appeared on his face. "Surprised to see me?"

She tried not to think of Juliette Beauvoir. Being jealous of the woman was ridiculous. Caleb had rarely looked in her direction, and yet . . . "As a matter of fact, I am. You were missing all afternoon." She gave him a silky smile. "But perhaps you were otherwise entertained."

Caleb didn't seem to catch the inference. "I've been busy." A note of sarcasm crept into his voice. "But then you've been rather busy yourself."

"Exactly how would you know?"

"Because I saw you. Out on the terrace with Mondale. I saw you kissing him, Lee."

Damn. She thought she had been discreet.

"That's right . . . there you were on the terrace, behaving like a harlot, and Mondale was lapping it up."

Heat washed into her cheeks. He had a way of goading her, making her want to lash out at him, and she couldn't seem to stop herself from doing it again. "Actually, Caleb—I *am* a harlot. *Your* harlot. In case you have forgotten."

His eyes went dark. "I haven't forgotten anything

about you. Not for a moment. I remember exactly the size of your breasts, the way your nipples tighten when I cup them in my hands. I remember what it's like to be inside you. It's you who seems to have trouble remembering." His dark eyes snapped with fire. "But perhaps I can remedy that."

He gripped her shoulders, dragged her toward him. She felt the heat of his mouth over hers as he claimed a hard, angry kiss. She should have pulled away, should have railed at him for believing the worst of her. She should have told him the truth about Andrew, that she had only been with him on the terrace because she was trying to help, but her nipples were already hard, her body begging him to continue.

He must have read her thoughts for a groan escaped his throat. The gown was low cut, not much of a barrier. Caleb shoved the shimmering fabric off her shoulders, baring her breasts, and captured the fullness in his hands. He palmed them, molded them, bent his dark head and took the weight of one into his mouth. Her nipple tightened, distended, sent a shaft of pleasure shooting through her. She swayed toward him, clutched his powerful shoulders to stay on her feet.

"Caleb . . ."

"That's right, sweetheart. This time, I want you to remember." His attack resumed, turned relentless. Deep, thorough kisses that stirred her blood and sent her arms up to twine around his neck. He kissed her as he shoved up her skirt, found her core, and began to stroke her. He knew exactly where to touch her, how to caress her, used his skillful hands until she was trembling, wet and ready, and begging him to take her, making soft little whimpering sounds in her throat.

One of his big hands worked the buttons on the front of his navy blue breeches and he freed himself. Caleb lifted her and she felt his hardness poised at the entrance to her passage. With one deep thrust, he buried himself to the hilt.

Oh, dear God. He was as hard as stone and so big he filled her completely. He eased himself out, then thrust back in. Deep strokes impaled her, rocked her against the trunk of the tree. He cupped her bottom, bracing her as he drove into her again and again. Pushing her skirt up out of the way, he wrapped her legs around his waist, began to drive deeper, faster, harder.

Her head fell back. Her body trembled, tightened. Pleasure rolled through her in powerful waves.

"That's it, sweeting. Let go." And she did, her body shaking, quivering, straining, the pleasure so intense she bit down on her lip to keep from crying out.

Caleb reached his release a few moments later, the muscles in his shoulders going taut as he spilled his seed. For long moments, he said nothing. Then his forehead dropped down, and rested against her own, and he just held her.

Reality began to drift in and her mind began to clear. She remembered where they were and that someone might stubble upon them, even out here in the farthest, darkest reaches of the garden. Caleb must have remembered as well, for he gently set her back on her feet.

He finished buttoning his breeches, then began to help her straighten her clothes. For a moment he paused, and she realized he was looking at the wine-colored, star-shaped mark on her left shoulder.

"I noticed this the last time we made love. What is it?"

She shrugged. "A birthmark. When I was little I prayed it would go away, but obviously it never did."

He traced the mark with his finger, looked down into her face. "I don't want you kissing Mondale."

Lee sighed. "Lord Andrew knows about the troop movements in Spain, Caleb. That is the reason I was kissing him."

"What are you talking about?"

"That's what we were doing on the terrace . . . talking about the war. I let him kiss me to take his mind off the conversation. I wanted to discover as much as I could."

"I don't believe this. You were kissing Mondale in order to get information? Dammit, I told you how dangerous that was." He wasn't happy, but she could tell he was relieved.

"Did Mondale say how he found out?"

"Apparently he received a letter from a friend in the army. I don't know if he is guilty of being a spy, but—"

"But it requires looking into."

"That's what I would say."

"What about Wingate? Did you kiss him, too?"

"Only once and it was awful."

"Dammit, Lee."

"I won't do it again—not even to get information."

Caleb ground his jaw and turned away, trying to bring his temper back under control. He sighed into the darkness. "I don't know what it is about you. Every time I'm near you, I seem to go a little insane."

She couldn't help a smile. "I don't know what it is about you, either, Caleb, but every time I'm near you, I seem to lose all my better judgment."

He laughed softly. She liked the sound. She had

very rarely heard it. Then the laughter faded and his expression slowly changed.

"Promise me you'll stay out of this, Lee. As much as I appreciate what you found out, it's just too dangerous. I don't want you getting hurt."

"I can help, Caleb. Maybe I already have."

"Don't you understand—this is dangerous! I don't want you getting involved." He shook her. "I want your word you'll stay out of this."

Lee sighed, recognizing defeat in the determined look on his face. "All right. But I'm still keeping my eyes and ears open. That is the least I can do."

Caleb bent his head and kissed her. "As long as you stay out of trouble."

"Whatever happens, I won't do anything without talking to you first."

Caleb's hard look warned she had better be telling him the truth.

"So you think Mondale may be our man?" Colonel Cox sat on the opposite side of the desk in his Whitehall office.

"I don't know, sir. According to my source, Andrew Mondale has information about Wellesley's troop movements in Spain. My source says—"

"And your source, Captain, would be . . . ?"

Caleb cleared his throat. He had hoped to leave Lee out of this. "Vermillion Durant, Colonel. A situation came up. I had to make a decision. Based on what I knew of the girl, I decided to trust her with the truth of my mission. She volunteered to help our cause and came up with the information on Mondale."

"I see."

Caleb just hoped he didn't see too much. "According to Miss Durant, Mondale got the information through a letter he received from a dragoon captain in the 60th Regiment."

"That's hard to believe. Those letters take weeks to get home. The information would have been old news by then."

"Maybe not. Maybe the captain had a friend returning to England, or maybe it was just a lucky guess."

"It's possible. No doubt about it. Still, we'll need to put a man on Mondale, see where he goes when he's not out at Parklands, chasing after Vermillion Durant."

Caleb wisely made no reply, since recently he found himself chasing after her nearly as much as Mondale and the rest of her lapdogs, a fact he found irritating as hell.

"Are you planning to rejoin Major Sutton this afternoon?"

"I've some errands to run first. I'll be heading back out there this evening. We'll be staying for the balance of the week." Or as long as they could stretch their invitation. He prayed something would break before courtesy required them to leave, but it didn't look good.

"Very well. I'll put a man on Mondale, though I can't say I'm happy about it. I know the boy's father. It will break the man's heart if his son turns out to be a traitor."

Caleb didn't disagree. He was thinking of his own father and how much it meant to the earl to have a son so well thought of in the army. Perhaps in a way he understood Vermillion's desire to please the aunt she loved like a mother.

Unfortunately, in Lee's case that meant leading the life of a courtesan when she deserved far better.

He worried about what she would do the night of her birthday. She still seemed uncertain. If she chose a protector, as she had earlier vowed to do, the odds were slim that she would pick him. Once his assignment was completed, he would be leaving, returning to Spain. He couldn't take her with him; he wouldn't do that to her or any other woman.

Military life was simply too hard, too grueling, too painful for a female. Even an officer's wife suffered the deprivation, the close quarters and lack of privacy, lack even of a decent bed. To say nothing of the misery of being shuffled from pillar to post during the long campaigns.

Caleb swore softly as he thought again of Lee and the decision she would make the night of her nineteenth birthday.

17

Dressed in her long white night rail, her hair brushed and plaited for sleeping, Lee stood in front of her bedchamber window, staring out into the night. She hadn't seen Caleb since last night when they had made love in the garden.

A warm flush rose in her cheeks as she remembered his angry, ardent passion. She could have stopped him. Caleb wasn't the sort of man to press himself on a woman, no matter how angry he was. But once he had touched her, kissed her, she hadn't wanted him to stop. She only wanted more. They had never made love in that way and she couldn't help wondering how much more there might be to experience—if only they had time.

But time for them was fleeting. Tomorrow night was her birthday ball. She was supposed to choose a lover, a protector, a man she would cleave to until one or the other of them grew bored with the affair. It was the sort of life her aunt had enjoyed, a life that offered a kind of freedom that few Englishwomen were granted.

But thinking of sharing a life, however briefly, with Andrew or Jonathan or Oliver Wingate . . . she couldn't even imagine it. After painful hours of deliberation, she had decided not to choose anyone at all, to somehow make a life of her own without the sheltering presence of a man. It was a decision that didn't come lightly.

In truth, she never would have made the choice if it hadn't been for Caleb. He had changed her in some way. Or perhaps he had merely shown her the person she had always been, deep inside.

It was a difficult decision. She owed her aunt and she wanted to make her happy. But in the weeks he had been there, Caleb had made her see that she also owed herself. She couldn't become some man's plaything, not merely to please her aunt. She would make a different sort of choice, one that took far more courage. She would leave her aunt's protective circle of friends and go out on her own. She had money. She could do anything she wanted. Somehow she would make it up to her aunt.

Still, in the quiet of the room, she found herself thinking of Caleb, wondering what it might be like if Caleb became her protector.

Lee sighed into the silence of her bedchamber. If only he weren't leaving. But in truth, even if she agreed to become his mistress, it wouldn't be for long. Soon he would return to Spain, and the risk of a broken heart would only increase if she spent more time with him.

The quandary spun round and round in her head as she stood at the window, staring down into the garden. She sighed and started to turn away, hoping sleep would ease her turbulent thoughts, but a movement below caught her eye. A slight, cloaked figure stole from the back of the house, slipping silently along the path through the shrubbery. One of the maids, perhaps, or one of the female guests.

Lee watched the woman make her way to the rear of the garden and escape through the wooden gate. Why would someone be leaving the house at this late hour? Why would they be stealing away like a thief in the night?

Unless . . .

In an instant, she made her decision.

Dragging her night rail over her head, Lee raced to the armoire and pulled on her breeches, shirt, and boots. In minutes she was dressed and flying out the door, trying to be quiet as she hurried along the hall and down the servants' stairs. It didn't take long to reach the gate at the rear of the garden. She made it just in time to see the slender, cloaked figure disappear among the trees along the path leading into the village.

Lee hurried after her. God's breath, she wished Caleb were here, but as far as she knew he hadn't returned from wherever he had gone off to, and she had no idea when he might reappear.

The path was well worn, the dirt track flattened from years of use, but it wound through the trees, making it difficult to keep her quarry in sight. She could hear the woman's footfalls on the path up ahead and the sound of her cloak brushing against shrubs and branches along the trail. The leaves were wet with dew and the dampness soaked into Lee's breeches as she hurried along. Up ahead, the woman raced on.

Lee tried to catch a glimpse of her face, but it was

hidden beneath the hood of her cloak. She worried that it was Jeannie, but something about the woman didn't seem quite right. Lee's heart pounded. Around her, the night air felt heavy and still and patches of mist hung over the earth. Crickets stopped their chirping as the woman ran past, and in the faint light cast by a fingernail moon, Lee could see narrow, feminine footprints pressed into the ground on the path in front of her.

The woman turned off the trail and Lee almost lost her. Then she realized the cloaked figure was heading for the Red Boar Inn. It loomed ahead, windows glowing with lamplight, moonlight glinting on the tiles of its gray slate roof. The woman didn't go inside, but rounded the building to the rear and disappeared. Lee hurried after her, stopping when she reached the tavern, plastering herself against the rough stone wall, then carefully peeking around the corner of the building.

There was a stairway behind the inn, partially hidden by ivy. She caught a quick glimpse of the woman's face as she climbed the stairs, lifted the latch on a heavy wooden door, and vanished into a room on the second floor.

It was one of the upstairs chambermaids. A woman named Marie LeCroix.

Marie had come to Parklands last year in search of employment. She was an exceptionally pretty young woman in her late twenties, with wavy dark brown hair, hazel eyes, and remarkable cheekbones. A number of the male guests had made offers for her time, but Marie had shied away from them. She was friendly to the men, but mostly she kept to herself.

At least that's what Lee had believed.

Now she wondered which of the men the woman was here to meet ... and why.

Uncertain exactly what she should do, Lee remained in the shadows, waiting to see if she could discover whom Marie had come to meet. Careful to stay out of sight, she pressed herself against cold gray stone and fastened her gaze on the room upstairs.

Caleb could scarcely believe it. On a black horse named Solomon that was his own mount, he was returning from London, riding past the village toward the lane leading to Parklands, almost to the Red Boar Inn when he spotted a figure running along the path that led from the village to the mansion.

Dammit to bloody hell, he knew who it was, knew there was never a lad who could fill out a pair of men's breeches nearly so well, knew that long red braid and exactly how silky it felt.

What the devil she was doing out here in the middle of the night confounded him completely.

Unless ...

His stomach muscles contracted. Sweet God, surely he hadn't been wrong. Surely Lee wasn't the traitor. As much as his brain cautioned him it just might be so, deep down he didn't believe it. As he watched her press herself into the shadows against the wall, his certainty grew.

Lee wasn't a traitor.

Instead, there was every chance she was out here trying to catch one.

The thought fired his temper. The interfering little baggage was sticking her nose into army business again and putting herself in danger. When he got her back to the house, he was going to wring her pretty little neck!

Tying his horse to a tree some distance away, careful to stay hidden in the shadows, Caleb started walking toward the small figure hiding in the darkness behind the inn.

From her place against the wall next to the stairwell, Lee could hear the creak of footsteps on the wooden floor in the room upstairs. If she thought she could see inside, she would sneak up the stairs and peek in, but the shutters were closed and only a sliver of light seeped out from within.

Lee rubbed her hands together. It was damp and cold and she hadn't had time to retrieve a cloak or gloves. Now it seemed as if the woman had been in the room forever. Lee shivered, tried to think warm thoughts and concentrate on discovering the man who might be trysting with Marie. If the fellow was a guest at Parklands, it didn't make sense. A visitor's privacy was ensured. If the woman wanted to spend time with one of the men, the two of them wouldn't have been interrupted.

Still, there were men in the village, wealthy squires, sons of wealthy squires. Lee figured she was probably wasting her time, that the maid was simply meeting one of them.

She wrapped her arms around herself and shivered, told herself that she should just turn round and go home. But what if Marie were meeting a traitor? What if she were the woman passing secrets to the French?

"Out for a midnight stroll?"

She jumped six inches at the words whispered into her ear. "Caleb! Good heavens, you scared me half to death!"

"If you are lucky, sweeting, that is all I will do. If you are here for the reason I think you are, I ought to put you over my knee."

Lee ignored him and the black scowl on his face. "What are you doing here, Caleb? I looked for you earlier but no one seemed to know where you were."

"I had business in London. As to what I am doing here at the inn, I'm doing my damnedest to keep you out of trouble."

Lee turned her attention to the room at the top of the stairs. "One of our maids is up there. A woman named Marie LeCroix. I saw her sneaking out of the house. I didn't know where to find you, so I followed her myself. I could hear more than one set of footsteps so I know she isn't alone, but I have no idea who might be up there with her."

"Maybe she's up there with Oxley."

"Oxley?"

"That's right. The lieutenant's been bedding her every chance he gets. I wonder what she's been receiving in return for her favors."

Lee glanced toward the top of the stairs, wondering how many other secrets Caleb had discovered about the people at Parklands. "I don't think she's meeting Lieutenant Oxley. He was still in the drawing room when I retired and if she wanted to see him, all she had to do was go to his room."

"Good point. So she's probably meeting someone who isn't staying at the house."

"That would be my guess." She shivered, the damp cold seeping through her clothes.

"Dammit, you're freezing." Stripping off his riding jacket, he draped it around her shoulders. The coat retained his body heat. She snuggled deeper into the warmth and her shivering eased.

"Stay here. I'm going upstairs." Before she could remind him Marie was probably there for nothing but a lover's tryst, he was halfway up the staircase. He banged on the door and waited, but no one came to open it. He pounded again, tried the handle, then came racing back down the stairs.

"There's probably another entrance inside the inn. You stay here. If he comes out this way, try to get a look at his face. Whatever you do, don't let him see you. He might not want any witnesses."

Lee thought of Mary and sank deeper into the shadows. Caleb took off toward the front of the tavern and she counted the time it would take him to get up the inside stairs. There must have been another entrance for a few minutes later, she heard the wooden floorboards creaking and guessed Caleb was in the room.

When he didn't come outside, she left her post and ran after him, racing round to the front, then shoving through the tavern doors.

The inn was crowded, the low-ceilinged taproom smoky, and noisy with the clink of glasses and the rumble of the patrons' conversation. One of the tavern maids laughed and the sound rang across the room. Careful to stay at the edge of the crowd, Lee headed up the stairs at the rear of the inn.

At the top of the stairs, a long hall yawned to the right. She hurried down the corridor, saw that one of the doors stood open. Caleb knelt beside a slatted bed. The moment he saw her, he came to his feet and started walking toward her. He had almost reached her when she spotted the woman draped limply over the edge of the bed.

"Marie!"

Caleb turned her away from the grisly sight and his arms tightened around her. "She's dead, love. I'm sorry."

Lee pulled free of his hold, her gaze careening once more toward the bed. Across the mattress, the limp figure of Marie LeCroix lay pale and lifeless, her pretty blue eyes staring up at the ceiling above her head. Lee started shaking. Tears welled in her eyes as Caleb pressed her head into his shoulder.

"The man was gone by the time I got here. The bastard used her, then strangled her."

She closed her eyes, trying to blot out the sight of the lifeless woman on the bed. "Oh, God."

"He must have left through the tavern. It's crowded and dark. It wouldn't be hard to get away without being seen. I would have gone after him, but the forest begins just behind the inn and there's no way in hell I'd be able to follow his tracks in the darkness."

"Why . . . why didn't he go down the outside stairs?"

"I don't know. Perhaps he knew you were out there."

Her head jerked up. "Oh, my God! If I hadn't followed Marie to the inn—"

Caleb gripped her shoulders. "This isn't your fault, Lee. Whoever did this likely also killed Mary—or had a hand in it. Perhaps they knew too much. Perhaps they posed some kind of threat—I don't know." His features turned hard and his fingers dug into her shoulders. "You're lucky you didn't climb those stairs. If you had, you might be lying next to Marie on that bed!"

He was angry. More than that, he was frightened.

He held her at arm's length for a moment more, then jerked her hard against him and his arms came around her. A slight tremor ran through his body.

"Come on," he finally said. "We need to send for the authorities. I've got to talk to the people in the taproom, find out if anyone saw the person who came down the stairs."

"Yes . . . or perhaps the tavern owner can tell you who rented the room."

He nodded. "Let's go find out." With an arm securely around her waist, he started guiding her toward the door.

"What about Marie?" Lee asked softly.

"I'll see she's taken care of. You don't have to worry about that."

Lee said nothing more, just let him lead her out of the room and quietly close the door.

Graveside services were held for Marie LeCroix the following day, a solemn occasion that briefly put a damper on festivities at Parklands. Since Oxley had been in the drawing room with Colonel Wingate all evening, he was not a suspect. The sheriff, not privy to army information concerning the spy ring, believed the woman had been strangled by a jealous lover, someone who had discovered Marie's affair. But no one had the slightest idea who the man might be.

Constable Shaw came out from London, but the only connection between the murders of Mary Goodhouse and that of Marie LeCroix was the women's brief employment at Parklands.

No one in the tavern had seen anything the night of the murder and, as the upstairs room had been let by Marie, there were no clues to the man's identity.

Lee's birthday ball was postponed. While the Parklands's staff, Vermillion and her aunt, attended a brief churchyard service for Marie, Caleb and Major Sutton descended on Lieutenant Ian Oxley.

It was obvious the young man was shaken and very deeply grieved by the news of the young maid's death.

"I can't believe it . . . I just can't believe she is dead." Oxley sat on the leather sofa in the study. The doors were closed and the few servants who remained in the house were given strict instruction they were not to be disturbed.

"What did you tell her, Oxley?" Sutton leaned over the younger man. "Colonel Wingate has already told us he had key information about Wellesley's upcoming campaign. You were privy to that information. Now tell us how much of that information you told Marie LeCroix."

Oxley's eyes filled with tears. He was a pale young man, given to shyness, and obviously in love with Marie.

"We just . . . we just talked."

"In your bed, you mean, while you were overheated and desperate to get inside her."

Oxley swallowed, his Adam's apple moving up and down. "She was interested in the war. I suppose I might have . . . mentioned a few things."

"She was French, Oxley." Sutton bore down on him. "Did the fact never cross your mind?"

He shook his head. "She was only a little girl when she came to England with her family. She was raised here. She wanted the British to win the war. That . . . that is what she said." He gazed out the window toward the garden. "She was so beautiful. She never talked to any of the other men . . . only me. I felt so lucky. I just wanted to please her."

Caleb swore softly. "Do you have any idea, Lieutenant, who Marie might have been meeting that night at the inn?"

He glanced up. The grief etched into his face made him look older than he had the day before. "I thought there was only me. I thought she loved me."

"She used you," the major said harshly. "Just the way that bastard used her. You know what they were doing in that room, Oxley? You know what he did to her before he killed her?"

"Don't," Caleb warned, ending the major's savage words. "The woman he loved is dead. She wasn't the person he believed her to be and because he trusted her, his career is over and he'll be facing charges. What we need to know is who killed her. We need the name of the man she was passing the information on to."

"I don't know," Oxley said with a shake of his head. "I swear I don't. I only mentioned a couple of things . . . We talked about Oporto. I told her Wellesley was gearing up, that it looked as if there would be fighting at Talavera. It didn't seem important at the time."

"You're a fool, Lieutenant," Major Sutton said. "You thought with your cock and not your brain and now you are paying the price."

Oxley made no reply. The misery on his face was enough of an answer. The afternoon wore on, but no new information surfaced.

One thing was clear: the spy ring's connection to Parklands had been severed. Marie was dead and no more information would be forthcoming. Perhaps Mary Goodhouse had also been selling secrets, or more likely she had figured out whom Marie was meeting. Either way, the women were dead and the leak had been stopped.

Unfortunately, the head of the spy ring had escaped, leaving no trace of whom he might be. Caleb wasn't sure if his assignment would continue once he returned to London, but his time at Parklands had come to an end.

As soon as Lee's birthday ball was over, Caleb, along with the rest of the guests, would be returning to the city. He didn't know how long he would remain in London, but at least he would have time to visit his family, see some of his friends. As he had before, he told himself to forget Vermillion, that interfering in her life would be doing her more harm than good.

Still, as the afternoon drew to a close, he found himself striding down the hall, stopping to speak to the butler, asking him to make it known to the lady of the house that he wished a word with her in private in regard to a matter of importance concerning her niece.

It was an hour later that Caleb was summoned to a small salon at the rear of the mansion. The butler, Jones, led him down the hall into a room done in soft shades of ivory and rose, then quietly closed the doors, making them private.

"You wished to see me, Captain?" Gabriella floated toward him in a gown a brighter shade of rose than the sofa and draperies, a warm smile on her face.

"I know you're busy. Thank you for making the time."

Her smile slipped a little at the serious note in his voice. "I thought this concerned Vermillion. Are you here in regard to the death of Marie LeCroix?"

"No. As I said, I'm here to speak to you about your niece."

One of her silver-blond eyebrows went up. "In that case, why don't we make ourselves comfortable?" She led him over to a brocade sofa, then sat down in a deep rose chair across from him. "Shall I ring for tea?"

"No, thank you. What I have to say won't take long."

"All right then, Captain, what is it you wish to discuss about Vermillion?"

"As you're well aware, tomorrow night is her birthday ball."

"That is correct."

"It is commonly known that sometime during the course of the evening she is supposed to choose a protector."

"Yes . . ."

"There is a chance she will choose no one at all."

Gabriella sat forward in her chair. "She has told you this?"

"We became . . . friends, during my tenure as a groom. She sometimes confides in me."

"I thought she might be having some doubts. Elizabeth and I discussed this very possibility. I had hoped, if she were unsure, she would come to me so that we might discuss it. I assumed whatever uncertainties she had must have been resolved."

"There is, of course, the other possibility—that Vermillion will decide to keep her pledge." His shoulders felt tight. He shifted a little on the sofa. "If that happens, I want to be the man she chooses."

Gabriella laughed. "Captain Tanner. Any number

of men find my niece attractive. Whether she will choose you to become her lover—"

"I am already her lover."

Surprise registered on Gabriella's face.

"The problem is eventually I'll be leaving London and returning to Spain. Our time together could be brief. Still, I believe she cares for me and that it would be in her best interest—should she decide on the latter course—for the man she chooses to be me."

Gabriella studied him closely. "You are telling me that you have made love to my niece?"

Caleb cleared his throat. "On more than one occasion. If my circumstances were different, I would be offering marriage instead of merely an arrangement." It was true, though he had never let the thought completely surface until now.

"Marriage?" The smile returned to Gabriella's face. "I assure you, Captain Tanner, my niece has no interest in becoming a wife—not yours or anyone else's. She never has. However . . . she must feel a great deal of affection for you if the two of you have become lovers."

Caleb sat forward in his chair. "Then you'll speak to her in my regard?"

"Vermillion has a mind of her own, Captain. I have taught her to use it. I'm not certain I should interfere."

"If you're concerned about money, I assure you I have more than enough. If, as you say, your niece has no wish to become a wife, then I make this pledge to you—I shall make it my personal duty to teach her all she needs to know to become the woman you wish her to be—the woman she has been pretending to be."

Gabriella's interest stirred. Pretty blue eyes moved slowly down his body, measuring his height and the breadth of his shoulders. "A tantalizing prospect, Captain Tanner. She'll want to take some of her horses. The others have agreed to that."

"That won't be a problem."

"All right. Considering the affection my niece apparently carries for you, I will do what I can to convince her that you are the man who should become her protector."

He relaxed a little. "Thank you, Gabriella."

"I warn you, Captain, it may not do any good. As I said, my niece has a mind of her own."

The edge of his mouth curved up. "Believe me, I know that better than anyone."

Gabriella could scarcely contain her glee. At last! For years she had been waiting for the day her niece would become a woman, when Vermillion would finally discover the incredible pleasure of making love with a man. And what a man her niece had chosen! Dear Lord, she couldn't have picked a finer male specimen if she had selected the man herself.

As soon as she could break away from the group playing cards in the gaming room, Gabriella sent word to Vermillion she wished to see her in the Rose Salon. She rang for tea and a few minutes after it arrived, the butler appeared with her niece in tow.

"Is everything all right?" Vermillion asked. "Mr. Jones said you wished to see me."

"Yes, darling. Do come in." Her niece looked

pretty today in a simple apricot muslin gown. For herself, Gabriella preferred more vibrant colors, but lately Vermillion appeared more inclined to the softer hues and in a way they seemed to suit her. "Sit down, dear, and have a cup of tea."

Vermillion took a seat in a rose velvet chair across from her and smoothed out her muslin skirt.

"I know you have a great deal to do before tomorrow night," Gabriella said, "so I won't waste much time. You have vowed to choose a protector the night of your birthday ball. Have you decided which of your suitors you will choose?"

Vermillion glanced away. "Actually . . . I've been wanting to talk to you about that, Aunt Gabby." She swallowed. "I was thinking that perhaps . . . I thought that I might not . . . that I wouldn't choose anyone at all."

"Really?" Gabriella carefully poured tea for both of them and handed her niece a gold-rimmed porcelain cup and saucer. "And what of Captain Tanner?"

Vermillion's teacup rattled in its saucer. "Captain Tanner? What about him?"

"The captain believes—since the two of you have already become lovers—that it would be in your best interest if you allowed him to become your protector."

Color washed into Vermillion's cheeks. The cup rattled again as she rested it in her lap. "H-he said that? Captain Tanner told you we were lovers?"

Gabriella waved away her niece's concern. "Don't be angry, darling. I couldn't be more thrilled. The man is obviously enamored of you. He knows that in time he'll be forced to return to Spain, but in the meantime he wishes nothing so much as for the two of you to be together."

Vermillion sat back in her chair, the tea in her cup untouched. "What else did the captain say?"

"For his part in the arrangement, he has pledged to do his best to initiate you into the world of pleasure."

Vermillion's eyes widened. "That is what he said?"

She nodded. "Unless you are dissatisfied with his performance so far, I would say it presents a great opportunity. And afterward, once the affair is over, you can take your time, decide then what it is you wish to do."

Vermillion shook her head. "I can't believe this. I can't believe he would tell you something like that."

"But darling, don't you see? He came to me for help. He wants to be certain he is the man you choose and not someone else. Surely it would break his heart if you did."

"Break his heart? I'd like to break his neck!"

"Darling, please. I wouldn't have told you if I thought you would be angry. I thought it was important you understood how highly you are held in the captain's regard and the length he has gone to in order to win your affections."

The color remained high in Vermillion's cheeks and her smile looked forced. "I'll keep that in mind."

Gabriella tried to think of something to say that would smooth the frown from her niece's forehead. "That is all I ask, darling. If you truly care for Captain Tanner, you should take advantage of his offer and enjoy your time together."

Vermillion merely nodded.

Gabriella thought her shoulders looked a little stiff, but perhaps it was only her imagination.

"Thank you for telling me, Aunt Gabby." Vermillion set the untouched cup and saucer down on the table in front of her.

"As I said, I thought you should know."

"Yes, well, now I know." Rising from the sofa, she made her way across the room and out the door.

Gabriella watched Vermillion leave, her spine unnaturally straight, and hoped she had done the right thing.

18

Vermillion's nineteenth birthday ball was a long-awaited event, a costume ball, a gala affair in the world of the demimonde. Though it was well known among the men that tonight she would choose a protector, there would be no formal announcement, nothing quite so tawdry as that.

Instead, when the birthday waltz was played, whichever gentleman she chose to partner her in the dance would become her lover.

Unless she decided to choose no man at all.

Which was exactly what Vermillion planned to do.

Last night and all of today, she had been so furious with Caleb she had purposely avoided him. She couldn't trust her temper not to spin out of control if she saw him.

Damn and blast the man! How dare he involve Aunt Gabby in so personal a matter!

In truth, it was amazing he had done so, extremely out of character for Caleb, who seemed in most ways a very private man. Did he really believe her aunt could convince her to become his mistress? And when had he become so determined? Once the head of the spy ring was caught he would be leaving. Whatever time they had together would indeed be brief.

Her stomach knotted at the prospect. She didn't like to think of Caleb going away, of never seeing him again. She didn't like to think of him fighting the French, being injured or maybe even killed. Instead, she summoned her anger and pushed those thoughts away. Ignoring a lingering thread of worry, she rang for Jeannie to help her dress for the evening ahead.

The task was lengthy. Being a costume ball, she would be gowned as Aphrodite, the goddess of love, beauty, and sensual rapture. The costume her aunt had commissioned for the affair was made of white satin and fashioned in the Grecian mode, baring one shoulder, clinging to her curves, and draping across her bosom. The sides of the gown were split, and when she walked, her legs were exposed well past the knee.

The entire effect was heightened by the Grecian designs embroidered in gold across the bodice and around the hem, the thin gold sandals that encased her bare feet, and the bands of gold encircling her upper arms.

As soon as she was dressed, she sat down in front of the mirror and Jeannie coiffed her hair, clipping it up on the sides with mother-of-pearl seashell combs while leaving the rest loose down her back in fiery red curls. As she watched Jeannie work, she tried to stay angry at Caleb, but her temper had cooled considerably and most of her fury had seeped away.

In truth, chances were good if he had known her decision—not to pick Mondale or Nash or any other man—he wouldn't have gone to her aunt.

Why had he? Did he really want her so badly? And if he did . . . ? If he did, what exactly did that mean?

Surely Caleb couldn't be in love with her.

She shook her head. It was impossible. Ridiculous. He was the son of an earl. His interest was only in the physical side of the attraction they shared. It wasn't love. It couldn't be.

But what if it were?

The question nagged her, wouldn't get out of her head.

As Jeannie fastened the buttons on her white satin gown, she told herself she was being a fool, a complete and utter harebrain, but the niggling thought remained.

Jeannie dabbed a little more rouge on her cheeks, urged her up from the stool, then made a sweeping assessment of her handiwork. " 'ow lovely you look, *chérie. Magnifique!*" Jeannie motioned for her to turn in front of the tall cheval glass and she made a slow pirouette.

Vermillion thought she looked exotic, that she looked sensual and seductive. That she looked like Vermillion and nothing at all like Lee.

And so this night, for perhaps the last time in her life, that was exactly who she would be.

She reached over and caught her maid's hand, gave it a gentle squeeze. "Thank you, Jeannie. You've been a very dear friend."

The older woman smiled. "You will choose the captain, no?"

Vermillion shook her head. "No, Jeannie."

"But why not? *Nom de Dieu*, surely now that you know 'e is not a servant, that 'e is—"

"I'm not choosing Captain Tanner or anyone else.

I'm going to lead a life of my own." Vermillion turned away before Jeannie could argue and started for the door.

The guests had all arrived. Everyone would be waiting downstairs. It was time to make her entrance.

The ballroom was in a separate wing of the mansion, a huge, high-ceilinged chamber illuminated by crystal chandeliers. As the guests walked in, each cut glass prism sparkled and danced, the colors multiplied a thousand times in the mirrors that lined the walls. Tonight the room had been decorated to resemble the sea from which Aphrodite rose the day she was created. Murals had been painted depicting the ocean, with white clouds above a rocky shoreline dotted with white-winged gulls. In the corner where the orchestra played, sand had been brought in to resemble a beach.

Pausing at the entrance to the ballroom, Vermillion pulled a white-feathered mask down over her eyes, then started through the door. Just inside, Oliver Wingate, costumed as a too-tall version of Admiral Nelson, offered her his arm.

"Good evening, my dear." His eyes moved over her seductive satin gown. "There are not words to describe your beauty, Vermillion."

"Thank you, Colonel."

Lord Andrew Mondale, extravagantly costumed as a sixteenth-century courtier in a doublet of deep orange velvet trimmed with ermine, doffed his matching ermine-trimmed hat. "Happy birthday, my beauty."

"Thank you, Andrew. You are looking quite dashing, as always."

He beamed with pleasure and settled his hat back on his head, hiding the gleam of his golden curls.

Jonathan Parker, Viscount Nash, was the third of her suitors to appear. It was obvious the men had been waiting.

"Ah, yes, Aphrodite. Quite appropriate, I would say." Wearing the tunic, jackboots, and the hat of a musketeer, Jonathan bent and kissed her hand. "Before the night is over, I hope to worship at your altar of love."

It was a rather un-Nash-like remark and she couldn't help a smile. "Why don't we join the others?" she said evasively, then, once they were immersed in the milling throng, excused herself to go in search of her aunt.

As she crossed the ballroom, making her way through the crowd, she tried not to search for Caleb. She didn't see him, but perhaps she wouldn't recognize him if he were there. He could be one of the several court jesters she passed or perhaps a Roman soldier. She recognized Sir Peter Peasley, costumed as Henry III, and beside him, Lisette Moreau in a tall silver wig, playing the role of Madame de Pompadour. Juliette Beauvoir was there, flirting outrageously with the actor, Michael Cutberth, but there was no sign of Caleb.

Vermillion continued toward the dais where Aunt Gabby stood next to Lord Claymont—a handsome Mark Antony and a beautiful, silver-blond Cleopatra.

Gabriella smiled, the golden serpents on her gown glittering as she moved. "We've been waiting for you, darling. Now that you're here, the party can truly begin." But of course it was already in full swing.

Vermillion thought of the long hours ahead, the boring conversation, the leering glances, the gossip she cared nothing about.

Steeling herself, she pasted on her practiced smile and accepted a dance with a skinny man she knew to be Lord Derry wearing a black hood and carrying an ax.

Caleb stood away from the crush of guests along a far wall of the ballroom. He wasn't wearing a costume, just his scarlet and navy uniform and tall black dress boots. His only concession to the masquerade ball was the scarlet satin domino that covered the top half of his face.

He surveyed the crowded dance floor, his gaze taking in the wild array of colors and fabrics, the plumed hats and rich satins and velvets. In the corner of the room, he spotted Vermillion, in conversation with her aunt and Lord Claymont. She looked beautiful tonight. There was no denying it. Every bit the goddess she portrayed. She was a sensual, stirring creature, the epitome of every man's fantasy, sophisticated and completely untouchable.

Only Caleb knew the sweet young woman she was underneath her façade. The innocent young girl he had made love to that first night in the stable. His loins clenched at the thought, began to fill, and silently he cursed.

Caleb watched her dance, first with a slight man in a black hood and then with Andrew Mondale, and cursed again, more savagely this time. For a man used to waging campaigns, his strategy in dealing with Vermillion had been a complete and utter failure.

He had made a tactical error in seeking her aunt's assistance and Lee refused to forgive him. For the last two days, she had avoided him. God only knew what she would do when she saw him tonight.

Caleb sighed as he watched her dance. He shouldn't have gone to her aunt. He knew that now, but at the time he hadn't been thinking too clearly. He had wanted her, been afraid he was going to lose her.

He should have known Lee would rebel, do exactly the opposite of what he wanted her to do.

Dammit to bloody hell.

The dance ended and Mondale returned her to her circle of friends. Oliver Wingate was among them. She looked up at him and laughed at something the colonel said. It was all Caleb could do not to storm across the room and drag her away from the man, haul her out of the ballroom, out of the house and off someplace private where he could make love to her until neither of them could move.

Instead, he stood there watching, wondering what she planned to do, feeling sick inside. He prayed that when the time came she would simply cry off, refuse to choose any man at all. She had said that she might . . . that she was giving the matter serious consideration.

One thing he was fairly sure of—if she decided to choose a protector, the very last man she would pick would be Captain Caleb Tanner.

The evening dragged on. Gabriella had let it be known that when the orchestra struck up the birthday waltz, whichever man Vermillion chose to partner would be the man who would become her protector. Aunt Gabby had also said that if Vermillion danced with Lord Claymont, it would signify she had decided against any of the men in the room.

As the dancing wore on, a fine tension settled in Vermillion's shoulders. The golden sandals hurt her feet and the shimmering threads in the embroidery chafed her skin. She wanted nothing so much as to retreat upstairs to her bedchamber and simply go to sleep.

Instead, she heard her aunt's joyful laughter and saw her smile, remembered how long Aunt Gabby had been planning this affair and how much it meant to her, ignored her aching feet and chafed skin and kept on smiling.

Another hour passed. Her face felt stiff, her lips brittle, as if they might crack at any moment. She had finally caught sight of Caleb and purposely ignored him, which only served to make the long night even more miserable.

At last the hour came. Midnight. Time for the birthday waltz. She spotted Lord Claymont and smiled, knowing he would be pleased with her decision. From the time they had met, the earl had wanted a different sort of life for her, had, on more than one occasion, tried to convince Gabriella that he could make some sort of match for her, the son of a village squire, perhaps, or a young man in need of a wealthy bride's dowry.

Gabby wouldn't hear of it, of course. Marriage was the dreariest future she could imagine.

For the most part, Vermillion agreed.

"Darling, are you ready?" Gabriella smiled and Vermillion's stomach knotted.

"As ready as I shall ever be," she said, the smile still stuck on her face.

"Come up to the dais, darling. Lord Claymont would like to propose a toast."

With more dread than she should have been feeling, uncertain what her suitors would do when they discovered she intended to break her vow, she nodded and stepped up in front of the orchestra.

The music stopped and people clustered around the dais. Lord Claymont clinked a silver spoon against his crystal champagne goblet and the room fell silent.

"I should like to propose a toast," he said with a smile. "To Miss Vermillion Durant on this, the night of her nineteenth birthday." He turned to her, held up his glass. "To you, my dear. All happiness in whatever course in life you choose to take."

"Hear! hear!" said Colonel Wingate, lifting his glass. Mondale chimed in and all of the guests lifted their glasses and took a drink. Several more toasts were made, then the strains of a waltz began.

Vermillion looked down at the men clustered around the dais, some she barely knew, and Andrew, Jonathan, and Oliver, the three with whom she was most familiar. Lucas Tanner stood a little ways away, eyeing her with considerable interest. She wondered what his brother had told him about her.

Her eyes swung in Caleb's direction.

He stood behind the others, the epaulets on his scarlet jacket glittering, taller than most of the men in the room, his posture perfectly erect. It was then she noticed that his shoulders were stiff with tension, his jaw set and looking as hard as granite. Though a scarlet domino covered much of his face, she could see his eyes, so dark a brown they looked like onyx.

There was something in them, she saw, something that compelled her to look deeper, past the reserve he wore tonight, all the way into his heart.

A faint tremor ran through her at the image that rushed into her mind.

It wasn't possible.

He couldn't care that much.

Not the way she did, not with a deep, yawning ache that never left her, a pain so deep that suddenly she knew exactly what she had to do.

She knew the choice she would make, knew that she would give up her precious independence. Knew that she would choose Caleb. And if their brief time together was all she ever had of him, it would be worth it.

She stepped down from the dais, reeling a little with the enormity of what she meant to do. She stumbled a bit and swayed toward Andrew, who steadied her with a hand at her waist. He smiled, thinking as everyone did that she meant to choose him. Instead, her gaze swept past him, fixed on Caleb. She saw the anguish in his face even the mask could not hide.

"Excuse me, Andrew," she said, politely easing away from him. For an instant, she caught a flash of anger as he realized he wasn't the man she would choose, but she kept on walking. A few feet away, Wingate was frowning, his jaw iron-hard. Beneath the folds of white satin, her legs were shaking. Her mouth felt so dry she couldn't have said another word if her life depended upon it.

She didn't have to. When she reached the place where Caleb stood, she simply reached out to him.

For an instant he didn't move and she thought that she had been wrong, that he didn't really want her as she had believed.

Then he stepped forward. One moment she was looking into his face and the next she was in his arms. She closed her eyes and felt a sweep of love for him so strong a lump swelled in her throat. The music swirled around them, urging them to dance, but Caleb simply held her and Lee clung to his neck. She knew people were staring, but she didn't care.

The orchestra began the waltz again. Caleb took a deep, shuddering breath and his mouth curved up in the softest, most endearing smile she had ever seen. Taking her hand, he led her out on the dance floor and swept her into the steps of the dance.

Other guests moved onto the floor beside them, falling into the rhythm of the waltz, the colorful congregation laughing, dancing with abandon as they whirled around the ballroom.

"I thought perhaps you would decide not to choose," Caleb said, his eyes locked on her face. "Or if you did, I would be the last man you would pick."

"So did I."

"Why did you change your mind?"

Because I love you. I love you so much. "You looked lonely. I thought you might need some company."

Caleb drew her closer. "I do," he said gruffly.

She smiled as he led her into a turn, but it felt a little sad. Caleb's *I do* was as close as she would ever come to a wedding vow. It had never mattered before.

It didn't now, she told herself firmly.

The waltz was coming to an end. "Let's get out of here," Caleb said softly. "We'll leave for London tonight."

She needed to pack. It was late and the roads would be dark. She didn't care. "Let me change into my riding clothes and throw a few things into a satchel. I'll bid farewell to my aunt and Lord Claymont, then we can leave."

"I'll have the horses saddled and brought round to the front." They left the dance floor, slipping away from the others, disappearing quietly out of sight. Lee said a brief farewell to her aunt, thanking her for the party and receiving a hug from Lord Claymont, then she left the ballroom and hurried upstairs.

She was leaving Parklands. She would have Jeannie pack the rest of her things and bring them to London once she was settled in. She wondered if she would ever return to the house she had been raised in, but she didn't think so. She was starting a new life, and though tonight hadn't gone exactly the way she had planned, it didn't matter.

She would be with Caleb.

She loved him.

She would stay with him until he went away.

Caleb sent a footman to rouse one of the grooms with instructions to saddle their horses, then waited at the bottom of the stairs for Lee's return. He couldn't stop smiling. He still couldn't believe his good fortune. Lee belonged to him. Until he returned to Spain, she would be his.

The smile slid away and a weight seemed to settle on his chest. He would be returning to duty and when he did, he would have to leave Lee behind.

A movement in the entry drew his attention to the familiar figure strolling toward him.

"Well, little brother, it would seem you are the man of the hour." Luc stopped in front of him, jauntily dressed in a full-sleeved shirt and tight leather breeches, a saber at his waist and an eye patch over one eye. The clothes of a pirate. Appropriate, Caleb thought, considering how many hearts Luc had managed to plunder.

"The man of the hour? I suppose you could say that."

"I assume the lady is your first official mistress. Congratulations on an excellent choice."

Caleb frowned. He had never thought of Lee that way and he didn't want to now. "I believe the lady chose me."

"Yes . . . so it would seem." Luc flicked a glance up the stairs. "I realize you are enamored of the girl, Caleb. I know you were her first and all of that, but the fact remains, you are the son of an earl and the girl is a Durant. Nothing is going to change that."

Caleb straightened. "If it's any of your business—which it is not—her social standing matters not in the least to me. However, the hard fact is, I'm an officer in His Majesty's Army. The war is far from over and I'll be returning to action very soon. When I do, my time with Lee will be over."

"Lee?"

Caleb made no reply. Luc didn't know her the way he did. He wouldn't understand that beneath her façade, Vermillion was simply Lee. He wouldn't understand that it was Lee that Caleb had wanted all along. That if there was any way to see it done, he would make certain that even after he was gone, Lee would be able to remain the woman she was inside, not the seductive creature everyone wanted her to be.

"All I'm saying is not to get too involved. You can't have her, Caleb, not permanently. You know it and so do I. Enjoy the time you have together, then let her go."

Caleb smiled thinly. "I appreciate your concern, Luc, but I'm not a little boy anymore. I haven't been for a number of years. My life is my own. I thought by now you understood that."

His brother looked a little surprised. As the eldest Tanner son, he had always watched out for his three younger siblings. But they were all grown men now. It was time Luc realized his job was over.

Luc smiled, the dimple appearing in his cheek. "You're right, Caleb. I suppose I should have figured that out a long time ago. I can't say I won't worry about you the way I always have, but from now on I'll try to keep my opinions to myself. Shall I tell Father he can look forward to a visit?"

Caleb nodded, relieved that Luc had let the subject of Vermillion drop. "As soon as I can get away I'll make a trip to Selhurst."

Luc clapped him on the shoulder. "Let me know when you plan to leave and I'll go with you."

"I'd like that," Caleb said, meaning it. He didn't get to see enough of his family anymore. It was something he missed. He would always regret not being able to have a family of his own, but his choice had been made long ago. The closest he could come was sharing a brief time with Lee.

Just thinking about it made him hard and he began to fidget as he resumed his vigil, waiting for the woman who would soon descend the stairs. His mind filled with exotic images of what he meant to do to her, once they reached London, of peeling her out of her clothes, tasting those luscious breasts, spreading her shapely legs, and—

Caleb forced the image away before his breeches got any more uncomfortable than they were already, but he smiled as he saw her at the top of the stairs. God, he couldn't wait to reach the city.

*   *   *

The party continued until well into the night. Elizabeth Sorenson, gowned as a medieval maiden in a long green velvet gown and golden girdle, a jeweled circlet over her short black hair, wandered into the garden. She was getting tired. She would have left the affair long ago if it hadn't been for the sandy-haired man in the black domino and black satin cape who had been watching her all evening.

Her husband, Charles Sorenson, Earl of Rotham.

"You look beautiful tonight, Beth." She started at his approach, surprised at his appearance in the garden at the very moment she had been thinking about him.

"Thank you, my lord."

"I would rather you called me Charles. You don't do it often enough anymore and I've always liked the way you say it."

She flushed. She couldn't remember the younger Charles she had known ever having been quite so gallant. "It was getting warm inside. I needed a little fresh air."

"The hour grows late. Perhaps it's time you went home. I would be happy to see you safely there."

She turned and looked up at him. She couldn't think of anything she would like more and anything she wanted less. "You don't have to bother. I came by myself. I can certainly return that same way. You needn't concern yourself."

"Don't I? I told you, Beth, I want another chance. I won't get that chance unless you find time for me. Unless you come to know me, to realize how much I've changed. Unless you can find it in your heart to trust me as you did once before."

Her defenses went up. He made it sound so easy when it wasn't easy at all. "Why should I trust you, Charles? How many mistresses have you had since the day we wed? How many women have you invited into your bed?"

"Too many, Beth. Too many faceless women who meant nothing at all to me." He reached out and gripped her shoulders. "But not lately, not for more than two years. Even before that, there was no one I wanted. Only you, Beth. Only you."

Her throat ached. She knew how good he was at seduction. He had seduced any number of females over the years. She couldn't listen to his honeyed words. She had to get away from him before he succeeded in convincing her to believe him and destroyed her yet again.

"You weren't the only one, Charles," she taunted as a means of self-defense. "I had affairs, as well. Men I made love to, men who wanted me the way you wanted other women."

He stiffened as she knew he would. Now he would go. The threat would be over. Dear God, why did it have to hurt so much?

"I don't care what you did in the past, Beth. I care only what happens in the future." He moved toward her, reached out and pulled her into his arms. "I don't believe there is anyone else. Not now. Not for a very long time. Let me make love to you, Beth. Let me be the husband I should have been from the start." And then he bent his head and kissed her.

She had expected an assault, not the feather-soft brush of his lips and yet that simple touch reached inside her, whispered over her very soul. Charles deepened the kiss and for an instant she kissed him back, kissed him as she had yearned to do a thousand times in the last ten years.

His arms came around her and his kiss turned fierce, but there was tenderness, too. A deep yearning welled inside her. She could feel his hardness, knew he was wildly aroused. He wanted her. And dear God, she wanted him.

But she wasn't the naïve young girl he had married and she knew what would happen if she let him into her heart again.

Elizabeth forced herself to pull away. Breathing raggedly, she turned and fled the garden.

19

❦

The night was still and quiet but a bright slash of moonlight shone down from above, guiding their way along the road to London. On his big black gelding, Solomon, Caleb rode beside her. They were halfway to the city before Lee thought to ask him where, exactly, they were going.

"There's a small hotel in Piccadilly. It's called the Purley. The accommodations are first cabin and it's known for its discretion." His black horse blew a breath into the cool evening air. "You will stay there until I can find you more suitable accommodations."

She didn't like the sound of that—the reminder she had agreed to become his kept woman. But a bargain had been struck. She would uphold her end of the arrangement.

"I usually stay in my father's town house whenever I'm in London," he continued. "Luc has a place of his own. Ethan is rarely in London and my father is mostly at Selhurst, so the house is generally empty. I'll find something nice not far from the house so it'll be easy to get there."

She was liking this less and less. "So you'll just stop by whenever you get the urge? Is that how it works?"

Caleb drew rein on the black. "Actually, that's exactly how it works. Look, Lee, this was your idea, remember? You didn't have to agree to any of this. You could have made a different decision."

Her chin went up. "Maybe I should have."

Caleb's jaw hardened. His gloved hands tightened on the reins. "And maybe I ought to drag you down from that horse and show you exactly why you didn't." He was scowling, looking like he meant every word.

The thought of Caleb hauling her down, shoving up her riding skirt, and making love to her in the middle of the road left her slightly breathless. Setting her heels to the sides of her horse, she started forward before she goaded him into actually going through with it.

"I made a choice," she said to him over her shoulder. "I don't plan to go back on my word."

Caleb made no comment. He knew how independent she was. He must have realized how difficult it was for her to put herself completely in a man's hands for the first time in her life.

It was nearly dawn by the time they reached London and Caleb procured a suite of rooms for her as Mrs. Durant at the Hotel Purley in Wilton Street.

Lee found the entire scene oddly depressing. Perhaps her dark mood was the reason Caleb accompanied her up to the suite but decided not to stay, simply promised to return later that afternoon, after she'd had time to settle in and catch a few precious hours of sleep.

Staring down at the street below the window, Lee watched him mount the black and ride off down the lane, her emotions in turmoil. Part of her wanted to call him back, to seduce him into making love to her. Another part was glad he was leaving. She needed time to collect herself, to think about the decision she had made and what it meant for her future.

For a while she padded around the suite, trailing her fingers over the rosewood furniture, examining a small silver box on the hearth, sitting for a while on the dark green velvet sofa. The bedchamber was large and airy, with a four-poster bed enclosed by elegant sea-green bed hangings that matched the draperies at the window.

Changing out of her riding habit into a night rail, she climbed into bed, but as tired and depressed as she was, she still couldn't fall asleep. Instead, she tossed and turned, finally gave up and returned to the sitting room. Thinking of Caleb's upcoming visit that afternoon cheered her a little—until she received a note telling her he had been summoned by his superiors to a meeting in Whitehall. He hoped, the note said, to see her that evening but he wasn't certain when.

For the first time, Lee began to understand the true nature of being a mistress.

More depressed than ever, she returned to bed late in the afternoon. She fell asleep thinking about Caleb and dreamed of him in bed with a sophisticated courtesan who looked remarkably like Vermillion.

"Congratulations, Captain Tanner. You and Major Sutton are to be commended on the excellent job you did in stopping the leak at Parklands."

"Thank you, Colonel." Caleb stood across the battered desk where his silver-haired superior sat working. "I only wish we had been able to prevent the death of Marie LeCroix and catch the man masterminding the ring. As long as he is free, the threat to England remains."

"I cannot disagree. However, that is no longer your concern."

"Colonel?"

"Your part in the investigation, Captain, has come to an end. You were chosen for the assignment because we needed a man who knew the business of horse racing. As a friend of your father's, General Wellesley was aware of your expertise. He was also acquainted with your very impressive service record. Which is why he has requested you remain under his command as a member of his specialist troops."

The colonel smiled. "The general has ordered me to extend your stay for two additional weeks so that you may visit your family. After that time you are ordered to return to Spain, where you will report directly to the general himself."

Two weeks. That was all the time he had with Lee. He should have been elated, overjoyed by Wellesley's continued interest, which practically insured future promotions and the chance for a brilliant career.

Instead, he felt sick to his stomach.

"Thank you, Colonel. That's extremely good news. However, I was wondering if it might be possible for me to remain in London until the investigation is concluded. As you know, my knowledge of the case is extensive. I feel I might be more valuable here than—"

"I'm sorry. I understand you may have come to feel personally involved in this, but orders are orders." The colonel came to his feet behind the desk. "Do not despair, Captain Tanner. Continue as you have been, and you will go far in this army."

Caleb forced himself to smile. "I hope so, sir."

"Enjoy your brief time off. Give my best to your father and at the end of your leave, report back here to me. I'll have transport arranged for your return to Spain and subsequent reunion with Wellesley. Till that time, you are dismissed, Captain Tanner."

Caleb made a smart salute, left the office, and returned to his father's Mayfair town house. He would be leaving London far sooner than he had expected. He had hoped to have more time with Lee, time to consider his options. Now he knew that wasn't going to happen.

As he stepped inside the imposing brick residence in Berkeley Square, crossed the entry and headed down the hall, the house felt cold and empty as it never had before. When he reached the study, he walked over to a sideboard and poured himself a drink. Carrying the brandy glass over to the desk, he sank into the deep leather chair, filled with an unexpected despair.

The question he had pondered all afternoon returned with relentless force. *What to do about Lee?*

Lee slept for a while, then spent the balance of the day wandering around the suite waiting for Caleb. The later it got, the more her irritation grew. She wasn't the sort to sit there doing nothing, at the beck and call of her lover.

Surely Aunt Gabby hadn't done that. Had she?

Surely Caleb didn't expect her to. Did he?

Then again, she wasn't sure what Caleb expected.

She was Vermillion Durant. It was Vermillion who had agreed to become his mistress. The notion bothered her more than it should have.

It was evening and still she hadn't heard from him. The longer she waited, the more her agitation swelled. By the time his second note arrived, telling her he wouldn't be there till nearly midnight, she was furious.

He wanted a mistress? Well, fine—she would give him one!

Storming into the bedchamber, she dragged out the satchel she had brought with her from Parklands. There wasn't much inside, but among the few items was the sheer, lavender silk nightgown her aunt had given her for her birthday. The sleeveless gown had a vee of lavender lace in front that ran clear to her navel. Lee rang for a chambermaid, who brought her scissors, thread, and a needle; cut out the lace; then cut off the ankle-length sweep of silk and hemmed it up. When she put it on, it exposed all but her nipples and barely covered the cheeks of her bottom.

Perfect.

She hadn't brought any face paint. The rice powder she could do without, but the kohl . . . In a moment of inspiration, she knelt in front of the hearth and swept a bit of coal dust into an empty glass. Carrying it over to the dresser, she sat down in front of the mirror and went to work, darkening the burnished color of her lashes, feathering the black dust carefully around her eyes. Though it made them look huge and blue-green, she still didn't look enough like Vermillion.

What to do . . . ?

A second inspiration struck. Tugging on the bell cord to ring for a servant, she ordered a bowl of fresh berries brought up from the kitchen. They were bright red and delicious, she discovered as she dipped them, one by one, into a little silver bowl of clotted cream and popped them into her mouth.

It was the juice she wanted and she found more than enough in the bottom of the bowl. As soon as she finished the fruit, she used the juice to darken her lips then watered it a little and used it to color her cheeks. Her bravado growing by the moment, she dabbed the last of the juice onto each of her nipples, rouging them as she knew a number of Cyprians often did.

Satisfied at last, she ran a brush through her hair, fanning the dark red curls out around her shoulders. Carefully surveying her handiwork, she grinned at the wild, seductive creature staring back at her in the mirror.

Caleb wanted a mistress. He was going to get one!

It was late, nearly midnight, before she heard the tread of his boots on the stairs. She was dressed and ready, pacing the floor in wait for him. At the light knock on the door, she took a steadying breath and pasted on her practiced smile. Turning the handle on the door, she jerked it open and invited him in.

He wasn't wearing his uniform, she saw, just a pair of fawn-colored breeches and a dark brown broadcloth tailcoat. His eyes briefly touched hers where she stood in the open doorway and for an instant he smiled. Then his gaze took in her kohl-darkened eyes, rouged lips and cheeks, and the smile disappeared.

Caleb frowned. "What the hell is this?"

Her lips curved even more. "Welcome home, darling. There's cold meat and cheese on the table beside the hearth. There's a nice claret to go with it, and brandy, of course. Why don't you sit down and relax? I'll fix you a plate and pour you a drink."

She turned to walk away, giving him a glimpse of her bottom. She hadn't got more than a couple of steps when Caleb caught her arm and spun her around to face him.

"Whatever game you're playing, you may end it right now. I don't think it is the least bit funny."

She battered her long, sooty lashes. "Why, darling, whatever do you mean? I am hardly playing a game. You are paying for this room, are you not? For the food we're about to eat, for the . . . entertainment afterward. I merely want to make certain you get your money's worth."

Caleb caught the tops of her arms and hauled her closer. "Stop it. Stop this right now." He shook her, not gently. "This whole thing was your idea, not mine. I never expected you to behave like a trollop. We both know you aren't one and you never have been."

Her smiled slipped a little. "But I will be, won't I, Caleb? After you're gone? And you did pledge to my aunt you would teach me all I need to know to continue in the role I will be playing."

His eyes darkened to nearly black. "I went to your aunt because I was hoping she might help me persuade you. I would have promised her anything in order to have you." The edge of his mouth barely curved. "But I have always been a man of my word. If it's a lesson you want, sweeting, I'll be more than happy to oblige."

Jerking her hard against him, Caleb kissed her. There was none of the gentleness, none of the care he'd shown her before. It was a fierce, demanding kiss, the kind a man claimed from the mistress he had bought and paid for.

And yet she felt the heat stirring to life inside her, burning between them, scorching like a fire in her blood.

She trembled, tried to draw away, but Caleb wouldn't have it. Instead he slid the gown off her shoulders, paused for an instant at the sight of her berry-stained nipples, then lowered his head and took the crest of one into his mouth. He laved the tip, suckled and tasted, then turned to her other breast and began to feast again. Each tug sent liquid fire pouring through her, drew damp heat into her core.

Her knees trembled. She tangled her fingers in his thick brown hair and fought to stay on her feet.

Caleb raised his head and the edges of his lips barely curved. "You want me to show you what a man expects from his mistress?"

She had pushed him too far. She could see it in the muscle flexing in his cheek, the hard set of his jaw. She had meant to goad him, but now he seemed like another man entirely and she was a little afraid.

She swallowed. "That is . . . that is what I am, is it not?"

Caleb didn't answer. Instead, he swept her up in his arms and strode into the bedchamber, tossed her down in the middle of the bed and began to unbutton his shirt.

He tugged it off and tossed it away, started on the buttons at the front of his breeches. "Come here."

A tremor of unease ran through her. "You're angry. Perhaps we should—"

"I said come here. Now."

She eased across the bed to where he stood with

his legs slightly splayed, his breeches unbuttoned and hanging open, riding low on his hips. "Turn around and get up on your hands and knees."

"Wh-what?"

"You heard me. Do it."

Her heart began to thunder. She did as he commanded, her hair swinging forward as she looked at him over her shoulder.

Caleb moved behind her. Reaching down, he slid the slick lavender silk up over her bottom and ran his hands over her hips. The anger was gone from his face and instead, she caught a glimpse of hunger. He didn't hurry, as she thought he would, just took his time, leaning down to kiss the back of her neck, biting an earlobe, pressing soft, moist kisses against her shoulders. All the while, his hands kept moving, tracing patterns, skimming over her flesh, sliding between the globes of her bottom. He slid his fingers inside and began to stroke her and her whole body infused with heat.

She was wet. Unbearably hot and wet. He stroked her until her hips arched, until she whimpered his name.

He moved closer. She could feel the heat of his bare skin, the strength of his arousal pressing against her bottom. Then he guided himself into her passage, gripped her hips, and thrust himself deeply inside.

She could feel the heat of him, the delicious fullness, and then he started to move. Long, determined strokes shook her, sent ripples of fire burning out through her skin. Deep, penetrating strokes sent waves of pleasure coursing through her. Gripping her hips, he held her immobile, pounding into her, impaling her as deeply as he could. Lee moaned at the sweet sensations sweeping through her, thick saturating waves that seeped out from her core and trembled over her flesh. Her body tightened around him and she heard him groan.

Caleb didn't slow until she reached release and even then he went on until she came again. Finally, he allowed his own climax to come, his big hands tightening around her hips, his body going rigid. Bare-chested, still wearing his breeches, he lay down on the bed and pulled her into his arms. As she curled against him, she could feel the rise and fall of his chest, the heat of his smooth, sun-darkened skin.

"You taste like berries," he said softly, his mouth just inches from her ear. "Even your nipples. God, Lee."

She started to smile. He had called her Lee, not Vermillion. *Lee.* The way he had before.

He turned onto his side, traced a finger along her cheek. "You don't have to be Vermillion, love. Not ever again. I never wanted Vermillion—I've told you that from the start. It's you I want, Lee. It's always been you."

Something burned behind her eyes and her lips trembled.

"You're here because you chose to be. You'll stay for that reason or not at all. You're no man's harlot and especially not mine."

She swallowed past the lump in her throat. "I'm sorry, Caleb. I've just . . . it's all been so confusing."

"It's all right, love. I'm a little confused myself."

He lifted a lock of her hair, toyed with it, smoothed it between his fingers. "Tomorrow we're going shopping. I want you to pick out a completely new wardrobe—the kind of dresses *you'd* like to wear, not something your aunt has convinced you to wear." He grinned as he looked down at the flimsy lavender gown that no longer even covered her breasts. "Though I can't fault your choice of night clothes."

She laughed. It felt incredibly good. And she couldn't find fault with the lesson she had received, since she had baited him into it. In truth, she could hardly wait for the next one.

"I think I should like that sort of shopping, but I insist on paying for what I purchase."

He cast her a look, started to argue, closed his mouth and sighed. "Fine, if it makes you happy, you can pay."

At the very least, it would help her maintain a little of her treasured independence. But the thing that most made her happy was Caleb. Dear Lord, she loved him a little more every day.

It was a terrifying thought.

He bent his head and nuzzled her shoulder, traced the star-shaped birthmark the sleeveless nightgown could not hide, bent and pressed his mouth to the spot. "I've seen a mark like this before. I've been trying to remember where it was."

Lee turned away, an uneasy feeling crawling into her stomach. She knew who carried a mark like this. Her mother had told her and so had her aunt.

"It'll come to me, sooner or later."

Lee hoped he never recalled, but even if he did, surely the mark he had seen had nothing to do with her.

"You must be tired," she said, changing the subject. "Why don't you finish undressing so you can get some sleep?"

His mouth curved roguishly. "I'm not tired,

woman—I'm hungry. I think I'd like a little dessert and I know exactly the thing." Bending his head to her breast, he whispered, "Some fresh berries would exactly suit my appetite."

It took Caleb three more days to remember where he had seen a birthmark the same shape as the one Lee carried on her shoulder. The dormitory at Oxford. The rusty-pink, star-shaped image rode in the exact same location on the shoulder, but the bearer of the mark hadn't been a woman. It had been a young student named Bronson Montague, eldest son of the Marquess of Kinleigh, who boarded in the room next to his.

Now that Caleb remembered seeing the mark on Bronson's shoulder, the memory continued to nag him. Could Lee be related to Montague in some way? Bronson was older, the same age as Caleb. He wondered if Lee knew anything about him.

It was the question foremost on his mind as he climbed the stairs to her suite at the Hotel Purley. He hadn't looked for any other place. He wouldn't be in London that much longer, though he still hadn't told Lee how soon he would be leaving.

He was acting as her lady's maid at present, enjoying the role more than he would have thought. He wanted her all to himself. He didn't want to spoil the brief time they had left together. Or perhaps he was simply trying to avoid the truth himself.

Whatever the reason, the days were slipping away, and Caleb was determined that when he left London, Lee Durant would be facing a better sort of life than she was living now.

Thinking about her brought a faint smile to his

face. Yesterday they had finished the last of their shopping, more fun than he had expected since Lee was so excited about everything she bought—an amazing assortment of gowns, walking dresses, morning dresses, riding habits, bonnets, gloves, mantuas, cloaks, pelisses, boots and slippers.

"I never liked shopping before," she told him. "It's different when you're buying things for yourself. Before I was buying clothes for Vermillion."

Something about the way she said the name gave his heart a little pang. It was clear she was Lee now, a new and different person, even more vibrant than the independent young woman he had first discovered in the stable. And even more enticing.

Last night they had gone to the opera and Lee had surprised him by translating the Italian lyrics for him.

"I've always loved opera," she said, a wistful look in her eyes. "Since the first time Aunt Gabby took me to see *Lucio Vero* when I was a little girl."

"Where did you learn to speak Italian?" he asked.

"My aunt believed in a thorough education. Aunt Gabby says it makes a woman more interesting to a man." She shrugged. "Whatever the reason, I am grateful. I also speak Latin, and of course I speak French."

Caleb smiled, no longer daunted by her ancestry. "My French is passable at best, but I'm fluent in Spanish. It's come in handy over the past few years."

The words brought a pall over the conversation and he wished he hadn't said them. He told himself it was time to tell her how soon he would be returning to duty, but she started smiling again and he decided to wait.

Today he was taking her to the house she often visited in Buford Street, to see Helen and Annie and the other women and children who had become her friends.

Earlier that morning, he had left to run a couple of errands. Sometime just before dawn, he had started thinking again about the traitor passing secrets to the French, and though he was officially off the assignment, a couple of things needed checking into.

Foremost among them, Lucas's recent discovery that Andrew Mondale was spending money as if suddenly he had buckets of it. Coupled with the fact the man had made mention to Lee of recent troop movements on the Continent, Caleb hoped it might turn into some sort of a lead.

He hadn't voiced his suspicions to Lee. He had told her he was off the case and had been granted a couple weeks of leave. He knew he should tell her that at the end of that leave he would be returning to Spain, and vowed that soon he would do so. In the meantime, he intended they should enjoy themselves, spend as much time together as he could manage.

Caleb knocked on her door and Lee pulled it open. He reached for her, swept her into his arms, and very soundly kissed her. "Did you miss me?"

She looked up at him and the smile in her eyes made his chest feel tight. "Miss you? You've only been gone a couple of hours—of course I missed you." She kissed him, drew him farther into the room.

"Guess what?" He didn't let her go, just closed the door with the toe of his boot. "I remembered where I saw a birthmark like the one on your shoulder."

She released her hold on his neck and eased away. "Oh?"

"It was a fellow I knew at Oxford. Bronson Montague. He's heir to the Marquess of Kinleigh."

"That's interesting."

There was something guarded in her manner that put him on alert. "You don't seem that surprised."

She shrugged her shoulders. "I don't imagine a birthmark is all that uncommon."

Caleb reached out and caught her chin, forcing her to look at him. "It is when it is exactly the same shape as yours and in the very same location."

She turned her face away, walked over to the mullioned windows, gazed down into the street. "Those things happen, I guess."

Caleb followed. In the street below the window, a young boy hawked newspapers on the corner. A donkey with a floppy felt hat over its ears pulled a cartload of coal over the cobbles.

Caleb rested his hand on her shoulder and gently turned her to face him. "You've never mentioned your father, Lee. I presumed you didn't know who he was. But you do know, don't you? You've known all along. Is your father the Marquess of Kinleigh?"

Beneath his hand, he felt her stiffen. "Don't be ridiculous."

"Don't lie to me, Lee. Not about something this important."

"Important?" Her eyes locked with his. "Why would it be important? It wasn't important when Kinleigh told my mother he was in love with her. When he asked her to marry him then got her with child. It wasn't important when he broke his promise and married someone else."

Caleb said nothing. He couldn't think of a single thing to say.

"You know why I've never been interested in marriage? Because I know how faithless men are. I know what happened to my mother. I know how the marquess treated her. Every day men just like him come to Parklands. They treat their wives little better than their livestock. Kinleigh is exactly the same. My mother died when I was four and she was still foolishly in love with him. The last word she spoke was his name."

Caleb wasn't certain what to say. Through his father and horse racing, he knew Robert Montague fairly well, had always respected him as a man of honor. He couldn't imagine the marquess seducing an innocent young girl, then abandoning her, but that was obviously what the marquess had done.

A sudden thought occurred. "Does Kinleigh know?"

"About me? I couldn't say." She nervously smoothed a lock of her hair. "I assume he does."

But maybe he didn't. Maybe he never knew his seduction had led to the birth of a child. Caleb couldn't help wondering what would happen if he found out. He gently drew Lee into his arms.

"I'm sorry about your mother. Sometimes things like that happen. But all men aren't that way. My father and mother loved each other very much. Father was devoted to Mother from the day they wed until the day she died. He misses her terribly now that she is gone. My brother Christian is madly in love with his wife. I don't believe he will ever be unfaithful."

Lee slid her arms around his neck and he tightened his hold. "Please, Caleb," she said softly. "I don't want to talk about this anymore."

Caleb eased her back enough to look into her face.

"All right. But I want you to know I am nothing at all like your father—or the men who come to Parklands. I want you to promise me you will tell me if a child should result from the time we've spent together."

She pulled away from him, returned to her vigil at the window. "That's right—you would accept your responsibilities. I haven't forgotten, Caleb."

"I would marry you, Lee." The words were out of his mouth before he could stop them. What surprised him was how much he meant them. His family would probably disown him. His brothers would think he was the worst sort of fool, but marrying Lee, raising a family with her, wouldn't be a hardship for him at all.

Her gaze swung to his face and he had never seen such turbulence in her expression. "You're a soldier, Caleb. War is what you do. You'd be gone most of the time. You wouldn't be much of a father."

She was right and both of them knew it. Not much of a father—or a husband. "Better than no father at all."

Lee made no reply. Perhaps she was thinking of Robert Montague, the father she had never known.

"The day is slipping away," she finally said. "If I'm going to have time to visit with my friends, I think we had better leave."

Caleb didn't argue. He needed time to evaluate the importance of what he'd just learned. But all the way to the house in Buford Street, a single thought continued to nag him. What would Kinleigh do if he knew about Lee?

20

In a velvet-draped bed in his mistress's extravagant suite at Parklands, the Earl of Claymont settled his head more deeply into the feather pillows. The room was a confection of pink and white, with ornate ivory and gilt furnishings, white and pink floral carpets, and pink velvet draperies.

Dylan had always felt ridiculously out of place in the overly feminine room. He wished instead they were comfortably ensconced in the big carved mahogany bed that had been in the master's suite at Claymont Hall for more than a hundred years.

Perhaps one day they would be, but he knew better than to pin his hopes on it.

"What are you thinking, darling?" Gabriella curled beside him, naked now, no longer wearing the sheer lace nightgown she had been wearing when she welcomed him into her bed. "You're a million miles away."

"What am I thinking?" He cocked a black, silver-touched eyebrow. "Aside from you and how much I enjoy making love to you? I was thinking of your niece ... wondering if she is happy with her decision." It was true. He had been thinking of Vermillion off and on since the night she had journeyed from Parklands.

"Why, of course she is happy. How could she not be? Captain Tanner is obviously infatuated with her. He is bound to treat her very well."

"I suppose he will ... as long as he is in London."

Gabriella rolled onto her side to face him, silvery blond hair spilling over a slender shoulder. "You don't think he'll be leaving anytime soon?"

"According to Oliver Wingate, Captain Tanner will be shipping out for Spain in less than two weeks."

"Oh, dear heavens."

"Wingate has made no secret of the matter and Lee's former suitors are all in a dither about it. You would think they would be discouraged, knowing she has obviously placed her affections somewhere else. Wingate is still furious, of course. Tanner is his subordinate, after all. As far as I'm concerned, the colonel is a pompous ass and I don't believe Vermillion ever seriously considered him."

"What about Lord Andrew? I've heard nothing of him since the ball."

"He was certainly in high dudgeon when he stormed out of the house that night—the lad is so bloody cocksure of himself. Now that he's had time to cool off a bit, I think he sees her as more of a challenge than ever. He'll be waiting at her door the instant Captain Tanner departs for Spain."

Gabriella scooted up against the ornate ivory headboard, propping herself against the pillows. "And Nash?"

"Jon isn't the sort of man to wear his emotions on his sleeve, but I'm certain he was very disappointed. Of all her admirers, Jon is the only one sincerely concerned with Lee's well-being." He cast Gabriella a glance. "He knew she was a virgin, you know."

Gabriella straightened. "What? He couldn't possibly have known."

"He knew because I told him."

"For heaven's sake, Dylan, why on earth would you do something like that?"

"Because I wanted her to be happy. I knew her innocence would appeal to Jon and that if she chose him he would treat her very well."

Instead of getting angry, Gabriella's expression softened. Leaning toward him, she brushed a light kiss over his lips. "You're a good man, Dylan Sommers."

"But you still won't marry me."

She only shook her head. In the light of the whale oil lamp next to the bed, her hair looked more silver than gold, and the pink of the draperies made her skin glow like roses. He couldn't remember a time he hadn't loved her. Before he had met her, he had loved her in his dreams.

"You know how I feel about marriage," she said. "Besides, it would hardly be fair to you. Your friends and family would spurn you. You would be banned from polite society."

"My true friends would be happy for me. As for Society . . . I'm an earl. You'd be amazed what a man of my wealth and position can do."

"We're happy, Dylan. If we married, things would change. We might lose the closeness we've shared all these years."

"Or we might grow even closer." But he knew she

wouldn't relent. He wasn't exactly sure why. She had never said she loved him and perhaps it was as simple as that. Or perhaps she was afraid, as she had said, of destroying the special bond between them. Either way, he wouldn't press her. He wouldn't do anything that might cause him to lose her.

"I hope Vermillion will be all right," Gabriella said fretfully. "Perhaps after the captain leaves, she should move back in here for a while."

"She's in love with Tanner, you know."

Gabriella rolled her pretty blue eyes. "Don't be ridiculous." He noticed fine lines in the corners, knew how much she feared getting older, though to him she remained as lovely as she was the first time he had seen her.

"I'm afraid it's true. As much as you might wish your niece were more like you, she is different."

"She's infatuated with him. I don't believe she is in love with him. And if she were, how would you possibly know?"

Dylan gave her a tender smile. "I know, my love, because Lee looks at Caleb the way I look at you."

The evening was dark, the cobbled street slick with mist. On the corner, the sign for Wilton Street creaked in the wind sweeping in off the Thames. Somewhere in the distance, Lee heard the clatter of carriage wheels. Inside her suite at the Purley, Caleb sprawled in the comfortable bed across the way, naked beneath the sheet and sleeping soundly.

Lee glanced at the mound formed by his big body and thought of the hours they had spent making love, the several times he had brought her to fulfillment. Caleb was a skillful, considerate, extremely passionate lover, the sort of man her aunt would have wanted her to choose. He was kind and caring, solicitous of her wishes, and wildly protective of her.

He would have been the perfect choice—if she just hadn't fallen in love with him.

Her heart twisted painfully at the thought. How much longer did they have? Weeks? Months? Whatever time it was, it wouldn't be enough. She was deeply in love with him. She had never thought it would happen, worked to guard her heart, but it had happened just the same. She was in love with Caleb Tanner and more than anything in the world, she wanted him to love her in return.

I would marry you, Lee.

For an instant when he had said the words, her heart had simply turned over. But marriage had nothing at all to do with love—she knew that far better than most—and Caleb had spoken out of duty, a sense of responsibility that was completely and utterly Caleb and had nothing at all to do with whatever he might feel for her.

She told herself not to think about it and most of the time she succeeded. But not tonight.

Lee returned to her vigil at the window, gazing down at the mist-slick streets, wishing there was a way to change the way she felt, wishing Caleb didn't have to leave, wishing any number of things that hadn't the remotest chance of coming true.

The notion weighed her down and a feeling of hopelessness settled over her. Tired for the first time that night, she started to turn away from the window and return to bed when a movement below caught her eye.

In the shadows at the side of the building next to

the hotel, she spotted the figure of a man. He was staring upward, toward the very place where she stood by the window, illuminated by the glow of a single burning candle.

Stepping back behind the curtain, she told herself she was mistaken, that the man was simply passing along the street and his presence had nothing to do with her, but an icy wariness trickled down her spine.

Lee blew out the candle. In the darkness, she inched nearer the window, looked down where the man had been standing, but there was no one there.

She should have been relieved that he was gone. She wasn't quite sure why she was not.

It was the afternoon of the following day that Lee returned to the house in Buford Street. Instructing the coachman to await her return, she waved a greeting to Helen Wilson, who stood on the front porch beside the open door. It was Lee's second visit to the house this week, but Helen's son, two-year-old Robbie, had come down with a pleurisy, an inflammation of the chest that kept him coughing all night, and Lee had returned to see if he had improved.

"I'm afraid he's the same," Helen said, her plump face lined with worry as she closed the door behind them. "He coughs and coughs. I'm just so worried about him."

"You mustn't fret, Helen. I stopped at the apothecary shop in Craven Street where my aunt usually trades. Mr. Dunworthy says there is some sort of illness going round. He says it is nothing to worry about. He sent some powdered mustard for a poultice along with these herbs." She handed Helen a small muslin bag. "It's a mixture of horehound, rue, and hyssop, combined with licorice and marshmallow roots. You're to place the herbs in a quart of water, boil it down to a pint, strain off the liquid, and give Robbie half a teaspoon of it every two hours."

Helen took the items with a grateful smile. "Thank you, Lee. It's hard when you're a mother. You worry about them constantly."

"I know it must be frightening whenever your child falls ill, but Mr. Dunworthy says he's seen a number of children lately with the same affliction and it doesn't last very long." She walked over to where the child lay sleeping beneath a soft woolen blanket on the sofa, his fat cheeks a little rosier than they should have been. "Is he running a fever, do you think?"

"I think he might be."

"Mr. Dunworthy says that's to be expected. He says the sickness seems to last about a week. Robbie should be better by then. Send word to me if he isn't and I'll get a physician to come round."

Helen took her hand. "You've a good heart, Lee. You always seem to be here when we need you. You'll never know how much your friendship has meant to me—to all of us." In a spontaneous moment, Helen leaned over and hugged her.

"You all mean a great deal to me as well."

Annie walked into the room just then. There were only four women now in the house and though it should have made things easier, Mary's presence was sorely missed.

" 'Ave ye any news of poor Mary? 'Ave they found the bloke what kilt 'er?"

"I'm sorry, Annie. There is nothing new to report. It seems there has been very little progress made in solving the crime. It's as if the man who killed her simply disappeared."

"We heard about that other woman who was killed," Helen said, "the other maid from Parklands... Miss LeCroix? Do you think their deaths were connected?" Marie's death had been reported as a small item in the London papers, but no link between the two murdered women was mentioned.

"I really don't know, Helen." That was the truth—she didn't know for sure, though she believed there was a very good chance there was. "All I can say is I hope they catch whoever is responsible."

"And 'ang the bloody bastard," Annie grumbled.

Lee made no comment since she staunchly agreed.

She didn't stay long, just made a last check of little Robbie and bid the ladies farewell. The women had sewing that needed to be done and Lee had other errands to run. As she made her way out to the carriage, she was thinking of the stop she needed to make at the dress shop for a final fitting of her new clothes when she spotted Andrew Mondale standing next to the rear wheel of the carriage.

"Lord Andrew—what a coincidence. Whatever are you doing here?" Mondale's snappy red high-perch phaeton, she saw, was parked directly behind the carriage that Caleb had provided for her use.

"I wanted to see you. I thought we needed to talk."

She frowned. "Then this isn't mere chance. How did you know where to find me, Andrew?" A memory returned of the man in the shadows. She thought of the late night vigil that Lord Andrew must have been keeping outside her bedchamber and her temper went up. "Have you been following me? Tell me you haven't been spying on me, Andrew."

Andrew sauntered toward her. Dressed more soberly than usual, in a dark blue tailcoat and silver waistcoat, he looked less foppish, older than the young man he often appeared.

"I told you I wanted to see you. I want to know what Tanner did to convince you to become his mistress." He stopped just in front of her. "You scarcely knew the man, Vermillion. Were you really so enthralled? Or was it something else? Money, perhaps? Jewelry? What was it, pet? What could Tanner give you that I could not?"

She lifted her chin, tried to think like Vermillion but it was getting harder and harder to do. "I chose Captain Tanner because he was interested in the woman I am inside and not some façade that my aunt created. Now, if you will excuse me . . ."

Heading toward the door of the carriage the coachman held open, she tried to brush past him, but Andrew caught her arm.

"Not so fast, my sweet. I won't be brushed off like a piece of lint on the hem of your skirt. I spent weeks courting you, Vermillion. We both know what you promised to deliver and sooner or later I intend to collect."

She didn't like the way he was looking at her, his mouth hard-set and his shoulders rigid. "I'm sorry if you were disappointed, Andrew, but you knew the game we were playing. Someone had to lose."

His mouth barely curved. "But the game goes on, doesn't it, pet—once Captain Tanner is gone." He reached out and touched a strand of her hair that had escaped from her bonnet, coiled it around his finger and tugged on the end. "This time I intend to be the winner."

Lee said nothing. For an instant, she was afraid of Andrew Mondale.

Then he smiled and let go of her hair. He swept her a bow, and his usual carefree demeanor returned. "Think of me, pet, when you are ready to play the game again."

And then he was gone.

More shaken than she should have been, Lee climbed into the carriage and leaned back against the seat. She thought of telling Caleb about the encounter but changed her mind.

Mondale was her concern, not Caleb's. And even if Lord Andrew became a problem, that wouldn't happen until Caleb had returned to Spain.

Nestled like a precious gem in the rolling green fields of Sussex, three stories high and constructed of creamy yellow Cotswold stone, the huge house dominated the landscape for miles around.

Kinleigh. Caleb hadn't been there in years, but he had never forgot the beauty of the home constructed by the Marquess's ancestors sometime during the seventeenth century. The entry was high, the ceiling vaulted and crisscrossed by heavy beams. The walls were paneled with different types of wood carved in idyllic country scenes and the windows near the top were fashioned of brightly colored stained glass.

As Caleb followed the stately, gray-haired butler across polished wooden floors inlaid in delicate patterns, down a wide corridor lit by gilded sconces to the room where the marquess would receive him, he thought of the man who owned the house, a longtime acquaintance of his father's, and wondered what he would say about the news Caleb had come to deliver.

The butler paused in the doorway to announce him. "Captain Tanner, my lord."

Caleb walked past him into an elegant drawing room done in black and gold. The butler backed out of the room, sliding the doors closed behind him. The marquess stood a few feet away, gray-haired and smiling, a kind man, Caleb had always thought him. But a kind man wouldn't have abandoned a young woman and her unborn child.

"Caleb, my boy! It's good to see you. How long has it been?"

"Nearly five years, I believe, my lord. I was here on the occasion of your son Bronson's twenty-third birthday."

"Yes, yes. I remember it well. Quite an evening, as I recall. I believe my son paid the price for that night for several days thereafter."

He chuckled, remembering Bronson's overindulgence that night. "How is he?"

"Fine. Beginning to think of marriage at last. I believe I have finally convinced him 'tis past time he wed and began to think of providing an heir."

"And Aaron? How does your younger son fare?"

Kinleigh sighed. "The boy is a handful. Spoiled rotten, just like most of his friends. But he fares well enough, I suppose."

Caleb digested this bit of news. If memory served, Aaron Montague was perhaps fifteen. Luc had once hinted at the younger boy's willful nature. Apparently it was true.

"Your father keeps me informed of your travels," the marquess continued. "It's unfortunate we don't see each other more often." Kinleigh walked toward an ornate black lacquer sideboard resting against a gold-flocked wall.

"According to Lucas, Father has been winning a number of races, which always makes him happy. Unfortunately, my assignment in London has kept me from paying him a call. I hope to journey to Selhurst the end of the week."

"Give him my regards, will you?"

"Yes, sir. I'd be more than happy to do that."

"Would you care for a drink? Brandy, perhaps or something else?"

"No, sir. Thank you."

"You won't mind if I have a glass, will you? Something tells me the reason for your visit isn't simply to renew an old acquaintance." The marquess poured himself a brandy, motioned Caleb over to the sofa, then sat down in a gold brocade chair across from him.

"All right, Captain Tanner, what can I do for you?"

Caleb shifted on the sofa. "I'm not exactly certain where to begin, your lordship. Let me start by saying I've discovered information you may find interesting. I can't be certain, however. There is every chance you already know, but I had to find out and so I am here."

Kinleigh took a sip of his brandy. "Go on."

"I realize you have two very healthy sons. The fact is, Lord Kinleigh, you also have a daughter."

The marquess straightened in his chair. "That is preposterous. Whoever told you that is lying. My late wife and I were together for more than ten years before she died. I never cheated on her. Not once. As to my more recent needs—"

"She is just turned nineteen, your lordship. Her mother was a woman named Angelique Durant. I believe the two of you were acquainted before your marriage to Lady Kinleigh."

The marquess's face went utterly pale. All the bravado seeped from his body and he sank more deeply into his chair.

"It can't be true. Angelique would have told me."

"From what I've learned, she discovered your betrothal to Lady Sarah Wickham, the woman you later wed. Angelique must have decided to keep her secret. She died when the little girl was four years old."

Kinleigh sat unmoving. A fine tremor shook the hand that held the brandy. "Perhaps the girl is mistaken. Perhaps her father is someone else."

"I don't think so, sir. She carries the same mark your son Bronson carries on his shoulder. I remembered seeing it when we were at Oxford together. When I pressed her about the mark, she admitted that you were her father. She told me the story of her mother and how much Angelique loved you."

Something flickered in the Marquess's eyes. He looked years older than he had when Caleb walked into the room. "If my Angel had a daughter . . . if what you are saying is true . . ." He shook his head. "Dear God, what have I done?"

His gaze fixed on the glass of brandy he gripped in his hand. He stared into the amber liquid as if it were a door leading into the past.

"I loved her so much. I knew about Angelique's mother, of course, Simone Durant. Everyone did. But Angel wasn't like that. She was sweet and gentle. She didn't want that sort of life. More than anything in the world, she wanted a husband and family."

"How did the two of you meet?" Caleb gently prodded.

"Simone owned a number of different estates. She was wealthy by then. One of her properties was a small manor house next to an estate my father owned in Kent. The Durant women spent time there in the summers. It was purely by chance that I met her daughter that day down by the stream."

His hand trembled and brandy sloshed up on the side of the glass. "Angelique Durant was the most beautiful creature I'd ever seen. Long red hair and the prettiest smile . . . this deep, warm sort of laughter. She had tied up her skirt that day and was wading barefoot in the water. I was enchanted. I fell in love with her the first moment I saw her." He glanced up and there were tears in his eyes. "And I will love her until the day I die."

Caleb looked away from the pain in the marquess's face.

Kinleigh's voice turned rough as he went on. "When my family found out I'd been seeing her, they were horrified. I was young but already a widower with a two-year-old son. The scandal would ruin the family, they said, ruin Bronson's life as well as my own. I didn't want to listen. I wanted Angelique. She was all I ever wanted. But I had Bronson's future to consider. In the end, I gave in to the pressure. I married Sarah—and regretted it the rest of my life."

The marquess looked up. "I never cheated on Sarah. The only woman I ever wanted was Angelique and I could not have her." The marquess struggled to collect himself and Caleb couldn't help feeling sorry for him.

"If you loved Angelique as you say," Caleb said gently, "there is something you can do to make amends. You can see to the future of your daughter."

Kinleigh stared off toward the window. "Tell me about her."

Lee's image appeared in his mind and Caleb felt the pull of a smile. "She is lovely, as you say her mother was, with the same fiery hair and sunny smile. She is independent in the extreme, with money of her own, and an education some men would envy. She plays the harp like an angel, she loves horse racing and manages her own small stable—and she rides like the wind." Once Caleb started talking, he couldn't seem to stop. "She never puts herself above anyone else. She thinks of her servants as friends and cares for a number of those less fortunate. Simply put, your daughter, sir, is quite unique."

The marquess watched him closely. "It's obvious you care for the girl. What is it you aren't telling me?"

Caleb's stomach knotted. This was the part of the story he dreaded. "She's a Durant, my lord. After her mother died, she was raised to follow in that tradition."

One of his silver eyebrows shot up. "Are you telling me my daughter is a courtesan?"

"No, sir." He cleared his throat. "The only man who has ever touched her . . . is me." Briefly he explained the mistake that had resulted in his daughter's loss of virtue. "If you want me to wed her, I will, but—"

"But? You tell me you have seduced my daughter and then seek excuses not to marry her?"

"My life is the army, sir. You know that as well as I do. And you also understand what that means. I'll be returning to duty in Spain in ten more days. The battlefield is hardly the place for a lady. I want your daughter to be happy. With me, I'm not certain she ever would be. Aside from that, I'm not the least bit certain she would agree. Vermillion doesn't much believe in marriage. I think you can understand why."

He flushed, color creeping into the gray at his temples. "Vermillion? That is my daughter's name?"

He nodded. "Yes, but she prefers to call herself Lee. That is her middle name. Vermillion Lee Durant."

The marquess's throat moved up and down. The moisture returned to his eyes and he stood up from his chair, walked over to the mullioned windows. "That is my name as well. Robert Leland Montague. Angelique always . . . she always called me Lee." His hands were shaking. He took a healthy swig of his brandy, then set the glass down on the mother-of-pearl inlaid top of a black lacquer table.

"If you will excuse me, Caleb. I need some time to adjust to this news you have brought."

"Of course, my lord. I'll be returning to London. You may reach me at my father's town house in Berkeley Square."

Kinleigh took a step toward him as if he wished to block his escape. "Is there . . . is there a chance you will stay to supper? I should like to hear more of this daughter of mine." He gazed off again, as if the past were right there in the room. "I always wanted a daughter. Aside from Angelique, it was my heart's greatest desire. If you would stay, perhaps we could arrange a time when it might be possible for me to meet the daughter I didn't know I had."

The pressure in Caleb's chest began to ease. "Yes, sir. I suddenly find myself inordinately hungry. I should be delighted to stay for supper."

The marquess simply nodded, his gaze sliding back to the window.

Caleb turned away and quietly left the drawing room, pretending not to notice the tears on the older man's cheeks.

21

You did what?" Standing in the sitting room of her hotel suite, wearing one of her new muslin gowns, Lee clamped her hands on her hips. "That is where you have been? You said you had an important meeting out of town that might keep you overnight. You never mentioned Kinleigh. You never said you were going to see *him!* You never said a word, Caleb. I can't believe you would do such a thing!"

"I told you I had an important meeting out of town and I did." He had known she would be angry, furious, in fact. Her eyes were bright and snapping, her cheeks as fiery as her hair. But there was no help for it. He'd had to do what he did. Now all he had to do was find a way to make her see reason. "He didn't know about you, Lee. Your mother never told him she was carrying his child."

"I don't blame her! The man is a blackguard. He is selfish and cruel and I hate him for what he did to her."

"And for what he did to you?" he asked softly,

knowing the pain she must have felt as a child, abandoned by her father, grieving for her mother. "Isn't that right, Lee?"

She spun away from him, walked over to the hearth, and turned her back to him. He could see a frantic pulse beating in the side of her neck.

Caleb walked up behind her, gently rested his hands on her shoulders. "I can only imagine what you must be feeling. My father and I never got along, not until after I went into the army. But he was always there if I needed him. I knew that. That kind of caring isn't something you've ever had, Lee."

She whirled to face him. "My aunt cared for me. She has always loved me. I don't need Kinleigh. I didn't need him when I was a child and I don't need him now!"

"Your aunt did the very best she could and I know she loves you very much. But you have a father, too. One who wants more than anything to know you, to somehow bridge the terrible years of loss you both have suffered."

"Tell him it's too late. I don't want to meet him."

"You're not the least bit curious? Not at all interested in knowing what your father might be like?"

"No." But she didn't look as certain as she had a few moments before.

"There's something I have to tell you, Lee. I know I should have said something sooner, but—"

"What? What else have you done, Caleb?"

"I got my orders, Lee."

"Orders? What kind of . . . ? Y-you don't mean . . . ?"

"I'm afraid so."

"But I-I thought you were staying in London until they found the traitor."

"I thought so, too, but Wellesley has ordered my return to Spain. I leave on Wednesday next. That's little more than a week."

Her throat moved up and down. "A week?"

"I tried to get them to extend the time but apparently the army believes I'm worth more to them there than I am here. I have to go, Lee. There's going to be fighting and I have to do my share. When I leave, I want to know there is someone here who will take care of you."

"I can take care of myself." But her face had gone pale and he thought he caught the faint reflection of tears.

"I know you can." But he hated the thought of her fending for herself as she had done before, of perhaps returning to Parklands, putting herself at the mercy of men like Andrew Mondale or Oliver Wingate. "I need you to do this for me, Lee. I need to know your future is secure."

She only shook her head.

He reached for her, prayed she wouldn't pull away, and eased her into his arms. "Just meet him. That's all I ask."

She looked up at him. "How can I meet him? What will he think of me? Sooner of later he is bound to find out who I am."

"You're not Vermillion, you're Lee. Your father knows the truth and he understands."

Her fingers curled over the lapels of his coat and she pressed her face into his chest. He could feel her trembling and his throat went tight. She meant so much to him. So much. He didn't dare tell her. It would only make things worse.

He kissed the top of her head. "Please, Lee."

She hung on to him a moment more, then dragged in a long, shaky breath and stepped away. "All right— I'll meet him. But I won't promise any more than that."

It was the news of his leaving that had convinced her. He could hear the sadness and defeat in her voice. His chest squeezed hard. He couldn't let her know he felt exactly the same. "Day after the morrow, then. We don't have much time."

She looked up at him and tears welled in her eyes. "No. We don't have much time."

Caleb made no reply. His throat ached and his heart hurt. He hadn't expected this, hadn't known he would feel this crushing despair when he left her.

He hadn't known until that very moment that he had fallen in love with her.

As lovely as Parklands was, it couldn't compare to the beauty and charm of Kinleigh. Creamy yellow stone gleamed like golden sheaves of wheat against the grassy knolls surrounding it. Tall mullioned windows glittered like diamonds in the late afternoon sunlight.

As the carriage approached the house, Lee counted dozens of chimney pots rising above the gabled slate roof. The front doors were tall and arched and they seemed to beckon her in. The Jacobean architecture was exquisite, the jewel-like setting almost too perfect to be real, though it was difficult to take in the details with her mind on what lay ahead.

Today she would be meeting her father.

Though she had never imagined it would happen, had vowed to Caleb to dislike the man on sight, there was some deep part of her that wanted to know him, wanted him to care for her as a father cared for his daughter, as she had pretended as a little girl that he would.

"Are you nervous?" The coach rolled up the impressive gravel drive and Caleb leaned toward her from the opposite side of the carriage. They had barely spoken since their argument the day before yesterday—since he had interfered in her life and had told her that he would be leaving.

"I'm not the least bit nervous. He is only a man, after all—not a god of some sort, or a king or a saint. Why should I be nervous?" But Caleb only smiled, knowing very well that she was.

"If you give him the slightest chance, you're going to like him."

"I shall loathe him."

Caleb straightened away from her. "I pray, for all our sakes, that you do not."

They said nothing more as a footman swung open the carriage door. Caleb departed the conveyance, took her hand and helped her down the narrow iron stairs, then they followed the golden stone path to the house. The butler, a stately man with gray hair and roses in his cheeks, ushered them in with grand aplomb, and the housekeeper, a sturdy woman named Mrs. Winkle, led them upstairs to their quarters.

Since Jeannie remained yet at Parklands, the housekeeper assigned a fair-haired young woman named Beatrice to act as her lady's maid. Beatrice was older than Lee, perhaps in her thirties, very efficient and pleasant company. She quickly unpacked Lee's traveling valise and saw to her comfort after the two-hour journey from London, helping her to freshen and change.

"These are lovely," Beatrice said, laying out her dresses for inspection after the trip. "Perhaps this one would do for your interview with his lordship." It was a gown of striped aqua silk with short, capped sleeves and a bit of ruching around the hem, the very dress she had brought for the occasion.

Lee smiled, determined to hide her nervousness and thinking that she and Beatrice should rub along very well for the brief time she would be remaining at Kinleigh.

"Yes, I think that will do nicely." With Beatrice's help, she was dressed and ready in record time, her hair in a thick plait the maid pinned into a simple coronet atop her head.

Her nervousness increased. She tried not to think of Caleb and that he was leaving and that his departure was the reason she was there to meet Lord Kinleigh.

"My, Miss, you do look quite splendid," Beatrice said. "Have you never met his lordship, then?"

"No. No, I haven't."

"I'm certain you are going to like him. He is ever so nice a man."

But she didn't really believe it. Not after what he had done to her mother.

"Is there anything else you need, Miss?" Beatrice flicked a telling a glance at the clock on the mantel.

"No. Thank you, Beatrice. I believe it's time I made my way downstairs." Leaving the bedchamber, an opulent suite done in pale blue and gold with molded ceilings and a silk-draped bed, as well as a charming little sitting room with a marble-manteled hearth, she made her way down the hall and descended the stairs.

She wasn't surprised to find Caleb waiting.

"You look lovely," he said, lifting her hand and pressing a kiss to the back of it. "Any father would be proud to have you for a daughter."

A shiver of unease ran through her. She had no idea what to expect from the man, so she prepared herself for the worst. "I suppose that remains to be seen."

Dressed in his immaculate scarlet and navy uniform, Caleb offered her his arm and she rested her fingers on the sleeve of his coat. His hair was freshly washed and still damp and it looked nearly black in the light of the sconces along the walls of the corridor. He looked so handsome it made her breath catch, made her think again of how soon he would be leaving, and an ache welled in her chest.

She took a deep breath and let him guide her down the passage, into an elegant salon of creamy yellow accented with pale jade green. The sofas reflected the colors, as did the serpentine mantel on the hearth. Like the rest of the house, it was a beautiful room, and at the edge of a deep Oriental carpet, the Marquess of Kinleigh stood waiting.

Caleb paused while a footman closed the door behind them, giving her time to assess the man who had sired her. He was of only medium height, she saw, but his body looked fit and trim. His silver hair was perfectly groomed and his burgundy, velvet-collared tailcoat fit precisely over his shoulders. He was still a handsome man, for his near fifty years, and there was a sense of power and purpose about him. She thought that perhaps she could see how her mother might have fallen prey to his charms.

"Good afternoon, my lord," Caleb said formally. "May I present to you Miss Lee Durant."

The marquess smiled. "Yes . . . I can see that she is indeed a Durant. And there is no doubt that she is Angelique's child."

Angelique's child, not his. The marquess started toward her and she stiffened, certain he meant to deny his parentage, to accuse her mother of lying.

"You look so much like her." He stopped just in front of where she stood, pale blue eyes assessing her from head to foot. "Your mother was perhaps a little taller, her hair a little brighter shade of red. But you are her daughter and of an age that you could only belong to me."

The admission stunned her. She knew she should speak but the words refused to come. What did one say to a father she had never seen? She thought to feel nothing but hatred but what she felt was far different than that.

"I loved her, you know," he said. "I loved her more than my own life. I gave her up because I thought it was the only thing to do. Because I worried about social dictates and I listened to the people around me. I should have fought for her. I should never have let her go. I've regretted it every day of my life for nearly twenty years."

Her eyes burned. She hadn't expected that, for him to admit that he loved her mother. That he ached for her loss as she had ached.

"My mother loved you," Lee said. "She was never interested in any other man. She whispered your name with her last dying breath."

Something glittered in the marquess's eyes. It took a moment for her to realize it was tears.

"She must have loved you greatly," he said. "She wanted a child very much. And I can see that you still love her."

She was aching inside. She wanted to turn and walk

out of the room, to leave the painful memories behind, to forget the past, forget this man she wanted to hate but somehow couldn't. She wanted to flee the pain his words caused but her feet refused to move. She felt Caleb's hand settle solidly at her waist and the ache eased a little.

"If I had known about you," the marquess said, "I would have brought you into my home the day she died. I would have raised you as my own."

A sob escaped. She couldn't help it. Caleb drew her closer and she could see he was fighting to keep from pulling her into his arms.

"It isn't too late," the marquess said. "You're young yet. I'm the one who is losing the battle with time. Say you'll at least give me a chance to know you. Say that you will consider staying at Kinleigh—at least for a while."

She wanted to say no. That it was impossible—inconceivable—for her to stay. She told herself to say the words. Told herself she owed it to her mother to deny him, reminded herself this man had abandoned her, abandoned them both. But when she opened her mouth, different words spilled out.

"I . . . would like that," she said. "I would like that very much."

He was standing closer than she realized. She hadn't expected him to reach for her, to pull her against his chest and simply hold her. She hadn't expected she would rest her head against his shoulder and simply hang on.

But that is what she did.

It was evening at Rotham Hall. The boys were in bed and the hour grew late. Elizabeth sat alone by the fire in the small salon she favored at the back of the house. Outside a summer storm had blown in, rustling the branches on the trees, tugging at the leaves. She hadn't seen Charles since supper, since he had joined her in the dining room as had become his custom of late.

She tried to tell herself it meant nothing, that he was simply being polite, but each time he arrived to take his place at the head of the table, each time he smiled at her and inquired after her day, listening to some small accomplishment the boys had made as if he actually cared, another tiny piece of the ice around her heart melted away.

She had begun to look forward to the evenings, to the time they spent together. She had begun to imagine that Charles felt something for her beyond duty, and a traitorous part of her had begun to hope that they might reconcile, as Charles seemed to want, and make their marriage more than one in name only.

As she sat on the sofa in the drawing room, her slippers off and her feet tucked up beneath her, those thoughts swirled around in Elizabeth's head. She wasn't a coward. And in truth, she still loved him—though she had tried to deny it for nearly ten years.

She loved him and she wanted him. She wanted him to be her husband and she wanted to be his wife.

And so when the letter had come, she had been crushed more deeply than she ever could have imagined. Because she had begun to believe in him again. Because she had begun to trust him.

Her hand shook as she reread the message that had arrived just after supper, a note for her, penned in a feminine hand. A note unsigned, but the author did not matter.

Your husband loves another. Do not be deceived again. It was signed simply, *A friend.*

She swallowed past the lump in her throat and wiped at the tears on her cheeks. She didn't hear Charles come in, didn't realize he was standing there in the drawing room until she heard his voice.

"You're crying. Darling, what is it? What's happened?" He strode toward her, was there by her side in an instant, gently drawing the note from her shaking hands.

His worried gaze left her face and fell to the sheet of paper. He read the words and his expression turned as black as the night outside. "This is a lie! A terrible, vicious, savagely cruel lie!" He waded the note up in a shaking fist and tossed it violently against the wall.

He went down on his knee in front of her, reached for her hand, gripped it between his own. "I was afraid she might do something like this. I should have warned you. I should have said something. I was afraid of what you would say . . . what you would think. I wanted your trust. I've tried so hard to win it. Now . . ." Charles shook his head.

Elizabeth swallowed past the knot in her throat. "Who wrote this?"

"There is only one woman vicious enough to do something like this. Moll Cinders wrote it. She came to see me in London several weeks ago. She told me she wanted more money than the amount I had settled on her when I ended the affair."

Elizabeth couldn't look at him. "I thought . . . I thought you did that some years back."

"Quite a number of years, in fact. Apparently, she is desperately in need of funds. She heard that I intended to reconcile with my wife. She came to see me, demanded more money. I refused. I had been more than generous already." He hung his head. "I should have paid her. If I had known what she intended—"

"You're telling me this note is a lie?"

"God, Beth. I love you so much. I don't want any other woman. I was young then, foolish. I rebelled against my father's dictates and the fact that the marriage was arranged. It took years before I realized what I really wanted ... what a treasure I had already lost. I love you, Beth. So very much."

She sat there stunned. He had never mentioned love. Not ever. Not in the beginning, not in the weeks he had been pursuing her. She didn't know what to say.

The corner of his mouth curved up. "I've surprised you, haven't I? That isn't an easy thing to do. You didn't know? You couldn't guess the way I felt?"

"If you loved me, why didn't you tell me?"

"I didn't think you would believe me. I thought that perhaps ... once we were no longer estranged and living again as man and wife, you would be able to see the truth."

She thought again of the note. "I want to believe you, Charles. I want that more than anything in the world, but—"

"But you don't." He stood up, towering over where she sat on the sofa, his expression hard now, oddly determined. Lamplight gleamed on his fine, sandy hair. He was so unbelievably handsome. "Moll Cinders means nothing to me. Nothing! I am a lot of things, Beth, but I am no liar. I haven't been with another woman in more than two years. I haven't wanted anyone else." He paced away from her, walked back. "You're my wife. If I can't convince you with words, perhaps there is another way, something I should have done weeks ago."

Elizabeth gasped as he lifted her into his arms, turned and began to stride across the drawing room.

"Where ... where are you taking me?"

"Upstairs, my lady. To my bed. From this day forward you will spend every night there. I am still lord here. Perhaps it is time I began to act like it again."

Every night with Charles. Every night in his bed, making love with him. More children, perhaps, the sort of life she had once dreamed of. It was all there—finally within her reach. If only she had the courage to grasp it.

Charles shoved open the door to the master's suite, carried her into his bedchamber and straight to his big tester bed. "If you are here and I am here, you will see that it is you that I cleave to. You I want and no other." He caught her chin, lifted it, looked deeply into her eyes. "I was always afraid of love. I had seen what it had done to my father, to other men of my acquaintance. But there comes a time, Beth, when one must put his fears aside and grasp the thing he holds most dear. For me it is you, my darling." And then he kissed her.

Elizabeth's heart squeezed. Melted. It was time, she knew, to put aside her own fears. No matter the outcome, love was worth the risk.

22

Caleb strode down the long marble corridor toward the marquess's study. Lamplight flickered on the walls, casting his length in shadow. Supper was over and Lee had retired upstairs to her room, but the marquess had asked to see him and he was on his way there now.

For the past three days, Caleb had remained with Lee at Kinleigh. The marquess had spent each day with her and the bond between them seemed to have deepened to a surprising degree. It was amazing how much they had in common: Kinleigh's love of music and Lee's gifted playing of the harp; the marquess's stable of beautiful, blooded horses and Lee's love of racing; they both loved children and animals; even their laughter at times sounded the same.

With Bronson in London and Aaron away at boarding school, the past was the only obstacle between them. Though Caleb had missed having Lee in his bed, he was happy for her. He had taken something precious when he had taken her innocence. In finding her father, he had tried to give something back.

Still, it was time he returned to London. He had promised to visit his own father at Selhurst and the days were slipping away. He had to return and though he wouldn't take Lee to Selhurst, wouldn't subject her to his father's scrutiny, he wanted her with him as much as possible these last few precious days.

Caleb knocked on the door of the study, turned the silver handle at the sound of the marquess's voice bidding him enter, and walked into the room.

"Caleb. Thank you for coming." Like the rest of the house, it was a pleasant room, paneled in walnut and lined with books, in a bit more disarray, perhaps, with several days' newspapers strewn over a rosewood table and a stack of ledgers perched on a corner of the desk. The marquess walked past it, over to the sideboard. "Brandy?"

"Thank you. I believe I will." There was something in the older man's manner that warned him he might need it. Caleb accepted the crystal snifter, then followed the marquess to a deep red leather sofa and chairs grouped around the hearth.

A small fire crackled in the grate. A summer storm had blown in, cooling the early July night, and outside the window, a layer of clouds crept over the valley.

"First, Caleb, I want to thank you. In bringing my daughter here, you have given me the greatest gift any man has ever bestowed upon me."

Caleb smiled. "I'm glad things have worked out as they have."

"Actually, things have worked out even better than you know." He leaned back in his chair. "You see, Lee has agreed to stay with me here at Kinleigh."

He was more than a little surprised—at the marquess for offering and Lee for accepting. "Won't that create a problem for you? Considering that Lee is a Durant?"

"It might. Even if it does, it will be worth it. But in truth, I hope to head off any problems that might arise before they occur. You see, I plan to adopt Lee as my daughter."

Caleb's brandy glass paused halfway to his lips.

"As soon as matters can be legally arranged," the marquess went on, "Lee Durant will become Lee Montague. There is no way to deny that she was born out of wedlock, but even should her mother's name be discovered, it will scarcely matter, once I have claimed her as my own flesh and blood."

It just might work, Caleb thought. Lee looked little like the Vermillion he had first met, the sophisticated courtesan who was the darling of Parklands. She dressed more simply now and no longer wore face paint. In truth, her entire demeanor had changed. The marquess's interest went far beyond what he had imagined, but it just might work.

"I'm a powerful man, Caleb. Even should people speculate, they would never dare offend her."

Caleb swirled the brandy in his glass. "That's extremely generous, Lord Kinleigh."

"Generous? It is nothing less than she deserves. Had I been more of a man all those years ago and married her mother as I wished, she would already carry my name and with it her legitimate birthright."

It was true, Caleb thought. And if Kinleigh claimed her, her future would be completely secure.

"As for you, Captain, and your relationship with my daughter—we both know you will soon be leaving the country."

"That's right, sir. In just a few more days." Caleb set

his brandy glass down on the side table and sat up a little straighter. "As I said, I would gladly marry—"

"I'm afraid I've changed my mind in that regard." The marquess's eyes fixed on Caleb's face. "When you came to me, you asked me to see to my daughter's welfare. As her father, that is exactly what I intend to do. You're an officer in His Majesty's Army. You'll be leaving for Spain and there is no way to know when you will return." *Or if you will return,* were the words that went unsaid. "Unless there are . . . consequences to your association with Lee, I don't believe a marriage between the two of you would be in either of your best interests."

He was right. Most certainly he was. So why did he feel this crushing weight on his chest?

"I know how much my daughter cares for you. In the brief time she has been here, she has certainly spoken your name often enough. But as you say, I want her to be happy. Both of us do. I intend to make that happen."

The marquess rose from his chair and Caleb stood up as well. He felt cold though the room was becoming overly warm. His heart was beating and yet it felt as if the blood had slowed to a crawl through his veins.

"You said at supper the two of you are planning to return to London on the morrow."

"That's correct. Even if Lee has decided to stay, she'll want to pick up her things and inform her aunt of her plans before returning on a permanent basis."

"I'm sure that is her plan. However, I am going to call on your honor, Caleb. As the gentleman I know you are, I am asking that you do the honorable thing where my daughter is concerned. I want you to travel at first light. I want you to leave Lee at Kinleigh. I don't want her hurt any more than she already has been."

He understood. In a way, he had expected this to happen. Lee was an unmarried woman and he was her lover. If she were his daughter, he would probably shoot the man who had stolen her innocence. But God, he didn't want to leave her. Not like this.

"I suppose it would be in Lee's best interest," he said, hoping the marquess didn't notice the rusty note in his voice.

"We both know it is. I'll make your farewells for you after you've gone. I'll tell her the truth—that I thought it would be less painful for you both." *And lessen the chances of his fathering a child.* The marquess didn't have to speak the words.

Caleb forced himself to nod.

"Then I have your word, Captain, as an officer and a gentleman? You'll agree to stay away from Lee until you leave for Spain?"

He couldn't breathe. He needed to escape the room, needed to escape the powerful emotions he hadn't expected to feel. Didn't want to feel.

"You have my word, Lord Kinleigh." He wouldn't make love to her again, wouldn't risk her future any more than he already had.

The older man relaxed. He walked beside Caleb to the door. "Do you still plan to visit your father?"

"Yes, sir. As soon as I leave here." He had planned to spend a couple of days with his father, no more. He didn't want to be away from Lee that long. Now it wouldn't matter.

"Take care of yourself over there, Caleb. And as I said, give my regards to Lord Selhurst."

He simply nodded, unable to manage any more words. Turning away from the marquess, he left the study. He didn't intend to wait till morning to return to London. He couldn't bear to stay in the house a moment more.

He wanted to go to Lee, wanted to say a final farewell, but he had given his word and he would abide by it.

It was going to be the hardest thing he had ever done.

Standing in the shadows outside the study, Lee pressed a hand against her mouth to still her trembling lips. Caleb was leaving. Her father had convinced him to go away without a word of farewell. She had been afraid something like this might result from the summons Caleb had received to join the marquess later in his study.

The thought had unsettled her so much she had slipped out of her room in only her night rail and wrapper. She had crept into the garden and sneaked up to the study window to hear what her father had to say.

Now, as she watched Caleb walk out the study door and disappear, anger poured through her. Her father was forcing Caleb to leave. She was furious with him! She hardly knew him and already he was trying to run her life!

But she had also seen the worry on his face, seen the protective look in his eyes when he spoke to Caleb about her future. He had asked her to come and live with him, told Caleb he planned to give her his name. It was beyond anything she could have imagined.

He was trying to protect her, behaving exactly the way a father who cared for his daughter ought to behave, and as hard as she tried, she could not fault him for it.

In truth, she felt deeply moved.

And she knew he was right.

Caleb was returning to duty. Any offer of marriage he had made had come out of duty, not love. He was leaving her behind and she had to get over him. A tearful good-bye would only make losing him more painful. It was better if she never saw Caleb Tanner again.

She repeated the words in her head. *Let him go. Let him go. Let him go.* And as she moved along the path toward the door leading back inside the house, she tried to convince herself.

Then a lamp went on in one of the rooms upstairs and she paused, guessing the room must be Caleb's. If she went upstairs and knocked on his door, would he let her in? He might, but he had given his word that he would stay away from her, and Caleb was a man of honor.

There was every chance the door would remain locked against her.

She told herself to keep walking, to ignore the lilac-covered trellis that beckoned her to climb up to the second floor balcony and slip into his bedchamber, as he had once entered her room at Parklands.

She tried to convince herself, but it was no use.

Reaching down, she grasped the hem of her nightgown and blue silk wrapper, dragged them above her knees, and set her bare foot on the first rung of the trellis.

*   *   *

Caleb stripped off his uniform and changed into a comfortable pair of buckskin breeches for the return trip to London. Dragging his satchel from beneath the four-poster bed, he began to stuff in the clothing he had brought with him to Kinleigh Hall. Downstairs, he had sent word to his coachman to ready his carriage and bring it round front. Now that his mind was set, Caleb couldn't wait to leave.

He was desperate to get out of the house, anxious to get away from Kinleigh. Away from Lee.

Just thinking about her made his chest ache. God, he'd been a fool to think he could escape unscathed when half the men in London had fallen in love with her.

But Lee wasn't Vermillion. She didn't pander to a man's ego, didn't play games. She didn't even look the same.

And he had foolishly believed he was immune.

Instead, he had fallen wildly, desperately in love with her, and now he had to leave.

Caleb closed the satchel, snapped the brass latches, and started for the door, anxious to be away. The night was cloudy and a little bit cold, but at least it wasn't raining.

"Caleb?"

The sound of her voice whispered through him, slipped softly over his skin. He turned to see her standing beside the door leading in from the balcony dressed only in her night clothes. He remembered the lilac-covered trellis. It was a long way to the ground. He didn't know whether to be angry or amused. In the end, even knowing he would have to send her away, he felt grateful she had come.

"You shouldn't be here," he said softly, afraid to

move closer, afraid he might reach for her, and he couldn't afford to do that.

"You were leaving. I heard you and my father talking in the study. You were going away without a word."

His eyes ran over her face, taking in the wisp of burnished hair against her cheek, the faint trembling of her lips, the look of regret in her eyes. He wondered if his own eyes looked the same. "You weren't supposed to be eavesdropping."

"I can't believe you would go away like this. I thought you cared for me . . . at least a little."

He cared for her. He loved her. So much it hurt. He cleared his throat. "Your father thought . . . we both thought it would be better this way."

"Would it?"

He knew he should lie. He looked into her face and saw the hurt there, saw the betrayal she felt. "No. Not for me."

She was in his arms in a heartbeat, bare feet flying across the carpet, her nightclothes sweeping out behind her. He held her. Just held her, his arms tight around her, pressing her into his chest. He inhaled her scent, felt the brush of her silky hair against his cheek. Her breasts pillowed against him. He could remember their weight and the softness, the way they filled his hands. He remembered how good it felt to be inside her and he began to go hard.

Gently, he set her away. "You have to go, Lee. Your father would be furious if he knew you were here."

"I've lived all my life without him. I can manage a little while longer." She reached out and touched him, went up on her toes and kissed him softly on the lips. "I'm going to miss you, Caleb."

He swallowed. "I'm going to miss you, too."

"I don't know what will happen to me. I'm frightened of the future. When I was with you, I was never afraid."

His throat tightened. "I know how brave you are. I know the marquess will take care of you. Already he loves you. He only wants what is best for you. You don't have to be afraid."

"Do you think . . . if I became the daughter of a marquess, things could be different? Between us, I mean."

Ah, God. He reached out, caught her shoulders. "Don't you know by now this has nothing to do with who you are. I can't marry you, Lee. I'm a soldier. It's what I do—what I am. I can't give you the life you want, the life you deserve." He reached out and cupped her cheek, ran his thumb along her jaw. "The war is far from over. I don't even know if I'll be alive when it's finished. I want you to be happy. You deserve it more than anyone I know."

She leaned her face into his palm and a painful longing tore through him. He was in love with her. God, it hurt to leave.

"I want you, Caleb. Make love to me one last time."

His hand fell away. He stepped back from her, wanting her, unsure how much control he had. "I can't, Lee. I gave your father my word."

Tells welled in her eyes and began to slip down her cheeks. The moon crept out from between the clouds and he thought how beautiful she looked, standing there with her fiery hair unbound, her pale skin bathed in the soft glow streaking in through the trees.

"I have to go," he said gently. "If I don't, I'll break my word."

She just stood there and for an instant, he wasn't sure he could leave her. In some primal way, she belonged to him. She was his, and he had come to need her in a way he had never needed anyone before. But it wasn't fair to Lee. She deserved to have a husband who would be there when she needed him. A man who would be a father to the children she would bear.

"I wish you didn't have to go. I wish I would wake up and find out all of this was a dream." Her eyes filled with tears and his own eyes burned. When she leaned toward him, he didn't push her away, just pulled her closer, held her until his throat closed up and the whisper of her name remained unspoken.

It took sheer force of will to set her away from him. He didn't look at her again, just reached down to pick up his satchel and started walking, one painful step at a time. Lee made no move to stop him. If she had, he might not have made it to the door.

Once he did, he turned to look at her one last time, saw the tears rolling down her cheeks. "Be happy, Lee."

She tried to smile. Failed. "Take care of yourself, Caleb."

He forced his legs to move. He didn't look back as he walked down the hall, descended the stairs, and walked out of her life into the lonely future that awaited him.

23

Life at Kinleigh Hall was as nothing Lee expected. In a way it was so much more. Her father was all that a father could be: gentle and caring, protective and loving. He began the legal proceedings to give her his name the day after Caleb left for London. He lavished her with gifts, had Grand Coeur and three other of her prized Parklands horses brought to his stable, and rode with her over the vast expanse of Kinleigh holdings nearly every day.

She was surprised at how often he spoke of her mother, making Angelique Durant seem real in a way she never had been before. Lee would have been happy—if it hadn't been for Caleb.

She tried not to think of him, tried not to let her heartbreak show. Her years of playing Vermillion enabled her to disguise her grief, but there were times she thought that her father suspected. After all, he had suffered the loss of the woman he loved. Perhaps he understood. If he did, he did not say.

She wondered why he hadn't forced Caleb to marry

her, as a man of his position surely could have, but she wouldn't have wanted Caleb that way and she was grateful he seemed to know.

There was only one fly in the ointment. Well, two flies, actually: Bronson and Aaron Montague, the marquess's sons. Bronson had loathed her on sight. He'd been aghast when his father calmly informed him he had a sister he meant to make a member of the family.

"Good grief, Father, have you lost your wits? The girl is the daughter of your former paramour, for God's sake! She is a commoner, scarcely a suitable addition to the Montague line!"

"Need I remind you, Lee is my child as well. And her mother was scarcely common. She was a descendant of French nobility. Had I married her as I wished, Lee would have been my legitimate offspring and I intend to rectify the situation as quickly as I can."

Bronson had threatened and they had argued.

"Lee is your sister," the marquess said, barely hanging on to his temper. "You will treat her with the respect she deserves or I shall cut you off without a farthing!"

"Perhaps Bronson is right, Father," Lee put in as Bronson stormed out the door. "I never wanted your family to suffer because of me. I have my own money. I can take care of myself. Perhaps—"

"Nonsense! You are my daughter. I intend that you should be treated as such."

Though his younger son, Aaron, had yet to arrive home from boarding school, Lee imagined once he did, the scene might be even worse. It would probably be better for all of them if she simply left Kinleigh and returned to Parklands, but she couldn't bear to think of resuming that sort of existence.

Thanks to Caleb, she was more sure of herself and what she really wanted.

Unfortunately, what she wanted was Caleb. If he had asked, she would have gone with him to Spain, though the army life wasn't the sort she would have chosen. She wanted a home of her own, a place in the country where she could raise her horses. More than that, loving Caleb had finally made her realize what she really wanted was a family of her own.

She tried not to think of him, to wonder where he was or if he had yet left London.

She tried, but she loved him so much it was simply no use.

The day was overly warm, the sun beating down from a washed-out, cloudless sky, the wind no more than a memory. Caleb walked between Luc and his father back from the fields toward the big Georgian house that was Selhurst Manor. They had been partridge hunting since early that morning. Caleb was dusty and tired, his long-gun heavy where it hung over his arm.

"What do you say to a brandy?" his father asked as they entered the house from the rear. "I know I could certainly use one."

"Sounds good to me," Luc said.

Caleb just nodded. He hadn't enjoyed the day the way he should have, the way he had as a boy. The sound of gunfire reminded him of the battles he had seen, the battles he knew were to come. But his father and brother had always loved the sport and once he had as well. Today, he was simply glad the day was over.

The three men went directly into the study. Dressed in their dusty shooting clothes, they were scarcely fit for a drawing room.

"It's good to have you home, Caleb," his father said as he walked to an ornate sideboard along the wall. He was getting older, Caleb saw, his once-brown hair mostly silver now, his shoulders a little less straight than they used to be. Still, there was command in his voice, and the smile he bestowed on Caleb still carried the power to move him.

"It's good to be here, Father. I just wish I had more time."

"So do I, son. So do I." He poured each of them a brandy and passed the glasses around.

"Any word of Ethan?" Caleb asked.

His father shook his head. "He is still at sea, I suspect." Ethan ran the family shipping interests. The sea had always been his love. "He has never been good at writing." The earl took a sip of his brandy. "You haven't mentioned the case you were working on. I heard about it, of course. There was a goodly bit of gossip going round for a while."

"Was there?" Caleb flicked a glance at his brother, wondering how much he had said, but Luc made a faint negative movement of his head. "How did you hear?"

"Jon Parker mentioned he saw you. He told me about the murderer you came home to help apprehend, though I am surprised they would send you all that way."

It was the story Caleb had told at Parklands, a flimsy tale at best, and his father was looking at him in that shrewd way he had of discerning the truth from a lie. But Caleb was too old to be intimidated the way he was when he was a boy.

"That was the story I told at the time. The truth is a bit more complicated. Unfortunately, I am not at liberty to discuss it, Father, not even with you."

"I see." The earl said it almost proudly, as if he admired Caleb's integrity. Perhaps he did. Caleb hoped so.

The earl took a sip of his brandy and they all moved over to the leather sofa and chairs. "There were other rumors, as well. Something about a young woman, as I recall."

He was fishing now. Caleb wondered how much his father knew, and a pulse in his temple began to throb. "And this also came from Lord Nash?"

"No. Just a bit of gossip I picked up here and there. I usually don't pay much attention. As this particular gossip concerned my son, I took particular pains to discover whether or not it was true."

Caleb was on guard now. He couldn't begin to guess what his father might have learned about Vermillion. "Exactly what did you hear?"

"That you have been spending a great deal of time with a woman named Vermillion Durant. There is speculation as to your feelings about the girl. As this particular young woman is known to be a courtesan of some renown—"

"That's not true. She has never been anything of the sort." Caleb fought to control his temper. Where Lee was concerned it was never an easy task. "It was all a ruse, one she mistakenly got caught up in that has now come to an end."

Luc stepped into the breach, for which Caleb would always be grateful. "Miss Durant is a lovely young woman, Father. Caleb helped reunite her with her father, who turned out to be the Marquess of Kinleigh."

"Kinleigh? Now that is interesting. I'll bet the news came as quite a surprise."

"Believe it or not, the marquess was pleased," Caleb said. "He plans to give her his name, though he is trying to keep the matter as private as possible."

"If the lady in question has that sort of past, I can understand why."

Caleb's temper inched up. "Lee is innocent in all of this. Her father knows that. He sees her as the person she truly is and he is grateful to have found her."

"Your defense is admirable, Caleb. I hope that is all it is . . . a dashing captain of the cavalry defending the honor of an innocent young girl."

His father had a way of grating on his nerves. For the past few years, since Caleb had gone into the army, they had been getting along very well.

But they had not disagreed in the past few years.

"I will tell you this, Father. The lady means a great deal to me. Under different circumstances, I might have asked her to marry me. But as you say, I'm a captain of the cavalry. Duty calls, and I must obey." He said this last with a hint of sarcasm his father must have noticed.

"I thought you liked the army."

He sighed. "I do. It's just that there are times . . ."

"Go on."

"There are times I miss the sort of life you and Mother had. I never really thought I ever would."

The earl took a sip of his drink, his eyes on Caleb's face. "Surely this war cannot go on forever. Perhaps when it is over, you will be able to return home and settle down, raise a family, as your brother, Christian, has done."

Caleb sipped his brandy. "Perhaps." But he didn't really think so. The truth was, there was only one woman who had ever tempted him to marry. He doubted he would ever feel that way about a woman again.

He took a last swallow of his drink and set his brandy glass down on the table. "I'm beginning to taste the dust of the day. If you both will excuse me, I think I'll take a bath and rest for a while before supper." At his father's nod, he turned and headed for the door. Behind him he heard the earl speaking softly to Lucas, but he couldn't hear what they said.

"He has always been hot-tempered," the earl said to Luc, "and often too quick to act. I worried when I heard he was involved with this young woman, a lady of questionable reputation."

"Caleb told you the truth. Lee Durant was never a courtesan."

"It really doesn't matter. The girl is a Durant. You don't think your brother is in love with her?"

Luc swirled the brandy in his glass, trying to decide how much to say. "Whatever he feels, he'll return to duty. He has no other choice. He leaves in a couple of days and he won't take her with him. He has told me what it is like for a woman over there. Once he is gone, things will return to normal."

"I don't know . . . Caleb isn't the sort of man to get involved so deeply with a woman." He sighed, took a long swallow of his drink. "Bloody damned war. I have worried about him every moment that he has been gone. I just pray to God he comes home safely."

Dressed in his uniform, Caleb strode into the colonel's office in Whitehall. Major Sutton was there, he saw, in conversation with Cox. Their attention turned his way as he closed the door.

"It's good to see you, Captain." The colonel beck-oned Caleb forward as he moved behind his desk. "Be at ease, gentlemen. You may both sit down."

Both Caleb and the major took a seat across from him.

"Your transportation has been arranged, Captain. Tomorrow morning, as scheduled, you leave for Portsmouth. From there, you will board His Majesty's ship *Nimble* for the trip to Spain. An escort will be waiting when you arrive. They will guide you back to your regiment at that time."

"That sounds good, sir." He shifted a little in his chair. "In regard to a previous matter, I've been won-dering if anything new has turned up on the spy ring."

The colonel shook his head. "Not much. We inter-cepted another courier day before yesterday but the man resisted, and in trying to evade capture, he was killed."

"What sort of information was he carrying? Was there any way to trace the source?"

"Unfortunately, it was the latest information on Wellesley's position, accurate down to the finest points. The hell of it is, at least half a dozen top offi-cials have access to that sort of knowledge. It is neces-sary for them to do their jobs."

"Have you considered feeding these people false information? Something we could trace back to a par-ticular person?"

"An interesting notion. Major Sutton made the same suggestion."

Caleb cast the major a glance, then returned his at-tention to Cox. "And?"

"I daresay it wouldn't be an easy thing to do. These men communicate with each other. The information is checked and cross-checked. Since we don't know who might be passing it along, we don't know which of them we can trust."

"I'm still trying to convince the powers that be," the major added.

"We're thinking of sending someone in," the colonel said, "as we did with you, but it would have to be someone in the diplomatic corps. Time is the problem." He sighed. "But all of this is neither here nor there as far as you are concerned, Captain. In a matter of hours, you'll be leaving for Spain."

They spoke for a little while longer, then both Caleb and the major were dismissed. Caleb walked with Sutton out to the street. This time of day, the roadways were bustling with hackney carriages, clogged with people and animals making their way across the city.

"I wish there were something I could do," Caleb said.

"Don't worry, we'll catch the bastard—sooner or later."

"I'd feel better if it were sooner."

Sutton nodded. "So would I." They walked along the street together, both men thinking of the days ahead. "Looks like there's going to be one helluva fight over there. You had best take care, Captain."

"I plan to, Major."

"You taking that little light-skirt you were seeing? I know a lot of men take their women with them. I figure that is what I would do."

Caleb clamped hard on his jaw. He had never liked Mark Sutton. Apparently that wasn't going to change. "I wouldn't drag any woman I cared about into a hellhole like that. And she is not a light-skirt. I told you that before. Unless you care to meet me with pistols at dawn, I would suggest you remember that."

Sutton's mouth faintly curved. "I remind you, Captain Tanner, dueling is illegal. Besides, you leave for Portsmouth at dawn."

Caleb gritted his teeth. "With any luck at all, Major, I'll be back. If I hear you've said one word maligning Miss Durant's character, I shall expect that meeting."

But Sutton just smiled. Caleb had the oddest feeling the man was simply baiting him, that he knew exactly how to prod Caleb's temper and he was enjoying the show. Why he would want to, Caleb had no idea.

It didn't really matter. Tomorrow he was off to Portsmouth. He was away to Spain and he had no idea when—or if—he would return. As he went to collect his horse, he tried not to think of Lee, but his mind drifted in that direction.

He wondered how many times he would think of her in the days to come.

The night seemed endless. It was cold for this time of year and a mean wind whipped through the trees. Lee read for a while, but the pages seemed to blur and she finally gave up and put the book away. Tomorrow was Wednesday, the day Caleb would be leaving.

Was he still in London? Or had he already gone?

She paced in front of the hearth, thinking of him, wishing they could have had these few last days together. Wishing she had left Kinleigh Hall as her heart had told her to do and followed him to the city.

Vermillion would have done it. If she had wanted a man, she would simply have gone after him.

But Lee wasn't Vermillion and the role was now

nearly impossible for her to play. Still there were times she could be just as bold and daring. In some ways, she was far stronger than Vermillion ever had been.

The notion gave her courage. Lee jumped up from the window seat and hurried toward the rosewood armoire in the corner. Ignoring the array of walking dresses, traveling gowns, ball gowns, cloaks and pelisses that had been brought to Kinleigh from the Hotel Purley, she pulled out a navy blue velvet riding habit.

Caleb was leaving. There would be fighting in Spain and he could be wounded or even killed. He had promised her father he would stay away from her, but she had made no such vow. If he didn't want to see her, she would return to Kinleigh and never think of him again.

But if he felt as she did . . . if his heart ached one tenth as badly as hers, then he would welcome her in.

Worried someone might try to stop her, she didn't ring for Beatrice but fought her way into the dress herself, grateful the garment buttoned in front. She penned a note to her maid, telling her she would return on the morrow and please not to worry her father. A few minutes later, she was on her way down the hall, descending the servants' stairs, making her way out to the stable.

She paused to light a lantern, then stepped inside. Grand Coeur nickered at her approach, then whinnied softly as she led him from the stall. She hadn't brought Noir or any of her racing stock. She still wasn't certain whether she would remain at Kinleigh.

"Whatcha doin', Miss?" It was Jack Johnson, the walker who had delivered her saddle horses. Lee had hoped none of the grooms would awaken.

"I have an errand to run." She turned to lift the heavy sidesaddle off of its rack, but Jack, a big, brawny man at least a head taller than she, reached over and hefted it as if were light as a feather. He settled it on Grand Coeur's back.

" 'Tis late, Miss. Ye can't be thinkin' of goin' off by yerself. There's a storm movin' in. And it's dangerous on the roads for a lady."

"I have to go, Jack. I'll be back some time tomorrow."

He shook his grizzled head. He was not a handsome man but there was kindness in his features. "I'll not be lettin' ye go, Miss. Not by yerself. If ye leave, I'll be goin' with ye." He didn't tighten the cinch and blocked her from doing it herself.

It was fifteen miles to London, but the road was well traveled and the inns along the way not far apart. She knew which house in Berkeley Square belonged to the Earl of Selhurst. It wasn't likely she would be assaulted, but there was no way to be sure. In truth, she felt a sweep of relief that Jack would be going with her.

"Thank you, Jack. Perhaps it would be better if you came along."

He nodded, went to saddle a horse for himself, and returned a few minutes later. "Mind tellin' me where we be goin'?

Lee smiled as she flipped the hood of her woolen cloak up over her head. "London, Jack. We're off for London."

A few minutes later, they disappeared into the misty night.

Caleb couldn't sleep. Tomorrow he would begin his journey back to Spain. He wished it were already dawn so he could be on his way.

Instead, a black, moonless night darkened the sky outside his bedchamber window. A harsh, north wind howled over the chimneys and a slick mist dampened the cobbled streets. Caleb paced in front of the window, paused to watch a lone carriage roll past, then walked over to pour himself a drink.

He thought of Lee and wondered what she was doing this night and if she had settled in with the marquess's family. He hoped so. He wanted her to be happy. It was his most fervent wish.

He removed the stopper from the decanter and poured some of the amber liquid into his glass. He took a drink, hoping the brandy might help him to sleep, started to take another sip when a light rap sounded on his door. Caleb crossed the room to open it, wondering what Grimsley was doing up well past midnight.

"You've a visitor, sir." The old man's ears turned slightly pink. "A lady, sir. She has come a bit of a ways. She says if you do not wish to see her, you should tell her so and she will go away."

His heart started thudding. Surely she wouldn't come all this way. Then he remembered her riding like thunder over the fields, the reckless way she had taken jump after jump. Of course she would come. He set the snifter down on a table beside the door, fighting to curb his impatience to see her.

He wasn't dressed for company. He wore only his breeches, no shirt or boots. He dragged his shirt back on but didn't bother to button it, just followed the butler back down the stairs.

Lee stood in the foyer, a small, cloaked figure with damp, windblown hair the color of rubies and cheeks rosy from the chill in the late night air.

"I took the liberty of showing her groom into the kitchen, sir, for a bite to eat. There is a pallet in front of the fire should he wish to sleep."

A groom. At least she hadn't traveled alone. "Thank you, Grimsley." But his gaze remained on Lee and he couldn't seem to tear it away.

She didn't say a word until the butler had retired, then she hoisted her chin. "If you wish me to leave, merely say the word and I shall be on my way."

His mouth curved. "So I've been told." He wanted to sweep her up, to crush her in his arms, but he was afraid if he touched her he would never let her go.

"Well?"

"I leave for Portsmouth at dawn."

"I know that. That is the reason I am here." She waited for him to say something more, to invite her to stay. When he didn't, she whirled toward the door and started walking. "I'm sure you have a great deal to do before you leave. I'm sorry to have disturbed you. Good night, Captain Tanner."

She reached for the door but he was there behind her. He caught her waist, spun her around, and straight into his arms.

"Too late," he said softly. "You had your chance to escape. Now I won't let you out of my sight until dawn."

She looked up at him, ready to push him away. Whatever she saw in his face changed her mind. Her arms went around his neck and she pressed her cheek to his.

"Caleb . . ."

For long moments, he just held her. He could feel her heart beating nearly as fast as his own, feel the faint tremors running through her body. She was here.

God only knew they would both regret these hours in the morning. Still, he swept her up in his arms and started up the stairs.

"I've missed you," he said as stepped inside his bedchamber and closed the door with his bare foot. "Every day that you have been gone I have thought of you and wished you were here."

He kissed her then, knowing he shouldn't, unable to help himself.

Wishing things could be different.

Knowing for him they never would be.

Lee could scarcely believe she was actually here, upstairs in Caleb's bedchamber. There was a time she wouldn't have been so bold, but that was long ago, before she had met him. Before she had become the person she was today.

She leaned toward him, went up on her toes and kissed him. "I've missed you, Caleb. So very much." She kissed his eyes, his cheeks, his lips. "I had to see you. I couldn't stay at Kinleigh, knowing you might still be here, knowing I might never see you again. I had to come, Caleb. I had to see you one last time."

His hand came up to her cheek. "I know I shouldn't say this, I know you're being here is bad for both of us, but I'm so very glad you came."

"I've thought of you every night. I've dreamed of touching you . . . of having you touch me. Once you arc gone, all I'll have left of you are memories." She kissed him very softly. "I want to spend the night curled up beside you. I want you to hold me in your arms. Make love to me, Caleb. Please?"

His hands shook as he framed her face between his palms, bent his head, and kissed her, a kiss so soft and sweet it nearly broke her heart. Reaching up, he began to pull the pins from her hair, then he combed the heavy curls out with his fingers.

"I can't make love to you—not the way you mean. I gave your father my word." But he kissed her again and began to unbutton her clothes and she reached down to unbutton his.

Outside the window, the storm was moving in. Lightning cracked and she heard the roll of thunder. The black night seemed to echo the darkness creeping into her soul.

Caleb removed the rest of her clothes and the last of his own. In the glow of the lamp flickering beside the bed, she could see the bands of muscles across his chest and she ached to touch them. She watched the way they bunched and thickened as he moved and she yearned to press her mouth against his skin. His stomach was flat, and ridges of muscle rippled in the faint, golden lamplight. His hips were narrow, his buttocks round, and his long, thick shaft jutted out from its nest of protective dark curls.

God, he was so beautiful. And she loved him so much.

Caleb lifted her again, carried her over to his tall four-poster bed, and set her down on the edge of the mattress. Propping an arm on each side of her, he bent and kissed her, a long, lingering kiss laced with the faint, sweet taste of brandy. She could feel the heat of his mouth, the softness of his lips, and an ache throbbed inside her. He was leaving. In a few short hours, he would be gone.

Caleb kissed her long and deep. He took and took and at the same time, the pleasure he gave was nearly unbearable. He kissed the side of her neck, trailed soft, open-mouthed kisses over her shoulders, bent his head and took one of her breasts into his mouth. Desire washed through her. Love for him welled up so strong it nearly made her weep.

Beneath his mouth, her nipples pebbled, turned diamond-hard and he rolled them around on his tongue. "Like berries," he whispered. "I shall forever remember the taste."

He cupped them almost reverently, massaged them as he claimed her mouth again, took her deeply with his tongue.

"I won't break my word," he said as he knelt between her legs, but she could see the hunger in his eyes, the hot desire and something else, something that matched the longing in her own.

She felt his mouth on her belly, his tongue in her navel and waves of pleasure washed over her. He eased her back on the bed and moved lower, pressed his mouth into the curls at the apex of her legs. Lee gasped as he parted her slick, woman's flesh and began to taste her there. It felt as if a torch had set fire to her blood.

"Caleb!" She tried to sit up but he coaxed her back down, began to kiss her again.

"I won't come inside you," he whispered. "But there are other ways that I can make love to you."

And so he began to show her. Sliding his palms beneath her hips, he lifted her against his mouth. He caressed her with his lips and his tongue until her body was on fire for him, until thoughts of Caleb consumed her, until she began to whimper his name. She fisted her hands in his thick brown hair, but he did not stop. Just held her hips immobile as he laved and tasted, stroked her again and again. There was reverence in the way he held her, in the way he gave and gave and did not stop. She reached her pinnacle thinking about him, wishing he were inside her. Pleasure poured through her. Even then he did not stop, not until she peaked again.

She was limp and sobbing when the sweet torture ended. Lifting her up, he settled her on the bed, then lay down beside her. He was still so hard she could see a faint pulse beating in the rigid length resting on his belly and she realized that what he had done was a gift.

Outside the window, the storm went on, a mirror of her own turbulent emotions. Lightning flashed as she reached out to touch him, wanting to give him the same gift he had given to her.

Caleb caught her wrist. "It's all right. You don't have to—"

"I want to, Caleb," she said softly. Bending over him, she tasted him, felt the smooth, rigid texture of his hardness, took him into her mouth. Her hair swung forward, pooled against his groin, and she heard his sharp intake of breath. She wasn't sure exactly what to do, but when she felt the tension sweep through his body, when she heard him whisper her name, she thought that perhaps it didn't matter. She cupped him and tasted him, caressed him more deeply, and in minutes he reached release.

She could feel the beating of his heart as he pulled her down beside him in the bed and nestled her against his chest. "I don't want to leave you," he said. "If there were any other way . . ."

She pressed her trembling fingers over his lips and ignored the painful lump in her throat. Caleb's arms tightened protectively around her and she felt the brush of his lips against her hair.

I love you, she thought. *I love you so much.* But she didn't say it. It wouldn't be fair to either one of them.

"I don't want to fall asleep," she said instead. "I want these last few hours with you." But she was exhausted from the tiring ride to London and he had pleasured her well. As hard as she fought to stay awake, sleep crept over her.

When dawn broke over the horizon and her eyes slowly opened, Caleb was gone. Inside her chest, her heart simply shattered.

24

Lee's return to Kinleigh Hall the following day went unremarked. If her father knew where she had been, if he noticed the despair in her eyes or the weary defeat that weighed down her shoulders, he made no comment and she would forever be grateful. Caleb was gone from her life. She would make a fresh start without him. Her father seemed to read her thoughts and he was determined to help her.

In that regard, he continued the paperwork that would make her Lee Montague, daughter of a marquess and nearly untouchable by Society. Though she never intended to go forward among the *ton*, she was thankful for the cloak of protection her father had placed around her.

She hadn't realized how strong it would be until she received a letter from Oliver Wingate, asking for permission to call on her at Kinleigh Hall.

"I think you should receive him," her father said. "You will establish very clearly once and for all, exactly who you are."

She smiled. "Lee Montague, you mean?"

His mouth curved into a smile that resembled her own. "Exactly so, and the daughter of a peer."

And so she had received the colonel for an evening quite different from those they had shared at Parklands. As if in reminder of those times, a note arrived the following day from Andrew Mondale, suggesting a rendezvous, his intentions far less sterling than Wingate's. Lee simply ignored it.

The only person who stayed away was her aunt. Aunt Gabriella had written a lengthy letter, explaining that for Lee's sake, she would not come to Kinleigh Hall. Gabriella wished her every happiness and said that once Lee was settled securely in her new life, they could begin to discreetly see each other again. She had been so happy when Lee had chosen Caleb. Lee hoped she wouldn't despair at this latest turn of events.

In her aunt's stead, Elizabeth Sorenson, Lady Rotham, came to call and Lee was thrilled to see her. She was even more thrilled to learn that Beth and Charles had reconciled.

"We're in love, Lee." The countess laughed. "I feel like I'm twenty again. Charles is a wonderful husband and a marvelous father. I never would have believed it but he loves me. He proves it every day."

"I'm so glad for you, Elizabeth. You deserve to be happy."

"I hated being married, Lee. I believed it was a life of penance, but I was wrong. Sharing a life with someone who cares for you . . . it changes everything. It makes you feel complete."

Lee tried not to think of Caleb, and Elizabeth made a point not to mention him. No one did. It was as if he had never existed. Like everyone else, in an effort to protect her battered heart, Lee tried to pretend he never had.

Other people paid a visit, close friends of the marquess who came to lend their support. Still it was a surprise when Jonathan Parker arrived at the house.

"I've known your father for quite some years," Jon said as they sat in the drawing room. "He's an amazing man, Lee. I'm happy things have worked out for you as they have." Everyone called her Lee now. Like Caleb, Vermillion had vanished like a ghost of the past.

"It's wonderful to see you, Jon. You've always been a friend. It's good to know that hasn't changed."

The viscount reached over and caught her hand. "I told you once I wanted more from you than friendship—I still do."

Her shock couldn't have been more profound. The viscount had wanted her as his mistress. This was far different. In a thousand years, she would never have believed both Nash and Wingate would continue their pursuit, though now it would require no less than marriage.

"I know it's too soon," the viscount said. "You and your father need this time together, but when you are ready, I hope you will at least consider my offer."

What could she say? Jonathan Parker was a member of the aristocracy, one of the most respected men in England. It was an honor of the highest order. "Of course I will, Jon. I can't tell you how honored I am. But as you say, I need a little time."

More than a little, she thought. It might take years to get over losing Caleb. She wasn't sure she ever would.

Unfortunately, there were other considerations. Namely, her two half-brothers, Bronson and Aaron, who continued to make her life miserable whenever they were near. Aaron had arrived home from boarding school and received news of the sister who had become a member of the family with even more outrage than his brother, throwing such a tantrum his father had threatened to birch him, which—it was more than apparent—was something that had never been done before.

Though her father had given her his name and his protection and had offered her a new and different life, there were strings attached, and not everyone—especially her brothers—was happy she was there.

More and more, she wondered if perhaps she should leave Kinleigh Hall. In a way she was more trapped there than she had been at Parklands.

The hot July days crept past. Caleb's trip across the dry Spanish landscape had led him to Wellesley's encampment near Talavera, but the fighting had yet to begin and the waiting seemed interminable as men and equipment poured in.

In the last few days, the atmosphere in the camp had changed, as if the troops sensed that now the time was right; the attack on Joseph Bonaparte's massive army was ready to commence.

Mounted on Solomon, Caleb rode at the head of the column making its way to the top of a rise that overlooked the battlefield below. For miles around, the ground was barren and dusty. For the soldiers of Wellesley's army, the march to Talavera had been an arduous one and food supplies were low. The heat was unbearable, the sun scorching down with merciless intensity. At night lightning cracked overhead but not a drop of rain fell to quench the parched earth.

One of the horses nickered. Solomon sidestepped and tossed his head, beginning to get anxious. "Easy boy. It won't be long now." Not long before the carnage began, before bodies littered the desolate landscape as far as the eye could see. Scattered along a defensive line across the field, Joseph Bonaparte's forty thousand men waited to face nineteen thousand of Wellesley's troops aided by the Spanish army commanded by General Cuesta.

Caleb had been assigned to the 4th Dragoons, led by General Sherbrooke, Wellesley's second in command. His squadron had been ordered to the rise, ordered to take up their position for the assault. For the past twenty-four hours, a calm detachment had been with him, a skill he had developed over the years. He used it now to study the tens of thousands of armed soldiers across the field, the dozens of cannon loaded with grapeshot, ready to rip men and animals apart.

He knew what he would face once the fighting began, knew he might not survive it. But today was the first time he had ever felt regret.

Regret for the life he had chosen, for all he had so readily given up. The keen ache of loss for the woman he loved and the children he would never have. He thought of Lee and prayed that whatever fate awaited him, she would be happy.

A bugle sounded. Caleb watched a sweep of men and horses rush down from the knoll onto the field at his left. Cannon roared. Guns began firing, clouds of thick black smoke filled the air. Horses screamed and dozens of men fell beneath the vicious barrage.

"Hold your position!" his commanding officer shouted.

Solomon pawed the earth. In minutes, it would be time. He wasn't afraid to die. Perhaps, in truth, he had been afraid to live.

In joining the army, he had found a retreat from the world and at the same time, a way to prove himself to his father. He had chosen this life, gained the love and approval he had always wanted and never had, but now he wondered . . .

If he could choose again, if he could start over, would the choice he made be different? As clearly as if a voice had spoken in his head, Caleb knew that he would not choose the solitary existence he lived now. He would choose a home and family. He would choose Lee.

But he had sworn an oath to protect his country. He was an officer in the British Army and he had a duty to perform. If only things could be different.

But it was too late for that. Too late the moment he heard his resounding command, "Charge!"

Caleb raised his saber above his head, urged Solomon into a gallop, and plunged off down the hill.

There was no word from Caleb. No letters, not even a note. Lee hadn't expected there would be. The newspapers were filled with accounts of the terrible battle that had been fought at Talavera and the costly victory the British had won. Lists of casualties were printed, more than fifty-five hundred British soldiers had been wounded or killed. Caleb's name had not appeared on any of the lists and for that she was grateful. Still she worried about him.

She thought about the traitor who had been passing information to the French and wondered if he had been responsible in some way for the high number of British casualties, but there was no way for her to know.

The days drifted past. August was slipping away. She was officially Lee Montague now, though the upheaval it caused between her father and his sons made her question whether the price was worth it.

It was a warm summer afternoon when the marquess called her into his study. Lee knew he wanted to talk to her about the problems with Aaron and Bronson, but she wasn't exactly sure what he would say.

Or what she should say in return.

"I cannot begin to tell you how disappointed I am in both of them," her father began.

"It isn't entirely their fault," Lee said. "They see me as an intruder. In a way they are not wrong."

"I know that's the way you feel. That is the reason I wished to speak to you." He indicated the teapot on the tea cart a few feet away. "Will you pour for us?"

She did as he asked, handing him the cup, nervous at the set of his features.

"Yesterday Jon Parker came to see me." Her head came up. "Jon has asked for permission to marry you, Lee."

She tried not to let her uneasiness show. She had known of his interest, of course. She wasn't certain he would actually make an official offer. "Jonathan is a very fine man," she said carefully.

"Yes, he is. He is kind and generous and very well respected. I think you should accept him, Lee."

The tea cup rattled. She steadied it with her hand. "I don't love him, Father."

"I know you don't—not now, but in time perhaps

you could come to love him." He set his untouched cup and saucer down on the table in front of him. "I loved your mother very much. I didn't believe I would ever get over losing her and in some ways I never did. But I found great comfort in Aaron's mother, Sarah. I never told you that. In my own way, I came to love her."

Lee mulled that over. Was it possible? Could love grow out of mutual caring and respect? Over the years, Charles had fallen deeply in love with Elizabeth. They were happy. Unbelievably so. In her life at Parklands, Lee would have chosen Jon as her protector. Why not a husband instead?

"Jon wants children, Lee. I know how much you would love to have a family of your own."

It was said that when one door closed another opened. Perhaps this, at last, was a door to the life she had finally discovered she wanted. Certainly she could be happier with Jon than she had been in the world of the demimonde, where she had never fit in.

"Jon enjoys racing," the marquess went on. "Your horses will have the very best of care."

She set her cup and saucer down next to his. "Do you really believe marrying Lord Nash is the right thing to do?"

The marquess reached out and captured her hand. "I have done all I can to protect you. Jon is aware of your former . . . relationship . . . with Captain Tanner and yet he believes, in time, you will come to care for him. As the wife of a viscount and respected member of the *ton,* your future would be completely secure."

His hold gently tightened around her fingers. "Shall I give him my approval?"

She thought of Caleb, closed her eyes and forced

his image away. "Tell him if he proposes marriage . . . if he is certain that is what he wants, I shall be honored to accept."

Lee could scarcely believe it. In only a few short months, her life had completely changed. She was betrothed to a well-respected member of the aristocracy and soon would be wed.

It was less than three weeks till the wedding when she made a trip to London for the final fitting of her trousseau. Though she missed Jeannie, her maid was happier at Parklands where she was more readily accepted. Beatrice was her lady's maid now, the two of them staying at her father's town house. She had buried thoughts of Caleb deep in her heart, never to be resurrected, and so she was surprised when, standing at the top of the stairs, she saw his brother, Lucas, striding into the entry.

The moment she realized who it was, a wave of fear hit her and the breath froze in her lungs. She flew down the stairs, her pulse hammering so madly she was afraid she might swoon. "Do not say he is dead!"

Lucas shook his head and relief rushed over her, so strong her legs went weak. Luc took her arm and led her into the nearest drawing room, urged her down onto the sofa.

"Caleb is alive, Lee, but I'm afraid he's been very gravely injured. There was some sort of mix-up and he was believed to be someone else. Word only reached us a few days ago."

Her hands were shaking. She clasped them together in her lap. "Where . . . where is he?"

"The hospital at Portsmouth."

She started to get up. She had to go upstairs, change into something for the journey.

Luc caught her arm. "My brother is in some sort of a coma, Lee. He has sustained a serious head injury. On top of that, he took a musket ball in the chest. He's been out of his mind with fever off and on for days. The hospital is a place of horrors, but they are afraid to move him. I came because in his lucid moments, Caleb calls your name."

Her eyes burned with tears.

"I heard you were here," Luc continued. "I thought that perhaps—"

"It won't take me a moment to change and pack a few things for the trip. If you would see me to Portsmouth, Lord Halford, I would be forever in your debt."

He gave her a weary smile. "I hoped you would say that." He looked tired. Faint smudges darkened the skin beneath his blue eyes and beard-stubble roughened his usually clean-shaven cheeks. "I probably shouldn't have come here, but if you are willing to suffer the horrors of that place and there is any chance you can help my brother, I can only say that I am grateful."

She simply nodded. Caleb was injured, perhaps even dying. Her throat ached and a film of tears blurred her vision. Turning away from Luc, she hurried out of the drawing room and raced up the stairs shouting for Beatrice.

In minutes, she had changed into traveling clothes, secured her bonnet strings beneath her chin, told Beatrice where she was going and asked her not to worry her father unless she had to. Then she hurried back down the stairs, tapestry satchel in hand. Luc took the bag from her trembling fingers and together they walked out the door.

Luc's carriage was waiting. He was the Viscount Halford and his crest blazed in gold on the door. He helped her inside and she settled against the carriage seat. They wouldn't reach Portsmouth before tomorrow.

She thought of Caleb and prayed he would still be alive when she got there.

The military hospital at Portsmouth overflowed with wounded men. The fighting at Talavera had been fierce, the casualties in the thousands. Some of the soldiers remained in hospital camps in Spain. Others, like Caleb, had been shipped home to England.

As Luc settled a steadying hand at Lee's waist and led her into the three-story brick building, she tried to prepare herself. But nothing could have prepared her for the moans of the wounded and dying men, the terrible stench of blood and death that hung in the fetid air.

"Are you all right?" Luc asked worriedly.

She knew her face was pale and her hands were shaking. Her stomach rolled with nausea and she prayed she wouldn't embarrass herself. "I'm fine," she lied. "This just takes a bit of getting used to is all."

Luc's face looked hard. "A good bit, I would say. I don't believe anyone ever gets used to a place like this." He took her arm, lending her some of his strength, and they walked down row after row of sick and wounded men.

Besides the bloodstained bandages and the odor of putrid flesh, she saw men with severed limbs and a number who had been badly burned.

"There was a grass fire after the battle. A lot of the wounded were killed in the fire or very badly burned."

She stopped, looked up at him. "Caleb?"

He shook his head. "The chest wound I mentioned and a saber gash in the leg. I'm afraid the leg is infected." Lucas caught her shoulders. "They may have to take it, Lee."

Her heart nearly broke. "Oh, dear God. Caleb would hate that more than anything. He's a cavalry officer. He needs to be able to ride." And she wouldn't let them take his leg unless there was no other choice.

Unfortunately, when she reached his bedside and saw how ghostly pale he was, saw the blood leaking through the bandages on his chest and leg, she thought removing the limb might be his only hope.

Lee knelt beside him, reached out and took his hand. It felt even colder than her own. The other, she saw, was bandaged.

"He escaped the fire himself," Luc gently explained. "He was trying to help some of the others."

"Caleb? Can you hear me? It's Lee." But Caleb said nothing. His eyes were closed, his cheeks gaunt, his complexion as pale as the sheet.

"He hasn't spoken in days," a tall blond man said from the opposite side of the bed. "I'm Christian, one of Caleb's brothers." The married one, she thought. "Our brother, Ethan, is out of the country. This is my father, Lord Selhurst."

The earl was mostly silver-haired, his shoulders slightly bent, and worry for his son was written in the lines of his face. "I'm sorry Lucas troubled you to come," he said a little stiffly. "I told him he shouldn't. This is no place for a woman."

She straightened a little. "Caleb asked for me. That is why I came. I won't leave him until he is recovered."

The marquess said nothing more but his gaze faintly sharpened.

"There seems to be a shortage of surgeons," she said, glancing around the room, thinking what an understatement that was. "Over the years, I have tended a number of injured horses." Actually, Jacob and Arlie had done most of the work, but at least she had been there. "Since there is no one else, I should like to take a look at the wounds myself."

"That is absurd," Lord Selhurst said. "I've sent for the best physician in London. Once he arrives, my son will be in the very best possible hands."

"That is good to hear, my lord. But until your physician gets here, I intend to do what I can."

"I'll help you remove the bandages," Luc said gently. "Father, why don't you and Chris get a breath of fresh air and something to eat? You've been here the past two days. Let Lee and me take over for a while."

The earl seemed unwilling to leave, but Christian Tanner gently took his father's arm and the two men left the building. Luc helped her unwrap the wound in Caleb's chest and the one in his thigh, then he stepped away.

Her heart squeezed. She was scarcely a physician. All she could really tell was that the injuries were severe. If Caleb were a horse, she would have at least some idea what to do, but he wasn't a horse, he was a man.

Then again, he had always been as stubborn as a mule.

"What do you think?" Luc asked.

Lee worried her bottom lip. "How long before the doctor arrives?"

"He was out of town when we sent for him. He is probably on his way by now, but there is no way to know for sure."

"We can't just sit here. Not when we don't know how long it might be until the physician gets here." She reached down, touched Caleb's pale face, and silently willed him to hang on. She turned to Luc, thinking of the mare several months back who had cut herself badly on a downed rock fence and trying to remember exactly what Jacob had done.

She gazed down at Caleb and took a steadying breath. "There are things I'm going to need. The herbs, you will find at the apothecary shop. The rest you will find in the nearest stable."

Luc flashed her a look of disbelief.

"Bring me pen and ink and I'll make you a list," she went on, as if she didn't see the doubt etched into his face.

Then very slowly he smiled. It was the first real smile she had seen since his arrival at the door of her father's town house. "I'll get the herbs. And there are stables right here with any number of horse supplies. You shall have the items you need as quickly as I can collect them."

True to his word, he returned not long after with milkweed and rue, boneset and dogwood, horse liniment, and fresh bandages. Lee took them gratefully and set to work, saying a silent prayer she could remember exactly what to do.

25

It was an endless night and most of the following day before the earl's physician finally arrived. In the meantime, Lee cleaned the wounds as best she could, then made salves and poultices, remedies old Arlie and Jacob Boswell had taught her, and applied them to Caleb's wounds. Still, during the night, his fever returned and he began to hallucinate.

Over and over he relived the terrible battle, and the pain in his voice made her ache for him. It was just before dawn that he whispered her name and when she heard it, her heart nearly shattered.

"I'm here, Caleb." She stroked his cheek with a hand that trembled and tears clogged her throat. "I'm right here, my love." But he said no more and by morning, she was exhausted.

She hadn't eaten since her arrival. Her stomach rebelled at the mere thought of food and her clothes were wrinkled and bloodstained and smelled of the same stench that hung like a shroud over the endless rows of hospital beds.

Lee was bathing Caleb's face, smoothing back his sweat-damp hair when she spotted the Earl of Selhurst striding toward them between the rows of beds. The man at his side, a thin man with a light-brown mustache, she presumed to be the physician the earl had summoned from London.

"Get out of my way, young woman." The doctor, a man Luc said was named Criffle, walked up to Caleb's bedside. "Let us see how much harm you have done."

Her hopeful smile faded. "I did what I could. I didn't believe it was in Caleb's best interest to wait."

The doctor harrumphed. Stripping away the dressings and poultices, he surveyed the wound in Caleb's chest, then turned his attention to the infection ravaging the gash in his thigh. He was frowning and Lee's heart began to thud with fear.

What if she had made matters worse? Dear God, what if she had done something that would kill him!

For the next half hour, Dr. Criffle worked over Caleb's still figure, cleaning and redressing the wounds. All the while, she stood fearfully between Lucas and Christian, praying Caleb would be all right.

Finally the doctor turned. "Young lady—I owe you an apology. You did an excellent job, considering what little you had to work with. I have no idea what exactly you used on Captain Tanner, but it seems to have helped the swelling in his chest and leg and some of the redness is beginning to fade. I do not believe putrefaction has set in as I had expected and whatever you used seems to have helped."

Relief made her weak and she felt Luc's hand close over her fingers in a grateful, reassuring squeeze.

"The problem now, I'm afraid, is the head injury he has sustained. For that there is nothing I can do. If he cares for you as his brother suggests, perhaps your presence here will make a difference."

She nodded, and prayed that it would.

It was a strange world Caleb lived in. At times the battle still raged inside his head. He remembered the cannon fire, remembered men falling beneath a barrage of gunfire and grapeshot, remembered the big French cavalry officer he had clashed with, the saber cut that had nearly unhorsed him. He remembered the searing pain of the musket ball that had slammed into his chest, the flames racing over the grass.

Most of the time, he lived in a world of darkness, an odd nothingness that engulfed him, made his body feel weightless, the days and hours seem to have no end.

But there were those few rare moments when he no longer drifted, when he thought he recognized voices. His father. His brothers. Lee.

It couldn't be, he told himself, but still he could hear her, gently calling his name. He wanted to answer, but he knew if he opened his eyes, she wouldn't be there. She was just an illusion and once he knew that for sure, then the pain of losing her would return and it was nearly as bad as the terrible ache in his chest.

"Caleb? Caleb, can you hear me?" She was there again, drifting through his mind. Peace settled over him and in his mind he smiled. He didn't try to awaken. Instead, he would far rather dream.

"I think we should take him home to Selhurst," the earl said.

"Dr. Criffle believes it's still too risky," Luc argued.

"He says Caleb should remain here until he is more fully recovered."

But Lee wondered if the earl might not be right. Caleb's wounds were healing. At Selhurst, he would receive the care and attention he needed. He hadn't yet spoken, but each day he grew stronger. His body was recovering very well. It was his mind that held him hostage.

"Let's give him another few days," Luc argued, and she thought that it was because she was there and wouldn't be with him at Selhurst. "Perhaps by then he will be lucid."

As she watched him sleep, she wondered what Caleb was thinking, wondered if he heard her when she spoke to him during the night. Sometimes she believed he did, when his mouth twitched at the corners and it seemed as if at any moment he would smile.

She wanted to shake him then, to shout at him and demand he open his eyes. And so that afternoon, while the others had gone off for something to eat and she had returned to his bedside, while she sat there speaking his name again and again, talking to him about Grand Coeur and Noir, telling him racing stories, her frustration mounted. She reminded him of the day they had raced and he had pretended to lose, told him he owed her a rematch, and bet him another week of mucking out stalls, and to her complete frustration, his lips faintly curved.

"You heard me! I know you did! That's it, Caleb Tanner! You open your eyes this instant! I won't put up with your nonsense a moment more!"

To her surprise and utter amazement, he did exactly that. For an instant, they simply sat there staring at each other.

"You're . . . really . . . here," Caleb finally said, the words so scratchy she could barely hear them.

"Caleb!" She hugged him so hard he groaned. "I'm sorry. Oh, God, I didn't mean to hurt you. Say something. Anything. Just so I know you're all right."

"Tired . . ." he said, but he smiled at her as his eyes drifted closed, and she started to cry.

Lucas found her that way, clinging to Caleb's hand, tears running down her cheeks. "He spoke to me, Luc. He knew who I was."

Relief eased the worry in Luc's handsome face. He leaned down and kissed her forehead. "Thank you. For coming here. For taking care of Caleb. For everything."

She nodded. She had done what she could and Caleb would recover.

She had tried not to think what that might mean and she refused to do it now. Instead, when she glanced toward the door, she saw Jonathan Parker striding toward her and there wasn't the least hint of a smile on his face.

"I can't believe you are here," he said, "in a dreadful place like this. When your father told me, I thought he had gone mad."

Luc stepped up beside her. "I brought her, Jon. I know it was a good deal to ask. I was fighting for my brother's life. I thought perhaps if Lee were here, it might make a difference."

Jon glanced down at Caleb, who seemed to be sleeping more peacefully than he had before. "Did it?"

"Yes. It looks as if my brother will recover. My family owes Miss Montague a very great debt."

Jon's amber gaze lingered on Caleb. "I've always liked your brother. I am glad to hear he's going to make it." He returned his attention to Lee. "Nevertheless, this is not a place where you should be. You are betrothed to me and in little more than a week, we are to marry. I'm here to see you safely back to London."

She didn't want to go. She wanted to stay with Caleb. But Luc was looking at her with pity, as if he knew that now that his brother would live, things would return to the way they were before.

"Come," Jon said. "I took the liberty of collecting your things from the inn. The carriage is waiting."

She forced herself not to look at Caleb, simply accepted Jon's arm and let him guide her out of the hospital. They didn't speak again till they reached his carriage.

"I realize you have feelings for Captain Tanner. But he is a soldier. Once he is fully recovered, he will be returning to war."

She stared down at the hands she clutched in her lap. "I know."

"I'll make you happy, Vermillion, I swear it. Once we are wed, you will see."

She raised her eyes to his face. "Lee," she said softly. "I would rather you called me Lee."

Jon bent his head and lightly kissed her. "Of course, dearest." His knuckles brushed along her jaw. "In time you will realize that this is for the best. It's your destiny, Lee. It always has been."

Lee didn't answer. She didn't like the way he was looking at her. Then again, she was tired and depressed. She ached inside and she simply wanted to be alone. Instead, she bumped along in the viscount's carriage, so exhausted she finally tipped her head back against the velvet squabs and fell asleep.

All the way to London she dreamed of a tall man in a scarlet uniform boarding a ship to return to Spain.

*   *   *

For the next six days, she hoped to hear from Caleb but no word came. Instead, a note arrived from Lucas, saying that Caleb was recovering well, that he was completely lucid and rapidly mending. He had been moved to Selhurst Manor to complete his recuperation. There was nothing to indicate Caleb wished to see her. Instead, Lucas wished her felicitations on her upcoming wedding and promised that he would attend.

Lee carefully folded the note and tucked it into her jewelry box. Nothing had changed. She should have known better than to hope for a miracle after the ones she had already been granted. Instead, Friday night, Beatrice pampered her with a bath scented with sandalwood oil and insisted she go to bed early.

Tomorrow was her wedding day.

Lee prayed that God would give her the courage to go through with it.

It was a nearly moonless night. A layer of dense black clouds hung over the streets and a thin mist hung in the air. The courier accepted the wax-sealed sheet of foolscap and slid it into the small leather pouch beneath his arm. Earlier, he had received a message telling him about the pickup and advising him this would be the last he would receive for some time.

Reggie Bags didn't care. He liked the coin well enough, but the risk was bloody steep. Already two of his mates had been caught, one of them killed when he tried to escape John Law. Reggie wasn't a man with much of a conscience, and he was Irish, not bloody English, so that part didn't trouble him, but riskin' his neck this way ... well, part of him was relieved his employer had decided to pull in his horns for a bit.

In the meantime, Reggie had a message to deliver and if he wanted the rest of his blunt, he would have to see it done.

He moved away from the rear of the tavern, off into the dark London streets toward the stable down in the East End off Smithfield Market, where he had rented a saddle horse. It was a long ride to Dover, but once he got there, he would leave the message in the usual place and his part in this rotten business would be done. He wasn't sure what would happen after that, but he figured from Dover, a man could row a small boat quietly across the channel to Calais and deliver the message to someone there. All he had to do was get to the coast.

A noise somewhere behind him filtered into his brain and Reggie stopped. The hairs on the back of his neck stood up, but when he looked, all he saw was darkness. Still, he had a nose for trouble and the scent was heavy in his nostrils now.

His heart hammered like a kettledrum as he hurried along the mist-slick streets and disappeared into a deserted alley. He paused a couple of times to look back over his shoulder, but no one was there. Then, just ahead of him, a shadow loomed out of the darkness and a tall man with curly black hair stepped in front of him.

"Hello, Reggie," the man said. "I believe you have something I need."

Reggie took one look in those cold blue eyes and his knees started to wobble. "Yes, sir," he said. "I believe I do at that."

"What the devil do you think you're doing?" William Tanner, Earl of Selhurst, strode toward Caleb, whose muscles strained in an effort to lift himself out of the deep feather mattress in his upstairs bedchamber at Selhurst.

"I have to go to London, Father. I need to speak to Colonel Cox." Caleb reached over and tugged on the bell pull to ring for his valet and that small effort made perspiration pop out on his forehead.

"Are you insane? You are barely well enough to eat. Your body needs time to recover. You can scarcely hie yourself off to London!"

Just then former footman Harry Prince, recently promoted to Caleb's valet, came dashing into the room. "You rang, sir?"

"I need a uniform. There's a clean one in the armoire. Help me get it on, will you, Harry?"

"You can hardly stand," William argued, his worry mounting. "What could possibly be so urgent you cannot remain in bed for another few days?"

Caleb's features shifted and an implacable expression appeared on his face. "I'm resigning my commission, Father. I'm leaving the army. I realize you probably won't approve, but this is something I've had a good deal of time to think about. I might have done it sooner, but there was a battle to be fought. There was the matter of duty and honor and the debt I owed my country. That debt has been paid and the duty I owe now is to myself."

The valet rushed forward to help him into his navy blue breeches. The effort cost him and he sank down heavily on the bed.

"Even should that be your decision," William said, "why can't you wait? It's obvious you're in no condition to travel. In a few more days—"

"I want to see Lee. There are things I need to say to her. Things I've already waited too long to say."

Lee. Vermillion Durant. William had been afraid of this from the moment Lucas had arrived with the girl at the hospital. "Things? What sort of things . . . ?"

"To start with, I want to thank her for helping to save my life. Luc told me how she stayed at my bedside for hours on end. There is no other woman like her and I mean to tell her so. And then I am going to ask her to marry me and pray that she will accept."

William's jaw imperceptibly tightened. He had been worried from the start that Caleb was in love with the girl. But a marquess's daughter or not, she was a bastard child with a blackened reputation and hardly a suitable match for his son.

He glanced up at the clock on the mantel. At two o'clock this afternoon, Vermillion Durant would marry Jonathan Parker. Luc had wanted to tell his brother about the marriage, but William had refused to let him.

"Not until he is back on his feet," he had said firmly. "As soon as he is, I will tell him myself. If he still wishes to intercede, he may do so then." Luc had argued, but concern for Caleb's health and William's words had finally convinced him.

"He'll want the girl to be happy and he knows marrying Nash is her best chance."

But William had never told Caleb about the marriage and he didn't mention it now. By the time he did, it would be too late.

By then, Vermillion would be Jonathan Parker's problem and Caleb would be free to make a more suitable match.

"I'll have the carriage brought round," William told him. "It will take you a while to reach Whitehall. I don't like your color. I think it would be best if I went along."

Caleb didn't argue. William could see he was trying to conserve his strength. As he walked out the door of the bedchamber, he thought of what Caleb might do when he discovered Vermillion belonged to another man, and a shiver ran down his spine.

You are doing what is best for your son, he told himself and headed downstairs to summon his carriage.

Lee finished dressing in her bedchamber at Lord Kinleigh's town house near Portman Square. Her friend, Elizabeth Sorenson, hovered over her, helping with the final details.

All morning the household had been frantic, the servants in an uproar as they scurried about completing last minute preparations before the family's departure to the chapel at Westminster where Lee and Lord Nash would be wed.

"Sit here, Miss," Beatrice commanded, barking orders like a sergeant in the army. "I need to finish weaving the ribbons into your hair."

Lee sat down in front of the mirror above her dresser and Elizabeth followed her across the room.

"You look beautiful," the countess said, surveying Lee's cream silk gown. Lee wished her aunt could have come, but it wouldn't have been seemly for her to appear in the marquess's house. She still wasn't sure Gabriella would come to the church.

Elizabeth knelt down to straighten Lee's train, her fingers sliding over the wide embroidered band of pale blue roses that decorated the skirt, the bodice, and the small puffed sleeves. Beatrice twined small blue roses and matching satin ribbons through her up-swept hair, then Elizabeth fastened a single, square-cut diamond, a gift from Lee's future husband, around her neck.

"I hope I'm doing the right thing," Lee said, speaking the words she had repeated to herself a thousand times.

Elizabeth took her hand. "Of course you are. Jon is handsome and charming and he cares for you so very much. He wants children and so do you. It's a good match, Lee. And in time, you will surely fall in love with him—just as Charles has fallen in love with me."

Lee didn't remind her friend it had taken nearly ten years for the two of them to find happiness together. Still, her choices were limited. She could no longer stay at Kinleigh. The discord she caused was making all their lives miserable and she didn't want that.

"He's a good man," Lee said, more to herself than Elizabeth. "I'll do my best to make him happy."

"Jon is in love with you. He has been pursuing you for months. All you have to do to make him happy is repeat the vows that will make you his wife."

Lee made no reply, just finished the last of her toilette and made the final preparations to depart for the chapel at Westminster. She prayed that in time, marriage to Jonathan would make her happy, too.

A measure of Caleb's strength returned as the carriage rolled toward London. He had a great deal to do and he was eager to see it done. Two days ago, he had sent a message ahead, advising the colonel of his decision to leave the army and requesting an appointment to see him. The interview was scheduled for one o'clock.

"I still think you should have remained abed," his father grumbled from the other side of the carriage. The coach wove its way through the crowded London streets but traffic was heavy and their progress was slow.

"I've waited long enough," Caleb said. "My enlistment is up and I am resigning my commission. I want to advise Colonel Cox in person of my decision. I've also written a letter to General Wellesley, thanking him for his support. Cox can see it delivered."

"And the girl? She is the reason for your sudden change of heart, is she not?"

"In part I suppose she is. Perhaps if I hadn't met her, I would have remained in the army. Now that I have, there is no way I can stay. Not when I have been given a gift few men are lucky enough ever to possess."

Caleb's eyes searched his father's face, hoping for a hint of understanding. "Mother has been gone for years, but I still remember the way you used to look at her. Do you remember that, Father? Do you remember how much you loved her?"

The earl sat up a little straighter on the tufted leather seat. "Your mother was special. There has never been any woman like her and there never will be."

"Perhaps not. But when I look at Lee, I see a treasure any man would cherish. I see a chance for the sort of happiness you and Mother had, the sort I never thought I would ever find for myself."

His father said nothing, but an odd look began to come over his features. "You love her that much?"

"More than my own life. I want to marry her, Father. I want us to raise a family together. I want that more than anything in the world."

The earl's eyes slid closed and he leaned back against the carriage seat. "Sweet God, forgive me." He straightened, took on the look of authority Caleb recognized only to well. "There is something I need to tell you, son. I think I may have made a very grave mistake."

But just then the carriage rolled up in front of Whitehall and a footman jerked open the door. "We're 'ere, Captain Tanner."

"I'll be back in a minute, Father."

"Caleb, wait!"

But he was already down the iron stairs and limping along on the lion-headed cane he had borrowed, heading toward the office Colonel Richard Cox occupied at Whitehall.

Cox was waiting. "Come in, Captain." He motioned for Caleb to sit down in a chair in front of his desk. "I'm glad to see you up and about. How's the leg?"

"I'll probably be left with a bit of a limp. Other than that, it's mending very well. I take it you received my letter."

"Yes, I did."

For the next few minutes, Caleb reiterated his reasons for wanting to leave the army.

"You're being promoted, you know. As of today, you are Major Caleb Tanner."

Caleb smiled. "That's nice to hear, but it really doesn't matter. My enlistment has been up for some time. I'm resigning my commission as of today."

"Are you certain this is what you want to do?"

"Very certain."

"All right, then—"

"Colonel Cox!" The door swung open and Mark Sutton strode into the room. "I'm sorry to interrupt, sir, but I believe we've found our man." Sutton flicked only the briefest glance in Caleb's direction. "Last night, our efforts finally paid off. As we suspected, Reggie Bags was carrying the false information we fed to one of our suspects."

"Who's Reggie Bags?" Caleb asked.

"One of the couriers who was passing information," Sutton answered.

"Major Sutton has what seems to be an endless supply of sources," Cox explained. "We have had Bags under surveillance for the past several weeks."

"Last night we were waiting for dear old Reggie." Sutton handed the colonel a folded piece of foolscap, the wax seal broken. "You know which man received this information?"

The colonel nodded as he skimmed the page. "Jonathan Parker, Viscount Nash, advisor to the Lord Chancellor of England."

Caleb's heart slammed to a very sudden halt. "It can't be. There has to be some mistake. Why would Nash turn traitor?"

"No mistake, I'm afraid," Cox said. "Personally, I was hoping we were wrong. But the fact is, the man got himself into very deep financial straits. He was able to keep his problems secret far longer than he should have been. The money he was being paid extricated him from his debts, but to continue his role would mean even greater risk than he had already been taking."

"I imagine that is the reason for his upcoming marriage," the major added. "Aside from his attraction to the girl, she has a good deal of money, enough to end his problems, at least for a while."

"Nash is getting married?" Caleb said, feeling the first stirrings of alarm.

"That's right," the major said. "I figured you knew, as you and the lady were once involved."

"When?" he said with growing urgency. "When is the wedding?"

"Two o'clock."

"Today?" he practically roared.

"Easy, Captain. Lord Nash may wed the girl, but he will never consummate the marriage."

"If he tries, she will soon be a widow," Caleb said.

Cox cast him a warning glance. "Major Sutton will take a contingency of men to the chapel at Westminster Abbey and place Lord Nash under arrest."

"Yes, sir!" Sutton said.

"I'm going with you." Caleb had already risen from his chair. He leaned a little on his cane.

"I thought you had resigned your commission," Cox said.

"I did, sir. At four o'clock this afternoon."

Cox just smiled and nodded. "Be careful, gentlemen. I remind you the man is dangerous, responsible most likely for the deaths of at least two young women."

Sutton led the way out the door, Caleb close behind. "My carriage is out in front," Caleb said to the major. "I'll meet you at the church."

Sutton grabbed his arm. "If you get there first, wait for us before you go in."

Caleb gave him a look that said he would do whatever he had to, turned and limped off toward the coach.

26

࿇

"Are you ready?" The Marquess of Kinleigh stood beside Lee in the doorway of the chapel, ready to escort her down the aisle to her waiting groom.

Lee nodded. "Yes, Father." In front of her, the small chapel held perhaps forty guests, mostly friends and acquaintances of her father or Jonathan Parker. But her aunt was there, she saw to her surprise and pleasure, seated next to the Earl of Claymont, who gave her a warm, encouraging smile. Two rows back, Lucas Tanner sat in a pew in the rear. He was dark and attractive and he reminded her so much of Caleb that for a moment she wished he hadn't come.

Lee took a deep breath and focused her attention on the altar, where Charles and Elizabeth Sorenson stood as witnesses to the event.

The organ music began to play. At the front of the chapel, rays of sunlight gleamed down through brightly colored stained-glass windows. Rows of candles had been lit and stands filled with pale cream roses clustered throughout the interior of the church.

"Have I told you how lovely you look?" her father said. "Have I said how proud I am that you are my daughter?"

The words filled her with love for him. She was so lucky to have found him. "Thank you, Father." If only the man waiting at the altar had been Caleb, this would be the happiest day of her life.

Lee fixed her attention on the man she would wed. In a dark gray tailcoat, silver waistcoat and black breeches, he was the epitome of an aristocratic male. Candlelight glinted on the few strands of gray in his dark hair and his mouth showed the hint of a smile. He was a handsome man, she saw, the sort any woman would be proud to marry.

She tried not to think of the wedding night that lay ahead, simply told herself she would get through it, just as she would have done had he become her protector.

"Who gives this woman to be wedded to this man?" The archbishop stood at the altar, a stately man in heavy satin robes. Lee hadn't realized they had already reached the front of the church.

"I do, her father, the Marquess of Kinleigh."

The ceremony began, the words and prayers swirling round and round in her head. When the moment came to repeat her vows, Jon gently nudged her or she might have missed what the archbishop said.

"Do you, Lee Montague, take this man, Jonathan Parker, Viscount Nash, as your lawfully wedded husband? Do you promise to love him, comfort him, honor and keep him for better or for worse, for richer or for poorer, in sickness and in health, to love, cherish, and obey him till death do you part?"

She opened her mouth to answer, but the words

caught in her throat. Jon cast her a look that held a note of warning and she started to speak again. "I—"

The door of the chapel slammed open. Every head in the room turned to look up the aisle. Caleb stood in the doorway, and her heart just seemed to stop. A thousand thoughts rushed into her head, foremost among them, *Dear God, Caleb has come for me. He loves me,* she thought wildly. *He's come to rescue me.* Secretly, she had prayed she would be saved from this loveless marriage and now he was here!

Her chest was aching. Her eyes filled with tears.

Caleb cast her a sideways glance as he strode forward down the aisle, fighting not to limp, his jaw granite-hard. But his gaze was fixed not on her but the man who would be her husband.

"What is the meaning of this, Tanner? You have no right to interrupt my wedding."

"There isn't going to be a wedding, Nash. You're under arrest in the name of the Crown—for treason against your country."

The guests erupted in a disbelieving roar. Lee looked at Caleb and with heartbreaking clarity, realized that he wasn't there for her at all. He hadn't come to rescue her, hadn't discovered that he loved her. He was there to finish the job he had started, and she simply wanted to lie down and die.

After that, everything happened at once. Lee's gaze swung to Nash, who still stood beside her. The viscount stepped closer, caught her around the neck, and jerked her back against his chest. The barrel of a tiny pistol appeared in his hand and he pressed it into the side of her head.

"Your timing is rotten," Nash said to Caleb. "Stand back. I wouldn't want anyone getting hurt."

"Let her go, Nash. There are twenty men outside this building. There isn't a chance in hell you're going to get away." From the corner of her eye, she saw Lucas Tanner ease out of his pew and flatten himself against the wall.

Nash grunted. "You don't think so? If someone shoots me, I'll pull the trigger. Which of those men outside is willing to cause the death of the Marquess of Kinleigh's daughter?"

Nash stepped backward toward a door at the rear of the chapel. Careful to stay in the shadows, Lucas crept forward. Then every door in the chapel burst open and a dozen uniformed soldiers rushed in. They took in the scene in an instant and fanned out around Jonathan Parker.

"Hold steady, lads." That from Major Sutton, the officer she had met at Parklands. "We wouldn't want Captain Tanner's lady getting caught in the crossfire."

At the mention of Caleb's name, her gaze swung to him. *Captain Tanner's lady.* Once she had been. Not anymore.

Caleb's face was slightly flushed, she saw, his strength not fully returned. But his jaw was set and when he looked at Jonathan Parker, the vengeance in his eyes was unmistakable.

"I'm warning you, Nash. You hurt her and I swear I will take you apart piece by piece."

Nash just laughed. "You've all been such fools. Why should that change? I'm leaving and Vermillion is going with me. Try to stop us and I'll kill her."

Nash's hold tightened around her neck and he started backing her toward the door. Her heart was racing, pounding painfully against her ribs. She had to do something. Sweet God, she refused to just go with him!

A candle flickered as he took another step back. She remembered there was a row of them in long wrought-iron candleholders along the pathway to the door.

"Let her go," Caleb repeated and she felt Nash's hold ease as he glanced behind him, gauging his route of escape.

Lee moved in that instant, turning and shoving with all her strength. Luc leapt forward and so did Caleb as Nash staggered, lost his balance, fell toward one of the candles, and the sleeve of his dove gray coat went up in flames. Nash screamed at the fire racing up his arm and a half dozen British soldiers rushed forward. Luc got there first and Nash went down beneath his weight.

In seconds the flames were out and Jonathan Parker lay immobile on the stone floor of the chapel.

Lee's gaze searched for Caleb and then she was in his arms, clinging to him and feeling such a surge of love and pain that even if she tried, she could not speak.

"It's all right, love, it's over."

For long moments, she clung to him. Dear God, she loved him so much. She closed her eyes and inhaled his scent, felt the fierce beating of his heart, and wondered how she ever could have thought she could be happy with any other man.

Caleb bent his head and very gently kissed her. "I didn't know about the wedding," he said, easing her a little away. "It's a long story." He handed her into the care of his brother, a bit reluctantly, she thought. "I'll be back in a minute." He flashed Luc a smile. "Don't let her out of your sight until I return."

Luc just grinned and she noticed there was a dimple in his cheek.

Lee watched Caleb walk over to her father, his

limp a little more pronounced. She couldn't hear what was said, but her father was nodding and when Caleb finished, the marquess' face lit up in a smile.

While the troopers and Major Sutton escorted the viscount out of the church, Caleb made his way to her aunt. Aunt Gabby started nodding and smiling, took out a handkerchief and dabbed at her eyes. Lee watched Caleb's limping progression back to her side and her heart squeezed almost painfully.

Hope had started rising. Perhaps he had come for her, after all. It was madness to hope for such a thing, but there it was, blooming to life in her chest.

Caleb paused to speak to the archbishop, then returned to where she stood next to Luc. By now the guests in the church had all sat back down and were waiting for the drama to play out. Caleb dropped down on one knee in front of her and took hold of her trembling hand. He looked unbearably handsome and there was so much tenderness in his expression, her eyes filled with tears.

His hand tightened around her fingers. "My dear Miss Montague. I would have stopped this wedding sometime back if I had known about it. I love you, Lee. More than life itself. Will you marry me?"

The audience gave up a collective sigh.

The tears in Lee's eyes spilled over and ran down her cheeks. "Caleb . . . I love you so much."

He lifted her hand and pressed it against his lips. "If that is a yes, my love, please say it so the archbishop can finish this wedding—this time with the proper man."

She smiled at him and spoke around the tears in her throat. "I'll marry you. I would have married you when I thought you were a groom."

Caleb's expression softened and something tender flashed in his dark eyes. He drew her into his arms as he came to his feet and she clung to him.

"I love you," she said. "I love you so much."

A man cleared his throat and she realized the Earl of Selhurst had walked up beside them. "I believe a special license has been procured from the archbishop so that this wedding may proceed."

Caleb cast a look at his father. Clearly, he was surprised to see the smile the earl wore on his face.

Selhurst turned the warmth of that smile in her direction. "It is a pleasure, Miss Montague, to welcome you into the family."

Caleb gazed at his father and something passed between them, something that seemed to bridge the differences they had had.

"You heard the earl," Luc said, with a dimpled grin. "Let's get this wedding finished."

Caleb caught her hand and brought it to his lips. There was so much love in his eyes a lump formed in her throat.

The wedding went forward as if it had never been interrupted, and when the archbishop instructed the groom to kiss the bride, Caleb made certain she knew which man she had wed. She was Mrs. Caleb Tanner. And this was, indeed, the happiest day of her life.

Epilogue

~◦◦◦~

Riding over the green rolling fields of Shadow's Keep, the estate in Surrey that Caleb and Lee had bought just after their wedding, Caleb pulled rein on his tall black gelding, Solomon. The horse carried several battle scars from the awful fighting at Talavera, but like his owner, the animal had survived.

Caleb smiled as he surveyed his surroundings. The land was beautiful, verdant and rolling, more than a thousand acres of prim grasslands, perfect for raising horses. And the woman at his side was Lee.

Caleb was happy. So very happy.

Still, he had work to do in the stable, preparing it to receive the new batch of mares they had purchased at Tattersall's just last week. He should be there now, but his wife had shown up with an overflowing picnic basket that smelled so inviting he couldn't refuse her invitation to share it with him.

"What's the occasion?" he had asked. "I know I didn't forget your birthday." He grinned. "I doubt I ever will."

Lee laughed. He had always loved her soft, smoky laughter.

"I've a surprise for you. Come on—we'll picnic in the grove at the top of the hill."

He couldn't resist her, of course. He never could. They reached the rise and Caleb pulled rein on his horse.

"All right, you've kept me waiting long enough. What is the surprise?"

Lee just laughed. "Not yet. I'll not be hurried with news as important as this. I'm hungry. This is the perfect spot for a picnic. Let's eat first and then I shall be more than happy to tell you."

Caleb swung down from his horse. "You little vixen. I want to know what you're keeping from me. You're torturing me and enjoying every moment."

"Of course I am. One thing I learned as Vermillion was how to tease a man."

Caleb laughed. He reached up and lifted Lee down from her sidesaddle. "That teasing goes both ways, you know." And after a long, lingering kiss that left them both slightly breathless, he thought he had proved his point.

Lee just smiled. "As soon as we finish our picnic, not before."

He kissed her nearly senseless. "Tell me now."

"All right. Aunt Gabriella has agreed to marry Lord Claymont."

"God's breath—she is finally putting the old boy out of his misery."

She grinned. "Aunt Gabby says she loves him. She says that after watching us make cakes of ourselves these past eight months and knowing how happy

Charles and Elizabeth have been, she has come to believe in happy endings."

Caleb nuzzled the side of her neck. "I'm really glad for them."

"Me, too." She went up on her toes and pressed a last kiss on his lips. "But that isn't the secret I came out here to tell you."

"What!"

She laughed and spun away from him. "This secret is a great deal bigger."

He started stalking her. With every step he took closer, Lee took a step away. "Give me a hint," he said. "I demand that right as your husband."

She rolled her eyes. "Well . . . it's something you've been wanting."

"I've got it! You bought me that stallion I've been hoping to talk Claymont into selling."

"Better than that."

"What could possibly be better? That horse is remarkable. He'll sire a line of Thoroughbreds that will make our racing stable famous."

She gave him a playful smile. "What else have you been wanting?"

"Right now, I'm wanting to throttle you—or better yet, drag you down in the grass and make love to you until you're too tired to give me any more trouble."

Lee laughed. Slowly the laughter faded. She walked closer, slid her arms around his neck. "I'm giving you a son, Caleb. Or perhaps it will be a daughter."

His heart stopped beating. He had to take a long deep breath to get it started again. "Sweet God, Lee." The kiss he gave her was fierce and yet he hoped she could feel the tenderness. "I'm going to be a father."

He could hardly believe it. As much as he wanted a family, he had never really believed it would happen. "That's the very best surprise I've ever had. Thank you, my love."

They talked of the future. She told him the child would not arrive for six more months, and they began making plans for its arrival. All the while, he kept glancing down at the soft curve of her belly and thinking that she carried his babe. Caleb didn't care whether the child was a boy or a girl; he simply wanted it to be healthy.

They picnicked in the small copse of trees, well out of sight of the house, and when they were finished, he stretched out on the blanket and pulled her down on top of him.

"I'm still hungry," he said, nibbling the side of her neck. "The chicken was delicious but I want you for dessert."

Lee laughed softly. She didn't resist when Caleb began to unfasten the front of her riding habit. He filled his hands with her breasts and noticed how full they were, wondered why he hadn't noticed before. He kissed her deeply, wildly aroused, wanting her even more than he usually did. She was his wife, soon to be the mother of his child. He wanted to imprint himself upon her, claim her in some primitive fashion and so, as he kissed her, he rolled her beneath him and dragged up her skirt.

"I want you, Caleb," she said, coaxing his mouth down to hers and kissing him again.

Caleb opened the front of his breeches and freed himself. "God, you are so sweet," he whispered. He slid himself inside her, felt her close around him. Like a schoolboy, he found himself fighting for control. Beneath her skirt, he cupped her bottom, lifted her against him, and slowly started to move.

Her soft flesh surrounded him, took him even deeper.

"More," Lee whispered, meeting each of his thrusts, urging him deeper still. He took what she offered, gave back what he could. He didn't stop until she reached release, then he allowed himself to follow. She was his. He wanted her to know it. She smiled at him as if she did.

It was late afternoon when they returned to their horses and started back to the house, a lovely sprawling stone mansion built in the shadow of what had once been an ancient keep.

"I never thought that in just eight months I would feel so utterly tamed," Caleb said with a feeling of contentment.

Lee just laughed. "I doubt, my love, that you will ever be truly tamed—and I wouldn't have it any other way."

Caleb just smiled. Under that sweet exterior, there remained a trace of Vermillion, just enough to keep things interesting. Caleb thought how much he loved her and hoped she never knew exactly the sort of power she held over him.

"Are you up for a race?" she asked, casting him an impish smile.

"What about the babe?"

"He is yet some months away. It isn't a problem."

Caleb grinned. "All right, then. Anytime you are ready."

Lee grinned and leaned over her horse. At breakneck speed, they set off down the hill.